PAULINA CHIZIANE

The Joyful Song of the Partridge

Translated from the Portuguese by David Brookshaw

archipelago books

First Archipelago Books Edition, 2024

Library of Congress Cataloging-in-Publication Data available upon request.

Archipelago Books
232 3rd Street #A111
Brooklyn, NY 11215
www.archipelagobooks.org

Distributed by Penguin Random House
www.penguinrandomhouse.com

Cover art: TK

This work is made possible by the New York State Council on the Arts with the support of the
Office of the Governor and the New York State Legislature. Funding for the translation of this
book was provided by a grant from the Carl Lesnor Family Foundation.

This publication was made possible with support from the National Endowment for the Arts, the
Hawthornden Foundation, the DGLAB/Culture, and the Camões, IP – Portugal.

Printed in the United States of America

To Domingos,
my eldest son, the source of my inspiration

To Aderito Leonardo Chiziane,
son of the sacred soil of the mountains of Namuli

The pathways of the world run between the legs of a woman.

Dya Kasembe, Angolan writer

1

A collective cry. A refrain.

There is a naked woman on the banks of the River Licungo. In the men's area.

"Eh?"

There is a woman in the solitude of the waters of the river. She looks as if she is listening to the silence of the fish. A young woman. Beautiful and resplendent like a Makonde sculpture. Her eyes fixed on the sky, she seems to be awaiting some revelation.

"Who is she?"

A black woman, as black as sculptures carved from ebony. Jet black, with tattoos on her belly, thighs, and shoulders. Naked, stark naked. Hips. Waist. Navel. Belly. Breasts. Shoulders. Everything on show.

"Where has she come from?"

In the sky over the town, the news spreads like radio waves. In this sleepy little town, almost nothing ever happens and everything is news. People talk of the foreigner who turned up and then left. Of the administrator's wife who got pregnant and gave birth. People talk of the rain that fell and the seeds that sprouted. Of the husband who did not fulfil his marital duties during the night that has only just ended. A naked woman is headline news. So everyone leaves their own little corner and joins a procession. They are going to see in order to believe.

"Who is the woman with enough courage to bathe in the private spot reserved for men, breaking all the local norms? Who is she?

The naked woman looks at the horizon. The horizon is a curtain of palm trees. She sees a stain. It is a swarm. Of bees? No, it must be hornets. Or chickens driven crazy by a grain of corn falling onto the granary floor. But the stain is gaining height, shape and ghostly movement. It is a stain that kicks up clouds of dust, like a stampeding herd over dry soil. From this babbling stain, she hears sounds of destruction, like subterranean dragons ordering earth tremors. Sounds that used to tell her things. Things she could understand. Other things that she could not understand. She senses the smell of milk. She hears a child crying — ah, so it is a band of angry women. She doesn't understand why they are there. She doesn't understand the reason for their procession, their fury. What do they want? To kill her?

The group of irate women rush toward her like birds of prey greedy for blood. A sizeable group. The march was driven by an instinct for self-defense. Anxiety. Within those frightened minds, myths emerge as the only truth in order to explain the inexplicable. They imagined plants withering up and rain falling and sweeping away all their crops. The cattle growing thin. Roosters becoming sterile, hens having no eggs to hatch or chicks to fledge. That presence was an omen predicting the disappearance of poultry. The naked woman's curves sent out messages of despair.

"Hey! What are you doing there?"

The crowd sees the woman seated on a throne of clay, by the river. She is in the lotus position, her intimate parts in the cool of the river. It sees her inner being budding, like a red anthurium edged with clay. It sees the tattoos on her mature woman's belly. It sees her slim, small body, full in the front, full at the back, sculptured by the gods. It sees her smooth skin. The hue of toasted coffee. Her thick lips like a medulla, full of blood, full of flesh. The eyes of a cat. It sees her smooth, full eyebrows, and her hair like silken skeins, like drops of water flowing down her back, like pearls of tears on a bride's garland.

"Disgusting! Be off with you!"

The naked woman's feet have counted many a stone on their journey. They have trudged here, there and everywhere, in her search for treasure. Like a woman condemned to a lifelong trek. They threw stones at her wherever she went. They chased her away with sticks and stones, as if she were some strange animal invading the property of others. Their voices willed her to disappear. But disappear where, if she had nowhere to go? She compares people to hyenas, vultures. She sees no difference. There is someone in the abyss begging for help. Human society rushes to hurl sticks and rocks, to stamp on the hand with which someone expresses their last wish.

The naked woman has raised her head. She adjusts her eyes between sky and skyline in the visionary gaze of a poet.

"Hey! What are you doing there?"

"Who are you?"

She looks at the multitude, her eyes vacant. She must be listening to the music of love. She must be re-living secret passions recalled from the other side of the world. Maybe she sees moving images. Or talking shadows. Within her, there must be jumbled up feelings, thoughts, voices, dreams, stories, lullabies, sowing confusion in her mind.

"Where have you come from?"

She is solitary. Exiled. A foreigner. She emerged from nothingness in the solitude of the waters of the river. She has come from nowhere. Her feet seem to have travelled through the entire universe from pole to pole. She seems to have been born there, a twin of the waters, the grasses, the corn and the mangroves. A being born from the earth's vegetation.

Rage and astonishment mingle in the same emotion. Lucky are the sightless eyes, who will never see the color of the terror inspired by this naked woman. Some women shield their eyes from such immorality. Such infamy. They look down at the ground. The profane utter loud, crude curses. The puritans cross themselves and place the palm of their hand over their face like a fan. They pretend they cannot see what they nevertheless manage to view through the cracks between their fingers.

"Where have you come from?"

The women prepare an apt sermon for the occasion, consisting of moral pronouncements and threats. She listens. She vanquishes their threats with a smile.

"Who are you?" The furious women insist.

People love identities. They even demand a birth certificate from someone they can see in front of them. Is there greater proof than my presence to confirm I was born?

"Why are you naked?"

The naked woman is too tired to answer. Too deaf to hear. She despairs. How many reserves of strength should a woman have in order to bear her torment, her anxiety and her hope, how many words will the eternal prayer for mercy contain when addressed to an unknown god, whose response will never come?

"Put your clothes on, stranger."

Her clothes are wet. Draped over the bushes like a parasol.

"Go on, put your clothes on right now, woman!"

"Woman, aren't you ashamed to show your face? Where did you sell your shame? Don't you have any pity for our children, who will be rendered sightless by your nudity? Aren't you scared of men? Don't you know they can use and abuse you? Oh! Woman, put those clothes of yours on, for your nakedness kills and blinds!"

She answers in the language of the river fish. She smiles. She looks at the ground. At the sky. With gentleness. With candor. Her eyes emanate a strong light and a myriad of colors. She is pleasant. She is agreeable. She has very white teeth. A full set of them. She is pretty. She has the smile of an angel. What is it that she can see beyond the horizon?

"Hide your shame, woman."

The image of Maria distorts the magical significance of the nudity of mermaids. She seems to carry the portent of a storm on the surface of her skin. Hearts dilate with pity. With fear. There are messages of danger hidden in the bare lines of her body. In the grains of sand. In the Milky Way. In the sun's beard. In the moon's eyelids. In the footsteps of some fisherman at the river's edge. In the gusts of wind. This woman has not turned up by chance. She is the messenger of ill fortune.

"Listen, woman: if you don't put on your clothes of your own free will, you'll put them on against your will."

They threatened her. Maybe like that she would be scared and get dressed. But she has settled down even more comfortably, there where she sits, a mermaid queen on a throne of clay. She sees the eyes of the crowd. Darker than the night, the rays of the dying sun dwell in those faces. Eyes full of tears and anguish. Hostile faces. She sees their feet sown in the soil as if the ground has given birth to shadows. Walking shadows. Moving shadows.

"Woman, get dressed!"

But the army of women is powerless. They were relying on the weapon of language. Of persuasion. Negotiation. It was a peaceful army. One of the women unleashes a yell to awaken her. Another looks for a stone to lash her. Another looks around for a stick to beat some morality into her. A wave of violence permeates the water's

< 11 >

surface. There are no sticks, nor stones. Only wet sand, clay, and mud, which the crowd brandishes as a weapon against this defenseless woman.

The voices of the crowd ululate furiously, breaking like a wave. It is superstition and fear bound together like threads from the same rope. Handfuls of sand fall on the naked woman's body like hail. Her breast swells with the strength of her fear. She exhales the air that the wind then gathers and hurls toward infinity. Then, she plunges into the river and navigates the swirling waters, like a nymph rolling through the waves. She dives down to the riverbed and then shoots up to the surface in the now-you-see-it-now-you-don't shuffling of moon and cloud. The water releases rainbow rings in a myriad of waves. Now far away, the naked woman hisses a venomous laugh that falls like a sword on the enemy's spears. And she celebrates her triumph over the multitude.

There goes the heroine of the day. Protected inside the fortress of the river. On a throne of water. A heroine who vanquished an army of women and threw public morals into disarray. Who defied the habits of the land and sullied the menfolk's sanctuary.

◆　◆　◆

< 12 >

When the crowd leaves, the mad woman returns to the same spot as before. She wants to listen to the voices lost in the waters of the river. The message would arrive, she was sure of that. At the same time as she sent it. By telepathy.

Maria das Dores — Mary of the Sorrows — is her name. It must be the name of a saint or a white woman because black girls like simple names. Joana. Lucrécia. Carlota. Maria das Dores is the most beautiful name, but it is sad. It reflects the day-to-day lives of women and blacks.

Ah, dear mother of mine! Here I am by the wayside. With only my friend the wind for company. On the banks of an unknown river. Persecuted by unhappy women. In their cries, I also heard yours, dear mother. Mother, were you in that crowd? Why is it that I didn't see you? Why didn't you show me your face, mother? It was you, yes, in that group of ghosts who were buzzing in my ears like a swarm of hornets. It was you and your group of ghosts, wanting to hit me, hurt me, hidden so as to rain their rabid blows down on me, but they were unable to, for I was protected by the waters. Because I am a daughter of the water. Am I really naked, mother? The nakedness they saw is not mine, it is theirs. They say I do not see anything and they are mistaken. They are the ones who are blind. They scream their own wretchedness at me and call me mad. But they are the mad ones, prisoners, covered in a thousand items of clothing like the skins of an onion. In the midst of all this heat.

I no longer quite know where I came from or where I am going. Sometimes, I feel that I was never born. Can it be that I am still in your womb, mother of mine? Everyone asks where I have come from. They want to know what I am, because I am nothing.

I am going where the wind goes, and my life is caught in the web of an unknown hope. The compass rose. My destination is that of the birds. To fly and fly until the final fall. My destination is that of the water. Always flowing in ever-changing shapes, sometimes a spring, other times a river. And yet other times sweat, or else tears. A flood. A drop of dew in a bird's throat. I am vapor warmed by life. I am ice and snow in a freezer compartment. But always water, movement is my eternity. I am an animal wounded by all things. By the song of birds, by the red of anthuriums, by violets in bloom. Wounded by dreams, by illusion. By hope and by longing.

Who am I? A statue fashioned from clay, in the midst of the falling rain. I hate clothes which limit my flight. I hate the walls of houses that stop me from hearing the music of the wind. I am Mary of the

< 14 >

Sorrows, Maria das Dores. The woman who defies life and death in the search for her treasure. I am Maria das Dores, and I know that a woman's weeping has the strength of a river at source. I know how many steps it takes for a woman to walk the perimeter of the world. How many pains it takes to make a life, or how many thorns it takes to make a wound. But I have no name. Or shadow. Or even existence. I am a deformed, colorless butterfly. When it comes to words, I recognize insults, and when it comes to gestures, I know aggression. I have a broken heart. Silence and solitude inhabit me. I am Maria das Dores, the woman no one sees.

◆   ◆   ◆

The women abandon the river and run swiftly to the house of the village headman to seek a solution to the enigma. They go to the headman's house, but he is not in. He has gone to the tavern to have an evening drink in the company of men. His old wife has abandoned her housework to come to the assistance of the startled crowd. Their terrified eyes converge on her. Sickly, incredulous eyes. And their voices all speak at the same time. They are raving hysterically. The old lady cannot even hear what they are saying. What they want. All she knows is that their spirits are suffering from hunger. She has to clap her hands and let out a cry to impose silence.

"What happened? What has brought you here?"

"You, lady, who know the secrets of this and the other world, the route to the beyond, the horizon's mysteries in all their detail, help us."

"Why?"

"That naked woman on the riverbank. She looked like a goddess, or a demon!"

"Which woman?"

"A stranger," shouts one of the women like one possessed. Why did she come and settle herself right there in the men's area? She is light, she swims like a fish. Can it be she's human? A mermaid? A nymph? A ghost? You, lady, who can see everything, tell us what disaster is coming: will there be rain? Drought? Sickness among our livestock? Conflicts worse than wars?

The women's voices are fearful flags fluttering in the wind. They had not seen anything real. They had seen the bogeyman. That is why they are making a noise and producing confused explanations.

Fantastical projections of stories told around the fire, about pretty,

< 16 >

considerate, obedient, hard-working girls who marry gilded princes, bear many children and live happily ever after. The bad, lying, disobedient, and slothful girls are punished at the end of these stories, don't get a husband, or have any children, living unhappy, spinster's lives for ever after, and end up mad. Such are their beliefs. In gifts and destinies. Plagues. Prophecies. Punishments.

"She said her name was Maria," one of the women explains.

"Can that really be her name?" The headman's wife asks. "Every Maria has another name, because Maria isn't a name, it's a synonym of woman. But tell me: what was she like?"

"She has the shape of a person but isn't a person. She looked like the angel of darkness. A messenger of disaster. She looked like a ghost, a creature from another world," one of the women says.

"She carried the winds of tidal races on her wings," another says.

The headman's wife soon recognizes the reasons for their collective anger and responds with the balm of a rainbow. Stories of life fly out of the archives of her memory like files from a computer. Each person has their journey, each one their story. The presence of that haunted soul has an obvious explanation. The world is topsy-turvy, depraved. Humanity is cast out at the drop of a hat, and people become savages, cannibals.

"Calm down, people. There was no prior warning of the war that ended a while ago, but folk died. The drought that has just finished was not predicted, but there was a storm. There were no mysterious prophecies before the plague of locusts that stripped our fields and made us die of hunger."

The voice of the headman's wife is like cool rainfall. It has the strength to placate multitudes. It has the power of waves gently lulling boats on the waltz of the breeze.

"Ah, lady! If you saw the mysterious form she took when she came! We insulted her and she answered us with amusement sketched on her face. We hurled stones and she escaped like a fish. She wasn't a person from this world, oh no!"

"Poor thing, she was no more than a mouse looking for a refuge. Or a cassava plant. A solitary being looking for its fellow creatures. Why did you drive her away?"

The crowd starts to rue its actions. She had a human form, they saw for themselves. She had been born from a female womb, just as they had, like the toads, the fish, the weeds in the marshes. The woman had her story, her marks, her scars. In her, she mirrored the fragility of existence. The multiplicity of journeys. Illnesses, torments, tears. Shattered dreams, anxieties, desperation. Only God knows where she came from. Only God knows the tears she shed. Only she can tell the joys she harvested. The roads she travelled. Only God knows how she came here. Maybe traveling on the backs of turtles. On the armored spines of crocodiles. In the mouths of fish, in the laciness of the algae. On the breeze's flurry.

"She bore good news written on her underside," the headman's wife assures them. "A message of fertility. That mad woman was the true messenger of freedom, my people."

The crowd is startled and the headman's wife smiles. From her honeyed mouth, she releases the most harmonious notes. From her small arms, she opens a cozy blanket like the wings of an eagle, where the multitude of women nestles like fledgling chicks. From her breast, she releases a wisp of courage carried to each and every one on the breeze. The crowd hears her voice penetrate it. Its smile blooms. Its mind begins to roam across the landscape of its beginnings. Fears are released. Minds placated. Spirits regain serenity. At first, the voice is heard nearby. Then from afar. Then even further away, like someone talking of love in the deepest of dreams. It is a song that reminds the youngest women of the most ancient things, the beginning of all beginnings. The story of matriarchy.

Once upon a time...

At the beginning of everything. Men and women lived in separate worlds across the highlands of Mount Namuli. The women used advanced technologies, and even had fishing boats. They dominated the mysteries of nature and everything... they were so pure, purer than children in a crèche. They were powerful. They dominated fire and thunder. They had already discovered fire. The men were still savages, ate raw flesh and fed on roots. They were unhappy cannibals. One day, a young man tried to cross the River Licungo, to know what lay on the other side. He was on the point of drowning when a beautiful girl appeared, his savior, and pulled him into her boat. As it was cold, the girl tried to revive the dying man with the heat from her body. The man looked at her body, a red anthurium edged with clay. There resided the marvelous temple where all the mysteries of creation were hidden. And then...

The old lady was an excellent storyteller. She knew the exact circumstances in which a particular image should be used. What should be omitted and what should be uttered. The points when she needed to make an impact, and the points requiring a pause. The beauty of a story depends on the tone of voice, and the gestures of the narrator. Telling a story means carrying minds on a flight of the

< 20 >

imagination and then bringing them back to the world of reflection. For this reason, she imposes a pause. And suspense.

"Why are you looking at me? What do you want from me? Do you want me to start saying lewd things in the presence of the children you are carrying on your backs? No, I shall not say any more, in fact, you know what is coming anyway. Now, go home and look after your children. Go home!"

The women laugh, tranquility has been secured. That story contains within it wondrous worlds. That is why they want to hear what they have known for years on end. Scenes of love and betrayal. Freedom and struggle. Attraction and rejection. They want to absorb the sweetness of the words emanating from that mouth and to dream like children.

"Ah! Great mother, tell us, finish this lovely story!"

"All right, as you have asked me, I'll finish it. The men invaded our world," she says, "they stole our fire and our corn, and placed us in a state of submission. They tricked us with their language of love and passion, but usurped the power that was ours. A naked woman next to the men? Oh, good people, she came from a bygone realm to take back the power that was usurped. She brought with her a new dream of freedom. You shouldn't have mistreated her and chased her away with stones."

Some women recall the tale and smile hopefully. The headman's wife sees that the fantasy of her words has taken effect. That mad woman reflects the new world of war, disease, social exclusion, of which they are all victims.

"Ah! But where did she come from, then?"

"And we, where did we come from?" The headman's wife asks.

"From far away," they all answer together.

"And where is far?"

They all seek the answer in silence. Their eyes scan the horizon, in silence. The headman's wife suggests some answers.

Far is the distance between your journey and your umbilical cord. Far is your mother's uterus from where you were expelled, never to return. It is the distance to your own innermost being, which you cannot always reach. Far is the place of hope and longing. The place to dream and remember. Far is the great beyond, which many set out for, leaving behind them endless yearning. Far is the twin of near, just as the beginning is the twin of the end. For everything changes when you cross the finishing line. There is now here, at the time of arrival. The future will be present. Tomorrow will be today.

"Where did we come from?" She awaits an answer that does not come, and then affirms: "We were from Monomotapa, from Changamire, Makombe, and Kupula, back in the first dawns of time. The power was ours. Do you remember those times, my people? No, you know nothing about them, no one remembered to tell you, you are still young. We joined the Shangaan, the Nguni, the Ndau, Nyanja, Sena. We waged war on each other and made peace. We were invaded by the Arabs. Waged war upon by the Dutch and the Portuguese. We fought. The wars with the Portuguese were the hardest and we ran hither and thither, while the slave ships transported slaves to the four corners of the world. New wars came. Of blacks against whites, and blacks against blacks. By day, the invaders killed everything, but made love during the pause between battles. They came with their hearts full of hatred. But then they drank coconut water and became gentle and their hatred turned to love. Women are like coconut, don't you think? Women were raped and wept over the pains of their misfortune with seeds in their womb, and they gave birth to a new nation. The invaders destroyed our temples, our gods, our language. But with them, we built a new language, a new race. That race is us.

That is how we came
From far away
From that place we left behind
And will never return to again

"We come from different narratives. Different wombs. Different places. Some were born among the sugarcanes, others on the road. Some on the high seas. Others in the gilded beds of princes. Some fled houses of mourning covered in fire. Fire lit. By demons. Demons who set the waters of the rivers alight. Others were born out of the solitude of warriors, the solitude of heroes. Vanquished and vanquishing heroes. We are heroes of the Atlantic, heroes of the crossing of stormy seas, bound for slavery in Guinea, Angola, and São Tomé. We have the blood of French, Brazilians, Indians from Goa, Daman, and Diu, and those banished to the palm groves of Zambezia. We came from the noble and the destitute. We came with the creeping gait of fugitives, or the prancing arrogance of conquerors. We were born multiple times and in multiple forms. We died on multiple occasions, silently, like mountains corroded by the winds.

"Collective thought travels far, there from where one can no longer return. To the time of bloody struggles, a time of suffering. With bands of people running hither and thither. Killing each other. Hating each other by day, at the hour of combat. Loving each other by night, during the lull in fire, and leaving behind evidence of our passage. Hatred generating love at the death of the sun.

"Each one recalls their own journey. The stones along the way. Joyous, unhappy, despairing, thorny journeys. And they start to think about the mad woman of the river with tenderness.

"Go back to your homes and forget the mad woman who was carried away by the waves. Remember that we are all children from afar, like that Maria whom you saw on the banks of the river. And always remember that nakedness is an expression of purity, an image of that ancient dawn. We were all fashioned from the clay of Mount Namuli. Black clay with red blood."

2

The mad woman of the river looks at the church at the top of the mountain, and it opens the route to her memory. I seem to have been here before. But when? In what circumstances? I went into that church, I prayed, at some point in my childhood. What is this place?

Years of memories converge in her mind. In tiny fragments, like the drops that go to form a river. Images obscured by time reveal themselves one by one, contoured and shuffled about like the pieces of a puzzle. As if an archaeologist of memories were digging among ancient photographs. I have a feeling I was once here, but when?

She looks at the landscape with greater attention. The range of mountains. The mountain top covered by the cloud's hat. A source, a river, growing, bound for the unknown. I have already climbed that mountain. What was I looking for?

Suddenly, she remembers José. Her father talking about life among the mountains. And she recalls that he left on the great journey after having travelled the perimeter of the world and returned to the starting point. It all began when she left home with the three

< 26 >

little ones in her arms. Many years ago. But it is as if everything happened yesterday, as if the twenty-five year nightmare had lasted no more than a day and night. In fairy tales, the sleeping beauty slept a hundred years that seemed no longer than a hundred seconds.

Time flew, and flew by. When she left, she did not have callouses on her feet. Nor did she have white hair. Nor any gloomy images in the archives of her memory. When she left, she had not travelled so many highways before, nor seen so many landscapes or people. She had no knowledge of life's terrors. Time flew by, for sure.

But how had everything begun? Begun or ended? In life, nothing begins, nothing ends. Everything is continuity. But it all began when her black father left, never to return. It all began when the white father loved her mother. It all began when her mixed-race sister was born. It all began when her mother sold her virginity in order to make some more money. It all began with a relationship that involved sex and bitterness. Children and flight. Inaction and absence. The scaling of a mountain. White soldiers in the defense of Portugal's empire. Money and virginity. Magic. Fortune.

She remembers everything, about the land and the world. Where culture dictates the norms governing men and women. Where money is worth more than life. Where the mulatto is worth more than the black and the white is worth more than them all. Where color and sex determine a human being's status. Where love is a poetic abstraction and life is woven with the yarn of hatred.

The image of her husband is the embodiment of her bitterness, she does not want to remember that. Her mother is the embodiment of her betrayal, and she does not want to re-live that. The family was a constellation of blacks, whites, all mixtures in between, based on hierarchies and false grandeur. That was why she fled it all and learned the secrets of solitude. To smile into the breeze. To converse with the wind and kiss the stars.

◆　　◆　　◆

She feels attracted to that place and decides to stay and take some respite from all the trails she has trodden. Without knowing that at this precise moment she is writing the preface for a new life.

She looks up at the world above. The rich town houses along with the hovels. Smoke from the kitchens spirals up into the air like giant mushrooms, columns, holding up the roof of the sky. Hills. Vaporous trees dissolving in space. She is present and absent. She has the delighted gaze of a wild cat that kills mice in the dead of

< 28 >

night. She absorbs all the smells of nature. The smell of the river. The stagnant waters of the ponds. The coolness of algae and stones. The smell of water lilies. The smell of the fresh green rice beds.

The headman's wife seeks the cool of the early evening in the narrow lanes of the town. Maybe she has come looking for the solitude and inspiration brought by the evening breeze. Maybe to contemplate the sun as it sets. She meets Maria, wandering, stark naked, along the bank of the river. A magnetic wave crashes over the two women. What words can bring back a mad woman in the depths of her absence? What use can her presence have when faced with a lost cause.

"Hello, Maria. It's a hot afternoon, isn't it?"

"Yes."

Tell me something, Maria, what did they do to you for you to end up like this, roaming silently along the streets, without a name, or a roof over your head? What do you do out on the byways, stuck to the soil like a slug, vegetating, arousing feelings of pity, repulsion, opprobrium, of nausea and rage in the face of your naked figure? What destiny is yours, you who feed such indignation, tyranny, suffering blows with sticks and stones from anyone, while competing for bits of food with dogs, rats, cats, from cans cast out on street corners?

What is this life you lead, which stretches into a ceaseless struggle against darkness, against feral animals and humans, against the devious snakes along the paths you travel? Tell me, Maria, where you have come from. What you eat. Who crushes you, who tortures you.

Scintillas of light flicker on Maria's face. The voice of the headman's wife is the sweet remedy that bathes the wounds of solitude. She replies to all the questions with a smile.

"Where do you sleep, Maria?"

"Me?"

She must sleep out in the open, abandoned like the destitute of the earth. Her mind must be full of dragons, dinosaurs, horrifying landscapes. She must have suffered terrible, destructive nightmares to end up like this. There have been many deranged people turning up and wandering through our town. People abandoned to the tranquil rhythms of the day. To the lethargy of sounds and music on the edge of the markets. They like to frequent public places, walking alone among the crowd. Modern societies produce ever more insane, marginalized people, like luxury goods. Wealthy families have an ever greater preference for giving their child a furry doll instead of a real sibling. They would rather have dogs and cats in their homes as companions in their solitude. For a cat or a dog does not complain. And they prefer to banish ever more humans to the realms of madness and marginality.

"Tell me, Maria. Where do you lie down to rest when the sun sleeps? Have you had anything to eat today, my dear Maria? Wouldn't you like to come and have a snack with me?"

"I'm not at all hungry," the mad woman replies in a distant voice.

The headman's wife studies Maria's profile. She seems a dignified woman. With good habits. With breeding. She lowers her eyes when she speaks, which is a mark of bashfulness typical of well-brought up women. She speaks quietly. And she speaks good Portuguese. She seems like a village girl. From the interior, tattoos on the body are a countryside thing. But she is not from the interior, believe me. She must be a city girl. From the big city. She is very hygienic, she doesn't eat with her hand. She begs. She begs for bread and a morsel of cheese. With a bit of butter. She's got the refined palate of city folk. When she is hungry, she leaves the riverbank and goes into town to ask for, to beg for sustenance. In a well-mannered way. Dropping to her knees in order to receive alms from men. Bowing her head to receive alms from women. And she looks tenderly at children in their mothers' arms. But where is her homeland? No one knows the womb that bore her. Or the firm hands that raised her toward the sky in the ceremony of the moon. No one, except for the solitary wind and its whispering breeze.

"Let's talk, Maria. Tell me about yourself, and your folks. Tell me anything you like, for I'm here to listen to you. Do you have any family?"

The confusion of races in her child's mind, all under the same roof, all in a muddling mixture, like milk and lemon in the same cup.

"And why are you here? Where is your family? How did you get separated from them before you got here?"

"The day my black father left, my mother didn't cry. She got drunk. The day my white father left, my mother cried and passed out."

"And what was your mother like?"

"Very pretty. She loved the whites. She wanted to be white."

When she talks of her mother, there is a sign of hatred and of betrayal.

The headman's wife tries to picture the mad woman's mother. There aren't any good people in this world. Nor are they bad. Life is a constant risk in search of a chance. The murderer thought it was better to kill. The thief thought it was better to steal. Maria's mother thought it was better to throw her into the abyss. Who is the owner of truth?

The headman's wife looks at her. She is algae. A medusa. A water lily. Her eyes are like the moon, which reveals itself, only to then hide, coming and going. She suffers from the illness of the moon. The moon is inside her. The moon is in fact her. The light from her eyes expands over the curves of the hills. Over the highway the birds use to cross the sky's empty spaces. Her dwelling place is misty but colorful infinity. She is like the ensign of a sailing ship as it flies triumphantly over the waters. Her real illness seems to be extreme anxiety. Let us hope she finds all she seeks in this world, so that her soul may encounter peace.

"You have beautiful tattoos on your belly. Can I see them? Who did them?"

The old woman arches her eyebrows as she looks at Maria's belly with increased interest.

The beautiful, geometrical tattoos resemble a web, a mesh, a lace belt stitched by hand, and covering only her belly. She examines the reliefs. Ridges. Recesses. She deciphers the message in each symbol and recognizes Maria's origins. They are Lomwe tattoos. She comes from the mountains, and in her veins flows the sacred blood of the rocks. She is a daughter of the land, returning from her great journey, summoned by the spirits. To cure herself in the waters of the Licungo or to climb the mountain of eternal repose.

These tattoos hark back to the time of slavery. That much the old woman knows. The African peoples had to stamp their bodies with marks of their identity. Each tattoo is unique. It is a sign of one's birth. On the body, a map of the homeland is drawn. The village. Lineage. In each line, there lies a message. An ancestral tree. Tattoos helped family members to reunite in São Tomé. In America. In the Caribbean. In the Comoros, in Madagascar, Mauritius and other places in the world. Times changed, Africans do not need tattoos anymore, for the time of slavery is over.

The headman's wife now knows Maria's origin. But she cannot do anything to help her. The old lady confirms the illusion of existence as she contemplates the corrosion and death of the edifice assumed eternal. Families were destroyed, dispersed, because of wars, and migration. In these new times, society has become corroded in the name of a modernity that has dragged hundreds of her fellow humans to the realm of marginality and madness. The world has adopted new challenges and battles new enemies.

She looks again at Maria's face. She is wearing the purest, most

< 34 >

stunning smile. Her gaze is fixed on the moon or on some other place. The old woman extends her hand to her. To hug her and give her some affection. But Maria avoids her.

"Maria, tell me the name of at least one of your ancestors."

"I don't remember."

"Where have you come from?"

"From afar."

"What are you looking for?"

"The children I lost."

The headman's wife searches for a word, an answer within her. She has known many stories, but none like this one. Maria must have been married, and then rejected. For being sterile. The obsessive idea of the woman as mother, removes the sterile woman from the human category.

Mad women create fantasies and pitch incredible stories out into the world. Can a mother remember the faces of her children lost twenty years ago? How long does a memory last? Can human feet journey around the perimeter of the world? How many steps do people take in twenty years? To lose a child is a pain that kills. To lose three is something that buries one in the deepest hell. No, this story cannot be true. So does it therefore reside in her imagination?

"Ah! Maria, such a brave woman who travels alone and faces all perils, in search of the treasure that has been lost in time. A child that wicked hands have cast out into the desert. Women of the world will take pride in your fearlessness."

"Do you think so?"

"Of course! Now, Maria, put on your clothes, for the nights are cold here. You're in the mountains, very close to God. You must get dressed."

The headman's wife remembers that Maria may have a point. In Zambezia, there are still people who have no experience of cotton or silk. Or any artifices. Adults go around in loincloths and children with their backsides exposed to the wind. The headman's wife remembers the clothes worn by the wives of the overseers in the olden days. Long skirts with thousands of frills, in the intense heat of the tropics. And they used to think the free and easy nudity of the local people was immoral. Times have changed a lot. Even the priests learned from the blacks to take a dip in the sea. White women learned from black women to go around in clinging loincloths, which they called miniskirts. Nowadays, it's these Europeans who go around in loincloths while the people rigorously wear clothes of another age.

"Maria, you must get dressed."

"What for?"

"To protect yourself and be like other women."

Maria's nakedness was a return to a state of purity. Transparency. But women are scandalized, because nudity in one of them is reflected in the body of another.

"Ah!"

In human cities, freedom is forbidden. Human beings must always be clothed, wear shoes, and carry their documents with them. People who are walking aimlessly along are arrested by the police on the grounds of vagrancy, as if anyone could tell exactly where each step was taking them. Why do people have to walk in a particular direction if all places are places for walking? Why do I have to walk at certain hours if all hours are hours for walking?

"You should cover your body."

"What for?"

What for, if she has nothing to hide under her clothes? She has nothing to hide, that is for sure. She is the daughter of a drop of water from the overflowing river. She was born from the algae. From the marshlands. From the flying fish that spawn among the highland rocks. She was born in the cane fields and the rice beds. She was born in the burning desert, without sweat or dampness. That is why she loves water. She is a lover of the water. She came like the foam on the eddies of the river. She came from nowhere.

"When are you going to return home, Maria?"

"Return? Never. I like it fine here."

She is right. Everywhere is good to be born. And die. The mother's womb is the only departure point for all the routes taken in the world.

< 38 >

3

The town of Gúruè has become a place of pilgrimage. New, interesting people arrive every day. This year has seen the arrival of Father Benedito and Dr. Fernando. It is said they are brothers. Ever since the war ended, there has been an increase in newcomers. With the construction of a paved highway, Gúruè has been brought even nearer to the world.

There are many outsiders who arrive in this mountain town covered in red anthuriums edged with clay. The beauty of the land and the tea plantations attract many migrants. But those two do not look like romantic adventurers, much less gold prospectors. Indeed, they came for other reasons. They came from afar, like those returning in triumph to the motherland.

The people venerate Father Benedito and weave myths around him. They say he has magical powers. One look from him cures all bitterness, which is why the people parade in front of him in order to be caught in the line of vision of those miraculous eyes. He is a man of tenderness, of deep passions, and of extreme humility. He has an open smile and a closed heart. During mass, he savors his words with the keenness of an orator. And he says beautiful things. About faith. About poetry. When he talks about his family, his father or his mother, he weeps. Maybe he is recalling moments of cruelty in this world. Maybe his father died in some battle. Maybe his family perished in some massacre. Something tragic occurred in his life. Or nothing happened at all. Maybe that was just how he was taught, for modern churches exploit the emotions of their congregations through theatrical performances.

Before, they had encountered elderly white priests. A young black priest is a novelty from the days of independence. For those people, procreation is the essence of life and sexual life is as vital as a drop of water. Being a priest, they acknowledge, is important, but more important still is to produce an heir for social security in difficult times. Many men were killed in the civil war and there are many widows in need of consolation, many single women waiting for love, so it is a serious crime for a man to sleep alone, whatever the motivations of his belief. It is painful to see young girls flaunting themselves in front of that saintly presence, trying to focus the male on matters of the flesh, only to end up frustrated like bees beating against the frigid glass of a windowpane.

< 40 >

There is nothing abnormal about the behavior of these women. It is these new beliefs that are puzzling and contradictory. The Bantu gods ordain that we should proclaim our virility and our fertility. Transcendence lies in sex. The gods of heaven also ordain that we should go forth and multiply, but insist that bodily purity can only be reached through celibacy. This is why black families do not take kindly to a son being ordained as a priest. Any handsome man should sow his seeds in the soil. And germinate. To fill the earth like stars in the skies, because eternity is the product of fecundity. That's why the women want to know more about this young priest.

"Father Benedito, are you from here, sir?"

"The land belongs to God. Like the swallows, I am from here, there, anywhere."

"Ah! Father Benedito, are you really a man, sir?"

He smiles. And he compares that merry banter to the song of the skylarks greeting the morning. An expression of freedom. Those women talk as if they are joking, but they both know that the best poison tastes like honey.

"I don't know. I'm the son of a rock. What do you think of me?"

"Have you ever fallen in love, sir?"

"Yes."

< 41 >

"Well then? Whoever has tasted that wine, never sleeps alone again."

"I don't drink. You know that."

"What a pity, Father!"

The women seek to free the tensions imprisoned behind the bars of the priest's heart, stimulating any weakness in his fresh young flesh. The most forward of them open themselves up to him, speaking their minds freely.

"Come on, Father. Commit a tiny little sin now and then, it won't matter at all. You can even do it with me, sir. Come on let's go, Father...!

"God's eyes are all seeing."

The women want to prove that they exist and that their presence is more important than all the beliefs and vows in this world. So that the priest may become aware of the real dimension of his body's needs. There are bits of the organism that do not feed on rice, or remedies and godly words.

"Did you choose this life of your own free will, Father?"

"It was destiny. My calling."

"Oh! What a pity, Father! What a waste! So much beauty just in order to serve God? No, it shouldn't be like that. It's a temptation.

Ordaining such handsome priests should be forbidden — because they leave the nuns, single girls   and married women in a tizzy. Oh, Father! You should show more charity, sir, and satisfy the thirst of all these unattached women around town!"

Dr. Fernando, the new priest's younger brother, is a man of about thirty. He is very different from the bourgeois elite of the little town, who seek refuge in the futilities of this world, showing off the latest fashion in cars and the grotesque jewelry of the newly rich, in their affirmation of imagined grandeur. He goes around in jeans all the time. Sneakers and short-sleeved shirts. He walks or rides a bicycle like any peasant. He has nothing at all to show off. Not even a gold ring on his finger. Nor do any complicated words tumble out of his mouth. He is as accessible and transparent as the waters of the Licungo, with its source in the high mountains. He is satisfied with what he has. Just his knowledge and strength, for his heart dwells in an inaccessible fortress.

The doctor believes in the magic of the mountains. In the myths that are told about the sacred, the profane, and magic. That is why he often goes climbing, in order to seek inspiration from the wondrous resident at the top of Mount Namuli. He also believes in the magic of love, and treats the sick with both the therapy of love and remedies.

The people venerate the doctor and claim that he has magical hands. It is enough to be touched by them to be cured. Women approach him full of desire. They lay siege to him.

"Our handsome little doctor! Have you got a wife, sir?"

"No, I'm single."

"Have you got a girlfriend?"

"No, I haven't."

"Why not, doctor?"

Those two shock the world. One cannot live without a drop of water. They live in a dried up sea, in a desert without a female soul to scare away bad dreams at night. The people seek an explanation and weave fantasies about rabbit bites causing sexual impotence, condemning men and women to nights of endless infancy. They make imaginary complaints about how both their parents must have kept rabbits when the boys were going through puberty, and as a result, the brilliant future awaiting the two creatures was ruined. People create flimsy fantasies and women are always on their guard.

"But are you really a man?"

"I am from the family of angels, I have no sex."

"Ah! But we could fix you up with a young girl for you to try. Or even me, if you want me, of course. It gets very cold around here, doctor."

"Angels don't feel the cold."

"You and your brother are so attractive. Enchanting. You have arms long enough to enclose a woman and make her feel she's inside a shell. Ah! How I'd like to be carried away in the waves of those arms. My handsome little doctor, any day you want...!"

In the hunt for love, women know they need to wait for nights when the cold is intense and the hearths are unlit. They need to wait for faith to ebb away and desire to re-emerge unequivocally, like a layer of oil in a glass of water. They need to wait for man the carnal creature to revolt and get the better of logic. At that time, the cute little priest and doctor will bend, for no man can triumph in the struggle against the laws of creation. When that moment comes, they will seek shelter, a shadow in order to soothe their wolfish fury. And children will be born, even if they don't want them. Any women in their vicinity at that instant, will be lucky.

Those two brothers are devoid of mundane sentiments, possessions, appreciation of the beauty of women and everyday vanity. They are healthy folk, who inspire morality in all the inhabitants. Their gaze hovers looking for something that flies, that provides relief, that takes their mind off the clouds, and anchors their feet in the soil. They have an air of absence, levity, it is as if they lack something ineffable in order to complete their existence. Maybe a feminine side to complete their masculinity, not in bodily terms, but in sacred, transcendent form, something which would make anyone feel fully alive and happy, even in the clothes they wear, or the way they smile. They seem to have the fragility of children who have grown up as orphans. They approach women, they offer them smiles and flowers. In this gesture of giving, it is as if they are seeking some long-lost residue in those women's eyes. Yes indeed, they dream of women, but women of another kind, another frame of thought. Perhaps a mother or a sister. Maybe a uterus where they might find protection from life's hard knocks.

They are always next to each other, uniting in some kind of resistance against time. Giving each other mutual protection so that they should never be separated. Always together watching the sun set every day. Talking to each other about their origins and about a world that only belongs to them. They say they are from there, but they know nothing about the geography of the area, nor about its history or lineages. They must be the sons of well-to-do families, old families that emigrated. They would know some more about them if the priest's cook were not dumb and the medicine man wasn't so discreet, never letting anything out. They could at least take a look at their bedsheets to confirm whether they are men or merely saints. Some people get together again and run to the headman's house in search of an answer.

"Lady spouse of our headman, mother of all mothers, who knows the history of the people here ever since the world was created, tell us something about these young men. Where have they come from?"

"The same question yet again? Didn't you understand my explanation? So you want to know where they came from, do you? And we, where do we come from? All right, once again let me tell you. The cradle of all Zambezia is right here, in the highlands of Mount Namuli. They have come here — this is for sure — to remind us of times when the land was ours and the mountains bore new life. Even though many say that we were born in a distant Eden, and from a foreign couple, these two young men have come to remind us of the slow deaths of our own myths. Of the times when there was no hunger, when the original paradise was alive in the womb of our mountain and the cradle of humanity, and all the species on the planet were right here. They have come so that we may be reborn. So that we may be reunited in communion with the Great Spirit, and may repose in the sacred soil of the mountains, because everything begins and ends here. Does Zambezia have borders? No, because this is the center of the cosmos. All of planet Earth is called Zambezia. The highlands of Mount Namuli are the womb of the world, the navel of the sky.

4

Delfina is crouching before the waters. There where the River Quelimane meets the Indian Ocean. She is trying to decipher the mysteries
of the night in the surge of the waves. She awoke at the rooster's first
crow and made her way here. To watch the sun rise and illuminate
her mind. Her expression is troubled and her mind full of anxiety.
In her dreams recently she has seen a landscape of mountains in all
its grandeur, and for Makua, Lomwe, and Chuabo people, to dream
of the mountains of Namuli is to dream about one's destiny. It is
the call of one's arrival or departure. End or beginning. Because the
mountains of Namuli are magic. Poetry. Prophecy. Delfina feels a
gust of anxiety in her mind. My time has come, the beginning and
the end. Will it be today? Will it be now?

She stays here until long after the sun has risen, like a monument
in the town square. She is like a beggar lying on a corner, waiting for
whatever destiny decides. Exhausted from so much trekking in the
desert. She has learned how many thorns it takes to feel pain. She
knows the size of her face by the tears that roll from her eyes down

to her mouth. When it comes to weeping, she knows the songbook all too well. She knows the dimensions of a cry by the number of times she has cried for Maria das Dores, wandering somewhere out there at the ends of the universe. Or in the depths of the earth. She is well aware of the number of grains of salt in each tear. Tastes? All she knows is that of bitterness, vinegar and alcohol. Her old drunkard's heart dreams of the endless joys she will feel on the day Maria comes back.

For years, she has been waiting for Maria to return on the crest of a wave. Including the time she lived between limbo and longing. But the cure for her anguish resides beyond the horizon, and in order to reach it, she will have to overcome the tumult of the rippling waves that glint in the sun like mirrors. She thinks of leaving for Gúruè, the town in the highlands of Mount Namuli covered in anthuriums. The road is good. The journey is long. Three hundred and fifty kilometers. In order to consult the mountain gods directly about the whereabouts of her lost daughter. She hallucinates.

"I had a daughter. Or I have one, I don't know. She was a beautiful little girl. She was born in 1953, but it seems like only yesterday that she was still playing mommy, taking care of her younger brothers as if they were dolls. She left in 1974, like a cloud, and she vanished into

< 50 >

the great palm plantation. I can no longer find her. I have searched it from top to bottom. I checked the crowds, one by one.

"Ah! Maria das Dores, I looked for you. On the backs of waves. In the heavenly hills and islands floating in the azure. In the grains of sand. I couldn't find you. You were stolen away from me in the beak of a stork, and taken up into the highest mountains, where I could never find you. And now, on the eve of a new century, I am still here, pining for you.

"I want to know about you. Where you set out for. I have been dreaming of you for the last twenty-five years, and I see you in all the people who pass by. I see you playing. Growing up. Wearing your school uniform. I remember the days when you would look up at the moon, while you combed your hair as thick as skeins of silk.

"My nights have been full of mountains lately. I sense that I shall soon be with you, in the beyond or in this world. I am tired of listening to my story, fossilized in molds of clay by the songs of the people. I am tired of popular justice, which accuses me and continually condemns me.

"I am one of those women who hibernate by day, in order to sing the symphony of night with the bats. I am a witch. I had all the men in the world. Two husbands, many lovers, four children, a brothel

< 51 >

and a lot of money. José, your black father, personified the institution of marriage by which I gained respectability in the eyes of society. Soares, your white stepfather, was my financial institution. Simba, that beautiful young black boy, was my sexual institution, my other self, capable of great leaps of the imagination, who left me to become your husband.

"I ruled. I spread terror. The only torment I have suffered in this wretched life was the pain of having lost you. Everything I did was a way of reaping vengeance. I stole men's love, leaving other women's beds to grow cold. I destroyed families. I dragged many young virgins to the abyss and made a fortune out of my brothel. I took all the magic potions to protect me from poverty and smoothed my face of all its wrinkles. I danced naked under the full moon and hypnotized all the men in the world, thus fulfilling my tyrannous destiny. It is I, your mother, who placed an inheritance of thorns in your hands, and built my own gallows to hang myself.

"It was my mother's fault, for she made me black and educated me to accept tyranny as the fate of the poor and to despise my own race. It was the fault of Simba, my lover and your husband, who fed me spells and destructive fantasies. It was nature's fault for endowing me with greater beauty than all the other women. It was the fault of José, a poor black man, who fed me flour and dried fish while I, Delfina, wanted codfish and olives. It's the fault of Soares, who raised me up into the skies and then let go of me in mid-air. It was my fault. For aspiring to what I could never be. It is the fault of the world, which taught me to hate.

"Ah! My God, bring me back my own Maria das Dores. My gods, my guardian spirits, take me to Namuli, my mountain, my cradle, my mother's womb!"

5

It is a peaceful afternoon. Even the partridges are resting their voices after their midday meal. Men and pythons in a natural gesture of idleness, wallowing in the shadows in order to digest their daily repast.

The doctor makes a superhuman effort and takes a digestive stroll to the clinic where his patients await him. He sees Maria das Dores sitting at the side of the road. She is crouching. Oblivious. He is assailed by a feeling of envy. He sighs quietly: if only I could be like her. Adrift and without commitment. Fall asleep and awaken without anyone waiting for me. Forever at a standstill in the march of time. Wouldn't that constitute happiness?

"Good afternoon, Maria."

"Good morning."

"It's no longer good morning. It's past midday."

"The day is twenty-four hours long, doctor. Good morning!"

"Ah yes, you're right, but even so, good afternoon, Maria."

An automatic response. Natural and genuine. Without all that bowing and scraping, and the hypocritical formalities with which

< 54 >

the people greet an educated man. The doctor is surprised. He stops for an instant. For the mad woman's words are shrouded in some kind of mystery. They provoke questions and demand answers, and the doctor doesn't have time to chat. He invites her to follow him.

"What are you doing there?"

"Nothing!"

"Wouldn't you like to come with me?"

"Where?"

"Keep me company as far as the clinic. It's not far. Just there, at the top of that rise."

Maria does not need asking twice. She gets to her feet and walks beside the doctor on his journey to the unknown. In that little town, everything is near. In a few minutes, they reach the clinic and sit down face to face. Without any barriers or formalities. Life's images become fixed when one least expects them. They merely occur. It is enough for the eyes to register objectively images forgotten in time. When talking about nothing in particular or something specific. Unaware of the importance of that encounter in a person's life.

"Tell me your full name, Maria."

"My name?"

She remains silent. A mask of shadows dances in those eyes of hers,

< 55 >

for her mind has traveled to other galaxies. To find herself again, she will have to rise into the heavens, and journey many light years there, with the help of bamboo scaffolds and wooden ladders.

"But I'm Maria."

"Is that all?"

"Yes."

"Maria is a woman's name, a mother's name."

What does a man feel in the face of a mysterious, ragged creature who is utterly out of her mind? Curiosity? Disgust? Pity? The doctor looks at Maria. What world might exist within her? What images, what nightmares might exist inside her? What shackles caused her to lead such a grim existence?

"Why do you want to know my name?"

"So as to get to know you."

"Why?"

"For us to be friends. So that I can walk over to you and call you whenever I see you. Take your hand and lead you home when night falls. It's not good for a woman to be alone in the dark remoteness of the open road, and you are always alone. Aren't you afraid of bad men, Maria? Aren't you afraid of wild animals? Or of rapists?"

Maria hears the boy's voice coming from some distant place. A

< 56 >

hand reaching out to the most precious part of her being. A voice emerging from an ancient dream, reborn from some faraway place.

"Then tell me where you live. I want to know where your house is."

"What for?"

"So I can visit you."

"Visit me?"

"Yes. And give you a little wood for your fire, so as to keep the dampness away on cold nights. To bring you some hot soup and a blanket. So that you won't get arthritis, or sinusitis, or the flu."

The doctor makes an effort to recognize the traces of humanity where others assumed it lost, like a poor child on a trash heap, trying to discover leftovers, scraps of food for his own relief. For he knows that by comforting someone else one comforts one's own self. We sleep more happily after we have helped a person to be someone.

Maria was a pilgrim seeking some distant voice.

"Where are you from, Maria?"

"Me?"

"Yes. You."

A typical question upon a first meeting. For people are like trees. They take root. People truly are trees. Joyful and fresh as the flowers of the field. Some are trees in arid land. Just as she is. Others are parched, without leaves or moisture, their branches bare like hands praying to the heavens.

"I've come from afar."

"Afar?"

"Yes. From a place that has no name."

"Oh!"

He tries to say something but is unable. It is hard for people to talk about themselves. Whoever talks of himself always lies. By layering bitter moments with sweet words. Placing flowers and candles in dark places so as to conceal the thorns on one's journey.

"Tell me the story of your life."

"I have no story to tell," Maria replies.

"Ah, but you're lying! Everyone has a story," the doctor insists, "every day has its story. Ah, Maria! You have your story."

True stories are in soap operas. They are also in books. Maria says this in order to try and foil the doctor's curiosity.

Maria feels her mind go dizzy. Doctors really are the twin brothers of priests. They are curious. They want to know everything other people are doing. In the consulting room. In the confessional. Some use words to treat sicknesses of the soul and others treat sicknesses of the body with medicine.

< 58 >

"Tell me a little about your childhood."

"My childhood?"

Maria goes back through time and rejoices at her childhood. She was the first to emerge from her mother's womb. She was a source of pride, ecstasy, in her mother's arms. She was the flower, the apple of her father's eye, who raised her on high to present her to the moon, crying triumphantly and full-throated: here is my daughter, my queen, my mother's soul!

"Tell me about your birth."

"Eh?!"

She has the sweetest memories of her earliest life. She says she is not any old black woman. She wasn't born in the bush or in the cane fields. Nor was it by happenstance or as a result of some accident. She was desired, awaited, her birth celebrated. She came into the world with the help of a white midwife, in the white folks' hospital. She was weaned on milk, honey, kisses, and plenty of affection. She was raised in her cradle of gold and in her lacy cot. She was fathered by a black man and raised by a white father. One day, her black father left, her white father arrived, and her life changed.

"So what about your childhood home?"

"Ah, my home!"

She recalls the house of her black father. It was cone-shaped. Like a mushroom out of the tales of Alice in Wonderland. Leafy trees of a deep, rich green. Mosquitoes. Plenty of food. Laughter and dreams. Pure happiness. Her white father's house was very beautiful. In the whites' area. With large windows and frosted glass. And a garden full of flowers. Electricity. Items of furniture taller than people that shifted like ghosts at night. Good food, and a lot of sadness.

"And your mother?"

"Ah, my mother!"

Maria recalls how deaf she was. She could never hear the cries of children or the supplications of the world. But she could hear the tinkling of coins dropped on the ground from miles away. She could hear the clink of bracelets and gold bangles as they jingled on arms, ears and ankles. And she could hear the dictates of her own mind. She was blind. She could see her image in the mirror. And no more. She was very beautiful, her mother.

"And your father?"

"I had two fathers. My black father was a man of courage. He usurped my mother from a white man's arms, in deadly combat. The white was a man of standing. He won my mother back from the arms of my black father. My black father was very tall and very handsome. My white father was very sweet and mild, short and tubby, like a barrel of red wine."

"Two fathers and one mother?"

"Yes."

"How is that possible?"

A story beyond the grasp of normal understanding. With refluxes of seduction and betrayal. Maria narrates this story. Without many details for she does not know them. It all happened long, long ago. Long before her father slept with her mother and caused her to be born. Once upon a time.

The black man and the white man were passionately in love with the same woman. They challenged each other, resorting to such terms as honor, virility, in order to camouflage their desire, and they both disputed her as if she were some trophy. She is my girl, my black woman, the white man would say, she is forever mine. The black man would reply: I am Adam and she is my rib which is the begetter of life, she will be my spouse, forever mine. They arranged to fight a duel on a moonlit night, without seconds or witnesses. Before the fight, both swore they would be victorious, using the same words: I shall kill or die for that black woman. For that black woman, I shall live, I shall vanquish. And so that is what happened.

< 61 >

They fought. The white man with fists of fury, the black man with fists of iron. They pirouetted along the spine of the earth in the dance of death. Tearing the grass from its earthen nest. Rolling in mud-laden puddles, reducing themselves to nothing, and fulfilling ancient prophecies. You are clay and mud. You come from dust and you will return to dust. Both of them on the ground gaining the color of dust and of clay, in an act of regression to their origins. Maybe in order to be born again. In the first generation we were the color of earth: all of us were black. Over time, the races became modified: because of climate, diet, ways of life, humanity diversified. That is why we are here today, in a collage of races.

The fight lasted until the roosters crowed. The white man's punches contained all the blindness of love. The black man's punches, all the jealousy and anger against the race of sailors, the hatred of colonization, slavery, the cracking of the overseer's whip. The moon paused to watch that night's miracle. A black man hitting a white man in a love duel. Unheard of. Incredible. Bravo! The name José dos Montes will be recorded in the memory of Zambezia as a maker of History.

The white man was ground into a mash of pulped carrot by the time dawn broke. Exhausted by so much fighting, they sat down side by side. In their love for the same woman, the two men embraced

< 62 >

each other as brothers. Whispering tired words to each other. The white man, macerated with pain, sighed, and asked: can a man conquer love with the strength of his fists? Ah, dear God, why did you bring me here to Eden? Why did you place before my eyes the most delectable fruit in existence, if I cannot hold her?

From on high, the Morning Star shone and cast its light into their minds. They looked at each other. They recognized in each other two wretched butterfly hunters. To risk killing or dying for something that cannot even be felt. They shook hands and sealed a pact, promising to keep their fight a secret. So much war in vain. In matters of love, all races are the same. A black heart, a white heart, the same madness, the same fantasy, and in their veins the same red blood. Why are we fighting? Why are we treating each other so badly? The white surrendered. You keep her if you want, but don't kill me. Let's leave it to her to decide who she wants to be with. She will choose me, the black man argued. I know that butterfly, boy, the white man said by way of a prophecy. She's a flying insect. A bloodsucker. She may choose you today. But for how long?

The white man's predictions would prove true later on. The two men followed the whims of her heart and body. After her white lover came the black man as her first husband. Then the white man

< 63 >

followed as her second husband. Then once again, the black man as a friend, lover, husband, or in some undefined role. Both men loving her forever more. Suffering for her until the edge of the abyss. So much was she loved that she ended up being abandoned, fulfilling the old adage: they who kill for feelings, die of feelings!

Having stopped fighting, they helped each other up like former adversaries, and walked off together like Siamese twins joined at the hip.

Both of them knew that a true woman is the one who journeys with her legs closed. She preserves her love in the strongbox of her heart. She holds her man's hand and supports him in the construction of their world. They knew this, they knew it well. They knew, too, that they were victims of the magical powers of a black siren. And they lived their life's course like heroes in the dance of the black man and the white man.

"What a story, Maria!"

"That's how it all happened, doctor. It happened just like that."

"How interesting!"

The doctor was expecting to hear a story of love that began with flowers in the garden and ended with thorns and torment, for it is in passion that the madness of most women resides. He was expecting to hear tales of princes and princesses, of castles and dreams. But he was completely mistaken. Maria speaks of other people's stories, but not her own. He begins to take an interest in her account. The root of the problem lies in the mad woman's family.

"How did you reach this stage in your life?"

"Ah, what a nice man you are, doctor!"

The mad woman goes back in time. She recalls that early evening which marked the end and the beginning. The arms of her mother's man who would turn out to be the man of her own life. Tears are born from her eyes which then flow like two abundant torrents as far as the gates of eternity. It was the birth of the Licungo and Malema, twin rivers flowing in opposite directions, offspring of the mountains of Namuli. They contain sacred myths regarding the feminine and masculine worlds that preceded the creation of humanity.

Her tears touch the doctor. And he sketches out a map of possible diagnoses. This woman must be from Quelimane, where mermaids fight each other to harvest a white man's semen, bear a child and fill the world with the color of a new race.

"What ill winds brought you this far?" The doctor insists with renewed interest.

"Ah, the things that happen in life!"

"What is life?"

"Do you really want to know?"

"But of course!"

"Life is loving and suffering. Traveling the labyrinths of the world blindfold. Trudging along highways, streets, and paths. It's seeing human faces, living faces, the faces of the dead, the lifeless and the aborted."

The doctor learns about the world's contrasts. This woman, who from afar, seemed stark-raving mad, up close appears human. With coherent words and clear ideas. In contrast to the individuals who from afar seem lucid, but up close reveal themselves to be crazy and despotic.

"Before I even came to understand the things of this world," the mad woman says, "the lights went out on my journey."

"Why?"

"The lights on the stage don't illuminate the whole day. When the light went out, the curtain fell. And I fell."

"So what is it you seek on your travels, Maria?"

"All that I never had. All that I gained and then lost."

"So do I, Maria. So do I. In this, we are all the same, isn't that so?"

The doctor senses he is facing a hermit and not a mad woman. We are all pilgrims on an eternal quest. Following the paths of chance until our lives are extinguished. At the end of one road, the beginning of another. Body and soul consorting with each other, divorcing, reconciling, imitating the love between the sun and the moon.

"She knew that was how my life was going to be."

"Who?"

"My mother."

He noticed the change in Maria's expression. A turbulent wave rears up in her mind, altering everything about her. Her gestures shrink. Her eyes are those of someone seeking something in the depths of her memory. He saw her consciousness transmigrating to some other space, some other time. The mad woman enters into some state of possession. Matoa. Madjini. Mandiqui. Or quite simply epilepsy. She unleashes a high-pitched voice, like the wolves that inhabit the caves:

"It was here," the mad woman shouts.

"What?"

"It was from this room that I left."

"Where to?"

The mad woman has overcome the barrier of time. She has reached the shores of the remote past, fulfilling the dictates of extinguished suns. The doctor panics. Metempsychosis is the realm of the medicine man. The mad woman is identifying a place and seeking something she had and then lost. Maybe it was from there that she had set off in pursuit of the moon.

"Where are they?"

"Who?"

"My children."

"There are only two of us here. No one else."

Maria abandons her chair and rushes down the corridor of the hospital. The doctor dashes after her. They go through the wards. The crèches. The consultancy rooms. Suddenly the mad woman stops and asks him sternly:

"Where's the doctor?"

"I'm here."

"No you're not, come on, tell me the truth, little black boy. It's no good lying. Stealing is worse still. I also played at being a doctor and a nurse and even a cook. People play such games when they're children. You're a big boy, you mustn't lie, tell me, where's the doctor?"

"Which one?"

"The white one. Old. Bald. Portuguese. It was also said he was a priest."

"Ah!"

A moment of lucidity flashes across Maria's mind. She remembers. There were soldiers at that time. She was in the middle of a war. Blacks and whites in the same army, assailed by invisible soldiers who would appear at night and mount surprise attacks. Liberators or terrorists. Guerrillas or warriors. She remembers being transported by white soldiers to a hospital where the doctors and nurses were white.

"Where did you get that white coat, black boy? Get out of here, this place isn't for you. Your place is at the entrance, in the corridor, carrying stretchers, washing the floor and changing the patients' filthy sheets. Your place is in the laundry, in the kitchen. Now tell me: where's that white doctor? And the white nun?"

The young doctor remembers. In the past, jobs obeyed racial hierarchies. The woman's memory has run aground like a galleon on the sands of time. She does not know the war is over, the whites have left and the flag has changed. She does not even know that there was a new war waged and a new peace signed under the new flag.

"The white doctor left and isn't coming back, Maria."

"Where's he gone?"

< 69 >

"To his homeland."

"Where?"

"Overseas."

"Over what?"

"Overseas. The other side of the ocean, up   north of the equator. We are independent now. Our land is on the map of the world."

The whites were here, alongside the blacks. Loving and hating each other like a husband and wife within a home. But anger and divorce succumbed to the miracle of time: the hatred of yesterday has turned into a new love, and yearning into the emergence of a new union. Where's my white man? Where's my black woman? He was here. She was here. Before that time. After that time. Where is he?

"I'm going there, right now. On foot."

"It's a long way! To get there, you'll have to cross the ocean."

"Desire will show me the way. I'll get there. That's what my life will be from now on. Finding a way there."

"Finding a way? Why?"

"They took away all that I cherish."

"Cherish?"

"Yes. My three children. And they replaced them with others that neither cry nor suckle. How long is it since they left?"

< 70 >

"Thirty-one years ago. I am the doctor and I am the same age as the nation."

"Thirty-one years? Is that all? Do you think that's a long time ago?"

The doctor tries to look at time, his time. Distant and cloudy. A dense, compact night, without any pinpricks of light in the sky. Our doctor does not yet know how distances in time are measured. Or in life. All he is familiar with is the long journey through an infancy spent in orphanages. The pumpkin soup served in colleges. The tasteless beans riddled with larvae and weevils. The boiled potatoes with their skins on in university residences, cooked and served in such a way as to preserve the shame and virgin purity of their nutrients. The flying saucers of sliced bread, turned into stones for slings, which made excellent catapults for birds. From afar, he recalls the coffee laced with sour milk. The bitter oil investing the carrots with a flavor of soap. Through time, he remembers the florid lettuces, with olive earrings, tomato bracelets and rings of onion. Nothing more than that. No birthplace, no dead loved one, no ancestor. No father or mother. A life made of books and attendance at mass. Studying every line and each paragraph in order not to fail his exams and so keep his place in college. So as to always have somewhere to eat a bowl of soup. To have a bed and a blanket. And to have friends. And the protection of the nun, his godmother. When it comes to the past, they have only one memory. They were brought into the world borne in the beak of a stork.

"Ah, my good, sweet child. You are the most intelligent boy I've ever met. My beautiful boy. Swear to me for the sake of your ancestors, your saints: you didn't kill the white man did you?"

"Me? Some were killed by History. As for me, none, I swear."

"My beautiful boy! One mustn't kill a man, even if he's white. Never!"

"No, I never killed anyone. Nor will I. When they left, I was still a child. I swear."

"Won't they come back?"

"No, never again."

"Avoid the word never, child. The sun that leaves, later on returns. Night too. Even the dead are reborn in new incarnations. The word never shuts the gates of heaven, child, avoid it."

"Why?"

Maria explains. The killer incarnates the spirit of his victim. The black who killed the white will leave on his knees for the land of the white. In order to pay the debt of blood at the tree of the dead man's ancestors. The whites who killed will come back. To kneel and beg our ancestors forgiveness. And they will be welcomed in our huts as brothers. Spilt blood brings people together in brotherhood, it ties a knot, and not even death can untie it.

"Are you sure, Maria?"

"Absolutely! It has always been so, ever since the beginning of the world."

The mad woman pursues voices of ghosts lost in the silence of time. She screams. Out of fear. Out of rage against a time that will never return. She unleashes all her despair there in the corridors of the hospital and the doctor is now able to confirm. It was from this clinic that she had left on the road to the infinite. The mad woman gets up. She runs. The doctor runs after her, without knowing he is running after his own destiny. He manages to seize hold of the fleeing mad woman, unaware that he holds fate in his hands. He tends to her until she has calmed down completely.

The doctor understands. The mad woman is well brought up, trying to face the world with a woman's strength. She has fallen into penury, but she is facing this burden with courage. Alone. On the moon. To travel the byways willy-nilly is not a sign of madness. She is in fact a cultured woman, living in exile from the world. Migrating to other pathways, other stars. They have killed her in the

< 73 >

name of happiness. Over the course of time, they have broken her inner equilibrium, her consciousness. She has lost her awareness of where she is heading. That is why she walks slowly, listlessly, in her search for the gates of paradise. She climbs the steps to the temple and encounters ruins and desolation. Wallowing in the rubble of ancient ruins.

A magical moment is generated between the mad woman and the doctor. The world untethers mysteries and leaves them suspended in gravity. Maria sees and hears: the nice doctor's voice is so gentle it awakens feelings slumbering in her mind. His eyes are little flashlights of enchantment. His smile, a full moon, limpid, cool, romantic, his face like that of a baby. Oh, if only I could hold him in my arms, nurse him like I did my own little boy! She sees in him a mask of sadness, his enigma. The solitude of a little boy without a mother. In the doctor's eyes, there is the image of an earth woman, containing all the trees and roots. Trees in bloom, out of bloom, bushes, grasses, fruit. He dreams. The body of a woman. Overhead. Sunshine and smile. River and blood. Bitterness. Flowers in a rainbow of color. The beginning, the end, the entire universe.

Once again, the doctor is a witness to human suffering in the face of the world's silence. That poor woman, chased away by everyone

< 74 >

like an owl, was nothing more than a little bird lost out on the highway. Poor thing! He treats Maria as he would his own mother, if he had one. I'm going to give this mad woman a warm top and a capulana. We are all trees with our roots displaced. Victims of this storm called life.

◆ ◆ ◆

It is Easter Day. Mothers and children are dressed in their best around the baptismal font. The church smells of milk, it smells of diapers. It smells of resin and incense. It smells of cheap perfume. The mad woman of the river peeps through the doorway. She pays attention to the words that penetrate her like drops of rain, as if that priest were invading her soul and sniffing out the pain corroding her.

This mass is a poem of praise to mothers. And Father Benedito enraptures.

"I love baptisms," the priest says. "When I see children in their mothers' arms, I am stricken with envy. When I see a child being disobedient, I am saddened, for I never had anyone to obey. When I see a son mistreating his mother, I suffer deeply, for I never had a mother to take care of me. I learned, through deprivation, the importance of a mother. I would love to have a mother to fill my existence with joy and fill this emptiness, this absence. A mother who might pass on to me knowledge of earthly things, of little things. Who might offer me a smile, a flower, and a lot of tenderness."

The mad woman listens to the priest, astounded: who was the mother who gave birth to that son and then lost him? How could a mother get separated from such a wonderful son? She longingly remembers little things. Placing the baby on her breast. Smiling at him. Changing his diapers. Caressing him. Laying him gently in the cradle and watching him fall asleep. Talking proudly about him with friends, family, and anyone who happened to pass by. He cries a lot. He's sweet, He's got a big appetite. He sleeps a lot. Yesterday's crying was worrying, but today's is a song, relentless, to strengthen his lungs. The mad woman feels like shouting, I'm also an empty-handed mother. My children were taken by the wind, by the earth or by the world and my only madness is that I miss them.

Now, the priest is talking about love and heavenly things.

The mad woman listens and reacts. No, Father, don't talk to me about love, for hatred has filled my whole life's course. Rather speak to me of dark, moonless nights. Speak to me of mothers like mine, who turn their daughters' bodies into bread baskets and money.

< 76 >

The priest starts talking about his mother again. He says every mother knows the names of the stars, because she is also a star. She is a dream, an invocation, poetry. He looks at the mad woman of the river peeping in through the window. His emotions are stirred. This poor woman has perhaps been a mother. Perhaps she has lost her children on the highways and byways of life.

Maria trembles, screams. Maybe she is inspired by the shame of not having been able to hold her children in her arms like those mothers in front of the altar. She feels the comfort of an arm around her shoulders. It is the doctor helping her to free herself from her torment. When mass ends, the mad woman is regaled with the attention of the churchgoers. Father Benedito dedicates a short prayer to her and invites her to attend mass, encouraging the worshippers to show her friendship, because she is as human as the rest of us. The mad are family, he says, they may be children, grandchildren, parents, siblings, anyone can go mad. He says all humans are mad, and Earth is a planet of madness. He goes on to say that the mad woman has not lost her senses at all, or anything else. She's only left for some faraway place, leaving behind this world of vanity, evil, in order to inhabit a distant paradise. That is why she lives in a world of purity, up there, in the realm of freedom.

6

José dos Montes would not tell this same story if he were here. No, he would not tell it like this. No man takes pleasure in telling the story of his own defeat. When one is a prisoner, a thick wall blocks one's throat, silencing one's vocal chords. Bitter feelings form dark clouds that end up producing a downpour of tears.

José's story begins like this. Which isn't the best way to start. For it begins in another place.

Once upon a time, some navigators set sail. They were on their way to India, in search of pepper and chilies, so as to improve the flavor of their dishes of salt cod and sardines. As they were sailing up the Indian Ocean, they got an urge to have a rest. Or to have a pee. To step onto dry land and gaze out at the sea. Maybe. Either that or they were attracted by the marvelous song of the mermaids. So they dropped anchor.

They found a vast land, with hippos, crocodiles, elephants and many blacks. The land had eleven mermaids. O'hipiti, which they called Mozambique Island. Nampula. Inhambane. Cabo Delgado.

< 78 >

Zambezia. Maputo. Niassa. Tete. Gaza. Sofala. Manica. Of all the mermaids, Zambezia was the most beautiful. The sailors invaded her and loved her with frenzy, in the only way a man invades a woman he loves. The gorgeous Zambezia, enraptured, shouted at the height of her orgasm: come, sailor, love me and I shall give you a child. You and I, forever together, creating a new race. Wherever we go, we shall leave traces of our love. We shall leave a mulatto in every grain of sand, in order to celebrate your passage through this world.

In the beginning of it all, the peoples of the land believed in Zuze, the god of the sea. They believed that all the wonders of the Promised Land could be found at the bottom of the ocean. They thought that the sea was the dwelling place of all the good spirits. This was why they viewed the navigators as the trusted messengers of the Great Spirit, because they had the light color of some of the fish of the deepest waters.

And so the kings dressed in their finest clothes to give the messengers of the gods an appropriate welcome. With drum beats, dances and everything. They set the prettiest young girls swaying to the tufo and the nhambarro. At the same time, the kings' subjects paraded with chickens, coconuts, bananas, papayas, gold and ivory to offer the visitors from the bottom of the ocean. Stay here, sailors, and fertilize these young girls, the kings beseeched. Release some of your seeds into this land for the eternal celebration of your passage through these tropics.

They took their visitors to the kraals, bowing and scraping before them, and begged: choose a bullock, sailor, choose a spotted goat, a white sheep, to be sacrificed in your honor! They prepared magic potions from coconut and gave them to the sailors. Any visitor who drinks these potions forgets his way home. They did everything to keep the visitors there. But those obstinate sailors left without so much as a goodbye. Black spells don't work on whites, they commented bitterly. How mistaken they were! Not long afterwards, the whites returned, with cannons, muskets, whips, and large quantities of wine, in order to purge the land and paralyze the troublemakers. They had found the Promised Land.

The navigators roamed from village to village, spilling blood, desecrating tombs, perverting history, doing the unthinkable. Zambezia opened its body and was left pregnant with thorns and gall. In the name of this love, women experienced moments of endless torment and their tears became a boundless river on their faces. Their birth pains became ceaseless, their sons were born merely to die, for they were destined to be cannon fodder. The people sought, in vain, to turn their hearts to stone so as to escape pain, death, oppression.

There was a logic to all this. The besotted man razes all in order to possess the woman he desires. That is life. First the pleasure of love in the incubation of pain. With nausea and vomiting to season pregnancy. The body transformed, torn, wounded. Blood flowing in the birth of the new nation.

That was how the story of José began many centuries before his birth. That is why he is there, sitting among the dunes, talking to the boats, the ocean and the waves. Remembering things from his childhood. Questioning things. Is the sling still there in its hiding place behind the granary? Is the little black cat, which my grandmother gave me, still alive? And what about the wild rooster that covered the hens in our coop and those of our neighbors? And my mother? Is my mother still alive? No one answers him. He yawns and sighs. Ah, how I yearn for my mountain, my cradle, my mother's arms.

He dreams.

Of building a little house at the top of the hill and marrying a lady who can cook good titbits, seasoned with coconut, cloves and cinnamon. With pepper and chilies brought by the sailors. A lady with a well-endowed body, whom he will garland with colored beads around her waist and her ankles. A lady who will bathe in the river and taste of algae and the flora of the river. He pictures himself standing at his front door watching the moon rise, round and romantic. Lighting a fire and lighting up the house. Eating dinner with aphrodisiac ingredients. Preparing himself for love. Watching her lie down naked on the rush sleeping mat, next to the fire's warmth, and starting her serpentine dance with an elegance already primed in the school of sex. And then lying down next to her, slowly penetrating the home of all life's mysteries, dousing the flames of desire with the rain of his flesh. And sowing his seed. He dreams of having a daughter. For women are born with a gold mine within them and pursue their sustenance in the sweat of men. He does not want a son, who will be born a slave, to be deported, and who will pursue his sustenance in the perils of the forest, become a robber and serve to increase the prison population. A man is born to suffer and dies far away, and that is why he does not want a son.

José feels an itch in the palm of his hand, and he massages it with the tip of a fingernail. The massage reaches his heart and awakens gentle thoughts — a sign of luck. He smiles. Human nerves have the

< 82 >

magical power to detect fair-weather tides and storms. It's a signal, he thinks to himself, a sign of good fortune, so they say. Today, I shall get some news. The sun won't go down before I have received my nice surprise. But what good news can a slave ever receive in life?

Maybe it's the message of the future floating in the air, reaching his nervous system like a succession of portentous waves. The dream of freedom is born in his mind.

◆   ◆   ◆

José wants to stay sitting there until nightfall. So as to watch the moon rising from the waters of the ocean. He wants to count how many stars there are in the blanket of night. He wants to choose the star that will lead him along the paths of freedom. He loves the murmur of the waves in the darkness. He loves seeing the gulls tracing geometrical paths, greeting the approaching night. A mermaid's voice can be heard coming from the deep. He listens carefully. It is the gentle whisper of a wave as it extinguishes itself against the anchored bulk of a lifeless boat.

"Hello, slave."

He turns his head slowly toward where the voice is coming from and does not see anyone. He rubs his eyes and gazes once more at the screeching gulls.

"Hey, slave!"

A woman appears out of nowhere like a goddess. In her gaze, there is a flash of lightning to pulverize men's hearts. My God, how pretty she is! Her whole being is a tissue of sweetness. The bullseye of lust. She must be Saint Valentina of the Despairing. My God how beautiful, how resplendent she is!

"Why don't you answer me, slave?"

José looks. He does not deign to answer. That kind of woman isn't worthy of trust. They are the eternal pursuers of their upkeep through the sweat of men. The sweat of white and assimilated African men has the flavor of money, but the slave's sweat smells bad. A black man's stink.

"Slave!"

There is temptation and entreaty in that voice, like a parched bird weeping for a drop of water. José puts his hands over his ears.

"Speak to me, slave!"

In the beginning, her voice is soft. Then it sours and becomes aggressive. At this point, José feels obliged to respond.

"What do you want of me if I've never seen you before?"

"Ah, slave! Then see me now."

"What do you want me to see in you, if I don't know you?"

"Then get to know me now."

"What for?"

"For us to be friends. For us to talk from time to time. You're always on your own, slave. Don't you need a woman?"

"Flutter off, butterfly, take your filth and go and land on some sailor's arm."

José understands. By her gestures. Her gaze. Her bodily curves swaying like the leaves of a palm tree. It was an invitation for momentary love, like a plume of feathers dissolving into ash and dust. Tumult, a plunge and then nothing. That kind of woman has love for sale but not to give. He doesn't have money to pay.

"Your feet are caked with mud, slave."

José looks at himself. His feet and hands are the color of soil.

"So what? What's that got to do with you?"

"Come with me, and I'll give you a bath."

Then, he hears the voice of loneliness and despair. And he discovers that he has a body and isn't dead. That after all is what a woman is all about. A blanket of fire on a cold night. The salt of life. A drop

< 85 >

of water in the inferno of the world. A tongue of flame in an abandoned heart.

"No. I don't like your kind of woman."

"Ah, slave!"

"I don't like women of your condition."

"You don't like me? Poor little black man! Milksop! Slave! Savage!"

José looks at her angrily. And he senses within himself the burgeoning of a storm that will cause him to burst out in all directions like the turbulent waters of the river breaking over dykes.

"Why do you provoke me?"

"Because you're a coward. Emasculated. You're scared of confronting a woman. You're not a man, slave."

The girl has waved a red rag in front of the eyes of a raging bull. José exhales fire through his nostrils. And he joins the fray. He looks around him and sees no sign of anyone, night is falling. He grabs her furiously and pierces her as if with a javelin, transferring all his energy into her body. He groans. At the height of his orgasm, José yearns for his mother, the only creature that links him to life. His father disappeared, like he himself did, along the byways of the world.

No, it isn't love he is waging. It is war on a virgin forest. And in that instant, she seems to have found a man who would placate the

< 86 >

fires of her anxiety, and who would make her forget the existence of other men on the surface of the Earth. She has also discovered that the ideal man is an unattainable treasure. To find one is a piece of luck few enjoy and she has been lucky this time.

José emerges from the waters like a shipwrecked sailor. A touch of magic transported him to a new life. For that is just what love is like. A secret like the birthplace of a breeze. Germinating anywhere, flowering in any thicket and dying wherever else. For it's the moon's twin and hides behind the clouds, teasing romantic sensibilities, while it comes and goes at the will of the tides, branding hearts with the record of its passage. At the instant when love strikes life is renewed.

"Where are you from, slave?"

"Me?"

In José's mind, there are memories of childhood, with the song of the partridges greeting the new morning. He feels a yearning for the notes of the marimba in the moonlight, imitating the song of the skylarks. Ah, my homeland, my mountainside, my mother's arms!

"Where am I from?"

"Yes, where are you from?"

His trajectory has been the same as all slaves. He was hunted down and shackled like a criminal, without knowing what he had done wrong. Living in the labor camp, those human castoffs forget about the idea of returning when night falls, huddled around the fire to escape despair, without the neon lights and cheap women. Just fire and alcohol. And the smell of raw tobacco. And cannabis. And they drink palm wine, quantities of palm wine, before doubling up into drunken dances, yelling like unhitched madmen, stamping on the earth, which rises in clouds of dust, praying to imaginary gods, releasing sweat that cures their eternal sadness. They were all dragged in the same chains to these lands. In order to break rocks and plant coconut palms as if they were the zombies of history.

"You're very quiet, what are you thinking about?"

"Me?"

He has nothing of the present in him. Nor of the future. Merely a past of sadness swathed in his memory. He does not know which year he was born. Nor will he ever know. Nor whether he exists or ever existed once. He is a grain of sand at the will of the wind. He was dragged along on the longest march in his life, walking barefoot for years on end. Gúruè, Mocuba, Lugela, Ile, Macuse, Milange, Quelimane, unknown places and people. He discovered that the land was a vast place, much larger than a mortal's gaze could take in. That the horizon is reborn the moment it is reached. That the point of arrival is always a point of departure. That pain makes a man harder, and yearning does not kill, but merely leaves a wound.

"How old are you?"

"Ah, how old?"

How old? How many steps do bare feet take during a whole life? How many dreams can a living man accommodate in his head? How many tears are there in a woman's eyes? How many offences can one heart suffer? How many drops of blood are there in a human body? How many years has he been alive? How many years of freedom did he enjoy, and how many years was he a prisoner? He does not know nor does he want to know. So many. He left the land of his birth when he was still a youth, but now, he has wisdom teeth and a growth of beard. He has been fed many a handful of rancid flour and given many a good beating.

"What's your name?"

"Me?"

Ah! How long are the routes across the sea! How parched the desert crossing! How far the afterworld of our ancestors! How beautiful is the land that witnessed our birth! How comfortable is a mother's uterus!

"How long have you been here?"

"Me? How long?"

He does not answer, because she knows all about it, she knows. She is a Chuabo and was born in the middle of a palm plantation. Her birth cries fused with the agonies of dying slaves, lashed to the tree trunks until they perished. She was born surrounded by pain and that is why she knows everything, she knows that a slave has no name or homeland. The sailors civilized the people by gouging out their eyes. They spread the word of Christ by fornicating with women in the forests. They built the new world with swords, guns and whips. They pacified the land by ripping the tongue from their mouths. The sailors' leader would yell to the four winds: that one's a thief, seize him. That one's strong, shackle him, sell him. That one's stubborn, kill him. Those ones are poisonous, lucid, they think and conspire, stuff them full of liquor. They're all big headed, idle, tramps, liars, enslave them.

"When will I see you again, slave?"

"When? Why?"

Again? Yes, he wanted to return to his childhood again. To the times of the myths he believed in that life blossomed at the bottom of the ocean, and that the most powerful God had built a diamond throne in its depths. To the times when all that came from the ocean was blessed. Fish. Thunder. The clouds. That the ocean was the center of divine creation, where the land came to an end and the clouds formed. He wanted so much to return to the times when the ocean was a road, paradise, secret and mystery.

"It was nice knowing you, slave."

"Eh?"

She gets up. She takes a couple of steps and tries to leave. José pulls her down again, like a pick furrowing the soil. He turns her body over with a planter's hands. And her body gains the porous softness of fertile earth, through which the river of life flows. He is both boat and sailor and she the high seas. And along they sail peacefully. Together, they remove the obstacles in their path and fly beyond the stars. José releases every note of love's song without knowing that he will sing those same notes in the song of pain.

They awaken from their dream and look at the world. The moon bids farewell in its flight, the sun is approaching. They part without a word or a kiss. They were sure they would meet again, like two prisoners inhabiting the same cage.

< 91 >

7

It was on one of those afternoons. Moyo was in his hut, surrounded by jars both big and small, plastic ones, enamel ones, ones made of glass, which he filled up with mysteries and the fruits of his knowledge. He prepared the herbs and roots he would use the following day, to help the countless clients who were seeking bodily and spiritual health. The hut smelled of fresh sap. He was hoping no client would appear that night, for he had had a particularly tiring day.

José dos Montes paid him a brief visit in order to hear the timeless wisdom of the patriarchs flow from that mouth of his and to radiate an image of the father he never had. If my father were alive, he would be as kindly as Moyo, he sighed to himself.

Moyo is the cornerstone of many lives. He is a short man. Chubby. A man who handles his magic objects like an artist, unhurried, as if he had all the time in the world. With magic wands intricately weaving the lives and souls of people coming from every direction to confide in him their most outlandish secrets. His hair is always uncombed in a Rastafarian style. A look capable of calming the most blazing heart. A man who gives anyone the benefit of his innocent smile, and a word of tenderness.

"Good afternoon, Moyo."

"You, here?"

The friendship between José and Moyo didn't just happen out of the blue. Many generations of enslaved, condemned men passed through his hands. He offered each and every one of them a word of hope. He was held in great respect by the people and feared by the system. On two occasions, Moyo's hands brought José back to this world from beyond. The first when he was bitten by a fearsome snake. The second when he was tied to a post and whipped as a punishment for trying to escape from the camp. His body was transformed into a purée of gore, which Moyo restored to life purely with his magic. He cared for him patiently, like an old woman absorbed in her needlework. And he rocked his spirit with magical stories of men, animals, monsters and everything, as if he were a child. José dos Montes owes his life to that man. A man who brought him back to this world from beyond. Who saw in him a little child without a father or mother, with nowhere to go, without hope. He had fed him for months without asking for anything in return.

"Where have you been, José dos Montes?"

"Here and there."

"You seem distracted, on the moon. Are you in love?"

"Me?"

Moyo's words fell like the hammer blow of justice and echoed in his heart. They pierced his innermost self with the ease of segments of an orange being pulled apart. José's eyes avoided the truth of the sentence and sought concealment in the emptiness. He protected the yearning he felt for that momentary love. For, yes, he was indeed in love. With a dream or a mirage. The image of that woman filled his memory.

"Yes, I'm in love."

"That's wonderful! Tell me about it."

"I love that woman."

"What do you know about love?"

"Only what I feel."

"Tell me where you met her and I will tell you your fate. At work? Your future will be one of toil and abundance. At church? Your life will be one of austerity and morality. On the quay? Whores, contraband, sailors, vices, and despair. What's her name?"

"I don't know. I don't even remember her face."

"What's she like?"

< 94 >

"Very pretty. She's like the moon. The ocean. The breeze. A star in the heavens."

"Ah!"

"She is the sunrise, the sunset. A sigh hidden deep in her belly."

"I understand. You're in love with an image, a shape, a ghost. You love a mirage, a shadow, an indefinite form. Where did you meet her?"

"Near the quay."

"At what time?"

"At nightfall."

"She keeps the company of bats. Fireflies. Vampires, oh dear!"

Love appears in many disguises. Sometimes one loves forms. Sometimes gestures, deeds. Goodwill and disaster are attracted to love's name. For love is a trap. For the sake of love, one collects a viper in a golden trunk and places it on a throne inside a house. Misery that makes us spiral in shame in the eyes of the world is drawn to love's name. It may be a thief, a murderer or a drug addict. As long as it has a beautiful shape and says I love you, it's enough for you to grow tender and forget all the crimes. In love's name, a lion may don a lamb's fleece.

"I love that woman, Moyo."

< 95 >

"You cannot love the unknown. Where is she?"

"I don't know, I've lost her. Help me find her, Moyo!"

"Listen to the voice of experience, my boy. The most beautiful piece of sculpture may bear a wasps' nest in its heart. The best breast isn't necessarily the most beautiful one, but rather that which produces good milk."

Moyo's eyes turned to the horizon in a look of concentration. A true prediction doesn't require cowries or conches. It is a radar capturing signals of the future emanating from the clouds or another planet. All that is needed is light, from the sun or the moon.

"I see her. She is beautiful, really pretty, she's that white cloud, can't you see? And she is coming to meet you, smiling, walking barefoot across a field of flowers. Now, I see you by her side, your image is white, but is changing rapidly. You seem like a hill, a plateau, an abyss. You darken like the storm of the centuries, you are rain and torment. Your gloom-ridden voice can be heard in an unbridgeable chasm. Why? Your image vanishes in the darkness. The woman dances naked to the sun and the moon. I see her. And I see myself. What am I doing on your path?"

Moyo's knees tremble. There is a change of mood in his expression and a fearful question:

"José dos Montes, who are you?"

"Me?"

"What fortune are you bringing me, what fate?"

"What?"

Moyo quivers. He forgets the present and travels along the pathways of the future.

"What can you see, Moyo?"

"I see myself on your path, screeching messages of doom, which you ignore. I see you calling for me, I stretch out my hand, but I cannot reach you. What are you seeking from me?"

"Me? Nothing, I have no idea!"

"Keep quiet, you cannot answer me now. Only in the future, do you understand?"

"The future?"

"Now go, leave me alone with my thoughts."

"Are you banishing me?"

"No, of course not."

"Don't banish me, Moyo. Can I come back?"

"You will come back. Water never forgets its course."

8

Delfina takes her morning walk. She sits down by the sea, not thinking about anything. Or about something. She sees boats and pirogues. Gulls. She casts her gaze toward the infinite. The same view she first saw as a child. When she opened her eyes to life, the world was already like this. A film without a plot. Blacks being tormented. Loading. Unloading. The crack of the whip. Strikes and deaths. Images that inspired melancholy and sadness in her. She walks along the paved roads with a lightness of foot. She admires the big colonial houses. Apartments. Buildings. Hotels. Life for the whites is fantastic. They killed the trees, they killed the wild animals and constructed glowing cities. They are fascinated by electricity, by lighting the night and subduing the moon's brilliance. The image of the grand old houses projects onto her mind a future of greatness and she vows: I shall possess the power of the ladies and mistresses, even though I am black!

She is sure, she does possess that power. It is a conviction born of intuition, of baseless presentiments, of an electric star or the flash of the distant lighthouse. Of nothing. Some oracle or other. One day, I shall have one of those houses, I swear. I shall be someone in this life. Delfina's heart creates cities full of neon lights. With plenty of food and a lot of wine. In her dream, she is a lady and lives in a stone city. With lacy dresses. Servants as black as she to treat like slaves. A white husband and mulatto daughters whose smooth hair she will comb and tie with silk ribbons. She will have the power of ladies and mistresses, even though she is black, she feels it. She will receive favors from the regime. Black women who marry white men rise in life. They eat salt cod and olives, drink tea with sugar, eat bread with butter and quince jam.

She looks at the streets. Girls of your age, daughters of assimilated blacks, go to school, neatly dressed. Wearing shoes. They learn things she could learn too if only her father agreed to change his life. But the school gate has remained closed. Because she is black and she is beautiful. A young girl. *Flashgirl*, according to the malice and gossip of the menfolk, because the girl shines like a flashlight. The same nun picked on her, eventually expelling her from the mission school. Because she was fleshy, pretty, and interfered with the boys' concentration. In church, she sat in the back row. The nun expelled her again. She distracted the faithful and filled the priests with sinful desires. The nun knew her secrets and shivered with fear of contamination by all that was satanic and forbidden. All because of that day when her mother had cast her like a gazelle into the cage of a carnivore. The old white man was in the darkened room waiting for her. He held her. Pummeled her. Sucked her. Outside, her mother smiled, and drank a glass of wine while she waited. It was a moment of intense conflict, in which she could not understand her mother's joy at her original sin.

She asked her father to apply for assimilated status, so that she could gain access to the state school, where the teachers were normal women rather than schizophrenic nuns. But her father refused. He said the assimilados were murderers. Delfina's father said no to assimilation, without knowing that the country's liberation would take place using the white man's language and without imagining either that the children of the assimilados would assume a leading role in history.

Delfina seethed with rebellious thoughts: why did parents interfere in their daughters' dreams? Sometimes it's in order to marry them off early, other times it's to make them work in the fields, and in her case it was to sell her virginity to an old white man in exchange for a glass of wine.

She tires of wandering through the city and turns into the streets leading down into the suburbs on her way back home. Vague sounds reach her ears like dogs barking in the distance. They are children repeating ditties learned from adults, inspired by hearts that had been embittered by life, assailed by hunger. As she walks down the streets, she inspires sarcastic comments, filthy words, poems composed for ring dances.

Centipede, oh centipede
Don't tell my mama
I slept with white man Sousa
On account of tea and sugar

In the upper city, there are the sailors' lewd wolf whistles. In the suburbs songs of scorn and malice. She feels a sudden loathing for the children who torment her ears, and for the women, their eyes fixed on their navels and on other people's business. That's where the difference resides. The poor put the whip in their hand, the poor put the whip in their tongue. It all hurts the same.

Centipede, oh centipede
Don't tell my mama

Furious, Delfina has climbed the mountain of life, looked down at the children from above and spat on the world below. Because she is famous. It is she who is the subject of conversations in bars and arguments between married couples. She is the most beautiful, best dressed, most desirable black woman. Always in a short skirt. A tight blouse and false hair. Her high heels pricking the earthen floor. A patent leather purse, now swinging from her left hand, now from her right. Buxom. Sensual. A bee harvesting its pollen.

Butterfly, butterfly
Don't tell my mama

They are barefoot children, cut adrift. Directionless. With no past and no future. Maybe without a father or a name, raising clouds of dust until their vocal chords get clogged from swallowing so much dust from the earth. Delfina's ears grow tired of listening to coarse words and her heart fills with bile. She explodes.

"Also tell your mothers I never slept with their husbands, because

< 102 >

they're foul-smelling blacks, who never wash, and stink to high heaven of tobacco, go on, sing that. Do you know what's wrong with you? You envy me my beauty, my freedom. Your mothers sleep on cold mats and I, Delfina Butterfly, have all the men in the world at my feet. Come on, sing it out loud!"

Seagull, oh seagull
Go and tell my mama

Children are wicked, that's true. With their innocence, they are able to aggravate the torment of adults. Hostile voices piercing one's ear drums like the buzzing of bees. Delfina rushes at them with the intention of giving them a good smack, but they take flight in a flock like quayside seagulls making for the highest branches to continue their insults. What do they sing? What are the words they keep repeating? And the gestures they make? A pornography of sound and the spoken word. And in their gestures as well. Children are sometimes horrible and immoral. They can turn an adult's peace into a horror show. She sheds a tear and continues on her way, saddened.

She launches forth into a mumbling complaint, and starts a private monologue on her fate. You people just don't know what it means to

< 103 >

lead a life like mine. A body without any secrets, which is grabbed, paid for, mounted and dismounted. If a woman's body could be worn out, I would have nothing left inside me, after having sold so much to seek my sustenance. How stupid these people are. They should look at their own selves, rather than at me, as if I had something to do with their own wretchedness. Do I have an easy life? My God, these people don't know what they are saying. I pretend I'm happy out of pride. It's out of pride that I wear this regal look when I view the world. Each man who climbs on top of me is another shovelful of earth that covers me. Each coin I'm paid is a thorn in my soul, it hurts. One can't be a nice girl in an unjust world. In an unequal struggle, it's better to surrender than to resist. What do they expect from me? That I should get up at the rooster's crow to go and plant rice? Give myself up to the palm plantations as a slave, in order to earn a cupful of salt after all that exhausting toil!? No! I prefer to offer the sailors the sweetness of my body and earn a few coins to feed my daily illusions. Nature gave me a granary in the depths of my body. A gold mine. Do they think I don't work hard in order to exploit all this to the full? Do they think the life I lead is easy? It's not easy to put up with the convulsed groans of any man on top of my body, expelling himself, renewing himself, freeing himself. I don't

< 104 >

want to die enclosed in darkness, I far prefer this life of illusion. It's my father's fault for refusing to try to be assimilated and for being unwilling to free me from this humiliation. It's my mother's fault for initiating me into the secrets of the pillow when I still dreamed of obtaining a diploma to teach in some native school.

She returns home with a heavy heart. A bitter taste in her mouth. Downhearted. She throws her purse onto her mother's lap like someone hurling a bundle of kindling wood onto the floor, to find some relief for their bodily fatigue. Serafina is startled.

"You're on edge, what's the matter?"

"I'm tired, mother."

"Of what?"

Delfina gives a deep sigh that is more like a puff of smoke from fresh firewood as it starts to burn. She fills her lungs with oxygen so as to project her speech.

"I'm nothing, mother. Nothing I do has any purpose to it. I was unable to study. I can't have any dreams. And when I do something to try and make my life better, the whole world mocks me and treats me like a criminal. The daughters of assimilados are treated with greater respect."

"Do you think I don't know what you suffer, Delfina? Ah, if only

I could open up my breast and show you the wound I have here inside me. It's painful being a black woman. A black has neither god nor country."

"I'm sick of being insulted in the street, mother."

"Ignore peoples' jibes, don't cry, dear daughter."

Moments of pain and rebellion. Her mental darkness transforms the color of children's dreams. Pain kills. Tears cure. Pain and tears hug each other in the expression of suffering. When the pain is deep, tears flow in order to wash sadness away. The moments of greatest turmoil in life drag us into the depths of the valley. Only those who know how to fly can escape the abyss. Mothers should teach their children to steer their way through the flight of the spirit, and leave their mind floating among the clouds. To look at the world from the highest point of their fantasy and swear: I must and will reach the peak of the world.

"One day, I'm going to change my life's course, you'll see, mother. These wretched blacks will see me rise from the ashes with a golden crown. With the world in the palm of my hand, studded with diamonds. You will witness that day, mother, I swear!"

Silence descends in the face of this strange revelation. Serafina is racked by a powerful tremor. Dreaming out loud is something the

< 106 >

mad do, normal people don't launch into flights of fancy, her daughter has been possessed by a demon and is going crazy. She holds her breath so as not to be overcome by the fright. And she stays like this for a long time. It is only with difficulty that she manages to start breathing again. She feels her belly with her hands, to measure with her fingers the size of the dream being incubated in her body, which after all is too small for such a sizeable ambition. Delfina is a strange creature, a new being in the process of revealing herself, she didn't emerge from me. Maybe she is an incarnation of the grand souls of dead rulers, of the ladies and mistresses and of so many spirits that roam throughout Zambezia. She fixes her gaze on her daughter. She sizes her up. Her body is rooted to the ground but her head is inhabiting unknown universes. Diamonds? A woman's dreams can't compete with the glitter of diamonds. Diamonds are stars. And a woman doesn't have wings, she cannot overcome the border between the sky and the earth. Only the mad can do that.

Gestation unites mother and child into one body through the umbilical cord. Delivery separates them and makes them two. Two paths, two destinies, two worlds. Delfina is following her own path.

"Don't dream out loud or you'll get hurt. Ah, Delfina! For us black women, expressing our dreams out loud is forbidden."

"What I'm saying is true. Don't you believe me, mother?"

Serafina is certain. The daughter in her belly was on loan to her. She held her in her arms on loan. Later the earth will carry her in its arms past unknown places, toward the horizon, and eventually swallow her up.

Delfina believes in that day. And she records every stage of her journey with words of bitterness.

"Mother, why did you make me look so dark?"

"Well, I gave birth to you."

Serafina feels pain in her heart. And fear of seeing her daughter plummet to the earth after such a wonderful dream. She feels a knot in her heart and asks God to give her a long life so that she may cushion her daughter's painful fall if good fortune does not favor her.

"I know many people who dreamed of the heights and sank to the bottom. Rein in your ambitions, Delfina."

"I shall overcome, mother."

Human beings trudge along the ground next to snakes. They weren't born to be free, which is why they envy the birds their freedom. They only have eyes for plunging into distant emptiness. They fly off into the heavens with their feet planted on the ground, and they experience their best flight when their eyes are closed. That is why lovers kiss with their eyes closed. Witches and magicians travel on flying carpets, winnows, and magic broomsticks. Human transcendence is the product of fantasy.

"Why didn't you make me look like a white, mother? Mulatto and white women are lucky because they were born with diamonds in their body."

"Why do you torture yourself so much? You're black and thank God. White sailors are strange, they are predators of the exotic and you are pretty! There'll be no shortage of white men dying for your love, my girl."

< 109 >

9

They are one man and one woman at the beginning of the world, facing each other in the circular space of a hut. Causing all the machinery of time and the movement of the planets and stars to stop. Creating disorder among all the things in the world so as to re-arrange them. Everywhere, there is evidence of a violent struggle. The bamboo bedstead is broken. Plates smashed. Blankets and sheets scattered around. Underwear fluttering about in the air like unfurled flags. Screams. Howls. Sighs. That is love. Bodies skirmishing in the original battle. No victor and no vanquished. Where a hug and a kiss seal a truce, the promise of a new battle.

"Delfina, that's your name. I sought your name among the stars in the sky. I have found you."

"Together at last, my José. It was your fault for turning me down. You despised me. The result was all this anguish, oh what anguish!"

They roam the streets without a care. Suddenly, love displays its colorful wings and the sweetness of its taste. They savor it. And it

< 110 >

leaves a yearning in the roof of the mouth. For love is the thief of peace, the thief of hearts. Love is powerful, it triumphs over strength of mind and conscience, and holds sway over all our senses. It opens up new paths and pledges meetings with destiny.

"Delfina, Delfina, what have you done to me?"

"And you, José. What have you done to me, what have you done to my life?"

They look at each other. And they delight in the defeat of their sentiments. In the expression of their love and their cry of denial, for help, they are like two sailors sinking in the deep waters of a lake. They recognize they are the victims of a cursed love. A love that has placed traps in their hearts, when they are ill-prepared for their encounter with fate, because love cancels out every individual.

"You provoked me, you sought me out, pursued me. Of course I should have guessed you were coming to rob me of my peace and quiet. And ever since I made your acquaintance, I have not been able to sleep."

"Yes, I provoked you. Because it doesn't look good for a handsome man to be on his own. And because I have desired you for a long time now."

< 111 >

"You're a tramp I hardly know. A loose stone in the middle of the road. And now my head is teeming with thoughts, my heart made captive."

In his tone of lament, there is an expression of despair. She also argues her case, with skill, for she is a victim of the same trap.

"Indeed. The same thing happened to me and I no longer know what to do. But listen, José," Delfina answers with anguish, "I too don't wish to expend all my energy on a slave. That much I want you to know. But I can't get you out of my thoughts, I just can't."

"Ah, Delfina! If you only knew what it's like to spend one's life, sleeping, dreaming, and waking up, while all the time thinking about the same woman. To see so many butterflies passing by and not being able to grab any of them because one's manhood has faded, only your image is important, as if you were some kind of queen, star or goddess, worthy of my veneration.

In that act, all the castles in the moon are demolished. Fantasies hanging in the clouds fall like drops of rain and are lost in the sand. They were convinced they were above base passions, masters of anything fate might throw at them.

"I drank some magic potions, the kind that kill passions," Delfina explains, "but they didn't work."

< 112 >

"I too consulted Moyo. Do you know what he said? That you represent disaster for me. That I should cast you aside and leave."

"Even so, you came looking for me. Why?"

They look for each other. Out of anxiety and anguish. Because love is a manifestation of fire. To love is to plunge into another body and float away to infinity. But the fire of love doesn't die, it just widens, like the ozone hole in polluted atmosphere. Advancing. Like a palm tree reaching heights. Love is cool and elusive like a breeze. Intangible. A game of blind man's buff. And when it is reached, it lasts for an instant and then veers away. When it is rejected, its stare has the icy force of a salamander.

"You should know, José, that ever since I met you, I view my clients as miserable, stinking wretches. They no longer please me because you are the only one for me. I'm losing business, they think I'm on edge, distracted, uninterested. My earnings have plummeted, José. All because of you."

"If you knew how much torture I've had to put up with. At the end of each working day, I rush to see you. Can you see these wheals on my back? I ran away from the camp and got punished, tied to a post and lashed. Look at my back, Delfina, look, fresh wounds, I was whipped just today and ran away again. I'm the worst treated of all the slaves. It's all your fault, Delfina."

"My God, why did I have to go and fall in love with you? I know men with power, with money. True men, with a name, influence and cash in their pocket. But I was betrayed by fate, slave."

"Indeed. I also lived with so many women . . . well, a few. And they loved me to death. I forced myself upon so many along the highways of life, who then gave themselves to me out of love, willing to give me children and to build a family. And then I had to go and fall in love with you, a quayside whore, the plaything of sailors?"

Both are mistaken, both he and she. Their relationship transcends the mere sharing of time. It is destiny seizing its moment, writing its history. They are in the garden of life, sowing each other with a bit of tenderness. Today, it is in their gaze. Tomorrow, it will be in their kiss. Later on, in their hug. A piece of sweetness for every passing instant.

"All I wanted was one moment. An adventure. I wanted to demonstrate my power as a man and avenge myself. Now, I've discovered that sex is a trap."

The best thing is to lay down one's arms and surrender. Discover an intelligent formula to break free of all this anguish.

< 114 >

"Well then, let's get married, and love will end. When our love is over and done with, each one will be able to follow their own path."

Marriage is the only recourse available to end their torture. Love is a bowl of soup served hot. When it has grown cold, it is no good. It must be eaten right away.

"What?" José exclaims in disbelief. "Marry?"

"Yes. Let's get married so as to destroy this love of ours?"

When love is too passionate, one needs to marry. To destroy Cupid's arrows. Love is a rose that lasts for only one season. A castle made of sand on the seashore. A swelling cloud that releases rain and then fades away. White foam in the gaps between the waves.

"Marry just like that, without more ado?"

"What else? Let's get married, and get it over and done with!"

"Is that a challenge?"

"Yes."

"Okay, let's get married," José answers. "We'll join in matrimony, me and you, before the shocked hoorahs of a crowd of guests, fired up by our kisses. From the throats of this world will come hypocritical speeches wishing us happiness here, long life there, when, deep down, what you and I desire is a cure to burn this illness away and allow us to separate in freedom."

José takes a deep breath and sighs. Let it be as God wills. Let the wave carry me like a dying shrimp into the marshes, the mangrove, the fishwife's scrawny basket or onto the queen's sumptuous platter. Or even into the sailors' rustic repast.

"Let's get going then."

"Where, Delfina?"

"To my parents' house, to announce our engagement."

"Right now?"

"Can you think of a better time?"

José quickly sums things up to himself. Where am I going if I don't even know who I am? My existence is one ceaseless adventure. A continual death and rebirth from life's womb. Here am I, ablaze inside me, but off I go. Because separation and yearning hurt. Anxiety also hurts. The fear of loss, in someone's presence, is also painful. It's better to accept the challenge and seize the moment, seize the body, clutch love before it can get away.

The two of them get up and start walking decisively. He has gone crazy and she is hysterical, completely besotted. They enter a lane and splash in a puddle of water. They pass some woodland. They leave one hut behind them, and then another, then some tall and small trees. There is a smell of topsoil, a smell of fertility, the fresh smell

< 116 >

of rice fields. What José never foresaw, has now occurred: fate has thrown its saddle over his back and love is riding him as if it were his new master. But how beautiful it is to die of love!

10

The wind fills her ears with sweet murmurings, like the babble of water from a spring. She has stopped work in the garden, got to her feet and looks into the distance. And she sees a lustrous, unprecedented image. Amazing like some romantic apparition on moonlit nights. But it isn't night, it is broad daylight. There is no moon, but a burning sun that makes the afternoon searingly hot. Serafina is intrigued. She wipes the sweat from her brow with the palm of her hand. She rubs her eyes to get a clearer view. It is her Delfina, walking toward her, hand in hand with a smiling stranger.

"Hello, mother!"

"Hey, what's happened?"

Delfina is leading home a fine upstanding stallion by the hand, her victory trophy. Her face exhibits the pride of a heroic horse breaker, while also being romantically tamed by passion. Their hands are

< 117 >

firmly sealed. They form a knot. A Gordian knot. Their palms joined, their life lines, lines of fortune and fate joined in one common line. Like two rivers together in one estuary, spilling out into the immensity of the world. Their held hands massaging each other's heart. There is confidence in the way they hold hands. Trust. Security. Of all the pledges of love, this is the most sublime expression. Serafina then recalls the old song: give me your hand and I'll give you mine. Like this we shall overcome the ghosts and thorns that lie in wait along the way! There is something mysterious about this masculine presence.

"Is there some problem?"

"No!"

She detects secret signals in the stranger's profile. An expression of bravura, of a person born to win all battles. A youthful look. The strong, muscular arms of world-building heroes. A well-shaped, unadorned man, pure nature. One who goes completely crazy for any woman, but whom life has transformed into a simple planter of coconuts.

"Who is this man?" Serafina asks, with an air of surprise.

"José. My fiancé. I want to introduce him. We're going to get married."

"Married?"

She puts down her hoe and sniffs the breeze a little. Her daughter has brought her various white male visitors, who did not displease Serafina because they left her a bit of loose change, bottles of wine, silk scarves stolen from a wife's wardrobe. Sometimes they even brought a container with a bit of salted cod and a few olives. What would that black man give by way of payment?

"Get married?" Serafina asks again.

"Yes, get married."

Her mother lets out a cry of alarm. Bitter alarm. As if a fish bone has got stuck in her throat. She chokes. Coughs. And starts talking again hoarsely.

"With that black man?"

"Oh! You don't understand! You're blacker than he is, mother!"

"Improve your race, my dear Delfina!"

She repeats unconsciously what she heard from the mouths of so many black mothers. And from whites. Get married to a black man? Confirming that sex is a weapon in a time of war. Marry a black man?

Words often heard coming from the mouths of sailors. That the blacks themselves adopt as unquestionable truths. Sentences heard etch themselves into the mind and become real. And so lies take on the shape of truth. For her whole life, Serafina has absorbed the

< 119 >

insults and jeers of the sailors, and these have become sewn into her conscience. Her conscience struggles with itself in a theater of war, in a battle without a winner. The stigma of race has left malignant seeds that multiply like the root of a cancer, and will kill generations, even after the sailors have left.

"Even so, you've alarmed me. Are you going to marry someone you barely know?"

"Oh, mother! What does it mean to know, for me who sells her body to the first client who shows up?"

"Ah, Delfina! Spare me from your immoral activities."

"Immoral activities that pay for your keep, dear mother!"

Serafina admires that daughter of hers. She has everything to be a queen. And she must surely have been one in some previous incarnation. Or was she destined to be one in some incarnation still to come. Because she is intelligent, beautiful, aggressive. She overcomes all obstacles and even overcomes herself when she gets in her own way. She's got a backside worthy of sitting on a throne. A face to be shown within the frame of a mirror. A neck slender enough for a diamond necklace. Abundant hair, good for harboring garlands, crowns, and diadems. She is one of those women who recognize the futility of life and live it to the full.

"We're in love with each other, mother."

"Delfina, since when have you started talking about love? And where did you learn it if I never taught you about it?"

José didn't know how one asked for someone's hand in marriage. His life had never permitted him such an experience. He looks down and seeks shelter in the scraps of sand. He realizes he is a poor black man who is a candidate for marriage, without a penny to his name. Without a ring, or a wallet. His slave man's pants don't even have pockets. He is a barefoot groom, writing indelible trajectories with the soles of his feet, the marks of his destiny on paper made of clay. He should have asked for Moyo's protection as a best man, the moment he had the chance. But he wouldn't have accepted.

"We love each other, mother."

"Love that good-for-nothing? A slave?"

Serafina loses all control of her emotions and her heart gallops. That boy's arrival has opened old scars. He is the bearer of a past, of the times when Serafina dreamed, sighed, and despaired. For the son who came, for the son who left. And when another black son is born, history repeats itself.

"I love a man. More of a man than any other man. Because he's my man."

"Delfina, why do you offend me?"

Delfina's words are seasoned with revolt. She knows she is holding something good in that hand. There is no virile man in the family, they have all disappeared mysteriously. All she has left is an elderly father and an exhausted mother whom she has supported on her adolescent shoulders. And in spite of this, she thinks life is good.

"I would never offend you, mother."

"He isn't what he seems."

The sun's rays burn with a painful force and José readies himself for greater insults. Or aggression. He is willing to put up with anything for love. Whips. Sticks, stones, knife assaults that might force him to take flight like a dog with its tail between its legs. That woman's words are as intense as thunderclaps. They fall as thick as darts. Anything to convince him that happiness is a gift from the most powerful and love a treasure that only the powerful can gain access to.

"What's your name, slave?" Dona Serafina asks.

"José."

Serafina's gaze remains fixed on the figure of José. He is of sculpted clay. A son of the thickets and the palm groves. Born from the dark womb of slavery. That figure awakens ghosts in her, resurrecting

< 122 >

ancient suns on a journey into the past. The backyard of the houses encircled. The granary in flames. People in panic seeking shelter in the shadow of a grain of sand. The land in tears. Folk running for their lives, caught, shackled. Blows from sepoys wielding sticks. The piercing shrieks of sons disappearing into the map of the world. Bodies dropping like ripe fruit. The locals resisting, advancing, killing, and dying while they yell: homeland or death, but slavery never! Three children torn from Serafina's arms to the sound of bullets, on that gruesome night of the sepoys. In Serafina's heart, there lies a contradiction. She is assailed by an irrepressible desire to hug, caress and fondle that young man with a mother's tenderness. But this desire is destroyed by spirits slumbering in the image etched into her memory. She turns to José and addresses him in an aggressive tone.

"What means do you have to marry my Delfina?"

"Me?"

"Come on, answer me, you pathetic man!"

"Answer you?"

Her words strike like angry whip lashes in José's mind and he quivers with surprise and alarm. Human beings have changed out of all recognition since the sailors arrived. The new regime's sword has expunged love from mothers' hearts.

"Have you looked at yourself in the mirror?" Serafina resumes her questions.

"Looked at myself? Ah!"

José knows his body's reflection through the ecstatic shudders of women ravaged out in the bush, as they sigh you are beautiful, you are a male, you are a man. He knows the image he projects in the concentric ripples in the waters of the rice fields, and which is akin to the worms, leeches, and other malign blood sucking creatures hidden in the slime. He senses some repellent creature in himself. Because of his slave's outfit. His skin that has become impregnated with the muddy smell of the swamps. His feet that have covered countless kilometers unshod, treading on stones, snakes, grasses, that have travelled along valleys and across mountains, forests and deserts. His muscular arms that have broken rocks and built highways. His whip scars. Scab marks. His calloused hands that have planted five thousand palms. Or ten thousand. Or a hundred thousand. That have planted rice, tea, sisal and cotton, sugarcane and beans, and shaped the empire's grandeur. At that precise moment he looks into his innermost being and identifies himself: I am an honorable man, a good man. My arms are strong, my feet bare. I have given my best in the construction of the world. I have given so much that I ended up like this, empty handed.

"Delfina, my girl, I was hoping you would tell me: I've got a white lover! I could accept that, you see, for there would be no lack of scraps on our dinner table, wine, salt cod, and olives. But a slave?"

"Glutton! Idler!" All you can think about is your next meal and your own peace and quiet. You never think about me."

Delfina answers back. Like all children, she knows nothing of this life we lead, nothing of this world. She hasn't yet learned that gestation is long and death quick. That black women have learned to view pregnancy with anguish and to put their ear to seashells to find out what the future holds. Will he live? He'll be as strong as iron, the shells whisper back. Will he be free or a slave? The shells answer with a laugh, amid the eternal silence of the stones. This one may live, the mothers predict, prophetesses of the future. Maybe this one will avoid being sold and banished, they pray. The one who left for the unknown on a slave ship, will he ever come back? Let's hope it's a little girl, a butterfly to bring happiness to my eyes. Delfina doesn't yet know that black women have invented a song and dance as magic rituals against bitterness.

"Delfina, are you out of your mind? Do you realize the step you're taking?"

"It's an expression of my love, dear mother."

"When you say yes, then your fate is sealed. Think carefully before you take such a step."

"I've already thought about it, Mother," Delfina answers with both war and peace on her tongue. Confident in her victory, while producing despair in her mother's heart.

"Think of me too. You are my bread and sustenance."

A timeless pain returns and gently settles in Serafina's belly. The same pain that has been present ever since the world was born, when children abandon the womb, abandon their mother's arms, abandon the home, abandon their homeland. For life is about arrival and departure.

"What is love for a black woman, Delfina? Tell me: what is love in this land of mail-order teenage brides? Tell me what love is for a woman raped by a soldier, a sailor, or a slave while on her way to fetch water? Stories of passion are for those who can dream. A black woman doesn't play with dolls, but real babies, once she reaches the age of twelve. Talk of love and virginity is for white women, not us. Why are you talking about love? Passion is dangerous, Delfina, don't place your trust in it. Love is as whimsical as the tides, they come

< 126 >

in and go out, hide, appear, fly off. If you want to create a solid base for a home, don't trust love, because when it vanishes, you'll destroy everything and set off in search of the next one. That's why love and passion should be forbidden to us poor, black women."

Serafina's soul sways in the approaching emptiness. The paths of suffering, the old bile returning. She is on the high seas, struggling courageously while trying to shape what nature forbids. Human hands stop everything in its tracks except for wind and pain. Love is still more powerful, human hands cannot reach it.

"Mother," Delfina says, trying to soothe the moment and take the edge off their argument, "this union is merely to exhaust our passion."

"I don't understand."

"No passion can survive in marriage, isn't that so?"

"That's true."

"That's why you must let me marry. So that love may be killed."

José holds his breath and hides his gaze in the ground. He steadies his feet like an old tree weathering the fury of a storm. His hand seeks refuge in hers. So that they may ride the same wave together in case the boat founders. She nestles more closely against his chest, demonstrating through her gesture what words cannot complete.

"Delfina, you're not even any good at lying, you can't fool me, oh

< 127 >

no! You're hopelessly in love with this black, this lowlife. I can see it in your words and in your gestures."

"Yes, we love each other. Very much. What's wrong with that?"

At that moment, Serafina feels like a dairy cow exhausted from nursing the world. From her past full of despair, she foresees an even darker future.

"Isn't it enough to watch your black brothers, enslaved and deported to the unknown, never to return? Oh, Delfina! I've shed many a tear in this life. Come on, get yourself a white man, and make some mixed children. They are never seized or mistreated, they are free and can go where they want. One day too, they will be bosses and will take the place of their father and your life will be saved, Delfina. Happy are the women who bear light-skinned children, because they will never be captured and taken away.

"You have lived through your pains, dear mother. Now, I want to live through mine, to have a story to tell my own children," Delfina replies, trying to console her distraught mother.

Serafina understands. But all she wants is a different generation, able to walk ahead without fear, free of the whip and forced labor, and to tread the ground with pride, even if it glances back ashamed of its origins, scorning the womb that has borne it and the black breast that has nursed it. Her despair spreads a whiff of sadness through the air.

"Tell me, slave. What does love mean to you, if you appeared out of the unknown and you're destined to die at any moment? Everywhere I look, I see hatred, death, blood, and fury. The men of the sea getting their revenge against a whole race. We have been landed with this tragedy all for the sake of love. Tell me, slave, what's love good for? Where have you come from, slave? You've journeyed through valleys and across mountains. You've met all kinds of women. Have you crossed rivers and oceans solely in order to steal my Delfina away from me? No, I can't accept such a marriage."

José pursues a hope hidden in a grain of sand. In a firefly's tear. All around him, there is darkness, the sun has never existed. In order to light up his way ahead, he will have to wait for night to fall and catch the pinpricks of light flashing from the eyes of a star.

"You don't love this black man, Delfina, no, you can't love him. He has imprisoned you with the strength of his witchcraft."

"You may even be right, dear mother," Delfina replies, somewhat unnerved by the atmosphere of bitterness.

"You will know poverty, Delfina! You should have got yourself an old white man, given him children and been a concubine."

"May God answer your prayers, mother. But you should be aware that a black man is a person as well. He may have power and money, mother."

"If a black man is rich, it's out of luck, but for a white man, it's his destiny. Rather a poor white man than a rich black one."

Serafina is hurt, and utters curses. When there is no hope for the future, it is better for love to be aborted right away. Let the forests of old die and the earth be sown with new seeds. Palm trees. Sisal, cotton and tea. Let the happiness in lovers' hearts be extinguished, to avoid disappointments and thorns tomorrow. May every black womb be sterilized, may the menfolk be castrated, so that black mothers may not spawn native sons only to be left empty handed, a pain in their breast and the marks of childbirth on their bellies.

"Delfina, are you really going to get married, you stubborn girl? Can you imagine the pain you've inflicted on my heart? In the empty bedroom you've left behind? In the chair now devoid of your presence? What will I do with your plate, your glass, your comb, your mirror? What will I do with an empty house without your smile?"

José begins to understand that vanquished woman now, in the process of self-abrogation and denial. A woman who doesn't believe in her own existence, and doesn't even bother to defend herself,

< 130 >

surrendering to her own self-destruction like a lamb on the sacrificial fire. Frightened like a mouse in the face of their marriage. It isn't her race she is rejecting, but that timeless pain tormenting her. She has been possessed by the specters of the men of the sea and she is trying to strike out the vestiges of a race with red ink.

"You're pretty, dear daughter, you deserve a better fate. You're one of those black girls white men like. You've got fleshy, full-blooded lips. Thick eyebrows like skeins of silk. Teeth of ivory and the eyes of a cat. You've got a full breast and the backside of a queen, all full and beautifully shaped. And you're about to waste all this treasure by giving yourself to a black man!"

Everyone is shocked by Serafina's attitude. For telling a stranger what no one has said before. Churning up all the secrets that silence conceals and only death sweeps away.

"Would you rather put me up for sale, dear mother?"

"Not for sale, but for rent."

"Does it make you feel happier to know that my life can be sold by the meter? Or the kilo?"

"A black woman's life is to serve, dear Delfina. In the rice fields. In the sowing and harvesting of cotton, so as to earn a kilo of sugar a month or a bar of soap that doesn't even fit in the palm of your

< 131 >

hand. A black woman's strength lies in her ability to serve in all manner of ways. You were very lucky to have been born beautiful, otherwise you would be suffering under a blazing sun, where unseen bloodsuckers provoke illnesses and death out in the marshlands. You're lucky, you can serve in bed, you've got more income. Why are you throwing your luck away?"

Delfina's father tries to intervene to mollify the moment, and quell the argument. He tries to douse the flames with warm, tender words.

"Serafina, please calm down. Why are you mistreating this boy? You can't say such bad things."

"I can and I will. Do you know what it's like to carry a child in your belly only to later feel the emptiness in your arms, the pain in your breast, and the yearning in your soul? If you knew what all the waiting was like, nine months of sickness, vomiting, pains! If you knew what childbirth is like, how hard it is and how painful it is to give birth alone, because the little baby's father has been deported to some corner of this world, one moonless night, to raise a baby all by yourself on your body's milk, only for someone you've never seen before to turn up and tear what is your most precious possession away, leaving only pain, silence, a vacuum. Can you ever understand? Do you know what it means to brave the vague shapes of the palm trees shrouded in the darkness of night, on the way to the maternity clinic, the health center or some healer, in search of a panacea for your child's endless fevers, in order for a storm surge of sailors to appear at any moment to take it all away, leaving you amid tears?"

Serafina's soul is left adrift in the torrent of her words like a stranded ship. She is wafted upwards like a bird with broken wings. For all to see. Her hurt is real, genuine. She suffers as only a woman can suffer. With a taste of blood and tears. With the stinging taste of bites in her navel, amid the clamor of all the women in the world, driven mad by the pangs of childbirth.

"If you knew the wakeful nights spent watching over each child's sleep, gazing at the stars in the sky, and then afterwards opening up your body to an occasional companion, making love that has nothing to do with love but rather hatred, only to fall pregnant once again, satisfying the womb's obstinacy in refusing to dam up the source of life! Have you ever wondered what a mother feels when she sees her sons leaving for a life of slavery? And you, Delfina, are choosing the path of suffering. You're going to marry a black man, you'll give birth to more black children or more tragedy. With so many white men who are fond of you. There's no problem at all if you eliminate your race in order to gain your freedom. We must resist, Delfina, we must resist. We must surrender to the life that has been imposed upon us, believe in their God, that invisible being who has no concrete form. I loathe all those ladies and mistresses, all of them mulatas, I hate those pious white women, always willing to elaborate beautiful speeches about the suffering, illiterate, poor little African woman. Where do the roads come from, the plantations along with all their wealth? And the beautiful houses, who is it that builds them? And the fine cuisine? And the white clothes, all starched and scented? From the hands of slaves like José, given birth to by black mothers. And what do we get in return? Scorn, insults, and expulsion to the fringes. Who are we black women in this regime devoid of hope. A black woman's fate is to lean against the door post weeping eternally before the indifference of the world, placing flowers on the imaginary graves of the children we have lost. Ah, dearest Delfina! At this moment, I weep for the children I have lost to the world. There are three of them. They came from the most sacred part of me, they came from afar! You don't know how much I suffered to bring them into the world. At the time, I lived two hundred kilometers from the maternity clinic. When I was six months gone, I walked all the way there, and I had to wait another three months to guarantee a safe delivery. Your father built a hut in an encampment that had emerged around

< 134 >

the clinic housing pregnant women who had come from all over the place. My mother-in-law left the comfort of her home and travelled with me so as to provide me with food, water, and firewood, while I waited. After I had given birth, I stayed there another month so as to be sure the child was healthy and would live. And all that effort was in vain, because my sons were taken away from me in the flower of their youth and carried off on a ship to unknown lands. Maybe they're alive. Or dead. I have a feeling I will never see them again. And they were fine young men, like this José standing in front of me here. Nowadays, I understand the suffering bitches and nanny-goats go through, when we humans take their young away from them, and send them out into the unknown before the impotent gaze of their mothers. But a day will come when the whole world will remember the suffering of the black mother and will ask us for forgiveness, for the children they tore away from us and stole in order to be sold."

José dos Montes listens to her embittered voice and feels pangs of emotion: this voice sounds like his mother's. This lament sounds like his own mother's lament. This pain, without a doubt, is the same pain his own mother feels. How I yearn for my mother!

"Ah, if God had given me more daughters, I might enjoy a longer life! Ah! If only this José of yours were an assimilado. If at least he

< 135 >

were a Chuabo, from a superior clan. But from what I can see, he's a Lomwe, a lowly slave, without any class or breeding."

When it comes to weeping, Serafina chooses the most romantic tone from the menu of lamentations. One with different notes. Gentle, breezy tones mingle with solemn, stormy ones.

"All I want is happiness and security for your Delfina," says José. "God is the one who knows, doesn't he? God isn't crazy, nor did he make a mistake in his formula for creation. If he made us blacks, he surely knows why. And if he gave us suffering by way of our fate, he's got his reasons for that."

"Try and understand what has happened, mother. I tried to resist such a step, but my heart betrayed me, mother."

"I wish you all the happiness in the world, dear Delfina."

A home is a garden where a couple sow flowers. A passerby comes, picks them, and leaves. That's the start of much torment. Human hearts shouldn't fall in love in order not to suffer.

"From this moment on, yearning will be my only companion. This visit is a door that is opening. This man is a thief coming towards me, ready to pick a flower from my heart with his strong hand. Delfina is gradually leaving. First, engagement. Then, marriage. Finally, absence."

Delfina's father says nothing, but he contemplates José benevolently, because he seems to detect signs of an honest man in him. Deep down, he gives thanks to God. At last, the savior has appeared who will rescue his daughter from vice and destruction. That is why he gives the final verdict.

"Well then, my boy, welcome to this house. From today, you are a member of this family. Marry and may you both be happy. Bring us many grandchildren and much joy in our old age. May God give you the happiness you seek. You have my blessing."

* * *

Delfina's father was pleased at the prospect of her departure. When children leave, a husband and wife return to their love of old. Giving each other succor in the autumn of their lives. When arms are released from caring for little ones, they are once again available for a new embrace.

"Ah, my dear Serafina! You've suffered many a blow in this life! Pain has shut your eyes. So much pain has made you lose your good sense. You're right. The faithful dog is domesticated by being given a hiding. You only think about your master, you don't exist. After

< 137 >

so many years of insults, a lie has become the truth. Now, you are in a state of self-denial, you cancel yourself out, you feel shame and fear in being black."

"Do you think so?"

"You ignited the fire of passion in the hearts of those little doves, dearest one. Love is a malignant disease, Serafina. The more you repel it, the more resistant it becomes. Refusing this marriage is like shooing away a dog with a nice fat bone in your hand. Children marvel at the colors of fire, and want to prove their strength with their own hands."

"Do you think so?"

"Words are grist to the mill, Serafina. There are words that should never be uttered. Feelings that should remain hidden. You spoke too much. You used every weapon to put an end to the dream. You went through the world in depth and on the surface. You swept away all the weather vanes, merely in order to snuff out the breath of life. It's lucky that love is free and doesn't obey any command."

"Is that true?"

"I saw the candle of chaos lighting up the girl's road ahead. I saw a road littered with despair in the boy's mind. Instead of separating them, you united them. You are the person responsible for their marriage."

Women dream of the day they will give birth, but they do their best to delay the hour of departure. And this happens because departure is another birth delivered.

"To love is also to open one's hands and allow them to leave. To love is to gain but also to lose. It's the acceptance that one sows oneself in order to germinate in some later incarnation."

"Ah!"

"My dear Serafina, you should smile and dream. You've got to believe in tomorrow. Oppression will come to an end. In future years, children will grow up next to their mothers, they will be buried in the family grave, next to their ancestors. They will never leave and families will grow larger. Women's wombs will bear millions of children to give new names to those who have left, resuscitate those who have died, as well as the young ones to be born in the future."

She looks at her daughter and then at her daughter's fiancé and recognizes that they both came from her. She comes to her senses. She is the uterus that opens and the creature who departs. All that remains are the wounds in her body so that life may go on. Sadly, in this world, pains weigh more than joy. Love comes, and in a flash, causes one to forget the anguish of the journey. For eternity is no more than an instant.

"That's enough tears shed over this whole affair, and now we must dream of our daughter's marriage. Don't you think it's a miracle? Yesterday, she was a prostitute and today a blushing virgin bride, walking up the altar steps with organ music and everything! It will make history, we've never had a wedding in our family. Don't you think that's a miracle, Serafina?"

"Yes, it is."

"Well then? Why so much anguish?"

Serafina begins to let her mind wander and her bitterness is dissipated. She thinks of her daughter being seen by everyone. She imagines the girl at the altar, dressed in white and carrying a spray of orange blossom. The church bells ringing, the organ playing the Wedding March, everything decorated in the girl's honor. She thinks of the envy of all those who threw stones at her. Yes, it's good that she's getting married so that the whiteness of the altar may wash away all the stains of the past.

"You're right, husband. Let our daughter walk up the aisle holding white roses, in a church bedecked with vases full of anthurium and bluebells," Serafina says, now feeling more cheerful.

"And later, may they have many children! Delfina should give birth to three sons. So that the brothers who left, never to return, may be

< 140 >

named anew. Then, let her bear two daughters and two more sons, in homage to her father and mother, father-in-law and mother-in-law. And then finally, some more, maybe three, maybe four, to give names to as she sees fit. Ten or eleven in all."

"Our family will grow, my dear friend. And you will be the patriarch."

"Indeed. But tell me: why were you so rude to the young man?"

"I was unfair, I know. It was fear, believe me, it was fear. I'm afraid of the whites. They are invincible. They are masters of fire, they are masters of water because they emerged from the depths of the sea. Our witchcraft is limited to the land, it cannot resist fire or water. That's why I give up, before they can kill me."

"One day, their power will meet its end."

Serafina remains silent. She recalls her dear Delfina, who was given to crying. She sees her, still tiny, placing her arms on her breasts, her shoulders, her lap, mother and daughter embracing each other, together, like that timeless image of the Virgin Mary. Now, she has exchanged her for a man. Children should never grow up.

"On reflection, things actually turned out better like this," Serafina admits. "A black son-in-law, black grandchildren, a harmonious family. As for the future, only God knows. Those mulatto

< 141 >

grandchildren I dream of, would they love me? Wouldn't they despise me? They might even ignore me, because I represent the roots they are trying to eliminate. It was better like this."

"Of course it was. Has it taken you this long to realize?"

"See, you crazy old thing, how it's better to have a daughter? Of the four children we had, Our Delfina is the only one left. And she's going to get married like white folk do. With a veil and flowers. Ah! My sons who have been lost in the sea!"

Serafina feels like dancing. Singing. Invoking the dead in a universal mukhuto, to celebrate her only daughter's marriage. May God bless her!

◆　◆　◆

The sweethearts walk toward the sea. Speechless, unsettled, like two ghosts emerging from the tomb. They get to the beach and sit down on the white sand. Their conversation is peppered with all manner of seasonings: honeyed kisses as fresh as the breeze. The caw of crows and the hiss of crickets to lend a bit of romance to things. The golden, red, yellow and gray hues of sunset. And finally, nightfall and the moon. They have entered the dance of the heavenly vault and they feel giddy. They wait for the fleeting breeze to carry away their bodily fire beyond the atmosphere. After all, pain has wings and can also fly.

In their eyes, there is the blue of the sky and the ocean. Gulls cast petals of wind into the air. On their palate, the sweet taste of passion.

"I love you."

"I love you."

"We love each other, then. Let us love each other in joy and in sadness, in health and in sickness, until death do us part."

The past returns and perches softly in José's mind. He looks for strength in the slumbering sun's rays. In the tender warmth of a mother's arms. José's thoughts plunge into the roots of time and speak to the wind. My mother who bore me. A mother who is mine or no longer mine. My mother a distant memory who chokes me with yearning and anguish. My mother, I hate you at this moment — he exclaims in mute delirium — for having brought me into this world without my permission and for having given me this pain by way of a destiny. Mother, where did you bring me from? Why did you bring me? Can't you hear my weeping in your silence? Are you impotent? You had the power to give me life, which I didn't want, now take it away from me, I want to die, come on, kill me, return me to nothingness, to the void where this world casts none of its light. My dearest mother, I hate you, yes I do, for having violated my right not to exist. I hate you for having given birth to me as a man rather than as a woman. For making me black rather than white. My beloved mother, my guilty mother. Why did you open your heart to the specter of my father? He was the main culprit. Who sang you the most beautiful love song and elevated you to perdition and then let you float away in the air with my life in your belly. Ah! My father, I despise you, I ignore you, because you don't exist. You are just pollen carried by the wind. The seed of a fruit in a bird's digestive track. A light drizzle that drips, moistens, and then goes on its way. A rooster loaned from the neighbor's coop. As you don't exist, dear father, you cannot be blamed for anything. The only one to blame is me, for not having deserted my mother's womb. I had a chance to abort myself, escape, raise my fetal arm and block the path to my birth, slip out of the midwife's hands and smash myself to smithereens. Nature is to blame for it gave me a sensitive heart destined to succumb to Cupid's arrows. The men from the sea are to blame, for they deliver punishment to all those who resist. Mother, here I am, unhappy, without the strength to abdicate from this life, mother, I

< 144 >

have your voice engraved in the depths of my memory, I know you are listening to me, I know you suffer, how I miss you, how I adore you, dear mother of mine!

11

The image of a perfect couple is reflected in the eyes of the crowd. The city has come to a halt in order to witness the unheard of: the marriage of a prostitute. Delfina makes her magical appearance. Shimmering. Sublime. Triumphant. She smiles to the four corners and adopts a victorious pose. She is dressed precisely as a virgin bride should be. With a veil, garland and orange blossom. José wearing a linen suit that fits him like a glove. Such is life. What is a dream for some, is reality for others. A throng of blacks and whites, people who attract and repel one another, is waiting at the door of the church, their eyes agog. They want to see in order to believe. The scornful mouths of the multitude are not blaspheming today, but are mute with astonishment, in the face of this converted Magdalene who sullied the altar of all the saints. The eyes of the womenfolk envy another woman. Who would have said? Rather me than her! How can a prostitute turn into a saint from one day to the next? The eyes of the menfolk envy another man. José is a hero. He's a proper man. He managed to tame the fury of the queen bee and conquer

< 146 >

the whole hive for himself. Tasty women are few and far between and shouldn't belong to one man alone. José, the poor fellow, is the luckiest man in the world.

They whisper among themselves that José won that woman in a fight with Soares, that rich white man, who owns the mines at Gilé. That white and his wife organized everything. With white godparents, photos and everything. A lavish reception. That wasn't a black folks' wedding, but pure revenge. Against the priests who harassed Delfina, but didn't allow her to attend church because they called her a sinner. Against the two-faced nuns who expelled her from school. Against the whole community that made ironic comments as she passed by. A ceremony with organ music and the Wedding March that not even the priests could stop. José, astonished, apprehensive, is floating on a sea of surprises. He is dizzy and his head full of colors. His suffering gradually drains away, while new sentiments awaken.

Delfina contemplates the world from on high and takes a deep breath. She rejoices. I'm a myth, I'm special. My medicine man confirmed my fate. He saw it all in his seashells and told me I would be the queen, reigning over all other women. He told me I would be a star. And today, I am. He said I would rule over the whole world. I have a feeling I shall yet rule, but I don't quite know how. I believe him. In spite of my lack of experience, he taught me many marvelous things: some magic potions to send my clients to sleep, and spirit away the wallets of those who were drunk. He made me a specialist in the most sought-after sexual delights, the type that paid the best, but today, I swear I shall abandon everything and do all that is necessary to build a new life. I have entered the church and climbed the altar steps. I want to have a fine family and a respectable name. I undertook this marriage to put some order into my life.

White women have rejoiced over this case up in the smart areas of the city. They sighed with relief at their freedom and sang the praises of José dos Montes. For he has reined in Delfina, and doused the fire in her body. For many of them, this marriage has come to represent the end of sleepless nights and the fear of losing their husbands to a black woman. At last, the Soares household is free of a threat. They send their sincerest good wishes to the couple. They wish them many children so that Delfina's body will lose its shape with each childbirth. They hope they will never be without food and wish the bride a hearty appetite, so that she may eat well and abundantly, and all her elegance turn into fat.

◆   ◆   ◆

< 148 >

José has just been born from his spouse's womb. A beautiful, special spouse, who has raised him from the ground to attain the loftiest of sentiments. She fought against her parents' opposition, overcame all the obstacles, to give him a new life. She brought him freedom and a new status, for he is no longer a slave, but a contract worker, a category gained by way of a wedding present.

Delfina and José dos Montes experience a unique, momentous love.

For a man, a honeymoon represents the conquest and legitimate ownership of an already familiar body. The previous kisses and embraces constituted credit, debts, a loan. For women, it represents the inauguration of her status as a serf. Bring me my coffee, now bring me my soup, now iron my clothes. And she lovingly ascends her throne of serfdom, as a queen of thorns. A honeymoon is a love ballad of sweet poems, into each of which a secret song is woven. My love! I love you too. But if you disobey me, I'll beat you to pulp. You are my wife. I am your husband. All yours. But this won't stop me from appreciating the young girl who passes by or giving a little joy to a sad widow. I will be your wife, your mother, your serf, until death do us part, of course I will. When this love dies, I shall get another one. In the iciness of this bed, I shall go on the hunt for fire. If I find a greater love, I shall kill you in the name of freedom in order to enjoy my new passion. Death will us part, oh yes, my love!

This dizzy passion causes José to gravitate towards the edge of the abyss. It is a kind of love that takes him by surprise and projects him into chaotic flight. It turns her into a mare, ridden to the perilous heights of the most sinister landscapes of passion. Anxiety. Insecurity. Longing. Jealousy.

All good things soon come to an end.

◆　◆　◆

The marriage shows the first signs of wear and tear. With each passing morning, the sweetness grows fainter. Because of the lack of money. Because there isn't enough sugar. Because of the absence of comfort. Mary Magdalene refuses to conform to her chastity, she reacts. She threatens to break out and return to the freedom of the dockside. Yesterday's passion starts to turn into yearning for the past. Delfina's voice starts to express a longing for the olden days when José presents her, at the end of each month, with five kilos of rancid flour, ten coconuts and a ten escudo coin, his wages as a contract worker.

"Do you think these wages are good enough for me?" Delfina screams. "You took me away from Soares, my rich white man who

< 150 >

gave me everything. Bring me proper money if you want me here."

"You're the one who decided we should get married, Delfina."

José is unable to escape his fate as the husband lover. The husband who allows himself to be devoured, and then regrets it. Delfina exerts the tyranny of the beloved woman over him, and turns her tongue into a sword.

"My stomach is bloated from all the rancid flour I eat every day. My whole body reeks of dried fish. How am I expected to put up with such a disastrous life for the rest of my days?"

"I don't know, my angel."

"Oh! So you don't know?"

José sighs and thinks to himself. The sailors made me a prisoner out of hatred. I walked into this prison out of love. Ah, Delfina! You impulsive woman, sweet Delfina. You who are only capable of making me feel anxious. You who turn love into a drama acted out between tenderness and confrontation. In the morning, seated on the bench, like a queen. Stretching lazily. Drying her beautiful face mask in the breeze. Avoiding the sun and heat in order not to crack it. Looking up into the azure, into nothingness. Or at the gulls soaring through the sky. Allowing her thoughts to wander through the dockside bars. Remembering scenes from the past. Rowdy music and

< 151 >

cold beer. The black women's armpits, and the white men's smells, in a jumble of sweaty odors. Yesterday's passion becomes yearning for the past and today's luster will become past.

"Ah, dear wife! Pretty when you laugh, pretty when you're angry."

"Oh! Is that so? Do you think I'm joking?"

"Next month will be better, I swear."

José knows he is lying, but he promises. Life has been controlled by the masters, and the people have nothing, not even dignity, not even land, not even any love in the hearts of their women. But Delfina forgets all this and dreams as if she were a free person. She is learning how many thorns it takes to make a husband. After all, love begins with a flower and ends in pain. His Delfina gets up early to take care of her own beauty rather than the comfort of her companion, for it is José who lights the fire and prepares his food before leaving for work.

"Make me some tea. Delfina."

"I can't. I've just put my m'siro on."

"All right."

Deep inside, this irritates him. What use are women? Why do people get married? Ah, black women spend hours and days taking care of their hair, but white women aren't like that, it's enough for them to give their hair a good comb. One or two touches and that's

< 152 >

it. Black women spend a lot of time in the bathroom, washing little bits and pieces. White women aren't like that. Black women are the vainest in the world! They know all about things to do with beauty and nothing about the sacrifices a man has to make in constructing the world. José is angry and then consoles himself. Of all my companions, I'm the only one who's married. It's good to love, and many will die without ever having been loved.

"You should be aware of one or two things right now," Delfina complains, "I'm with you legally and also by accident. An accident of the heart. I'm with you in order to cure an illness, a passion. And another thing: I've never lacked money, I've always had enough. Remember that. I am Delfina, sought after by all men."

"I'll fight, I'll make every effort, Delfina. One day, you'll have an answer. One day."

"One day? When exactly?"

"One of these days."

"Don't worry, dear José. You're young, and so am I. We can resolve the issue of our fates in various ways. We're both at the start of our lives."

José is suffering. From love. From the insecurity of losing it. He shouts and curses the heart that has turned him into the plaything

< 153 >

of a chancer. Who forces him to go and get her money in order to keep his love, goodness knows how. He can't even steal it. But blacks only have bananas and coconuts, and Delfina wants gold. Stealing from whites risks him being banished into slavery once again. And so the first signs of revolt begin to appear: curse colonization, curse the hour I was born a black. If I were a white, I'd lack for nothing. There are one or two feeble formulas that enable us to be less black: creams, clothes, the texture of the hair.

"I'll do everything to give you the home you deserve, my dear Delfina."

He comforts his lady with incoherent words. I'll carry you away. I'll give you away. I'll do it all. Dear oh dear. He is gradually turning himself into an overstrung slave. I'll kill. A discourse of submissiveness. I'll do it all.

"What will you do to get all this, my angel?"

"I'll work."

"Work even more? You'll gain nothing by doing that. My exiled brothers worked themselves to death, they earned nothing and never came back!"

José is overcome by a sense of estrangement. And rebellion. What is this life, in which a man's greatness is measured by his wife's image?

< 154 >

By the girth of her gold necklace. The softness of her skin. Her wide curves. Her smooth, uncalloused hands. The number of capulanas she wears every day, seven in total, all wrapped up together on her backside, making huge cushions like those embroidered skirts women wore in the olden days. Delfina lived well, my God, she lived well, for she had her white lover, her own money, her punters, why did I bring her here?

"I shall buy you a rickshaw, my treasure. I shall carry you along seated like a white woman, my little queen. I shall buy you many beautiful clothes, so that all the women in this place will die of envy."

"Ah, my dear José, if you don't fulfil your promise, I will boycott sex! You'll die of cold, you'll see!"

Women and sex, their instrument of torture. A madness men struggle with from birth to death. A strike over sex. A besotted man consigned to the catacomb of the world. They fell in love for sex, they married. What sort of life will he lead without sex?

"Delfina, you ungrateful woman, can't you see how much I suffer for your sake? I took you away from the streets of bitterness. I gave you dignity and a name. You are a respected, married woman. For you, I became a dogsbody. The boss's bodyguard, a planter, an informer. At the time of day when I should be with you, I'm learning to read and write, so that you should be proud to have a literate husband. Why do you treat me so badly?

"I'm aware of your sacrifices, my love. But for me to live, I need so much more."

"Delfina, you sourpuss! You've got such a lovely voice when you're angry!"

José's life is turned into a war of feelings. Sometimes, love is pure. Other times, it's hatred and suffering. When he's with her, there is tenderness, but hardly have they separated than bitterness returns. And his mouth is filled with laments. I'm poor, I'm weak, I'm black, Delfina is going to be taken away from me. The day is long, work is intense, while I'm absent, they'll sleep with my Delfina. Oh God! Give me a strongbox to hide my Delfina away. I haven't got a sword, I'm defenseless, they'll kill me to take advantage of the sweet attentions of my Delfina. In his mind, he sketches out new hopes: maybe this poverty will come to an end. And colonialism will be over. And the whites will leave, so that Delfina will be mine alone!

"I know where we can find the good fortune we need, my love."

"Do you?"

"Yes. All we have to do is apply to the authorities for assimilado status. It's the only option."

< 156 >

José learns the pain of being a man. To build the world with the strength of one's arms. To break stones in the depths of the tunnel, and turn them into bread. But to become an assimilado?

"Assimilados are murderers, Delfina."

"So what? If you're a black, you either kill or die. If you don't kill, they'll kill you. What's the difference?"

"Do you think that's a satisfactory solution?"

"I'm sure. You've every right to refuse, but remember this: I wasn't born to be poor."

José's thoughts brighten with the idea of a respectable little house, where Delfina can play the queen. People to work their garden and to cook. To capture her heart with nice presents. To buy her hooped skirts, complete with interlining and padding, of the type that fill a whole bathtub, and then when she walks along, she can lift it up in that sexy way European women do as if they wanted to undress and show off their legs, but only let you see their red patent leather shoes and a flash of silk stocking. He wants to give her beautiful skirts to wear on religious holidays, to make neighbors murmur as the couple pass by and to needle their hearts with pinpricks of envy.

"You may be right, Delfina. But to become assimilated?"

José muses over the magic luminosity of appearances. Blindness in pursuit of the paths to the abyss. That's precisely what colonization is. Switching the course of the river. Killing off the fish, waterweeds and corals. José plunges into the new current and is drowned among the leaves of the weeds. He's doing it for love, he believes. But even without love, the lock gates close, and whoever resists, dies. To colonize is to close all doors except for one. Assimilation is the only road to survival.

◆　◆　◆

Whoever refuses to kneel before the might of the empire will never be able to ascend to the status of citizen. If you don't know the words of the new speech, you will never affirm yourself. So come on, swear on all you hold dear that you won't utter another word in that barbaric tongue. Swear, renounce, sweep it all away, so that you can be born again. Abandon your language, your tribe, your faith. Come on now, burn your amulets, your old shrines, and your old pagan spirits. José takes his pledge before a magistrate, in a ceremony that is more like a pledge to the flag. With few formalities in front of a half-drunk official.

"I swear," he repeated.

"Do you swear to abandon all those savage beliefs, that backward language, and your barbaric life?"

"Yes, I swear."

"Good boy. Now sign here."

José signs the document that turns him into an assimilado. Even without reading it. His educational abilities don't allow him such luxury. He just signs it. Speechless, he awaits the results, the new orders given before long.

"You're now an assimilado. And from now on, you'll be a sepoy."

"A sepoy?"

"Yes. You've got plenty of fiber in those muscles. You're an ideal black for a sepoy."

"But…"

"Sssh, be quiet. You don't ask questions here. Do you want to be an assimilado or not?

"It's just that I don't know how to be a sepoy."

"Don't worry about that, you'll learn in no time, it's easy."

The official hands him a sealed envelope containing money for him to buy clothes worthy of his new status. A lot of money.

"What's this for?"

"To buy clothes suitable for your new status."

< 159 >

"Yes, boss."

He goes shopping for the first time in his life. Clothes, soap, perfume, white sheets. He tries everything on and stands in front of the mirror. Sitting on the bed, Delfina observes her husband changing identity like a snake shedding its skin. She opens her eyes wide and gasps every time José tries on a new set of clothes. The white shirt accentuates his gleaming black skin, making his eyes and teeth shine more brightly.

It takes only one occasion for young damsels to lose their innocence. For love, all it takes is the first kiss. All it takes is for the first fuse to be lit for the dynamite to explode and for men's dreams to go up in smoke. All it takes is the first gesture. The first blow. The first drop of blood, to destroy the peace in human hearts. José looks at himself and smiles. The most striking recollections flow along the thread of his memory. The first time he travelled in a car. There he was, sitting. Traveling. With the trees flashing past. Traveling meant one's body could vanquish the wind, gravity, distance... In his mind, he recalls the confusion, the dizziness, and the bouts of sickness he suffered. He understood nothing about the dynamics or mechanics of bicycles, much less automobiles. Today, he laughs gleefully. He recalls the first time he set eyes on wrapping paper, far more beautiful than his goat-skin loincloth. He wrapped it around himself and showed it off to his friends as his new outfit. But then, a huge downpour dissolved his clothes along with his dream, leaving him stark naked, shivering with cold, while his pals made fun of him. The first time he saw a tarred road, he stood there powerless for hours on end, scared to cross it in case he got run over. The first time he saw a building, he shook and didn't even go near it. For fear it might fall down on top of him. The first time he held a radio, he turned it over and over, to try and understand the magic of it and discover the people who were speaking inside it.

He looks at himself again in the mirror, he passes his hands over the curve of his shoulders and then gently downwards as far as his knees, savoring his new clothes with his eyes and his sense of touch. The well pressed creases are like the edge of palm leaves, and they cut like knives. For the first time in his life, he feels good about how well he is dressed.

And for the first time, he is wearing new shoes, for the ones he wore at the wedding were old and borrowed. He takes a few steps and then stands once again in front of the mirror. He doesn't like them very much, for they stifle the ability of his skin to breathe. He prefers the direct contact with the soil, his footprints left in the sand.

He enjoys splashing barefoot in the cool, marshy rice plantations.

And for the first time, he eats salt cod and doesn't like it. He prefers the dried fish of his homeland such as the Malawi chambo, the blue and Mozambique tilapia. The olives are sharp, very sharp, but they leave a sweet aftertaste in the mouth, a pleasant sensation. The wine, acid at first, turns out wonderful! As for lupin nuts, he can't bear the taste, but it's what civilized folk eat. He'll have to learn to like them.

The eyes of the couple exude the burgeoning consciousness of those who have chosen the path of assimilated status. They walk haughtily, gazing down at the world from on high, plunging headlong into the prelude of History while trying to stifle tomorrow's liberation. And José discovers that the leaves of the palm trees are a vivid green in color and the flight of the swallows is one of complete freedom. Delfina has tried on her long silk skirt, with its slip and lining. She likes her new image. And her José's image too. She likes that smell of starch, soap and their new life. She embraces José affectionately in order to celebrate the moment and to be sure that this transformed man is truly hers. And they sigh to each other: how good it would be if time and the crowds disappeared and left them alone in the world!

"Delfina, my goddess, I love you. You who saved me from death and caused me to be born again. You love me. More than God. More than my mother, who brought me into the world to experience enslavement, and to know what it's like to be a slave, without at least teaching me to see the world in all its hues."

"Thank goodness you trust me."

"There are no ugly people when there's money. It's poverty that makes folk aged and unsightly," José says with a sigh.

"Why did you dig your heels in for so long?" Delfina asks, satisfied. "You could have become an assimilado long ago, and your life might have been different by now. You wasted your time with ideas about resistance, trying to affirm some lost identity. Dignity in the midst of hunger. Slavery. Death."

"Ah, Delfina!" He takes his wife in his arms and repeats his litany of tenderness. "Is there anyone better than you under the sun?"

Can it be that Delfina is the reason for his decision? No, it wasn't because of her. Adrift among the clouds, he got a sense of how turbulent his future was going to be. Like the swallows, he predicted the storm and saw that the time had come to seek shelter. Those who didn't know the new language wouldn't be able to get on. Whoever fails to incarnate the spirit of the new rulers will never know the colors of the new sun. The song of generations will be silenced. The soul will be a battlefield between the old and the new. Only after many generations of contention will there be harmony. Tired of penury, he gave his rustic peasant's hands over to crime. Delfina had merely added the briefest of brushstrokes to the formation of his thought. The decision to seek assimilated status was his as a man. Because he wanted to live. He had agreed to it in the name of his own heart, in order that Delfina should not look somewhere else for what she didn't have at home.

◆　◆　◆

The day José held a rifle for the first time, he wept. The icy feel of the metal ran through his body. His spirit weakened, and he got agitated like a child. This rifle reminds me of my dead friends. My father. It reminds me of my mother's tears. This weapon isn't what I wanted, nor this dagger. Nor this stupid uniform of a second-class citizen. Love is my only ambition. And also peace. I wanted to satisfy myself with life's crumbs, like birds pecking at bits of bran. How did I reach this point, how? Oh God who made me a man, how can I injure the soul of my people? With this weapon, I'll be the one shepherding lines of slaves to the harbor. To their exile. To lands I shall never know. He looks at himself, at his new khaki uniform with its

< 164 >

silver buttons that go with his watch and his thick leather belt. On his chest, the copper star. The reins of his new passion have made him gallop and have left him vanquished. I abandoned my nest, I left the orbit of familiar things, I'm far from my homeland, my father and mother, spurred on by the steely power of these weapons.

He finally understands the real breadth of his new state. He ponders on the changes taking place in his life, and prepares himself mentally for the great encounter. His hour has come. The army of betrayal and death has gained another recruit. He is going to become his own enemy. To look at his own race and be tormented by it. To kill men and protect the palm grove.

He dons his khaki shorts. His tunic. He puts on his tall boots and his fez. He places his rifle on his shoulder. In a weak impulse, he seeks the approval of his beloved. He stands before her and says without conviction.

"Delfina, I'm important. I'm a sepoy. I've got money in my pocket."

"Ah, my dear José! It's still not enough for a bicycle. I'm sick of walking."

José's heart is a boat on a choppy sea. Will I reach a safe harbor? I'm a husband through love and not by chance. It was Delfina who stretched out her tentacles and hugged me to her as dockside women are wont to do. I wouldn't have the courage to ask for such a grand lady's hand in marriage. He starts to have regrets. Without wanting, he has usurped a white man's concubine, but he cannot satisfy her desires.

"I thought you would like this new outfit of mine, my treasure!"

"Me? And don't you like it yourself?" she answers without looking at him.

José takes a deep breath. Of bitterness. His is a soul in the midst of a terrible conflagration. He goes to the bedroom, takes off his clothes and hides his tears. He attempts to order words into a prayer. What gods will heed the lamentations of a traitor? Even so, he prays. Frantically. My gods, I am faced with this fire, this madness, protect me from my bitter feelings. In whom will I confide my anguished thoughts? What fate have you in store for me? Look into my eyes and see how wracked with pain I am. Listen to these laments I address you with. You deserted me, casting me out into the world and its whims. Why did you allow them to place this dagger, this rifle, in my hands? All I wanted was my daily bread. Victory. Prowess. Adventure. I have sought refuge in the most shadowy corners to eke out my existence. I have agreed to help them eliminate my own people in order to survive, but I shall never be one of them. In this world, I am nobody!

< 166 >

"Tell me something, Delfina!"

"About what?"

"Ah!"

"Stop being such a gutless wonder, be a man! And stop asking me such petty questions."

He despairs. For she does not put his mind at rest. Deep inside him, it's all fire and angst. He misses his mother. Only mothers understand the simple things going on in their children's hearts. And they douse the flames with one look. A smile. He pauses for a moment and thinks. Am I not on destiny's path? Life's changes occur when fate ordains. He smiles grimly: in my hands, the whip will sing and lives will dance. My dagger will cleave a muscly man with one thrust. Life and death are the preserve of the dead. Blacks and whites are the inventions of God. What powers do I have to alter my path? If I don't kill, I'll die.

He abandons himself to his fate, like a minnow at the whim of the current. Surrendering to the whim of the waves, his fears are now useless. Let God's will be done. And that of the other gods too. Let the waves take me to the depths of the oceans.

12

It is 1953, deep in the colonial night. José dos Montes leaves for war. Not as a soldier, but as a sepoy. A soldier is a man's thing, bravery is the stuff of sailors, and he is nothing more than a second-class citizen. Repression is taking on new forms. Folk are going round with fantasies about liberation and are hatching plots. Every black man is a possible opponent, and they need to crack down.

José experiences a violent shudder. Fear inhabits his belly. He feels shivers. It is desire and destiny battling each other inside him. Shaking his body. One saying yes, the other no. But the law ordains. To kill or die for a flag. For a symbol. A piece of cloth. A rag. He complains. I'm too young to die. Too timid to kill.

The lights dim within him and he has to embark on a mighty struggle to face up to the approaching terror. He would need a rush of air to fill his soul with hope. The adult man shrinks. And he yearns to be kissed and coddled on his mother's lap.

He walks over to Delfina and intones the poem of farewell.

< 168 >

"Delfina, whatever happens, please know that I will love you until the end of my days."

"I love you too, my dear José."

"I can't live without you. I shall return to love you."

"Can't you live without me? So what about if I'd never been born?"

"Eh? What?"

"Your mother never drew up any contract whatsoever with mine, before we were born. Yes, I love you, but I wasn't born to look after you."

Delfina unsheathes her tongue and starts to fence. She is perfect in the precision of her moves. She cuts. She slashes throats. Her word is the deadliest of weapons.

Delfina takes José in a farewell embrace. But her kiss is icy. They hug each other, unfeeling and silent. José discovers the strangeness of love in its different phases. From a distance, it is desire and nothing more. When they are with each other, there is irritation and argument. It's even as if love were both desire and its opposite. He gets the impression that Delfina wants him absent, far away from her, dead.

"Until soon, Delfina."

"Have a good trip. And bring me some gold earrings so I can favor you with a child."

< 169 >

José gets the message. He is now convinced. She doesn't want anything more to do with me, I'm nothing to her. The only thing I don't get is why she throws herself at me so voraciously. I'm a moving meatball. I'm a kilo of chorizo she got weighed and is using up one slice at a time. She doesn't care for my body as a whole. And she has no interest at all in my soul. She's only interested in one part of me. The only part. I must be the sexiest of men. This gives him courage.

"Bring me a present from this war of yours."

"A present?"

"Yes. A souvenir. A bracelet of rare gemstones, so I remember you each time I look at it."

"A bracelet? From the war?"

He closes his eyes and takes a deep breath. He mutters something to himself. This woman thinks I'm a fool. It was she who sought me out and took possession of me. She does whatever she likes with me. I think I belong to her but I don't. I can't tell anyone except for myself about this anguish. I feel I'm with her, but with each passing day I'm more alone. She will become a widow and be free. She's biding her time at my expense. She insults me on a whim and I weep. The moment I hear her voice, I run to meet her like a faithful little poodle. I don't want anything more to do with her, let me go off to war and

< 170 >

die. She plays with me as if I were a pumpkin and I don't know what comes over me. But I'm going to be honest with myself. I love that woman. I'm her slave, her plaything. I take pleasure in talking ill of her, but when I'm on my own, it's her I think about.

"All right, I promise I'll bring you one."

"Don't forget."

"Delfina, you're just like your mother. Stupid. Bad mannered and insensitive. If she didn't want me as her son-in-law, why did I marry you?"

"Because you can't live without me."

José dos Montes starts imagining his Delfina in the other man's arms. He begins to torment himself with jealous thoughts. Fantasizing. And feeling harsher torture than the agonies of death.

He swears. He will do all in his power to get rid of this obstacle to his enjoyment of life and happiness. To make that woman Delfina so insignificant, she'll fit in the palm of his hand. Stuff her belly full of children and leave her beauty diminished. And he'll bring her all the gold in the world so that she will forget her former white lover. In Gilé there are huge quantities of gold, tied around the waists of the womenfolk. In tins buried in the earth, under the soldiers' camp beds. In Mocuba, in…

José dos Montes joins the murderous march of all the conquests, which advances toward Maganja, Namarroi, and Lugela. He is one of the nameless soldiers in a battalion of many men. In the early evening, they set up their camp on the banks of a river. They shelter. He is trembling because nightfall will herald their first assault.

From their hideout, José hears sounds. Songs. Sounds that were part of his life, part of his own being, his past, those songs that transcend the ears and are heard through the blood, the soul, as a call to the ancestors.

> *Though they may torture us*
> *We shall return*

He ponders on the reason for his presence there. He thinks about his Delfina. The songs get louder from over there. They are the voices of his brothers, friends and family. One sole bloodline, one united race, one pure race. Fear engenders new conflicts in his heart. He surrendered up his weak body, but his soul feeds stubbornly on the past. On nostalgia. José tries hard to eliminate the past like someone

< 172 >

shedding an item of uncomfortable clothing. He recalls the recent oath he has taken. I believe in the future. I swear. I'm done with the here and now. I shall forge ahead to the there and then.

The spirit of the lion, which devours everything, has been aroused, the spirit of the dragon to fight for the homeland and for life.

> *Though they may expel us*
> *We shall return.*

The song causes the darkness of the forest to quiver, in the ruddiness of the fires that have kept the ghosts of first light away. It is the pain of the people in one verse. Pure poetry. A soul has the face of a phoneme after all. Of the first bar in the song of sunlight. He stifles the old song in order to give life to the song of the new man. With new clothes and good food, cooked by black folk, and his wife's sexual gifts. With money jingling in his pocket to pay for little pleasures, wine, and sex with other women. José sighs. Free are the slaves who stick to their condition and fight among themselves with conviction. Ah! But then there's that old song, that stubborn song that won't leave me alone for a single second. The song of freedom, the song of resistance that torments my thoughts. His soul sways in the wind, unsettling the battle taking place in his mind. I'm one of them. But one doesn't abandon one's nature with the flurry of a signature and one doesn't change one's race with an oath. Not even with the most perfect disguise.

Though they may kill us
We shall return!

Night falls. They advance. They hide while waiting for the hour. In his line of fire, José sees folk, seemingly without a care around the fire, breathing in smoke and dust. Dancing. No doubt prepared to spend another whole night in that useless babble of voices, with which he has been so familiar ever since the beginning of the world. Tattooing fantasies onto their minds, which they will later believe in. The sound of the drums raise the dead from their slumber. He sees silhouettes dancing. Masks of divinities. Nhaus, mapikos and other pagan dances. Painted masks. He is assailed by inexplicable feelings and prays for silence. In the beginning we were just one people. One family, one army of resistance. Then, all of a sudden, we were different. Them over there, and me over on this side. They convinced me that nobility can be found over on this side, and I believed it. He looks at those people in their frenzy and laments. The gods are deaf and sleep through the middle of the festivity. They will answer the people with muted words, when destiny signals it is time.

Despite this enslavement
We shall return

The commander takes a few steps. He fires the first shot. This is followed by the scream of bullets ripping through the air. José's heart is beating in his chest. The women run away in disarray clutching their children. The men grab their spears and arrows. José fires at the men wielding spears, who fall like flocks of birds. In bunches. He treads firmly on the reddened earth. The menstrual earth. The earth in its birth pains. He feels the umbilical cord rupture deep within him and his image rising endlessly towards the sun, which the night conceals.

…
We shall return!

The voice of the people of the Zambezi can now be heard much louder. Desperately fighting for their beloved Zambezia, their homeland of lofty palms, sown by the hands of slaves as witnesses to history. They defend the Zambezi, their river, where tasty fish frolic like water lilies flowering among the waves. In spite of their suffering — so the song goes — it is good to be born in Zambezia. The ground is of marble, gold and mother-of-pearl, it is good to live in Zambezia. The grass is of a vivid green and the hills covered with anthurium. The whole land is a flowering flagstone, which invites us to eternal rest. It is good to die in Zambezia.

...

We shall return.

The Nharinga, those Zambezians from Maganja da Costa, pride themselves on their fighting skills, resolute warriors who refused to pay the hut tax. They have no fear of death and fight to their last drop of blood. They never surrender. You kill one and ten appear, never-endingly, just like those mysterious bees emerging from the hive.

The Nama ya roi, those Zambezians from Namarroi, are even more terrible. They are magicians. They fight with the magical force of the serpents of the goddess Nathériua, the all-powerful enchantress of serpents, whose palace is guarded by all the varieties of snake in the world, which she charms, plays and even dances with. In her presence, even the most poisonous reptiles are tamed and obey her command. The arrogant voices of men grow silent in the presence of the goddess and the sailors die of fear. This woman urged the men to fight against the occupation and against slavery in the tea plantations.

José dos Montes tests his bodily strength. What a strange life! My strength, my arms. The cervix bearing lives. The barrel of his gun selecting lives. Men's hands deciding who will die by the barrel of a gun. Random deaths. Planned deaths. Prison and torture. Exile.

The Zambezians defend themselves with the ancient spirits of ferocious lions, the Zambezia of talking trees that tell magical stories to all wayfarers. Land of the sacred soil of Namuli, cradle of all humanity. Land of the sierra of Morrumbala and of Mount Thumbine, with their dragons of fire and water, bearers of humidity, clouds and rains, and all fertility. Of the wondrous Mount Juju, Mount Ile, and Mount Gilé, pregnant with fertility, with magical gates that open when disaster strikes, in times of war and drought, in order to protect human life.

< 177 >

...

We shall return.

The memory of the song invites José dos Montes to return to his old life. The life of a slave. A plantation worker. Free to eat with his fingers and sleep on the ground. Walk barefoot and feel the magical power of the earth strengthening his bones. His conscience advises him to take part in the struggle against the invaders, but he has turned his back on his folk and is on the other side of the trench. In the middle of the struggle over land, bearing an alien flag. All he thinks of now is about dying. There's no point in thinking about a non-existent love. Nor in dreaming of a tomorrow that will never come. Nor yearning for a past that has already gone. It's better to eliminate once and for all the anguish of yesterday and today. Free the body from ancient pains. The hunger of centuries. Smash once and for all the heavenly mirror so that his image will never again be reflected.

...

We shall return.

He thinks of Delfina's body. He imagines the goddess in the arms of other men. In his dizziness, feelings mingle together. A good dream and a bad dream. A nightmare. A smile. Chance and luck. An unhappy ending. The pendulum of existence swaying between life and death. He begins to hallucinate and plunges, clutching his weapon, into the business of creating a new world. Yesterday, humanity was the offspring of clay. Tomorrow, it will be the offspring of a bullet. Selected and protected by the fire coming from gun barrels choosing their seeds, sweeping, irrigating, so that the new nation may grow. José dos Montes praises weapons. Fire. The brave men accepting they will turn into clay in the defense of their land.

Who said God created the world in seven days? Wasn't the world being created now? So, why all the wars, storms, earthquakes, and floods? No, the world hasn't been created or even completed. More wars are needed until blacks and whites mingle in only one race. Only one nation.

◆　　◆　　◆

He leaves for war and joins the dance. The dance of slaughter. The dance of a brave man. In each death, his sense of power and long life is renewed, animated by the frantic love he feels for Delfina. The lives of others don't matter, what counts is power. For human shoulders are the steps men climb in narcissistic pursuit. His people and he go head on in successive battles. José surpasses himself. He commands. He lays waste. He makes his triumphal entry into a criminal career. He is at the peak of the pyramid. He has fulfilled the regime's orders with supreme efficiency. He has tortured. He has massacred. He has captured many Zambezians, and put them in shackles for work on the plantations. He has put many on the ships to exile. Then came harmony. Enjoyment. Vastness. The world is his at last.

What José doesn't know is that his deeds have made their mark, have made history, the stuff of myth and legend. They will change the world. Without the complicity of the assimilados and the sepoys, the land would never have been colonized.

Women take pride as bearers of life. Men, at least some of them, can take pride in stealing lives away among the shadows. That is why they organize themselves in legions, platoons, armies and terrorist movements.

◆　◆　◆

< 180 >

The name of José dos Montes begins to feature in folk songs and in the lamentations of slaves. These are the wave-battered years of glory, which the future will record in fables, legends, songs of scorn. Colonialism is virile, it made your wife pregnant. It stole your sweetheart's kiss and your children's smile. Oh, the white man's whip is a caress, it doesn't hurt! The true whip is the one hissing in your brother's hand. A slap from a white man is a sponge against your skin, it's nothing. A black man's hand is full of callouses, scars, tattoos, thorns. It is as hard as iron. It stings, dents, injures, breaks. And it hurts even more because it's your brother's. A white man's insult is foreign, fleeting. But your brother's is prickly, the black man José has gone over to the white man's side.

The blacks are victims at this point in time. But weren't they before? What will become of them when the system changes? Blacks are weaving the tapestry of their own destruction in order to fashion, with shards of clay, the imperial sphynx bearing the face of a behatted, mustachioed white horseman, and place him on a stone plinth in the middle of a square.

For José dos Montes, the songs of the people are a mere murmuring of the waves. They scare, but don't kill. Mild compared to his embittered heart. Of the thousand women who offered themselves up to him as vassals, his heart chose Delfina, a malign mermaid. A woman who involved him in a game of Russian roulette. Turning him into a shooting star, a minor planet, orbiting around her, the greater sun. José dos Montes dreams of the day when Delfina will surrender and kneel, like true women kneel before their husbands. He begins to have his regrets. He should have married a submissive woman who would gaze upon him as if he were a god, so that he could feel more of a man. He should have married an older woman. Ugly. Insignificant. Invisible. One of those women who spend their life in the kitchen so as to woo their man through the tastiness of a dish. What José dos Montes hasn't yet realized is that Delfina was the artist and he the piece she was sculpting. He is going to find it hard to free himself.

That is why he needed blood to create his own outward grandeur. There's nothing wrong with that. A human being is a quintessential parasite. He tears the mother's womb and sucks her when he's tiny. He sponges on the father's wallet when he's a boy. He seeks pleasure and transmigration, while riding another body when he's an adult. He sucks animals and vegetables to sustain himself. Tyranny is a stage on the road to sovereignty.

He has been distributing favors on behalf of his bosses amongst the weeping people. Causing a head to roll every day. Letting out a tear and a curse. And he has heaped his plate with glory.

"Boss, I need to go and catch the snakes in their lair, I need your permission. I need to take out the leader. Boss, there's a strike in the rice and cotton plantations. The disturbance is spreading to the palm groves. I know who's behind it all, I've been making inquiries among the dockside prostitutes, I know all the details, absolutely everything! I know the bastards who are the ringleaders, I'll sweep through the place with your permission, I know their hiding places, I was one of them, I did forced labor, I've been a contract worker, and now I'm an assimilado, a Christian and a sepoy, I was married in church, I've risen in the hierarchy of life, the only thing I never experienced was outright slavery because it had already finished by the time I was born, I'm only too familiar with these folk, you know, boss."

The slaves' resistance plans no longer take place around the fire. There is a dark phantom emerging from the middle of the flames, as in Aladdin's lamp. Deaths increase in their intensity, colonialism has dressed the land in its colors.

"Let's carry out a bit of irrigation, boss. With gunshot. Let's

< 183 >

fertilize the land, boss, with real blood, blacks are manure, boss. The human body has many bones. Let's build a tower, with the ivory of the dead, so that we can climb to the top and shit on the world."

The black demon is on the loose along the streets, and death isn't only the realm of the sailors. There's a potential killer lurking in every black man. All he needs is a weapon. Ambition. A license to kill. It's no longer possible to seek refuge anywhere, evil is in the middle of our fire and knows all our hiding places.

"Boss, they've got too much to eat, they're fat, their movements are slow and they're not working hard enough. With your permission, I'll reduce their rations, and set them to work until the sun has gone to sleep, I'll order them to put their nightly fires out, they'll be able to dance once a week, but not every day because they disturb your sleep and that of your wife, boss. No, I'm not exaggerating. I was also a slave, a bondman, you know that, boss, a black man doesn't just die like that, a black man is tough, boss! The important thing is to keep the men's sexual energies alive so they'll fertilize their women. Otherwise, come the next generation, we won't have any slaves."

Without blood, the empire is anemic, lifeless, insignificant. Blood rejuvenates when drunk. When it's not drunk, then it's sung. In the national anthem. Or it's spilt. On the tunics of kings. On the red carpets of the generals, marshals, and guards of honor. The flags of the world always have a touch of blood on them. For blood represents vitality, strength. New blood is injected into the army and the institutions of the State, not to mention soccer teams. Spilt blood. Verses. The discourse of liberation. Lamentations of the people shaping monuments to rhetoric. Combat poems. Revolutionary songs. Inspiration.

"I told them to pick the best fruit for your wife, boss. I told them to choose the finest rice for your family, boss."

There's never been a better executioner in these lands. Never a more skilled one. You don't need to be a sailor to be bloodthirsty. Resistance has died for good. The slaves have surrendered once and for all. To kill a people, you have to crush them guts and all.

"Do you want a virgin black girl, boss? I've got one all ready for you. A genuine black girl, pure coal, first class, for you to break in, sir. Those butterflies along the docks are old, dirty, full of sores, you could pick up a disease, boss. I can fix you up with a virgin every week, you're a good boss, you deserve one, boss, the same girl no, why, what for? Black girls are born by the dozen like pumpkin seeds, you're a hot-blooded man, boss, you don't need used goods, you need to break them in, dignify them with the magic of your touch, and they'll be well satisfied. Every young black virgin dreams of being sexually initiated by a white man as an honor, because here, it's dishonorable to be deflowered by a black man. Every black woman dreams of having a mulatto child, you know what it's like, boss, when it comes to sowing crops, we need to select the best seeds, the fertile ones of finest quality, in order to improve the species, you know that only too well, boss."

❖   ❖   ❖

At the police station, the colonial regime's police assess their actions and talk in low voices. They are dying of heat, humidity, and yearning for their homeland. Under the intense heat, their white skins take on the ruddiness of carrots. They breathe all the air they can get in the atmosphere, they strip off their shirts and surrender. That's what Zambezia is like. A hothouse for fattening rice and mosquitoes. They stand there distilling the delicate perfume of their armpits.

They abandon the police station and seek refuge at a bar room table. They drink glasses of cold beer and sigh. There they are. Young saplings torn from their mother's womb with promises of greatness. That is why they take it out on the black slaves. Some of them know that just like the enslaved blacks, they will never again see the hues of their native land, or their mother's arms, for they will die here. Those lucky enough to return will find their wives with other men. That is why they are getting their revenge. Some of them will go mad. Others will return paralyzed, limbless, blind, or disabled for the rest of their days. That is why they suffer and get their revenge. For the empire they are building is an invisible edifice. A dream on the peaks of the clouds. Untouchable. Unreachable.

They talk about José dos Montes. They praise him. He's a good black, a loyal black, the best there's ever been. If he wasn't a kaffir, he could even be a gentleman, a general. He sets a fine example. Even white women sigh over him.

"He's excellent, but he's a black, don't you think, sergeant, sir?"

"Yes. And he's better than you lot put together. But he's nothing more than a slave."

"He put down the hardest rebellions with the skill of a general. He crushed those rebels from Maganja da Costa, Namarroi and Macuse, like fleas, sir."

"Yes, of course. Because he has our weapons, our technical back-up and his own brains. Because he thinks. He'll go far. He's worthy of respect, yes indeed."

"Far from what, sir?"

"Our empire would go far with men like that. Soon, he will be conscious of his greatness and our weaknesses. What will happen after that?" The sergeant asks grimly.

"Revolt."

"Exactly. Revolt. Can you picture that kind of man in the enemy trenches?"

In the squadron's mind, there is an image of blacks who have gone from mere existence to transcendence. Who have scaled the heights and hurled thunderbolts from the mountains of glory. Who commanded the rains, like Makombe, Monomotapa, Kupula, who have now been silenced. Some of them conquering power with much blood and by force of arms.

"You are right, sir. He may be the perfect rebel leader. If he switches sides one day, he will be a danger to our race."

"It's a good job that's what you think. But, later? Are we going to endlessly praise the prowess of that worm?"

They are suddenly buffeted by a cool gust. There is a black cloud

< 188 >

hovering above. Then, a torrential, magical, unexplained downpour that has come out of nothing. Not long afterwards, the cloud disappears and the sun returns. But it was enough to cool their spirits and start thinking about survival.

"Well, let me tell you something," the sergeant asserts, "there shouldn't be a man left in the palm groves. We need to transform those bodies out there into shadows, and that's why we're carrying the cross and the sword. To tame the mind and wear down the body. Do you know how to do that?"

"Not very well, sergeant."

"Then you're not men."

"We are, sir."

"Don't you know how to tame a woman?"

"How, sir?"

"Bunch of milksops," he shouts irritably, "by attacking her, violating her, for everything she's done, for everything she hasn't done, and for whatever she might one day think of doing. We shape our children by giving them a good hiding, and for dogs, we beat them with a stick. Blacks are tamed with wine and a good whipping, get that into your heads. That's why we carry a cross and a sword in our hands."

< 189 >

José should be transformed into mist, into the dust he should never have left. For a good black is one who has been domesticated. The one who trembles and bends before the whip. It's important that he shouldn't have a mother, or a homeland, or an umbilical cord, and that only recollections and uncertainties should hover around in his mind.

"Should we kill him?"

"No."

"So why not?"

"We've got to use him until he's worn down."

"Arrest him?"

"No, there's no need for that, you thickheads. Every strong man has a weak point. He's married to a nymphomaniac, that girl Delfina who's already serviced us and will continue to do so for all of us. She's very talkative. He lives for Delfina's love. He'll die of love for her.

< 190 >

13

The heat is gentle in the shade of the jujube tree. Only the noise of the sea gives any sign of life. And two people sighing. Sighs of love projecting beyond life. Delfina confides in her love.

"I don't feel well. Something has changed in me."

"Malaria?" José asks her, attentively.

Then, she tells him. In every detail. For days on end, she has felt fluttering in the pit of her belly, with nausea and morning sickness. It was then confirmed. It was the hand of the creator kneading the clay of creation in her woman's body. It all began that day when she was walking along the narrow streets of their district. She came across a man picking bananas and papayas. She asked for some. The man didn't answer her but gave her some. Delfina saw in the man's silence something mysterious in his gift. At that very moment, she ate the banana and the papaya. And she was sick. For the banana has a man's shape and the papaya that of a woman.

"You must see a nurse."

"We're going to have a child, José."

"A child?"

This is precisely what they call a surprise. A woman's body is a trap where a man gets caught. And at the end of it all, the woman declares he has left bits of himself inside her, which will turn into vertebrae, a face, a soul. Whoever first goes there always returns and ends up being a father without planning to be one. For a woman's sexual organ is the only place in the world where a man is happy.

"That's right. A child."

José dos Montes is as wide eyed as a child. As if he didn't know. The world is on the move: men arriving, men leaving, others dying. Children are born from women's wombs, as anonymous as young goats. Everyone knows who the mother is. But the father is always an outsider who came and then went.

"A child of mine? Can that be true?"

"Yes, we are going to have a child."

"Ah!"

Sweet words introduce the dance of honey in the blood. Eyelashes turn tears into a shower of pearls. He looks toward the horizon where the clouds proclaim fertility. Today, the gulls are flying high, and life is beautiful. José's thoughts soar into the air, like a hymn to the wind. His dream raises him up into the heavens, in an ascent that

< 192 >

lasts as long as a kangaroo's leap. For the future conceals the beautiful hues beyond the horizon.

"That's wonderful news, Delfina!"

"You don't seem happy."

"But I am," he replies in a melancholy tone of voice. "I braved life and death just in order to have a wife, a child and a home with a roof of straw. Ah! If only I were a bird. A fish in the ocean. A water hyacinth in the river.

Without wishing to, he reproduces the words of his mother-in-law, Serafina, which lie embedded in his subconscious. A black child belongs to a generation of slaves. The workers in the palm groves. The sugar plantation. He will write his life's journey with the sole of his foot. He will erect heaven's pillars with his black hands. He will abandon his mother's arms and leave for a life of torture. Will his son have his father's fate? A contract worker, exile, mistreatment? Or an assimilated killer?

"If you're happy, at least give us a little smile."

"Smile?"

"Yes."

"Ah, Delfina! Sometimes a smile can take the form of tears."

José's musing both shrinks and amplifies. What's the use of a child?

< 193 >

What am I going to do with a child? Build a house for him? What for, if life is never-ending migration? From the father's body to the mother's womb. From the mother's womb out into the sunlight, into the land. From the homeland to the unknown. Everything migrates. Birds. Grasses. Seeds on the wind's journey, pollinating themselves, transforming themselves. So what use is a child if we are born to travel? What is a child? It is a sacred relic of one's blood on the road to tenderness.

"I'm worried, that's all."

"Worried? Why?"

José doesn't yet know that one offspring is never the same as another. My child, another man's child. A female child, a male child. A prickly child, a sweet child, who tattoos its parents' hearts with tenderness.

"What would you like? A son or a daughter?" Delfina asks, to lighten the moment.

"A son? Ah, Delfina! A son?"

A man is about being on the road. Guillotine. A prison cell. A pair of handcuffs. A shotgun, a bullet, a military uniform, a grave in the belly of the earth. A man is a dangerous, sinuous path. A rocket tearing through the unknown. With the birth of a male child comes

< 194 >

the illusion of continuity. A family name. What is the importance of a name if the world is autonomous and a man anonymous? Does God know the family names of all the stars in the Milky Way? Maybe a family name can be compared to the name of the constellations. And the constellations take the shape of a tribe.

"Don't you want a son?"

"No, Delfina, not a son. I would rather God blessed us with a daughter."

José dos Montes closes his eyes and takes a deep breath. During his brief absence, he meditates. And he makes a request. May it be a girl, yes! A prostitute, a butterfly of the docks, flesh for the sailors. May she be a piece of sex for sale, priced by the gram, or the kilo! May she sleep with the white man in return for salt and sugar! May she be a goddess of love, a sacred cow! May his offspring be anything except for a man! I want a little girl, yes indeed, to fill my life with joy. I shall kill and die for that child. I shall light all the fires for her and say every possible prayer to keep her by my side. For her, I shall wage all manner of wars in order to provide this nest with warmth and sustenance.

"If it's a daughter, she will have my mother's name," José dos Montes says.

"Your mother's name? Certainly not. We are assimilados now, and we live the life white people lead. You swore you would abandon kaffir traditions, have you forgotten?"

José dos Montes does not answer. He understood a long time ago. Life's path is too long. Life's path is too short. The pain of existence is too strong. We have come from afar. We have completed generations, without anyone to tell us the reason for so much disorder if the world has been completed and is perfect. Besides, he does not need an offspring at all. He had never thought about setting up a family before, or even having children. All the planning and embroidery belong to Delfina. Let her do what she wants. The child is hers, her womb belongs to her. He is going to become the father of her offspring because that's what she wants, so let her do as she likes.

"And her re-naming as a way of resurrecting the dead, isn't that a concern for you?"

"Oh no! Stop all these superstitions!"

"Wouldn't a homage to your mother be a noble gesture?"

"No, not her. She was always against our marriage."

"Well, in that case, my mother's name."

"I'm going to choose a lovely name for our little girl, you'll see, José."

< 196 >

What name will my daughter have? What heritage? José imagines a difficult future. The sailors arrived without any invitation, and were welcomed by us. They disembarked triumphantly from their ships, boats and instruments of torture. We greeted them with canticles and they replied with deadly gunfire that dragged us into the abyss. We are lost souls floating in the abyss. The land is no longer ours. I don't have a past anymore. Not even a single legend has survived, and even myth has sunken into the belly of the future. Darker days are on their way, that's for sure.

"I would like our little girl to have my mother's name."

"Oh! I've already told you countless times, no!"

He is left breathless. He seeks oxygen in ancient sayings. I was a son, and I shall be a father at the change of seasons. Stories of his ancestors, lineages and continuity build their nest inside his heart. And for the first time, he misses his father. To teach him what a man should say when his wife tells him she is expecting his child. He learns through practice and through the meaning of eternity. In the seed of the first cashew in the whole wide world, which became a tree, fruit, and seed, for generation upon generation. Ever since the beginning of the world, one tree dying and another being born. Continually. One son following on an older son. All of them living one at a time, a little at a time, without ever living beyond their time.

"How I wish my father were nearby and I could speak to him!"

"What for?"

"Nothing. I just remembered him. Besides, I'm going to be a father too."

José dos Montes gazes at the parapet of the horizon. At the gloomy frontiers of the future, behind gloomy iron gates. The future is impenetrable, but there is a fog-shrouded crack through which prophets can peer.

◆　◆　◆

Pregnancy is always about the rebirth of new life. New hope, life does not die, it is like the sun which is born every day. Dona Serafina forgets death and pain in order to experience the pleasure of rebirth.

"Don't start being lazy, Delfina, pound flour, tend to the crops, go down to the river and carry jars of water on your head, and this will help the baby to come out. Get some exercise so as to make the delivery easier."

Delfina casts her mother a defiant look and replies with scorn.

Because her mother sowed bitter words in a field of thorns. And they have germinated.

"My baby is black and you wanted a mulatto, Mother. Why are you worried now? Why must you offer an opinion?"

Serafina soon accepted reality. She switched from her dream of racial mixture to one of racial purity. The purity of appearances because the spirits of the Chuabo and the Lomwe, two enemy ethnicities overcome by the strength of love, will fuse in the new being. Serafina's desires alternating like the sun going down and the coming night. Alternately. Eternally.

"Forget yesterday's angry words. You are mine and you belong to me. Your happiness is mine as well."

"You insulted my husband, you insulted me, but I married for love. I am a woman who is loved. I'm a lady, mother, I have servants, I don't need to walk anywhere or go to the river like a slave. José treats me like a queen. I wasn't born to suffer."

"You could at least use your feet a bit. Go to the market, go shopping from time to time."

"I can do without your advice, let me lead the life I want. I don't need any interference from you."

"When it comes to matters of motherhood, you're still a child.

Childbirth is the same for all races anywhere in the world. A slothful body opens up the possibility of total disaster in the final battle."

Her mother's words perturb the dreams of this newly civilized woman. Serafina floods her soul with revolt. For her words fall on a barrier that becomes more impenetrable by night. She and her daughter are engaged in the fight between generations.

"Oh, my dear daughter, childbirth is a scream, a gust of wind. The world has two major rivals: woman and the earth in a dispute for life. If you fail, the earth wins and your child will be buried. Delfina, prepare yourself for war!"

Against Delfina's wishes, Serafina has organized all the rituals. She lit candles, knelt, offered flowers, mealie flour, snuff, and liquor, in a prayer that mingled beliefs. She invoked the good gods and the good spirits. She invoked angels and saints. Gods of good fortune and fertility, gods of motherhood and of healthy birthing.

◆   ◆   ◆

Childbirth, the original Olympian contest in which mother and child struggle with each other over the possession of life. In this combat, the baby must leap over the barrier with its eyes closed and project itself into the world by defeating all the obstacles. Challenging the mother's body. Torturing it. Tearing it. Causing it to bleed. Bringing it to heel. Triumphing over it. Taking away its life if need be.

The mother has to expel her body's invader. She has to defeat it. Expel it. Kill it if necessary, in order to preserve her own breath of life. There are many mediators in this combat. Matrons, doctors, nurses, assistants, in a ceaseless coming and going, while refereeing this game of life and death. There are yells and oaths encouraging the woman to be brave: stretch, breathe, push, fight, defeat, expel it, out with the invader! Out there, the whole world is waiting for you, don't forget that. You can't leave here without the promised victory. Mother and child, listen to the anxious voices of your family. The final decision over your folks' fate is in your hands. Choose between light and darkness. Smiles or tears. Hope or despair. Come on now, my courageous ones, get separated, and declare your victory!

At that very moment, the midwife senses a whirlwind of images, faces, voices, moments, feelings, landscapes, dreams, destinies. Sometimes she sees light, sometimes darkness. Rain, wind, a flash of lightning, water, trees and stars all join together in that instant to ensure the new life is born.

< 201 >

Every live baby is a victor. That is why it is born with clenched fists, in the image of the great gladiators. It keeps its mother's soul as a trophy, because from then on, she will be its slave. It emits full-throated victory screams, forcing its serf to nurse it, give it its victory feast.

In this combat, there is crying and a sigh. The contest ended in a draw, mother and child both gained life.

Sometimes there is crying and silence. The child killed the mother and stole her soul by way of a trophy.

Sometimes, there is a sigh and silence. The mother killed her child and preserved her life.

Sometimes, there is complete silence. The contest ended in a draw, mother and child killed each other in the fury of combat. The earth gained a grave and a feast.

< 202 >

14

Delfina stretches out on her throne of smiles, before the enslaved world. Everything has been adorned and she has been proclaimed a heroine. For child birth is the triumph over anxiety. Over death. A future has been inaugurated. She is surrounded by prying eyes. From her lofty throne she observes life's bustle and she is shocked: is being a mother so important?

"What a lovey baby! Is it a boy or a girl?" Her friends and neighbors ask.

"A girl!"

"Ah, a girl! You're really lucky. Sons don't fill the world. It's better to have a girl, so the family will grow. Congratulations, Delfina."

"Thank you."

Delfina smiles and feels she is transmigrating beyond life.

"A beautiful child like the mother. There's nothing of the father in her," they keep repeating these time-honored words of triumph.

These words sound to her like a victory. And they lift her up in ecstatic flight.

< 203 >

Serafina, the grandmother, is an efficient concierge, reporting little titbits of information, spreading news about the tiniest occurrence to all four corners. That the child was born without any problems, and weighed three kilos. She was born healthy, and must grow well, so that the next one may be born as soon as possible. She has a hearty appetite, cries a lot, and shits plenty. Her Delfina has plenty of milk, she was a brave mother, and gave birth without screaming or crying. The little creature has her grandfather's fingers, her father's eyebrows, her grandmother's beauty, herself in other words, her mother's hands, so tiny they reminded her of Delfina when she was small.

Serafina's mind wanders. Her Delfina's belly delivers healthy children. Let her release from that fine womb of hers more black souls, who may turn into upstanding folk, teachers, farmers, who knows maybe some of the brave heroes who will free their land may issue from her belly? She dreams of freedom day, when her grandchildren can fill every corner of the land, running through the fields free from the fear of being deported. At this moment, all Serafina yearns for is freedom. She travels back into the past, to the beginning of it all, when all was peace, love, with the presence of a serpent. She travels forward into the future, when there will be peace once more, but without a serpent and evil.

"I've prepared some herbal tea for you. It will do you good, it will purge you of all impurities. Drink a lot of coconut water. From a green, tender young coconut. Give some to the baby as well. In no time at all, the umbilical cord will fall and your wounds will heal."

"I'm not taking any of that. I've got the antibiotics José brought from the pharmacy."

"Delfina, there are ailments that the white man's medicine can't cure. I always took these herbal remedies and I survived."

Mother and daughter, two generations ill at ease with the laws of nature. But a tree is always a tree. The timber, wood, degree of shade may vary. But it's always a tree. A remedy is always a remedy, for all races, just as the sun is always the sun in whatever corner of this world.

We were all fashioned from blood. We were born in the midst of blood. Menstrual blood runs   red in all women.

"I shall never turn back. I shall never again take these witches' brews that blacks make. Doctors solve all problems."

"Tell me honestly, Delfina. What do you know about white people?"

"Lots of things, my dear mother."

That's how the world is. The pursuit of what we don't have. Tossing

< 205 >

all you have out of the window, in order to later turn the world upside down searching for everything you once had and allowed to fly away. A sleepwalker, in the pursuit of all the distances you have left behind, seeking roots that have been lost in time.

Serafina feels exasperated. A curse on those women who destroy their nest with their own hands.

"Those medicines you trust came from these plants. If the doctors had an answer for everything, our people would only have been born today."

"Mother, I've already said I wouldn't! Can't you see everything has changed? The sun's beams have shattered inside your world. You're behind the times! Superstitious! Obscurantist! Doddery old folk lost in time! Can't you see the new dawn that's coming?"

"When the sailors arrived, they found people here and they had to work really hard to kill them. There were many of us, we were like ants. There were no white doctors or nurses. Look at our sons. See how strong they are. Do you know why your brothers were deported? Because they were as strong as bulls, thanks to those remedies you now reject."

Delfina looks down at her parents. Her mother's face seems strange to her. Her father, a despicable creature without a face, devoid of expression. That is why her tongue has become a blade, so as to cut her ties with her past. This was how it always was. Mothers and offspring at war with each other ever since the deep night of time. Rupture between the generations is a violent process.

"Ah, Delfina! You're going blindly on your way like a sheep. Can't you see the hole you're buried in? Don't fall in love with the stars, they're so far away, they're beyond reach."

"You're the one, mother, who set me off on this journey. You led me by the hand into the abyss. I was initiated into this way of life by the sailors. You made me see that everything good came from them. Do you regret it now?"

Relations between the generations have come to this. Forever arguing over ideas, experiences. Without any agreement. Treading on quicksand on their journey into the unknown. The spirits of the sailors and the Bantu have set the stage in the black man's mind. And the blacks pull up their own roots, just like ageing birds at the end of the season. Growing ever further away from themselves. Their essence. Trees with their roots exposed, swaying in the breeze. Without anything to sustain them. Mother and daughter have learned to deal with the world of appearances as if it were a science.

"We must organize a birth ritual; to give the little girl luck,"

< 207 >

Serafina suggests at last.

"No, I can't do that."

"Do you know what this means?"

"It's because I took an oath. I renounced all those primitive practices and I live the life of white people."

"I was the one who suggested you marry a white man. You didn't want to. And now you live the life of white people? Married to a black man? Tell me in all honesty, Delfina. What do you know about the white people's world?"

"They like flowers and give them to their wives."

Mother and daughter only know whites from afar. All they know of their world is olive oil. Salt cod. Their barrels of wine that dulls the senses. Delfina only knows white men by their kisses. Through fleeting conversations between the four walls of a room. She knows the coarse words they hurl at her when paying for her body. The sailors were poor. Like them. They had abandoned their people in order to die there, in unknown lands. It is their nostalgia that fills them with ire and the illusion of greatness. It was the construction of this invisible empire that inspired them to abandon everything. But they know nothing of their good spirits, which gave them victory in all their battles, and their bad spirit which causes them to hate the other half of humanity to the point of robbing them, colonizing them.

"Spare me your indecent thoughts, Delfina."

"Then let's finish this uncomfortable conversation, dear mother."

"Delfina, you can prevent bitter ordeals, disappointments, listen to the voice of experience, listen to me. You can strew the little girl's path with flowers, listen to me. You can hold a flare and light up the entire firmament, please, my daughter, just stop and listen!"

Your opinion, Delfina, is irrelevant as far as I'm concerned. We will organize a ceremony, yes we certainly will. Serafina dreams of a lavish ceremony. One that begins at nightfall and finishes at sunrise. With men on one side drinking nipa and rum, manly drinks. And with women drinking beer and palm wine, female drinks. Around a great fire and a full white moon in the sky. Lifting the child up on high and greeting the world, yelling full-throated incantations, showing the moon that in spite of our pains, life goes on.

Serafina's enthusiasm fades. She experiences the bitter taste of nostalgia. She decides it isn't worth it. She weeps and mumbles: no,

I can't do anything. The frontier is closed, for me, it's all over. There are no longer any fantasies for my times as a young girl. She decides to silence today's anguish with that of yesterday. Delfina may despise me, but at least she's nearby. It's better to feel her anger than the endless yearning for her departed sons. She realizes how useless her existence is. Her departure for the great beyond before long. The dreams in her mind dying along with her body.

Delfina's father gives her a bitter look of resentment. He sees a young mother's hand casting weeds and thorns on her own daughter's path.

"What is the future you seek, Delfina?" her father asks. "To live in two worlds is the same as living in two bodies, it's impossible. You are black, you will never be white."

"I've changed my life, father."

"What have you changed, if you are no one? Where do you think you're going if you have no greater plan? If you want to exist, you'd do better to fight for your territory. So that this patch of land can belong more to you, and so that your race may be your home. You are black, and apart from that, a woman. How can you love what will never be yours? Are you really assimilated? What pleasure can you feel in being treated like a second-class citizen?"

"Father, I've already told you I'm not a child."

Delfina's father despairs and embarks on a long lament. For he discovers how long the journey is to one's innermost being. How painful it is to see his daughter leave, never to return, to her tomb or to another world. A daughter considers herself an adult, without knowing how many suns and moons it takes for a human being to achieve maturity. What does it mean to grow up, if you need love, care and affection throughout your life? Even the lilies of the valley need the sun in order to burst into flower. High mountains need the rain to dull the volcanoes lurking inside them. The sea needs the wind's caresses to move. Even the dead nudge the living into a drum dance, a ceremony with candles, snuff   and chicken's blood, just so that they will be remembered. She says she has chosen her road. Does she know how many successes and disasters there are in the course of a life? She says she has taken her decision, but her eyes are closed, she doesn't know who she is or where she's going.

"My dear Delfina, there is no particular age when we become adults, and we remain children throughout our lives. My father used to tell me, don't go down that path. But I would follow it because I was stubborn. Nowadays, I sing to the waves empty handed. As much a child as I am an adult. As poor as I am old. If my father were here, he would tell me what to do, how to do it. He would say magical words to me in the wisdom of silence. In the distant expression of his gaze, he would transmit a message of knowledge. I'm old now and don't have a mother to give me affection and a bit of advice. Delfina, you should hold on hard to your mother's love, and not allow it to escape."

A period of silence follows, the challenge has won a moment's pause. They look at each other. They concentrate their thoughts. The scars of time are reflected in each other. Parents and offspring, adversaries in the centuries-old battle. Serafina decides to clear the air to revive the atmosphere.

"Delfina, your father is going to organize a mukhuto to inform the dead about this new birth, whether you like it or not."

"There you go with your superstitions."

"These are the myths that bind us together. A prayer won't do anyone any harm. Even God likes them."

"I've already said: I don't want it!"

Delfina's father assesses the dimension of the conflict. He learned long ago that a whip is a manly instrument that transforms men into women. He also knows that violence engenders resistance. In the new world, money is worth more than life. The number of properties

< 212 >

is more important than the number of children one has. Solitude will be better than company. Her father makes his calculations with regard to the birth. Life is short. One doesn't return to one's mother's womb and the umbilical cord is cut. For Delfina, her change in life style has become a matter of urgency. She wants to overcome her previous state. She wants to surpass herself. Choose new friends. Treat her parents with disdain. Whoever climbs the pole, sees the world from above. It's natural.

"Have you prepared the naming ceremony?" Delfina's father asks his daughter.

"What for? There's no need for that. My daughter's name is Maria das Dores."

"Maria das Dores? Why?"

"It's a simple, pretty name. It's the name of an actress in a photo novella. I liked it. Don't come and tell me I can't give my own daughter the name I want for her."

"But why give such a beautiful child a name that speaks of sorrow?"

Human beings join together in groups and create bulwarks against solitude. Even mountains cluster together in cordilleras. Over there on the horizon. Sorrow is the loneliness women feel when they have lost their husbands or sons to the plantations, the high seas, or exile.

Sorrow is what a father or a mother feels when separated from a child on the pathways of the world. Sorrow is what Delfina's father feels today and in the here and now. And so he speaks to his little girl in order to soothe his pain.

"Maria das Dores, my pretty little girl, just like your mother. What are you holding in your clenched fist? Sorrows or joy? You've got fingers as long as claws. It even looks as if you are fated to grip your prey. Are you perhaps a witch or a miner scratching away at the earth? You've got huge, clever eyes. What for? To run away from the predator? You have a big foot, a wayfarer's foot! It could even be that your destiny will be to walk along valleys, over mountains, over the whole world, in order to placate your sorrows, yes indeed, my little one! Your mad mother will one day mortgage your life and drag you along the pathways of sorrow, yes indeed, Maria das Dores!"

Delfina nervously resists, by adopting the strategy of palm trees. Who's never seen a palm tree on a stormy day? It's as if the wind is going to blow it down, but all its efforts are directed towards toughening its canopy and enabling it to resist the most violent gusts of wind. That is why she digs in her heels in defense of her beliefs.

"Stop this talk, dear father."

< 214 >

"No, I won't stay silent. The cord of time will string you up on any small tree. Your madness has nothing to sustain it."

Autumn comes and all lives slow down, sluglike. Winter is almost here and Delfina's father penetrates the heart of his memory. He recalls all the dreams the wind blew away, endless night is approaching, dense, long, without limit. He raises his eyes and on the horizon glimpses a world darkened by what is to come. He lights his pipe in despair, and blows smoke rings in the air.

"You are right, Delfina. Our life is full of pain and sorrow. The life path of blacks is one of sorrows. The destiny you have traced for this child is one of sorrows."

"Father, I have a right to choose new ways ahead, to open up new paths. Let me build my own world."

"Yes, you are right, my dear daughter."

For the young, the future will always be better than the present. For the old, the past was always better than the present. The old father sails in dark currents, without a boat, or compass, or oars. He curses the dreams of the new generations. For the names they desire remind him of things that have been carried away by time and wind. António is the name of the white who whipped him until he

< 215 >

was at death's door. Macário is the sinister name of the black sepoy who made the whole village seek refuge out in the bush. Francisco, another sepoy who killed blacks.

"Delfina, my girl, these names you like so much are full of hatred."

"Oh, father! You've told me these stories so many times. Forget the old days!"

Mothers like to give their children extravagant names. Names of travelers, of vagabonds. It all started in the earliest times. The Arabs came. The blacks were converted. And they started to call themselves Sofia, Zainabo, Zulfa, Amade, Mussá. And they became slaves. Then came the sailors with their cross and sword. Other blacks were converted. And they started to call themselves José, Francisco, António, Moisés. All the women were called Maria. And they remained slaves. The blacks who were sold started to call themselves Charles, Mary, George, Christian, Joseph, Charlotte, Johnson. They were baptized. And they remained slaves. One day, other prophets will come, bearing red flags and messianic doctrines. They will deify Communism, Marx, Marxism, Lenin, Leninism. They will demonize Capitalism and the West. The blacks will start calling themselves Iva, Ivanova, Ivanda, Tania, Kasparov, Tereskova, Nadia, Nadioska. And they will remain slaves. After that, people

< 216 >

from all over the world will arrive, with money in their pockets to donate to the poor in the name of development. And the blacks will call themselves Soila, Karen, Erica, Tania, Tatiana, Sheila. They will receive money from these people and they will remain slaves.

Adventurers will come and go like people who take a bath and don't get wet. And what about our languages? They'll learn just a few sounds. Names? They'll invoke one or two. Beliefs? They'll desecrate all of ours. We'll learn everything: Arabic, Portuguese, French, English, Norwegian, Russian, German, and so many other lesser known ones. And we shall remain slaves. We shall wage war among ourselves. We shall kill one another. We shall elect presidents. We shall hoist flags. We shall change flags, hymns, symbols. And we shall remain slaves.

< 217 >

15

Moyo paces round and round his house. He is trying to measure his backyard. He enjoys the pleasure of treading the soil barefoot. He discovers that the earth is as ripe and fertile as a black woman's womb, awaiting semen for the prolongation of life. Ah, my virgin Zambezia, adorned with palm groves! My Zambezia of unparalleled beauty, which inflamed the sailors' hearts with love!

He looks up at the tops of the trees. The mango trees are laden with fruit and the pregnant cashews are a promise of abundance. He prays for the rain not to fall for a little while, so as not to interfere with the flowering of the fruit trees. He thinks of the rice in the valley and changes his mind: the rice needs water. A lot of water. For the rice alone, a spot of rain would be good.

His eyes survey roads over yonder on the horizon and he exclaims: Ah, how beautiful life is! He gazes at the horizon and gasps: how vast the sky is! He dreams. If he could, he would journey into that immensity. If he didn't have all this fat and weight about him. If he didn't have this corroded body or these knees in constant need of

< 218 >

repair, like the parts of an old bicycle. Would that I could return to my days as a child!

He feels the earth vibrating under the soles of his feet, and this massages his chest, provoking a slight tremor, and his thoughts rush wildly. Heavens! It's a stampede. Horsemen, whites, sailors. Deportation. He listens attentively and concludes. No. It's neither horses nor an army. It's just a man running. A fugitive looking for a hiding place here. My God, for how much longer will I lead this life of a wizard, always playing tricks in order to hide folk on the run from the police? How much longer will I lead this life of wounds, fresh blood, bitterness? Oh, how tired I am! If only I lived in a wild, barren desert, free from the greed of the men of the sea, ah, my Zambezia of the sailors!

Over there in the distance, the cloud of dust dances at the whim of the waves of fear. And it is coming toward him. Moyo's eyes open wide in surprise: it wasn't a fugitive, but a sepoy, armed and in uniform, running like a madman, asking for help.

"José dos Montes?"

"Yes."

"What's wrong? Come, sit down, relax, tell me what's up. Do you want a glass of water?"

< 219 >

Moyo grabs him by the hand, leads him as far as the shade and sits him down in a chair. The man is in a state of shock. His heaving breath subsides like the waves coming to rest, exhausted, on the sands of the beach. Sweat runs down his skin. Powerful people don't seek out the poor in moments of affliction, for they are saved by weapons, laws, and the whites. They only seek out a medicine man when they have reached the edge of an abyss on their life's journey.

"You were running, José dos Montes."

"Yes."

"Did some snake bite you?"

"No."

"Were you running away from a lion?"

"Likewise no."

"So why were you running?"

The afternoon breeze soothes the man's fury. Moyo observes this strange presence. He displays none of the airs of an assimilado nor the arrogance of a sepoy. None of the violence or brusqueness of an armed man. He is merely a human being. A scared child seeking a life raft in his father's arms.

The sun sets too quickly in the west. Women returning from work,

< 220 >

in groups, chatter more noisily than a flock of birds. Moyo waits for the noise to abate before their conversation begins.

"The white man's religion is no use to blacks," José dos Montes raves, "their gods are far away and ours are near. Their angels exhort them to pray and our dead answer us immediately. God speaks when he feels like it, while our dead will give us an answer straightaway and at any moment."

"Do you think so?"

Moyo begins to have his suspicions. José dos Montes ascended the heights and found a perch on the moon's back. He is a lunatic. That's why he has come rushing here all out of breath just in order to declare his love for pagan gods. Proving in addition that he has already born witness to the efficiency of the dead and seeks their renewed blessing.

"How do you feel, José dos Montes?"

"Scared, very scared. I feel like crying."

"What are you scared of?"

"Of nightmares. Of fearsome shapes that constantly pursue me. Whether my eyes are closed or open. Whether at night or during the day."

< 221 >

José dos Montes has gone there hoping for a miracle. Willing to pay any price in order to relieve the pain he feels at that moment. Moyo is in a dilemma. How is he to treat a killer using the therapy of words? How is he to open his ears in order to inject the music of life into his soul? He searches for the best strategies in the encyclopedia of his memory. In the arsenal of his words, he selects the most learned ones to give his patient a good rap over the knuckles. He practices the magic breath that will issue from his throat and says:

"Nightmares are important in re-ordering the mind. They are your conscience keeping a close eye on you. Do not fear them."

"They're powerful, they want to kill me."

"They don't kill, they just make you aware. Their hidden voices are an omen. Listen, listen carefully, they aren't shapes, they're men."

"There are so many of them, they're right there, can't you see them?" He yells, pointing at the road. "They're waiting for me to leave so that they can pursue me again."

"How many people have you tortured, José dos Montes?"

"Me? I don't know. I never kept a tally."

Moyo's heart is filled with acrimony. But also with tenderness. This visit is the start of the great march backwards. To the grave or to the abyss. With much raving and incoherent speech. José dos Montes,

< 222 >

a murderer or a thief, is a human being asking for succor, and his duty is to cure and not to judge. He feels sorry for him. A fine man of iron. A royal steed. Born in the wrong place and the wrong time. And into the wrong race. With wrong thoughts. Using the wrong methods to survive. Born to triumph, but ending up vanquished. Transformed by the circumstances of life into a ridiculous sepoy.

"Ghosts don't exist," Moyo assures him. "Sometimes, mental turmoil projects fearsome shapes onto our field of vision. Don't be frightened. They are the cries of protest uttered by the men you whip until the point of death. These ghosts are the friends who reside in your conscience, and who want to bring you back to your senses."

A silence falls between them. José dos Montes is bent double. Maybe to hide the traces of his destiny mirrored in his eyes. Maybe trying to protect the deep secret that should never be revealed. Or merely rent asunder by the fury of the confrontation that oppresses him. Or perhaps he has positioned himself better to absorb the truth that has dawned on him and has begun to take the blindfold from his eyes. Moyo, astonished, seeks to rescue the man of reason drowning in the world's massacres. Incapable of accepting the harsh reality with which his old friend is struggling, he just sighs. How precarious the highway of life is! How deceptive the signs along the way. José dos Montes has been defeated. The dead will be avenged. Madness has taken its first steps inside his mind.

"Come," Moyo invites him, "we need to talk in safety. You must tell me how it all began. The wind is treacherous, it may carry our secrets to the four corners of the world."

It is no distance at all from the backyard to the hut. Moyo takes José by the hand and realizes how weak his muscles are and how he staggers like a soldier vanquished in invisible battles. The doorway into his hut is as narrow as the gateway to Paradise. They go in. José dos Montes's eyes are adrift in a sea of ancient memories. He feels ecstatic and gains vitality. In the middle, the fire flickers serenely on a bed of ashes. The half-light inside the hut provides his tired eyes with respite. He breathes a sigh of relief: I distanced myself from this aromatic world of my own free will, but how I missed these live smells of roots, smells of my childhood, smells of my mother's hut!

"Tell me how it all began," Moyo asks.

José talks of his emerging depression and the pain reborn from the roots of time. Of the reek of death haunting his sense of smell. Of the black birds dancing their macabre waltz around his field of vision. Of the hatred of the plantation blacks spilling over his shoulders. Of the suspicions of whites spilling over him. Of the children calling

< 224 >

him a monster on any street corner in the black quarter. Of his vain search for peace before the altar of the parish saints.

"Ah! This is a long conversation we are having, Moyo concludes. "Why don't you stay and have dinner with me? I shall tell you some stories from the olden days. I'll soothe you with a song. Roast you a chicken. Let's drink a toast with a drop of rum so as to lay our fears to rest."

"I don't want to eat."

"Are you going to leave me to eat on my own?"

"My palate is no longer used to black folks' food. I now eat refined food."

"What?!"

Tension hovers in the air on this early evening. In the middle of a straw hut. Gaining the fluidity of dark clouds. Threatening to unleash storms. Causing a beautiful conversation to be interrupted. Moyo pulls out a cigarette. He smokes for a while and his anger is dispersed. He takes a deep breath and concludes: this snake is dangerous. He begins to feel more comfortable and his strength is revived.

"Today, I need a ritual," José dos Montes confesses, "I need a spiritual immersion."

"Your soul is cold, my old friend!"

"Yes. I need the heat of a huge fire and the roll of an enormous drum. That's why I remembered you."

He's come to listen to my voice. To seek his evil deeds in my remedies. Submit me to his madness. Turn this house into a market where everything is bought and everything is sold. The man dreams of climbing up onto a pedestal through another man's strength, totally unaware of the perils that lie ahead of him. That is why he hurls icy words at him:

"You have come here in search of yourself and not to meet me."

"Why?"

"The patient never prescribes his cure."

"You can surely do me this favor. And I shall know how to reward you."

"One man alone doesn't perform a ritual. Two hands are needed to play a drum. Another two to keep a fire going. The feet of many women to dance wildly. As you can see, today I'm on my own."

Today's lamentation is the offspring of yesterday's weeping. Today's sun follows on from another sun. Before you, there were other men. Men who dreamed and died in the darkness of the abyss. In the

< 226 >

brazen pursuit of glory. In the pointless exhaustion of slaughter. José dos Montes, open your eyes!

"Stop mistreating the people, José dos Montes."

"I can't, I have to carry out my orders. Whites punish even more harshly and no one complains.

Why does punishment only hurt when it is administered by me? Because I'm black and they think I'm their brother?"

Not a drop of remorse in his tone of voice, proving that José dos Montes is declaring himself the victorious sower of chaos. Moyo has a bitter taste in his mouth from having to swallow professions of wickedness he is unable to digest. He tries in vain to understand this strange discourse. It is of no use. The madman opened his mouth wide and spat on the world. Moyo feels crushed by a huge wave of disgust and feels utterly at a loss: how to cure a man who is neither alive nor dead, but is death itself at large on the streets?

"What do you seek in the suffering of the people, José dos Montes?"

"Strange displays of affection. Bread. Power. I think I was born to destroy."

The icy thrust of a speech hovers in the air. Moyo feels a lack of air and he struggles with an excruciating attack of breathlessness. He discovers that he has just been contaminated and he is drunk with fear and terror. Before his eyes, he sees a parade of shapes, ghosts, nightmarish figures, that are no more than the reproduction of one shape alone, just one ghost, no more than that. He rubs his eyes to rid his sight of this sudden affliction. And he discovers the causes of his visions: it is José dos Montes, now already transformed and removed from the category of a human being.

With great difficulty, he cries out:

"You lead your life like a drunken driver, José."

"Ah, Moyo! I scared you with my words! I didn't mean to, I promise!"

He uttered the deep secrets that are normally unexpressed and he was rewarded with a moment of freedom. Reflection. It is Moyo's magical words that provide him with the mirror in which he can see his own image, hidden away inside himself. And which cause him to realize that all his victims are human beings. Just like him, born from love or hate. He recalls the eyes of the crowd bulging with fear at the imminent slaughter. He now understands that it is the howls of those condemned desperados imprinted in his mind that have taken on fearsome shapes. Stunned, he now begins to see

< 228 >

what he was blind to before: yes, it is those people I killed who are now rising up within me, demanding the lives I stole from them. How powerful they are! They engage me in combat, limbless and without weapons. Without sounds or syllables. At night and during the day, they pursue me with their wind-blown bodies. He falls into a trance and a fit of madness. He kneels and curls up to hide his face and weep. But his tears seep into the soil.

Moyo remains silent until the crying ceases. For a man's tears are a remedy against fear and anguish. He leans that weeping man's great head on his shoulder, reuniting all the fragments of that being dispersed to the four winds. After the bitter tears, the tentative beginnings of a conversation.

"Tell me about your family, José."

"We already have two children, and are expecting a third."

"As good looking as you, no doubt."

"They take after Delfina."

"Ah, yes! Delfina is a very beautiful woman."

José dos Montes's heart is tossed unawares between the world's extremes, like a ping-pong ball. From East to West, alternately, without a pause in between. His heart is thumping because he has mentioned Delfina by name, his love, his passion, his raison d'être.

"Tell me about Delfina. How is she?"

"Well. Very well."

"But your eyes suggest otherwise, José. Tell me the truth: is she perhaps the cause of all this torment?"

No, it wasn't all her fault. She was reared in the cradle of an affliction. She had picked up her morals on the streets of life. These provide sustenance in the goldfields of sex, where fidelity and infidelity are two sides of the same coin. No, she cannot be incriminated. She is too generous in the love she has to give and to sell. Delfina, a woman of contrasts, conflicts, confusion, and contradictions. She couldn't be the cause of this torment. Maybe it was God and fate. Maybe José dos Montes himself, who invented such fantasies about love and turned her body into both his vessel and anchor, without any safe port. At that point, he has a clear view of his insignificance in the carnivalesque pretense of love.

"Give me a remedy to cure this love, this passion."

"You are seeking a remedy against fear. There isn't such a thing."

"Cast a spell that will hold Delfina's heart in check."

"Hold a heart in check?" Moyo asks, startled. "Love in the world of magic isn't sincere, it doesn't last long and it causes bitterness. It's not worth it."

< 230 >

"When it comes to love, all means are justified, Moyo!"

Love, that old favorite song. It embellishes the songs in ring dances and the crazy dreams of poets. Love, an eternal prisoner in the hearts of lovers, a treasure that is sought and guarded, even if possession of it causes huge pain. It fills the heart with vain promises that lovers cherish as the truth.

"White men go crazy over her," José bursts out. "They molest her."

"Ah, Delfina! She knows how many threads it takes to sew love, and how many sighs it takes for the strongest of men to go crazy. Are they molesting her? Are you sure?"

"They're going to drive her into prostitution again."

"She is both the stage and the artist. The whole theater. She always was."

José dos Montes fills Moyo's ears with all the impotent verbiage of love's fanfares. My wife, the cross I bear and my punishment. My heart turned to ashes, to flames. My flighty woman of the streets and the dockside. In the skirmishes of feelings, the heart is a toy with which we play the game of love and passion, even though we know it is a relic that can break and not be mended.

"I wept for you on the day you were married. Delfina will be your perdition."

< 231 >

"I love Delfina."

"I understand."

"I admire the courage of lovers, sightless volunteers of fire and torture. Love, the twin of hatred, expresses itself in the very same actions: pain, torture, despair. People live but also kill for love. Who were the authors of the crazy theories of love? If love is good, why does it cause so much pain?"

"Cast a spell that will make me the only man in Delfina's life."

"The human heart is a free territory, and no one can penetrate it."

"But you can find a way to penetrate it, Moyo."

"To bewitch a lover's heart is a woman's thing. You led her to the altar, and placed a diadem of pearls on her head. She is yours. Hold on to her if you're a man."

"I tried, but I can't."

Although saddened, Moyo smiles. He recalls his past as a dreamer and a romantic. He put up with many a beating for peeping at women bathing in the rivers of Zambezia. He courted married women and was caught red handed on countless occasions.

"A man with any self-respect seeks his own freedom and not to be imprisoned by a woman's heart. The more you love her the more she'll punish you. Why did you marry her?"

< 232 >

"You don't know how I feel, Moyo, you just have no idea."

"Oh yes I do. I was once your age and suffered from the same madness."

Many folk look for solutions that deliver love by magic. Disturbing the sleep of good souls and clairvoyants. For they exist. Bringing together all the magicians in the world to resolve their problems.

"I too drugged myself with fantasies. I too set off in search of the moon for the sake of love, but I discovered that its surface consisted only of stones. The moon seen from among the palm trees is the most beautiful sight in the world. I'm a romantic, José dos Montes!"

"You can save my home, you can," he implores, "you stop the rain when you want and turn the sailors' bullets into water. You've got arrows of thunder in this hut, in a little clay pot, because you command the thunderclaps, we all know that."

"Don't exaggerate. I'm a mere mortal and am no one's savior."

José dos Montes tries to sing his praises with clumsy words. Yes, he wants to soar into the sky with the magic wings of all the witchcraft in the world, which will make all his actions magnificent. To ascend into the fantastic world of those who govern life, audacious like all heroic deeds. Like a piece of wizardry. An act of enchantment.

"With your powers, I can rule the world."

"What for?"

"So that Delfina will see that there's no other man after me. Only God and I reign supreme."

José dos Montes: a bull. Muscles hardened during the arduous training undergone by sepoys. His powers unlimited, nourished by powerful arsenals of fire, gunpowder, madness. Begging me for all the witchery there is in order to suck yet more blood. No, I shan't give him anything.

"You kill folk at random. What is it you seek in the death of others?"

"A great deal. Power. Freedom. Glory. I want to be a hero."

"How?"

"The heroes of legends always kill. That is why they are proclaimed kings."

"And what heroic deeds would you carry out?"

"I would kill all the whites so I could live in peace with my Delfina. I would make each person kneel before me, just like the mistresses, the ladies, the landholders, and the owners of companies do. Make me the greatest of them all, you have the power to do that, Moyo!"

Power. A ceaseless bluster in moments of fantasy. What kind of power, and for what purpose? He chuckles at Montes's ingenuousness.

< 234 >

Power can't be picked up in the street, nor is it sold by the kilo at the witchdoctor's stall. Fortune isn't measured by the meter, nor is it stored away in the medicine man's container. I can even raise him to the pinnacle of life. Through magic. I can reduce Delfina's sexual power, and turn her into a good spouse, I've got herbs for all that. I've got the murderer in my hands, I can disable him, by breaking one of his arms or a leg, and turn him away from the world of crime for good. But no, I won't do anything. My spirits will never be placed at the service of crime. I wasn't born to serve kings or regimes. Who am I to interfere in the world's course of events?

"When someone is hailed king, it is his inner power that frees him. Greatness lies within people," Moyo explains. "There is no witchcraft to guarantee greatness."

"Well then, give me the good fortune to be the most esteemed, and best-liked of all the sepoys."

"What you want is a remedy for unimportance. I don't have one."

"You're lying, Moyo. You give people like yourself magic to avoid raids by sepoys and not to pay taxes," he censures him, "you hide fugitive blacks here in this hut, because you have already hidden me. You protect everyone, I know that. You have the power to disappear. You transform yourself into an ant, a fish, a bird, whenever you want.

You transforms warriors into bees, fish, flies, playing havoc with Portuguese plans for invasion.

"Don't exaggerate!"

José's tone changes, acquiring the melodious sounds of a beggar. Moyo is perplexed. He is shocked by the anxiety expressed in the endless search for all that is intangible. He is shocked by the obsession insatiable hunters have for everything that doesn't exist. He laments the destiny of those disciples of the mechanical philosophies of this new world, which glorify and empower all those who are the most effective at squeezing the trigger of their firearms. He laments the fate of those who skip in the air when they have no wings to fly. He laments the fate of José, whom he loves like a son.

"My good José, in the old days you used to ask me for cures for your bodily injuries. You would ask me for a remedy, and then my blessing, protection for positive things in life. You've changed a lot, José!"

"I was a child, now I'm an adult and I want to be even greater now."

"Greatness lies in our soul, José."

"Are you by any chance an opponent of the regime? A terrorist?" José asks, somewhat irritably.

"Are you suspicious of me? Why?"

"You're known to be a pillar of the resistance. You always talk

< 236 >

about independence. You don't want to attend to me because I'm a sepoy. The whites are all about progress, and this regime represents the future. Why are you against it?"

"In this independence we dream of, the world will not be the same. Yes, we shall liberate the soil, but we shall never be the masters. The rulers of the future will have white heads on a black body. When that time comes, the sailors will no longer need boats, because they will have built secure dwellings inside us. Colonialism will inhabit our minds and our bellies and freedom will be nothing more than a dream."

Moyo doesn't live for the present. Nor does he aspire to the future. Nor distant pasts which he never knew. Maybe he aspires to the justice that inhabits the dreams of poets. Maybe paradise, that tourist resort priests, prophets and believers preach to us about, but that only the saints can enjoy. He defends human freedom and not systems shaped by imported models with ideas of supremacy, nor the material world of the dead who scream commands to the living in the voices of seashells. In all regimes there are condemned prisoners in cells and starving old people trudging through the world each almsgiving Friday. In every regime there are folk eating from trash heaps, sleeping in the open air, freezing at the mercy of the dew on cold mornings. There is also lust for power. And fights. And blood. Marxists. Colonialists. Socialists. Communists. Masochists. Fighting for power that is never conquered or to dominate the united people who will never be defeated.

"My territory is the silence in which I am reflected," Moyo explains, "my space is my time, where I reproduce myself and from where I depart, thus completing the cycle of life."

"Why do you refuse my request, Moyo? Are you aware I could denounce you?"

"And you, even with all the magic potions in the world to protect you, will be no more than a black at the back end of life."

"You treat me with scorn. Are you any better than me?"

War is declared between the two men and they are heading for disaster. In both, there is a feeling of impotence. Moyo is pained by impotence as he watches his son leaving for the abyss without being able to save him. José dos Montes is pained by impotence because he is armed, fighting against a defenseless old man without success. They defy each other. Eye to eye. They reflect each other. The submission of one in the other's lack of submission, both in despair because of their fear of the future. They envy each other. José envies the other man's tenacity, his ability to defend his principles even though it may cost him his life, obeying the dictum, "it is better to die than to yield." Moyo envies the other man for his frivolity, the superficiality that makes him sufficiently versatile to adapt to the savagery of the world.

In trying to achieve the impossible to save his son, José's words are an appeal to his conscience. Moyo thinks. I was born to treat the world's wounds. Destined to live between my hut and the bushlands, which are a paradise for remedies. I was made from love and it is for love that I exist.

"We are the same, Moyo. Killing and curing, servants of the same regime. Both of us expelled from the world. You wearing your loincloth and living in your hut, while I wear this khaki uniform, these tall boots and a rifle, a ridiculous citizen with a red fez on my head."

"We are not the same, boy, no, we are not the same."

"Are you sure we're not the same?"

Moyo rummages around in the bag of time and discovers the relics of his own journey. Where did my life begin? Where does it end? He tries to add up the number of lives he has saved. The sick he has cured. The offspring of barren wombs his roots made fertile. He keeps counting and then stops. Can the number of drops of water in the Zambezi be counted? Can the number of grains of sand in all the

< 239 >

waters of the Indian Ocean be counted? He discovers that his life is both ocean and river on one and the same path. It is immense. He no longer knows how many women he has loved and how many he has kissed. Of his wives, he lost two and was left with four, and he has never been a widower. As for his children, there are twenty six. He cannot remember how many aborted offspring there were, or still births. And when it comes to grandchildren, there are seventy nine. He was born on the day when a boat full of shackled blacks arrived to build the port on the banks of the Quelimane River. He was born on the day when they began to build the first tarred road. He is the same age as most of the white folks' houses. He is the brother of that old palm tree at the entrance to the house, planted in his honor at the time of his birth. He is the twin of everything: the bridge, the highway and many palm trees.

He came of age at the time when surviving men had the spiritual duty to get down to work and make fertile women pregnant in order to preserve the species — for the husbands were imprisoned in labor camps, exiled, or slaughtered. He helped create the palm grove, and he was a slave. He was whipped, shot at, knifed, and was always saved from death thanks to the spiritual power of his roots. When a boat

< 240 >

full of whites was wrecked at Macuse during the First World War, he was already a soldier.

"Moyo, you used to be my friend."

"I still am."

"You did everything I asked of you."

"Everything you ask of me is within you. Free yourself."

"Is that a refusal?"

"Yes."

"Is that your last word?"

"Yes."

Upset, José dos Montes unleashes all his strength from deep inside him and mutters to himself: you crazy old man. You don't know who you're messing with. My temper always gets the better of me, I've been like that ever since I was born. I'm a thug, a street fighter. A rebel. When I was a child, everyone was scared of me. I conquer everything with the strength of my punches, and work off all my anger with my fists. One puff of breath from me and everything turns to coal. I'm a dragon.

"Well, you can be sure of this: no one is innocent in this regime," José dos Montes cries. "I'm active and you're passive. I destroy and

< 241 >

you mend, each one of us in his own way under the illusion that we are building something."

Displeasure approaches José dos Montes with the certainty of a soldier's march, stirred up by his growing agitation. He places his hand in his belt and feels the cold metal of his dagger. Sinister thoughts hover in his head like a nest of wasps. He pulls it out. He places it across Moyo's throat. With this gesture, he is begging for pity. Obedience. To force the old man to yield to his desires, and accept the language of the new age, and to bring him to heel.

"No one refuses a request from me, Moyo. I'm not going to leave here empty handed. I'm an important person."

"Are you important? What is the nature of your importance?"

"Yes, I am. I'm a sepoy! I'm assimilated, a Christian, and I've been married in a church."

"What you are is a hero defeated by a bunch of ghosts! You're so important that you can't even feed your wife in your own bed!"

Words of lucidity and madness in the blazing fire of a fight. Among the stock of caustic terms, these men in battle with each other, each seek the best arsenal. Moyo feels suddenly tired and a deep desire to die and forget the bitterness of that encounter once and for all.

"Why do you speak to me with such disdain?"

"What reasons do I have to respect a sepoy?"

José has taken the first step on the great march towards the abyss. It's going to be hard to make him return to the present and make him part of everyday things, which are born and then die. In order to belong to this world, José would have to be born again.

"You don't know what I'm capable of, Moyo. I came in search of help and you refuse me. I came in search of peace, and you insult me. I came in search of a dream and, instead of encouraging me, all you offer is scorn and hatred. If you possess power, so do I. So be sure of this: the power of weapons is greater than all the witchcraft in the world."

The cold dagger presses against his flabby neck. Memories of a long life flash across Moyo's mind. Sweet memories of José as a boy, whose wounds he treated and then he fed soup to with his own hand. He sighs and changes his mind. No, my God. No, this isn't the boy I reared. Nor was it to these ears that I sang the most beautiful lullabies. The boy I saved won't come back, for he is buried in a heart of stone. The sweet words I taught him were carried away by the wind, leaving this killer who now threatens me.

"Who are you, José? What are you doing here? What do you want from me?"

< 243 >

"Do you really want to know?"

Moyo nods. Madness has built its dwelling in a man's troubled mind. At the pinnacle of torment, forgiveness. Flashes of lucidity and fellow feeling flood into Moyo's mind like the oil for a lamp. And this imposing father figure emerges into the light at the last moment. Although he is suffering from insanity, although he has the role of a killer, although he is convinced about his assimilated status, José dos Montes is still a noble-hearted man, capable of the deepest love. In his search for life, he became derailed. In his search for love, he got hurt. A killer who, haunted by ghosts, flees from his acts, proving there is a dormant saint within him.

"You have known me ever since I was a child. You always knew who I was, but now, let me tell you: I'm José dos Montes, the killer!"

"I am immortal, José dos Montes. Do you want to kill me? Then kill me. But I will live on inside you forever. I shall be the permanent inhabitant of your conscience. I will be your nightmare, your greatest ghost on moonlit nights. I shall be your star, in your ascent and in your fall."

Moyo receives the price of his love at the point of a dagger that José dos Montes manipulates with skill over his body. The killer suffers the cost of his anxiety, pain, and despair. That is why he extracts

< 244 >

through malice everything he was denied for his own good. With the point of his blade, he searches for material assets. Gold and silver relics. Plinths, pedestals, the laurel wreaths of champions. He discovers that the empty carcass contained nothing, and that it was the same as the carcass of an ox. With a lot of blood, many muscles, bones, innards, dung. Just matter. Not even the blue blood of nobles. The brain, just a jellied mass, lacking the firm white brain of a coconut.

And so he decides to unveil the mystery of life. Where did this dead man's wisdom come from? His heart, head, or genitals? Where did his brilliant mind come from? And the light in his brow? Where was his vigor? Where was the joy and the pain? And what about love? And hatred? And the source of his honeyed words? And where was his long life of good fortune and ill luck?

He examines the whole body in vain. He finds no diamond in any of the cells. Nor even a pearl. Nor even the imitation of a star. But when alive, the body had luster and mystery. In his searches, he discovers the great mystery of the ethereal nature of the soul and wisdom: the death of another man achieves nothing. He was involved in a useless tragedy, condemning himself to the impalpable sentence of the gods on the day of judgement.

< 245 >

He suddenly feels the unbearable pain of a child without a father. His weeping is a song of sorrow. Moyo, your image was a gentle caress on my chest. What have I done to myself? I tried to pocket the sun, and in so doing, I turned the light of my world into darkness. I wasn't even conscious of my acts. The blame for this lies in my rage that got out of control and fled from me like a pack of wolves on a moonlit night. You are to blame, Moyo. Why didn't you scream for me to calm down? If you had screamed, I would have stopped, I swear. Yes, it's your fault. You gave me no sign. You didn't warn me of the danger. You gave me a last mocking smile, as if it gave you pleasure to die at my hands. This blade is to blame, this metal phallus that drags me into orgies of bloodshed. This female blade is to blame, this blade of both and neither sex, my companion at macabre times, my sweetheart, accomplice in my misfortune.

He stops weeping all of a sudden: it's no use now. Maybe pray and ask for forgiveness. But he still possesses the urge to inherit the man's boundless powers. The powers that turned to vapor in the last breath he took. Ah, Moyo! My father whom I killed, place within me all that I took from you: the gleam in your eyes. The beauty of your heart. Come on, get your revenge, make me your slave, but let your good spirit take carnal form within me so as to take away my enslavement to love, to these ghosts that pursue and destroy me.

Outside, the moon grows, bursting with mysteries. The ghosts get ready for their great jamboree. A shower of unknown stars frolic above the palm grove. The desert has just penetrated the soul of a killer and the evil shadows dance freely.

◆　　◆　　◆

What is being celebrated today?

Two processions heading in opposite directions. One celebrating the end, the other the beginning. One crowd crying, the other laughing. One heading west, the other east. Both marking the death of the same man. They reach the meeting point and look at each other. They defy each other. And there is some murmuring.

Among the marchers heading east, there is merriment and laughter. Who killed the wizard, the witchdoctor? It was José dos Montes, an exemplary black, a visionary who recognized that times were changing. On his own, he entered the wild animals' redoubt and eliminated the most dangerous of all the terrorists. The wizard was confronting the regime with souls from the other world. He was mobilizing the rabble against the might of our empire.

Among those marching westward, there is gloom. Who killed our saintly patriarch, Moyo, he who healed the wounds in our bodies and souls? It was the traitor José dos Montes, in an act of ingratitude. Because he wanted to possess the impossible. Because he didn't want to listen to the voice of reason. No, he wasn't mad. That was a trick he used in order to carry out his abominable deed.

Moyo's body is lowered into the ground to the rhythm of somber drumbeats. At the same moment, José dos Montes climbs onto the pedestal. Guns and cannons in the fanfare of victory. A military parade. Upon the death of a man, the sailors after all award a copper star, which embellishes the shoulders of their brave men.

In his victory speech, José dos Montes declares that everything he did was for the fatherland. But his conscience tells him a different story. I didn't kill anyone, I killed myself. He feels a sudden nostalgia. He remembers. In Moyo's death agony, the key words. Ascent. Fall. A star. The flimsy badges they place on his shoulders carry the weight of a man. For they represent his ascent; they have stars. All he wanted was to tear his own heart out in an act of suicide.

Songs of the people, the intoxication of pain and grief. In their eyes, there are gloomy shadows, as the future is inaugurated. The waltz of change. The sacred symphony of new words. From now on, the word freedom has been killed. Let slavery be called discovery. Let slaughter be called civilization and humiliation be termed conversion or Christian baptism. Let submission be called fidelity. Let all the humiliated submit themselves to those elegant gods who live in the heavens and the clouds, far from the mud and the dust, represented on the earth by the god fishes who have disembarked from the caravels. That's how it will be forever more. From this day onward, we shall call them molungo, mulungo, nungu, muzungo, muzimu, meaning he who comes from the sky, heaven itself, the greatest God, the white god, heaven, paradise, in all the languages of our land.

The people dance at the funeral of their Moyo knowing that, although he is absent, he will send them messages from under the earth, in the drops of dew and of rain. They know he will always be near, to help the living to unleash the rain, rejuvenate the flocks, to pray that the hens may lay more eggs and that famine may end. They know that although he is dead, he will help the country to become free of the sailors' exploitation, so that children may grow up free

< 249 >

from slavery. They know that the country's dead return to clay, because ascending to heaven is to become dust and air pollution, a dark stain in the immaculate, fragile ozone layer.

They lay the body in the shade of a tree. And they scatter flowers for each memory. With sonorous words, they weave myths that elevate Moyo to the pinnacle of eternity.

Under the earth, the words of the prophets, only heard by those chosen by the whispered voices in the depths of conches: you are only bewitched by those who know you. Without the collaboration of blacks, colonization would not have been possible.

16

He feels his left eye twitching. Bad luck.

There's an enigma at the heart of nature — José dos Montes confirms — today the sun won't set before something has happened to me. There's a gray stain in the subtle colors of the horizon. There's an itch on the bottom of my foot. Piercing barks from the dogs as I pass by. A cat crossing my path. Yes, something is going to happen today. But what is it?

He feels an enormous chill inside him and looks for a reason. All he finds is the reflection of his own anxiety. But I am at ease with the regime. I've got ahead in life. He who owes nothing has nothing to fear. But something bad is going to happen to me today. His mental disquiet causes him to fantasize. His irrational side concocts superstitious thoughts and his eyes start capturing invisible signs. No, nothing can happen to me!

He leaves his post and returns home, apprehensive. Judging by his father-in-law's presence, the day has one or two mysteries in store for him. There is Delfina's father in his favorite patch of shade. Sitting

< 251 >

in his easy chair, as if he were waiting for him. He gets a shock. He hurries toward him.

"Good afternoon, father-in-law."

"Eh?"

Delfina's father hasn't managed to emerge from the abyss into which he had sunk. For a father's career leads him along unexpected paths. Every day, there's some new story, a new path, a new destiny. Starting with childbirth, diapers and fevers. After that come episodes of joy and sadness, scandal and shame.

"How are you?"

"Me?"

"Yes, it's you I'm talking to."

"Oh, I'm alright."

He sighs bitterly, uttering cries of disgust in his silence: how could he be alright? I've put up with childbirth, menstrual blood and infidelities on the part of her mother, I pretended not to notice, but I felt it. Now, this whore, an adulterous wife, bearing races, tribes, and castes all in the same womb. Why do I have to put up with all this? Where is this career as a father leading me?

José dos Montes notices. There is a thick cloud in those placid eyes. Why?

"Well then?" José makes an effort to break the silence.

"Sit down and have a drink, son."

On hearing his father-in-law's slow, hoarse tone, he understands the nature of the mystery. One or two truths that are hard to reveal, and that need some liquor to come to the surface. José takes a mouthful. Then another and another. Silence descends on the two men.

From inside José's house, the cry of a newborn baby tears through the air like cannon fire. Those screams have the solemnity of a command, the cry of children born to rule the world. José smiles.

"Well, then, father-in-law? My daughter has been born. My third child. Why didn't you tell me?"

"It's my granddaughter who has been born. My granddaughter!"

"And my daughter!"

"I said: my granddaughter!"

Dense, compact words. A declaration of life with deathly tones. Why? He seeks to explain such a phenomenon. Cold words on a hot afternoon. Words that humiliate and reject him. Why?

"I'm going to see the child."

"Have another drink first."

< 253 >

After each mouthful, José dos Montes pauses and asks a question: why was the child born at home? Why can't I see the child? What's happening in there? Is the child a monster?

José gets up impatiently and makes to rush into the house. His father-in-law's steely grip stops him.

"Wait."

He obeys and stops. Maybe the midwife is bathing Delfina. Maybe they're still cutting the creature's umbilical cord. Maybe they're just getting the child ready for the father to be able to see her. His father-in-law tries hard to get him drunk and time lingers on. Soon, it will be night. José is desperate.

"Why all this delay? Why are you trying to get me drunk?"

"Our Delfina has just given birth dishonorably."

"Dishonorably?"

"The delivery went fine, according to her mother. It was a healthy baby. But she gave birth to our dishonor."

"If she's healthy, why is it dishonor?"

"Have another drink and relax." His father-in-law looks down as he speaks. When the news is good, there are smiles. When it's bad, eyes seek refuge in a grain of sand.

"I've had enough!"

< 254 >

"Ah, my dear son-in-law! Put off your disappointment for just a little while longer."

"Disappointment?"

His father-in-law doesn't have the strength to put off his sadness any longer. He lets him dash off towards the cause of his dishonor. For his soul to feast on its meal of thorns. He brazenly climbs up onto the stage of his dishonor. He enters the house, with his heart thumping to ancestral drumbeats. Delfina hurriedly conceals the child's face. José's body sways erratically and he leans against the wall. Sweat flows, hot and fine. He enters the beating heart of the abyss.

José uncovers the child and looks. His eyes absorb nature's phenomenon with crystal clarity: the birth of a new race. The body is covered in a thick film of dew, distilling vapors, smells, waves of heat. At first, silence reigns. Then he stutters. After that, words flow in a cascade.

"My God! Place flowers on my grave, I've just died!"

The child is white like an eggshell, the bosses have just presented him with an offspring. In order to add color to his home and remove the stigma of blackness from the family. My God, a mulatto daughter for a black couple. Whose sperm was it? The boss? The owner of the plantation?

< 255 >

From José's throat comes the neighing of a dying horse. Ah! The sailors have turned sex into a weapon of war. They have won and everything belongs to the regime: sperm, egg, blood, the arms of the menfolk and the sexual organs of the women. That is why Delfina has sown the seeds of the future: the race that Eden hadn't planned for but that love created.

Bitterness brings ancestral voices to his mind. Moyo's prophecies that the world of hierarchies would be based on skin color: white at the top, mulatto in the middle, and black at the tail end of History. When the white leaves, the mulatto will assume command. After independence, we will still see the mulatto enjoying the freedom of the streets. In shop windows. In the aquarium of a brothel. In the aisle of an airplane. As the hostess. Coffee, sir? Tea, madam? Behind the counter of a bank. Bookkeeper, economist. On the catwalk at beauty pageants, because the beautiful girls will be the ones who have inherited their skin tone from a sailor. They won't have to put in much of an effort to be people, to have a good job, a nice house, a good life, because power is their inheritance. The black, as hard as a coconut, will have his pride of place in digging clay up in the hills, carrying goods, toiling in the kitchen. That's why a black woman

< 256 >

will seek to have a mulatto child. To lighten the black man from the burden of his skin, just as a person lightens the burden of their having to wear mourning clothes. Independence will come one day, but there will still be a need for a thousand and one revolutions for centuries to come. The black will have to be the victor in all these revolutions to restore the world's equilibrium.

José plucks up courage and asks in a plaintive murmur.

"Delfina, was the creature born prematurely?"

"Why?" There's no sign of apprehension or fear on Delfina's face. Only endless joy and a smattering of pity for this tortured man.

"Her skin! There's no color in her skin. Is she an albino?"

"She's neither premature nor an albino."

"Tell me, Delfina, tell me it's all untrue, tell me that underneath that white skin, there's melanin budding, which will burst into blossom in the sun and dye the girl's skin the color of clay. Come on, tell me she was born raw, that she needs time to ripen like the fruits of the fields that are born green but gain the color of the soil when the sun shines on them."

The child launches forth into more screaming. She is like a white spider waving her paws around in the wind. In that creature's face lies the death of a family. A white larva at the very core of life, announcing the death of a family. José's arms flop down in defeat. In the endless dance, the palm trees celebrate the might of the sailors.

"Tell me, Delfina, tell me what happened? What did you lack? What didn't I give you? Don't you know how much I suffered for you?"

Incoherent words. Raving. A song of fire crackling within him. His head droops onto his chest like a fallen tree. He raises his head and looks from side to side. The dagger on the wall. The hammer on the table, inviting him to macabre orgies. All he needs to do is to stick his hand out and open his palm. The soft pillow inspires other secret thoughts. All he would need to do is to hold it down firmly over the nose of the adulteress. As for the newborn, the open palm of his hand would suffice to give her the ruddy skin of a corpse.

"Delfina, why?"

She thinks quickly. And then she decides. It's better to tell him everything in one go. Hurt him. Come out with the whole truth and not one bit at a time. Give her husband a merciful death and finish his suffering in one fell swoop.

"It was that time you were away, over toward Maganja and Lugela and all that bushland. While you were killing black children, I was conceiving a white man's child. It was as if it was all part of a plan. Hardly had you left, your boss turned up and pestered me. Then he took me to the most beautiful places in this world and treated me like a queen. Sometimes I get the feeling God arranged everything so that this child could be born. It's my good fortune, it was all written in the stars, don't you think, José?"

"You betrayed me."

"Me?"

"And what about the love I feel for you, Delfina?"

"Ah! Love. Does it still exist? Haven't you forgotten about it?"

"Delfina!"

"What do you want, José? Do you want me to abandon my lucky fate because of you?"

"You swapped me, Delfina, you've gone back to being a prostitute, you're a woman of the streets, you're never going to change. Selling your body is your vocation. I paid a high price for your love, can't you see that?"

"You've got your ambitions and I've got mine. You go around killing people on your own account and not on mine, I have nothing to do with that. You make me scared, you disgust me, and I feel no pleasure in being the wife of a murderer."

< 259 >

José dos Montes extols the virtues of courage. Delfina is an obstinate woman. Haughty. Vomiting stark words like bullets. Stabbing her husband in a display of suicidal bravado. José dos Montes discovers marriage is a theater of war between the sexes. He has lost all the arguments.

"You're a tramp."

"I prefer to be treated like a tramp than as the wife of a killer. Besides, you knew the life I led, José, and in spite of that you married me. You knew this would happen one day, you knew that as well. One never forgets the nice things."

"Ah, Delfina!"

"From now on, my status has improved! I'm the mother of a mulatto girl. A white man's concubine. Never again will I live at death's door, for this daughter represents my security. I shall flaunt this creature like a white flag, waving to the sailors and shouting: I'm all yours! I fused my blood with yours to create a new race. I loved you, sailor, I fulfilled my promise, here's your child! I have made your passage through this land eternal. I've brought happiness to my black mother's heart. Security for my father in his dotage. A right to a piece of land to build a little house and plant cabbages and onions, without having to pay the hut tax, in a space that is our own by divine right. This child will free our dear Zezinho from the fate of a litter bearer or a coconut planter for some white man. She will save Maria das Dores from becoming a prostitute for sailors on the quayside."

"No, Delfina!"

"You don't have the power to satisfy my yearnings. I'm sorry."

"I'm a new man, Delfina."

"You've changed, that's true, but only in the papers you carry. You've got to take many a bath before you start looking like a white man. You're black, you're poor, my dear José, you don't have any money in your pocket."

Delfina's smile was hostile, exasperating in its indifference. Today, her voice is especially cold and it can be heard all the way from the mountainous heights of her victory. She knows that one day the world will tell her story and celebrate the heroism of the women who produced the miracle of a race from their own belly.

"Those white men are married, Delfina."

"So what? It's better to be a white man's lover for an instant than a black man's wife for one's whole life!"

"Think of their families, Delfina."

"Their wives are saintly and as cold as fishes."

The sailors' wives are saintly and abominate sin. Invoking their

< 261 >

saintliness, they wrap themselves up in countless bits of cloth in the tropical heat, without even imagining that their descendants will parade naked on the deserted beaches, enjoying the tropical breeze. Delfina is a proper woman. She knows how to use her body to swat away men's tedium, and incinerate their desire, reducing it to ashes so as to make their money fall like drops of rain into the palm of her hand.

"There's no cure for your problem, Delfina."

José feels the pain of humiliation. A grown man whose life is dependent on the hooped skirts of a harlot. Shackled to perversion to guarantee his survival. Life demands that he should be like a stone in order for his heart not to suffer.

"Why didn't I make you wear a chastity belt?"

"Would you have been capable? And where would those smart new clothes you wear come from? And what about your protection? And the promotions that get better day by day? Where would the salt cod and olives that you eat without question come from? And the good wine you get drunk on?"

José could have put a stop to her betrayal, it wouldn't have been hard at all. He could have beaten her, humiliated her, killed her any time he wanted. He could now cut off the ear or the nose of

< 262 >

the adulterous woman, a traditional expression of vengeance by wronged husbands.

"Oh, my God! Melt this woman's icy heart!"

His voice assumes the high-pitched whinny of a dying horse. He is a lizard in the middle of the fire. An ox shooed away from its kraal. He is downcast. Disorientated. Conflicting thoughts well up in his conscience: where shall I go? Where shall I go and seek repose from my exhaustion if the invader has installed himself in my nest? He travelled the road of bitterness like a bull thirsting for the way to water. He knew this was going to happen one day, and its delay gave him the illusion that it never would. He knew things would be painful, but not to such an extent. While he travels down this long road, he takes stock of his sad existence: the power of a black man can be summed up in his long list of losses. His mother's lap that was stolen from him. The endless forced marches through unknown lands just in order to love Delfina. The friends who have perished at his hands. Killing his brother in order to exist. Being a cannibal of his own race. Love is a dream that can never be achieved, because love is the child of freedom.

It isn't jealousy that assails him, nor the fury of a betrayed man. Tomorrow, he will have to put up with the mocking looks of the

< 263 >

black palm grove workers. He feels bitterness towards everything. He has just discovered that he is the most solitary of men. And so he runs to seek peace and quiet in the heart of the palm grove. He walks along the seashore until night falls.

The voices of distant spirits disturb his mind. He hears magical drumbeats and the songs of the dead. Tongues of fire grow in his chest. He raises his eyes to the heavens seeking God, but he sees other miracles. High above, the coconuts are the skulls of the dead laughing at his shame. He panics and begs. Wind, take me to the peaks of the mountains of Namuli, the world's lookout. I want to return to the fetal age. Penetrate my mother's womb and go to sleep! But the wind replies mockingly and embraces the palm trees in a waltz, rustling ancient mutterings of sarcasm in the middle of the ring dance. Sea, the graveyard of waves, be my graveyard too.

The ocean is too cool when he reaches it. He takes off his shoes. He hurls himself into the waves, in a mighty race to the sea's endless depths. He feels death is cold. Liquid. It tastes of salt and the fluidity of the waves. To add to his even greater shame, the sea sweeps him away, vomits him up afar, holds him in contempt.

< 264 >

Human beings may strip off their clothes, but they never strip off their acts. Rancorous images become embedded in the cornea like tattoos.

José dos Montes howls his delirious thoughts onto the red of his chest and into the blackness of night. I have put up with long marches. The hissing of serpents. I followed the rocky path on a carpet of thorns. He looks at the skies above, maybe searching for God. He sees a star growing, filling the dark gloom of his heart with light. He sees Moyo sitting in the dunes, only a few meters away.

"Moyo?"

"Yes, my darkened soul. It's me, the eternal inhabitant of your conscience."

"Ah!"

"Get up, you wretched soul. The roar of the ocean is fearsome, but the sand undoes the waves with a fairy's hands. Don't be afraid. Get up and walk."

José dos Montes recognizes the voice of the star. He gets timidly to his feet, moved by astonishment. So it wasn't a star after all. It was Moyo making his magical entrance by causing his soul to take the concrete form of a lit candle.

"So you didn't die after all, Moyo?"

< 265 >

"I inhabit your conscience, I never died."

"What have I done with my life?"

"The problem isn't just yours. All human beings rush headlong into the ocean, while leaving their body on dry land. Only birds can fly, my poor José."

"Why so much bad luck?"

"The pathways of the world aren't straight."

"I want to die, Moyo!"

"Death isn't the end of life, but the beginning of it. Stay on earth until the gods call you."

He remembers the fables of his childhood. The frog that wanted to be an ox. The toad that wanted to be beautiful, and jumping into a pot of hot oil, scalded itself. The swift hare that fell asleep during the race allowing the tortoise to win. Suddenly, he makes up his mind and shouts to all four compass points. I'm tired of this world. I want to die today, right now. In the middle of this palm grove. At the top of a palm tree. I want to sway in the air next to the coconuts to which I dedicated my whole working life. I want to be nearer the clouds. Nearer to God. The stars. But palm trees don't have branches. José dos Montes feverishly looks for a solid enough palm tree for him to hoist his gallows.

< 266 >

"Moyo, palm trees don't have branches. All they have are arms, palms   and fingers. Why?"

"So that sailors can't use them to hang blacks. So that you don't hang yourself from a palm tree."

"Why are they forever dancing?"

"They are daughters of the wind. Like blacks, endlessly celebrating death and pain that occur at every turn. You should celebrate too, José dos Montes, come on, get up, sing, dance!"

"Why is a coconut wrapped in so much fiber and a hard shell?"

"Because it's Zambezia's twin brother. In order to exist, the native of Zambezia must be as hard as a coconut. To which one should add to the basic features of his character the ability to lie, the strategy of a rat, treachery and cowardice. He should live at the very pinnacle of summits and be inaccessible like the highest coconuts, so as not to be enslaved by his fellow men."

"What do the palm trees say to the world in their song?"

"That the art of living can be found in the pliability of palm trees which adapt themselves to the whiplashes of the wind and resist life's hard knocks."

"I dreamed of everything: money, good health, love."

"Like the palm trees, you should dream of the sun and the rain.

< 267 >

Love is the child of the moon. The moon that comes and goes, promises and lies, and enraptures with the sweetness of lovers. Then, it disappears."

"I kept falling. Falling. Today, I have nothing, Moyo. Life no longer has anything to offer me and has turned into a desert."

"The desert is within each one of us. In this land here, there is no desert, everything is green and smiling. A desert is the contrast between the wealth of Zambezia and the poverty of the people. Zambezia will be a desert after the colonial pillage and the degradation of the forests by global predators who will leech off all the trees, timber, and shellfish that belong to you in order to then bring you all the creeds about managing the environment and the doctrine about the perils of deforestation. It's your world that's a desert, you who have been blinded and are unable to see the way ahead. The world will be a desert when polygamous marriage is opposed in the name of progress in order to defend monogamous marriage between people of the same sex in the name of modernity. Zambezia will be a desert after the wars that are bound to come and the epidemics that will kill more than slavery. It's you who are the desert for having sold yourself to a system in order to burn your own grain store and spill the blood of your motherland. The desert is within you."

< 268 >

José dos Montes understands. Each palm tree is a black man, his arms raised to the sky in search of redemption and freedom. A palm tree is a monument, a sign, redemption, and that's why the palm trees of Zambezia cannot die.

◆　　◆　　◆

From his veranda, Laundryman Silveira witnesses the birth of the stars. In the silence of the house, his noisy grandchildren are fast asleep. He sees a boat drifting. This way and that, rudderless. No, it's not a boat, it's a man adrift. He is walking along the deserted beach, like a crab bowled along by the wildness of the waves. He tries to regain his balance in the sands of the dunes. He sits down, gazing at the sea in the darkness, and buries his head in his arms. There in the place chosen by those contemplating suicide before they plunge into the water for the last time. That man must be desperate. Laundryman is saddened. Life has brought down yet another. Memories that the wind had long blown away, come flooding back. He too had sat there, seeking his own end at the hour of his despair.

To bring the person on the brink of suicide back to life, all that's needed is a shout. He can unleash one from there. Laundryman

< 269 >

knows that perfectly well. Why save him? The life or death of one more human isn't going to make any difference to the statistics of the world. He thinks about diverting his eyes away from witnessing a macabre act. Maybe the man will kill himself. He returns to his room and tries to fall asleep.

The man on the beach is José dos Montes. He is thinking about Laundryman Silveira, the black man chosen to envision his own bitter feelings. Among so many folk, he had been chosen. For he had advice to give, a story to tell. He wants to know how many pills are needed to cure a pain. The color of the remedy one takes against betrayal. He wanted to hear the other man's words to mitigate his own soul's hunger.

A heavy body turns half a kilometer into an eternity. He leaves a slug's trail in the soil. He walks. He climbs the steps up to the house and knocks on the door. When there's no answer, he shouts.

"Open, it's me, José dos Montes."

"The sepoy?"

A visit from a sepoy at night? Trouble, prison, deportation. Payment of the hut tax. Laundryman Silveira gets ready to raise the

< 270 >

white flag. Life is a thread of hair. Brittle, Precarious. People live in permanent fear.

"We're peaceful folk, Sepoy José," Laundryman replies. "We pay our taxes regularly and go to mass on Sundays. We're assimilados."

"I'm not on duty. I'm alone and unarmed. I need help."

The lamps are lit in the house in order to receive the messenger of the regime. Laundryman is alarmed as he opens the door and comes face to face with a spectacle from the other world. A man sheathed in flames and wounded by life's dagger, in search of a refreshing shower of consoling words.

"José dos Montes? You're hurt, covered in dirt. What happened?"

"I've been expelled from the world. They killed me."

"Who?"

"The whites."

It's because we look alike that he remembered me, Laundryman thinks to himself. Transformed when the season changes, we shed one skin and put on another, on our difficult mission to survive. We swallow pains like sacramental bread to gain the right to look at the sun and yearn for the prophecies of the new world.

"Have you lost your job?"

"No."

"What happened then?"

"My Delfina."

"What has she done?"

"She's given me a mulatto daughter."

They look at each other face to face. Each identifying in the other the scars of the same trajectory. One man's past in the other man's present. Just as the world is round, just as history is repeated from one sunrise to the next.

The two of them sit down in the comfortable living room and José dos Montes allows the stink of his misfortune to linger in the air. He is ready to listen to the parade of wise words that will reach the shattered pieces of his soul. He looks around him in the hope of finding some inspiration for a new life. Laundryman is the epitome of a well-to-do black man. He even wears a pair of white taffeta pajamas. A Chinese silk dressing gown. On the table lies an ivory pipe.

"When was the child born?"

"Today."

"Was it a good delivery?"

"I don't know. Nor do I want to know."

"What do you want from me?" Laundryman asks.

"Your advice."

"Ah!"

Every adult is a natural doctor. Comparing histories, experiences of life. An episode here, an episode there, giving the soul consolation with the cure of words.

"She's a great lady, your Delfina. Mulattoes are a good race. They bring luck. You'll never go without a crust of bread in your home. That child represents your security."

"What?"

"Don't feel so hard done by, man. The construction of a new world has begun today in your life. Take a grip on yourself, get used to it."

"So what have you got to tell me?"

"Calm down, man! Look at the matter in a positive way. With a child like that in your household, you gain many advantages. You're exempt from the hut tax. Your black kids can go to school and you won't have to pay anything. You'll never be disturbed by police raids. You'll get presents at Christmas, Easter and New Year from the administrator. At church, the best place will always be kept for you. Above all, think of the good things."

Laundryman Silveira offers him a drink in a gold-rimmed crystal glass. He seizes the opportunity to show off the gold rings on his fingers, with their clean nails, and smooth hands. There is a glint of fascination in José dos Montes's eyes. That house is bathed in affluence, everything points to it. A surge of attraction drags him in the direction of new ambitions. They say humanity is made in the image of God, but this image here is that of a white man. In the clothes he wears. In the elegant language he uses. In the wine he drinks. In the jewelry he exhibits. He is a classy black man. Civilized par excellence, overcoming the stigma of his race. With the name of a slave, which destroys in one fell swoop all the attributions of his class: Laundryman de Francisco da Silveira.

This was a name he had gained in a police interrogation after a fracas on the quayside. He had been charged with insurrection, and when arrested he had said that his daily routine consisted of washing the clothes of his white lord and master, Mr. Francisco da Silveira. Many Zambezians got their names in similar fashion. Names reflecting a dislike of everything that humiliates, such as intimate items of clothing and other banalities. António Knickers, Júlio Pettycoat, Lucas Shirt, Raul Shameful, False Comb, José Handyman, Lisboa Lettuce, Bonito Monday. All the women were called Maria.

"God hasn't yet finished creating the world, my good José. Races should mingle together to bring a new color to the world. The whites overcame the oceans in their search for peppers and new races. They won new lands for themselves and new families during the course of their journeys. You and I have gained the supreme privilege of celebrating the future within our own homes."

"Do you think so?"

"Yes. We celebrate supper with other beings. Blacks and whites in the same bed, at the same table, in the same land. Mingling their smells, sweat, semen, and shadows in the act of inaugurating the future. The world of equality among the races is destined to come one day."

These are theories invented by him and he is convinced of their truth. Inventing superstitious dogmas about the creation of the world. Sculptors inventing stone images. Prostrated before them, they make offerings of flowers to them. And they call them saints, miracle makers, protectors.

"This is why you should forgive Delfina."

"No, I can't."

"Yes you can."

"I shall never forgive her!"

"That's your mistake! For life is a permanent process of reconciliation. Even white and black tastes in food are reconciled when the table is laid. It's cod and chicoa. Sardines and pende. Cashew and apple. Manioc and potato. Black sex and white sex."

"That's all but impossible."

"It will take many years to construct this new, expanding race. And there will be destruction as well. Metamorphosis is always painful."

Am I one of the chosen to participate in this construction of the world? This is the consoling speech of a cuckold, for whom the word honor means humiliation, while comparing himself in some crazy way to the gods of creation.

"Within the walls of this house, I have created many races."

"Was it easy?"

Laundryman Silveira raises his eyes to the sky. And he navigates through the rich constellation of his memories. Recalling the forlorn nights when, surrendering his own dignity, he would close his ears to the caustic murmurings of the world.

"I bore the shame of having been born a man. I carried my weakness on top of my head, a never-ending cuckold. Like the palm trees, I bent in the face of the battering wind. I allowed my dreams to commit suicide, while I myself survived. And here I am before you. Triumphant. A survivor."

Laundryman Francisco da Silveira had a beautiful wife who

< 276 >

provoked the lust of his boss. He made his calculations about life with rustic cunning and came to this conclusion: if I resist, the white will have me deported just so as to have her to himself. If I give her up to him, I'll be a cuckold, but I'll avoid trouble. He put his wife in the white man's bed. She got pregnant and brought home twin mulatto girls. How could he refuse them if they represented his ticket to freedom, his shield and his survival? At first, he was in despair. Then he got used to it: hiring out his wife to any man in exchange for clothes, flour, and soap. That's why Laundryman has children of many races: two kids fathered by a white, two black children, and one with an Indian father. Then, he explains himself.

"The name I use is that of my white boss, Francisco da Silveira. My eldest children were fathered by him. This house was a gift from him. My black children had their schooling paid for by him. I have an easy life thanks to him. Under this roof, all races mingle and mix. Of my twin daughters, one married a black man and the other a mulatto. My black daughter married a white man. My black son married a mulatto girl. My Indian son will marry one day, only God knows which race he'll marry."

"You talk of this Francisco da Silveira as if he were a savior. Can one love one's enemy?"

"Francisco da Silveira was a good man. He saw the color of my despair in my face. He realized I was a human being and was suffering."

"But to give your own wife up to him? Hire her out? Were you capable of all that?"

"Yes, I was. It was a condition of my existence. Women share the heart of the same man. They suffer, but they share him. I did the same. That's all it was."

What words of love does one use to convince a wife to accept such a pact? Was it not a long awaited opportunity to express openly her libertine's instinct? Can love really lead to such degrading acts?

"I can't deliver up my wife, Laundryman," José dos Montes says with a shudder.

"My gifts earned me a house, a vegetable garden and a palm grove. My children married well and I don't go hungry. But in spite of this, if I hadn't handed her over, she would have acted on her own account, and I wouldn't have had any benefit from it."

These are unusual declarations, almost worthy of psychiatric analysis, and José ponders over them with the greatest attention. They are made with intense, deep words. And they are proof that Laundryman is lying. They show that in order to survive, one needs to fabricate the truth on the tenuous edges of untruth. As he handed his wife over to his boss, he became the victim of his own gesture. José dos Montes understands: if we don't turn a lie into our truth, what will become of us? He forgets the problems of the moment and his thoughts range wildly in the face of the incredible. He throws inquisitorial glances, and starts asking forensic questions.

"Was it easy to bring up a family with various races?"

"At first, the house was a battlefront. A symphony of children all seeking the same explanation: Why are blacks so black? Why are whites so white? Why are we like this, half light-skinned, half dark?"

"What answer did you give them, Laundryman?"

"Easy. I told the blacks: you are dark because you came from me. To the mulattoes, I would say: you are light because you came from the sea and the moon, a grafted seed, renewed life."

In Laundryman's voice, there was the song of all the vanquished. His body was adorned with all the finery of submission, but deep within the man, there is a bitter voice.

"What does it mean to have a family made up of many races?" José dos Montes asks.

"It was a college, an army barracks, a classroom."

Laundryman's mind travels down the spine of memory. The good

< 279 >

and bad moments. He had never felt himself to be a father, but a broker in disagreements and a guiding light in journeys, a true director of a college. He recalls the different phases in this journey. His black children felt their space had been invaded and complained: go back to your Portuguese father's house! The white man's children answered back: there are a lot of blacks in this house. The Indian man's son didn't say much but created mayhem.

In a second phase of life, stratification occurred. With dispersal, rivalry and jealousy. The mulattoes were at the top of the pyramid, but dreaming of being white. They were masters of the food and the home that the blacks sponged on empty handed. The blacks harbored the secret dream of being mulattoes. The family had the solidity of a cobweb. There was a lot of envy, treachery, lying, intrigue at that age.

"They must have kept you very busy."

"Oh yes! Very busy!"

He remains silent for a few moments. Recalling the most troublesome part of the journey. The sleepless nights when his children were going through adolescence, discovering their identity, the capers and confusions, his inability to rein them in when their different natures came to the surface. He decides to break all his inhibitions. With renewed vigor, he continues his story.

"On one occasion, his mulatto children overheard the adults talking behind a closed door. From the complicated dialogue, they understood the word strike. As they were familiar with the malign power of uprisings, they ran to their father's house to warn him a plot was being hatched. As children don't lie, believe it or not, the police clambered out of an assault vehicle not long afterwards, and burst menacingly into the house. I was forced to invent some story full of the names of false suspects, just to save my skin. Then came the bloodshed and settling of scores: seven blacks were strung up. They were my best friends. You can't imagine how this still weighs on my conscience, José dos Montes. On another occasion, the son of the Indian, sick of his siblings' high jinks, invented his own story involving witchcraft, which damaged business. The Indian traders were in uproar, and started throwing their weight around and threatening, eventually breaking into my house and smashing everything up.

"So what about your black children?"

"They were the bearers of tittle-tattle. Between Indians and whites. Between blacks and whites. So as to get tips, chocolates, bijouterie. I found it hard to control things at that time, José dos Montes."

After he has finished talking, there is silence. José feels empathy. He sees something of the hero in him. In this man's family, there

< 281 >

are no stories around the fire. In his own home, he puts up with permanent warfare for possession of territory. A home, the lessons of submission, tyranny, and supremacy are acquired on the mother's lap and in accordance with one's race. A home governed by outsiders, where their own children are turned into the regime's agents, listening to conversations behind closed doors. A home characterized by rejection and dependence among siblings of different origins, who often refuse to recognize the blood kinship that unites them.

He now understands that Laundryman is a wounded man, which explains his self-effacing life and isolation. He is a solitary soul. A man of few words and few friends.

"How did your children treat you?"

"They realized it was good to have a father, whatever his race. They realized their biological fathers were merely visitors and their social father was the true inhabitant of their lives. Today, they respect and love me."

"Which ones were your favorite children? The blacks or the mulattoes?"

"At first, we were proud of the children with the white father. They represented our survival, our ascent, the food on our table. We put up with the Indian, because he represented credit at the

< 282 >

shop and we thought the chili pepper there of good quality. The blacks? We ignored them for some time. But in the end, we loved them all equally."

"And what about society? How did the world treat you, Laundryman?"

"Society? I never paid any attention to the world."

That family was theater, its actors performing a mute play. At the center of the stage, the figure of vanquished man, personifying domination, shielded by the skirts of beautiful women, wearing a crown of horns, just as kings proudly wear their crown of glory. But he was a hero. He held firm at the helm of his shame, braving all the storms, and guiding his ship to a safe harbor. His children give him great joy, because the human family is, after all, made up of different races.

"How do you see yourself, Laundryman?"

"Do you want to know the truth? I'm the unmistakable image of impotence, you know that. The woman who was mine belongs to everyone. When I walk down the streets, society laughs at me behind my back. But I don't care. I merely follow the path God set for me."

"What about your black children? Are you sure they're yours?"

"How can I be sure? When it comes to procreation, only the

< 283 >

mother counts. Paternity is an accident. The children are hers and she knows where she got them."

José dos Montes gives up in the face of this enigma. He is stunned by it all. The quiet containment of pain. Between the fire and the frying pan, the distortion of thought. A lust for life that draws one towards the abyss and the path of death. He closes his eyes, overcome with the giddiness of it all. From between the cracks in his memory, voices of old begin to flower. And he travels through the green ocean of the palm groves. Along the countless paths trodden in the direction of disaster. He allows his mind to fly in the company of the clouds until it comes to earth on the sacred soil of the highlands of Mount Namuli. From the summit of the mountain, he lets fly his disapproval.

"You raised the son of an Indian just to get some chili powder?"

"Have some respect for chili powder, José. Have some respect for pepper and all that oriental stuff. It was because of this that we ended up in this slavery. The Portuguese were on their way to India to fetch those spices when they decided to come ashore, to repair their ship or for some other reason only they knew. As for me, with neither a voyage nor a broken ship, I ended up hosting the whole of India in my home thanks to my wife."

The craven words of the inhabitant of a strange, purposeless world,

< 284 >

who in fleeing one death, embraces another. Willing to compose a ditty that serves to console his yearning for a future that never comes and a sun that has vanished. Assessing his life with contradictory measurements.

"No, my friend. The whites sing their songs on the graves of our souls. They hoot like owls while perched on the crosses over our tombs. And we gradually die, a little every day. I would rather die suddenly."

"Don't talk nonsense, José dos Montes. I know it's hard to make progress when the body lives in this world and the soul roams around in the other one. That's what resistance is all about. Human existence is really onerous. Deep within us, there's something that causes us to resist. Another life, perhaps. Another body. Another soul."

José looks at Laundryman with astonishment. In trying to flee one source of pain, he embraced another. In that old soul, the will to exist has the strength of a diamond. With pieces of difference, he constructed a blanket of unity. He once again regards him with disdain. And what he sees in him is a worm, who has never faced up to danger, has never killed a snake or even a fly, a useless experience for a man of courage. And he reaches a sad conclusion: a man's dignity is measured by his woman's contours.

< 285 >

"I admire you, but I cannot accept that I should be like you. I gain my living by the strength of my arms. Killing people, killing lions, seeking my wealth through the power of my physique. For me, you are useless, a worm who accumulated your wealth by peddling your wife's sex."

José has heard enough for one night. The image of Moyo comes to his mind, the man who just loved his people and was happy. He gets up from his chair and takes his leave with a few brief words.

"Thank you for these few moments, my friend. I don't want anything else, no children and no family. Nor do I need philosophies of race that are born and then die. All I want is to love my little patch and forget."

"My good José, no matter how complex your dilemma, there's always a way out."

There was fellow feeling as they shook hands. Between them, there was a look of complicity. At the end of the day, they both had the same dream: freedom. A flash of envy sparkles in Laundryman's eyes. He envies those wings of freedom as they retreat and close, thus avoiding a flight back beyond torment.

◆　◆　◆

Back on the seashore, José dos Montes laments his fate with words of high drama. I could have been a king, I have power. I could kill Delfina and her mulatto daughter. I could castrate the white who stole my bed. What's the point of going on living, if my soul has abandoned my body and we continue our journey as if on two parallel tracks? He pauses to recall the other José, married to the imaginary lady with her scent of algae, up there on the mountain peak. An enchanting lady, beautiful, gentle, loyal to the end. He thinks of a carefree José, a barefoot José, serenely taking his goats to pasture.

Life, take me back to the mountains of Namuli, where pain does not exist and oblivion reigns supreme. Take me to the source of the Licungo and Malema rivers, where the waters of forgiveness bubble. Ah, how I miss my mother! He feels a sudden urge for the depths of the ocean. He senses the waves summoning him for a new embrace. He strips off his ridiculous sepoy's clothes. He frees himself from his boots and his dagger. He strips everything off, but he cannot strip himself of the acts engraved in his mind. He faces absence and time. He walks into the sea to be picked up by some wave and begin a new life beyond this world.

< 287 >

17

When morning comes, Simba leaves his hut and lazily wanders around his backyard. Maybe he wants to feel the fresh air in his face. Maybe he wants to greet the sun in the ritual of wishing the day well. As a precaution, he checks to see whether his home has been visited by the thieves of the night. He notices a sculptured figure near the entrance. In his favorite patch of shade. Is it real or his imagination? He rubs his rheumy eyes to clear his vision. Can it be a mirage? A man or a woman? Who can it be? He rubs his eyes again, but they just confirm the same again. It's Delfina, yes. It's really her. At this time? Or has she slept there? What does she want of me at this hour?

He stops and appreciates her from afar. A wandering gaze of someone contemplating the mysteries of the world. Ears enraptured by the sweet music of the morning as it awakens. A meditating air, that of someone who has a question and wants an answer so as to break free of life's worst nightmare. He calls her.

"Delfina!"

She smiles. His voice sounds like cool water dousing the fires of her anxiety. A gruff but friendly voice. Simba is surprised. Before it was he who ran along highways and byways looking for her. Today, here she has come stealthily, first thing in the morning, to beg a ray of sunshine from his wizard's wand.

"Good morning, Simba."

"Couldn't you at least have waited until I was fully awake?"

"I thought about you all night."

He stands there gazing at her intently without moving, trying to establish why she was there. He turns his back and continues his morning ritual: a cold dip in the stream, two hundred meters from his house. Washing out his mouth. Combing his hair. Returning to the house to dress appropriately. For his daily outfit, he chooses red capulanas, men's capulanas. Smooth ones. With luminous stripes down the edges, like regal gowns. He feels light-spirited, enlivened. Possibly inspired by her presence.

"So tell me why you've missed me so much."

"I want to lead a new life."

"A new life? I'm not God, my dear."

She seems open to influence. But from the word go, he can see she harbors an enigma within her. Simba tries to evade her. To understand a woman is like plunging into a labyrinth with no beginning and no end. It's like going underground with your eyes shut. Diving into the depths of the sea and kneeling by the deep roots of water lilies. But he senses something tying him to that web making escape impossible. He is gripped by mystery. Or fate. Or her.

"No one is born more than once," Simba explains.

"Don't talk nonsense. You're a magician and you know what I want."

"Have you had news of José dos Montes?"

"I haven't come to talk to you about him."

"He's still your husband."

"He's a lost cause. He's probably mortified by what happened, but... what can I do?"

"So what about the love you felt for him?"

"Love? I enjoyed it and it ran out, I don't have any more to give."

"What happened?"

"It's simple. One man alone doesn't produce a fortune. One garden alone won't fill your bread basket. I went and looked for a friend to help pay the bills, José dos Montes's wages aren't enough, life's expensive."

< 290 >

These are passionate words. With much fire in their belly. With many poisoned arrows sent flying in different directions. Perhaps she is unaware of the consequences of her tongue-lashing. Simba's sleepy brain is shaken by the violence, as if some deadly rope has been coiled around his neck. He stares at the speaker and recognizes her at last. This is the Delfina of old. She is like the moon. All glitter on the outside, but on the inside all trash.

"What do you want from me now, Delfina?"

"A remedy to make José forget me. So that he'll never come back. A remedy to make another man love me. I need to renew myself, to become rejuvenated."

"What's the reason for this change?" Simba asks, by now more curious.

"Times change, can't you see? The world changes. We all change. Why can't my feelings change?"

In her words, Simba sees reflected his own fate and laments the other man's destiny. There is nothing more he can do. It was José's heart that had experienced the greatest mishap. He was a romantic. That's why he is now treading the bitter paths of disenchantment. He discovered there was a wild beast in the eyes of his beloved. That the hiss of the serpent was hidden behind the mermaid's song. He

< 291 >

died of fright when he discovered that everything is vapor, clouds, water, so ephemeral and fluid that you can never hold on to it in the palm of your hand.

"I've discovered a mine," says Delfina.

"What mine?"

"A gold mine."

"Where is this mine?"

"Soares. The white man."

"I don't see any link between Soares and this mine."

"You really don't understand?"

"That white man Soares doesn't deserve this."

"There's no malice at all," Delfina assures him. "All I want is to show the world that a black woman can have a white husband. I want to show the world that love overcomes the frontiers of a race."

Her voice is as languid as someone in the throes of a dream. A melodious voice, leaving in its wake traces of fascination and certainties born from nothing. Revealing that within her there resides a slumbering visionary. There is something beautiful in a woman who dreams. Even though she may fail, at least she fights. Simba watches her open expression with fondness and then he is surprised: where did such power, such strength come from?

< 292 >

"His wife is a saint, she doesn't deserve such punishment, Delfina."

"Saints don't sleep silently all through the night. They also wake up to groan with love or pain on a cold night, just like you, just like me."

"Think carefully, Delfina."

"I want the old man for myself."

"You're so cheap, Delfina, you suck. José, your husband, wasn't much good, oh no, he certainly wasn't! The hideous methods he used to get ahead disgusted me. But you're worse than him, Delfina, you suck!"

Those ideas of hers, that brazenness, they are what surprise him. Delfina is different from other women injured by life, who seek medicine men to deal with domestic disagreements. Even prostitutes search for success that is compatible with the aspirations of common mortals. She turns up at a wizard's consulting room, lays out her case, decides what she wants, and gives the orders. She has eliminated the word problem from her lexicon. All she talks about are solutions. She outlines projects. She acts on them. No matter whether they are simple or complex. She is too direct. Why should he have to get involved in useless speeches, when she is so objective, so set on her course? Call death by its true name. Hatred likewise. Don't stain your tongue with hypocritical words.

< 293 >

"What are you accusing me of, Simba?"

"You killed a man."

"I didn't kill him, I freed him."

"You killed him, that's what you did."

"It's my dream to have a white husband. If José were to be lucky enough to be able to marry a white woman, he wouldn't hesitate to abandon me, for I know how ambitious he is. Just like me, all he thinks about is getting on in life without worrying about scruples. I was the one with the luck, so why are you condemning me? Because I'm a woman?"

"There's no gender in an error, Delfina."

In the face of her declaration, Simba weighs up his abilities and competences. He succumbs, despite the predicted painful impact. He is faced with the orders of a woman who is asking him to perform an extremely sensitive task. To light a fire in known and unknown homes. Mutilate the sentiments of a living man. Destroy the home of a noble man. Play with other people's lives in exchange for money tossed on the ground like grains in a hen coop. He is being asked to destroy. A word that is apocalyptic in its terror, and will push his life over the edge.

"Delfina, you are so cruel because you're always after the impossible."

"But of course. If my wishes were humdrum, I wouldn't ask you for any help. I would resolve matters myself. But be in no doubt, I'm a lucky person. Fix me up with some magic and we'll make a profit, I promise."

"I would find it easier to accept if you asked me to make Soares your grandfather. Don't you think he's a bit too old to be your husband?"

"Yes. But it's not his age that matters. What's important is that I should be that white man's wife."

It's a fascinating challenge, but casting a spell on a white man is an attack against the regime, against public order, making the perpetrator liable to arrest, deportation and death. That woman is an adventure, a permanent state of emotion, causing the blood to surge from one surprise to the next. An emerging artist in survival. Delfina, the ideal woman for that regime. Who kills and gets away with it, a heroine of survival. In war, feelings don't count. All that matters is victory.

"What do you want to do, then?"

"I want to steal him away from his bed. To be mine and mine

alone. His marriage has already lost all it magic and he's gotten old. I want to make him young again."

"With my spells?"

"That's what I'm here for."

"Black witchcraft doesn't work on whites," Simba declares conclusively. "Don't give me that nonsense, Delfina."

"Have you ever tried?"

"Never."

"Well, here's your great chance!"

To cast a spell on a white is the greatest of heresies, as far as Simba is concerned. He is assailed by fear and alarm. He trembles. It's at this point that he realizes there are gaps, lapses in his professional experience. In the field of witchcraft, he has tried a bit of everything — flying on a broomstick, penetrating the realms of light and darkness like someone going in and out of his house. But cast a spell on a white? It never crossed his mind. When it came to Indians, he knew a thing or two. They often visited him to improve their businesses and increase the flow of customers in their shop.

"That man doesn't deserve your cruelty," Simba declares somewhat condescendingly, "he's the best white I've ever met."

"You and I are good too. All we Zambezians are good. That's why the sailors exploit us. Do you know why lambs get all the praise? They're dead easy to catch. They go to the barbecue without so much as a groan. And because they're just as weak, chickens have become food for the human race. And you pity that white?"

Simba is alarmed but enraptured by this woman who thinks. Who challenges and bends all the rules of the game. Women like Delfina are rare. Fascinating. Prostitutes attract him because of their practical outlook on life. With them, everything is calculated in detail, everything is negotiated, all is prepaid or paid on delivery. They turn a man into their adversary, their weight and measure. They defy. They excite. Whether they win or lose. For Simba, wives are boring, without any fascinating qualities, true machines in their obedience, swinging to the left and to the right at the whim of their master. That's why, whenever he feels a desire to display his manhood, he rushes off to see prostitutes. Life only has any allure when someone is a source of excitement.

"Don't count on me in your act of madness."

"Whites have firearms, Simba, but they can't escape the magic traps set by our spells. You can cast a really good spell on those guys.

< 297 >

Come on. Bathe me in the blood of the dead using your conches. Find the truth of my fate in your seashells. Give me a broomstick to fly through the night, and bring Soares back to my bed."

"I'm not taking you anywhere."

"I'll pay you, I promise, this business is going to be really profitable. I'm looking for something, do you hear? I want a life with money jangling in my pocket."

"How are you going to pay me, Delfina, without a husband or a penny to your name?"

"This business is going to pay well. Do you remember my time on the dockside? You found me clients and protected me. Then we divided the cash. I always paid you well, or have you forgotten?"

Simba remembers the past. In relation to the present. He looks at her. It isn't a dream but the truth. There she is, the Delfina of former times, a woman of unusual behavior. She has turned up to remind him the struggle shouldn't be constrained by limits. Audacity shouldn't have boundaries. In war, it is better to kill than to die.

"You're the Delfina I know. Crazy. Daring. Ready for any blow. Women all seem the same, but they aren't. You're out of the ordinary."

"Ah, my pimp, my fancy man from my quayside days."

< 298 >

Simba studies Delfina's profile with the eyes of a poet. In her body, he sees the movement of untamed waves. Blood courses swiftly like the waters of the Zambezi over the cascades of Cahora Bassa. To enrapture, she has the glint of stars in her eyes. To lull, she has her melodic voice. To seal the deal, she has the warmth of her body. That's Delfina. An air of magnetism that makes a man wander in dreams of transcendence. Moving hearts with fire, breezes, storms. Her presence inspires music, dance, rain. No man remains indifferent to the call of a star.

"Have you any idea of the gravity of your intentions? What will become of me if the authorities discover this plot? I shall be killed right away or deported. Acts of wizardry are prohibited by this regime. As far as these whites are concerned, magic is the work of the Devil."

"You won't be the first or the last to be deported. There have been so many before you. Killed as heroes or deported without killing or injuring anyone. In this world, those who do good end up in hell."

"I don't want any trouble with the regime. Leave me alone."

"Simba, are you really a man?"

"Do you doubt me?"

"Totally. There are no men in Zambezia. That's why the invaders came and established themselves here. And they sleep with your women. José lost me because he wasn't man enough."

Delfina waves the red rag in front of the old bull, and the man reacts immediately like an injured animal.

"Is that a challenge?" Simba falls into the trap and lets all his resentment show. "I'm good, Delfina, I'm still young, but don't despise me. I'm the best there is in this place. Do you want to know what I can do? You'll learn one hell of a lesson from me. But... what will you give me in exchange, my dear Delfina?"

"Stop talking and show me. Show me you're a man, if you really are one!"

"I've got no shortage of women," Simba comments disdainfully. "Beautiful virgins appear every day. You are old and worn out. You've been pummeled so much, you only please crazy old men who've lost all their teeth."

Simba looks at her with rare fascination. There is magic in beauty and barbarity. Delfina is the kind of woman he would have married if the spirits had approved. But women with vices don't enter the domains of the ancestors. They want damsels with a pure heart.

Pretty. Obedient. Hard working. He was much younger than her. No, she was excluded from such a possibility.

Simba closes his eyes and navigates the platonic spaces of dreams. He treads lunar surfaces without end, in the sweet dream of an earthbound future. A well-defined time span. All he needs to do is to cast a good spell. And she will be garlanded with anthuriums, diadems of gold. The anthuriums of a black queen. Then he dreams once more of a better house. And he sees that it is a dream full of promise. And that is why he decides to ally himself to her fantasy.

He weighs up the business proposition and decides to accept it. In return for money. He invests his man's dreams in her. And he goes for the high stakes, where victory will confer on him the highest rewards. He ponders on his life as a wizard. Every day the same things. Small and more complicated spells, invariably paid with chickens, manioc, but rarely a goat, because his clients are always poor.

"Make your magic work for me. Bring the man to my bed, Simba. I'm an ideal black woman for a white man. I want to demonstrate that a black woman can be someone, and can overcome racial barriers. If you help me in this project, you'll be well paid. With real money. Even properties. I'll give you half of what I get."

"I want a house with a tin roof, Delfina."

"You'll have everything, I swear." Delfina talks with total conviction. "Oh yes you will! The old man only has eyes for me. He can't stop thinking about me, you'll have the house you want, I promise."

It's an attractive proposition. Even if he doesn't succeed, he senses that he will emerge more of a man, and with greater insight, from the experience. The prospect of earning some money by participating in the stunt gives him the impetus to overcome his fear. He ponders her offer. A house with a tin roof would be a tremendous improvement in a place where it rains so much. A cement floor rather than one of beaten earth would be very handy in that marshy soil.

"So what if it doesn't come off?"

"It will come off. The old boy only has eyes for me."

Simba experiences the humiliation of renewing his dreams as a man through the dreams of a woman. He dreams of a wood-tiled floor on which he could use a bit of red wax polish. Should he become an assimilado for the purpose? No, he can't, because of his profession as a medicine man. Once he became assimilated, he would have to renounce his spiritism. The spirits would then avenge themselves and he would die. He has to live in that depressing world. Feed himself with roots and raw seaweed. Undergo long periods of sexual abstinence. Carry out magic rites when required.

"I trust you, Simba."

"Witchcraft brings success in the form of credit," he warns sternly. "Over time, it decays, Delfina, and everything is worse than before."

Simba gazes at her with renewed passion, but says yes. A man in love can never say no, even if it costs him his life. I shall earn a fortune with this crazy woman. She will be my hostage, the shield that will bring me victory. I shall reap profits through this mad woman. By the time she discovers the plot, I will have my nest egg. And a lot more besides. He is aware that something unites them, something he cannot decipher or visualize. Something that is stretching towards him like a life raft.

"Ah! I knew you'd accept, for you're a great man."

"I promise we'll win this war, Delfina. But if you don't deliver on our agreement, you'll know the power of my vengeance. I'm a wizard, remember."

He announces the rules of the game from the outset and experiences the ecstasy of their pact. He discovers that he desires Delfina far more than the money she owes him. He realizes that being a sorcerer is to go forward without leaving footprints or a shadow. It is about managing other peoples' lives from a subterranean lair. There's no doubt it's an exciting adventure. And he gives far more than he's asked for. His embrace, his sixth sense. Magic for any service. And all his manly heart.

◆　◆　◆

And so war is declared between two women. One black and one white. Women who turned the arena of love into a field of battle.

Delfina entered the war disposed to kill or die. She included various items in her arsenal: lies, blackmail, magic, old tricks made new. She attracted the white man and shut him up inside a bottle. She pledges to stifle him with love and witchcraft. She also pledges to make as many children as nature allows. She's not going to let go of her goose that laid the golden eggs for one single instant.

Soares's wife fights using the weapons of honesty. She goes on strike over sex: she tries to stop her husband from being enveloped in the dusky arms of a black woman. She cloisters herself away. She fasts, prays and lights many candles to the static, porcelain saints. She cries and rants and raves.

< 304 >

Both women know that a promise of love doesn't last, and there's no remedy or cure for love's pains. In the challenges of love, truth never wins, nor does logic count for anything. The intrepid courage of the strumpet is the winner, for she fights without rules or morals, free of all preconceived ideas.

Soares, a tubby old man, just ate and slept. He felt fulfilled in this world, everything he had done over the course of his seventy years had rendered good results: his fortune, his solid business enterprises, wonderful children, buildings and the palm grove. But everything changed that day he rediscovered the world in the luster of the moon. And he saw that life is beautiful, and life is short. He remembered that he had not experienced all of life's emotions, so busy had he been building his future and ensuring there was bread on the table.

Assailed by a sudden clarity of vision, he started to develop senile prophecies. He saw that an old man renews himself over and over again while a woman is in a permanent state of aging. He returned to adolescence. He had erotic dreams. He went off in a sulk and did daft things. During his quests, he found Delfina, who aroused a part of his body that lay sleeping and she gave him a daughter as if thus affirming to the world his renewed virility.

His old friends, astonished and green with envy, patted him

amicably on the back, hoisting him even higher into his lofty dreams: the old dog is back, he's alive and i   n top form! He managed to put that fiery mermaid in the family way! What a macho man!

And so he became infatuated with Delfina. He yearned for her at all hours. An enamored old man, he swore to use up all the cartridges of his virility before the end of the season and enjoy the last paranoid fantasies of this world with his darling Delfina.

Soares makes his escape gently, dismissing his wife with the utmost tenderness: you stay there and take care of everything, woman. Go on, go and do some crochet! If you get tired of that, do a bit of embroidery, you're so good at it. Don't forget to see to the alms for the church, look, have a word with the priest, you can both start preparing Christmas for the poor. Don't wait for me for dinner because I won't be home till late. Don't forget to make sure all the doors are locked when it gets dark, I'm going to talk to my friends all night, and won't be back.

His wife is faced with the dilemma of a cycle that is coming to an end. Her children leaving home. Her strength waning. Dreams dying. Her husband running off. She sits on the veranda and does her needlework. Stitching together her best words to gently justify the man's mad antics. Embroidering her words of consolation: it

< 306 >

was I who enjoyed this man's best years. It was for me he devoted all his energy. It was to me and me alone that he gave his best: four wonderful children. Dignity and honor belong to me, and I'm not going to kick up a fuss over the childish behavior of an old man in decline. These women he gets involved with are getting the leftovers of what I ate, just like pigs.

She struggles and fights, but is also in despair. In her quest for comfort, she unleashes heartfelt laments to trusted friends.

"He's abandoning me," she raves, "he's leaving me on my own, in a cold bed, and to eat my meals by myself. Sometimes, I feel like going after him and dragging him home. I feel like insulting the woman who has led him astray, using the ugliest words in this world. One day, I'll pull off her wig and fight the whole night with her. I feel like throwing her in the mud and fighting openly for my man, my home, and my honor."

"Dignity and honor are yours, you are his legitimate spouse!"

"Sometimes I wake up in anguish: where is my husband? And what if he's dead? Even knowing he's enjoying moments of happiness, I torture myself imagining the details: where are his hands resting? On the black woman's ass? Where's his mouth? Inside hers? And the rest of his body? Then I feel sick and almost throw up."

"All men are billy goats. No matter how distant the pasture, they always go, but never fail to return."

"At first, he would home back completely drunk and sleep in the sitting room. Then, in the kitchen. After that, on the veranda or in the porch because he couldn't open the door. It was as if his key had grown too large and the keyhole too tiny. Lately, it looks as if he can't find his key or the door. He stays out more than he comes home."

"A man never grows up. The older he gets, the more childish he becomes."

"I've lost all my charms, and grown old. All I have left are tears. I cry over everything I feel, everything I once had and lost. Abandonment hurts, repudiation hurts, oh, my God, being a woman hurts!"

"Eagles soar into the air, cross borders and continents, but they always find the way back."

"I'll go to the very depths, if needed, to salvage what is my home."

"No, you shouldn't do that. Stay up there on your pedestal. It doesn't look good for a woman of your class to descend to such a level."

"I know what I'm going to do. I'm leaving for a new world. I'm going to shield my children from all this immorality. I'm going to

< 308 >

find freedom in Lisbon, no more superstitions, no more myths, or magic spells."

"Leave your man in this jungle? No, surely not!"

Soares's wife surrenders in the face of Delfina's power. For she secures a man with claws and uses him up until he is forever doomed. In spite of her jealousy, she admires her. Soares seems happy. Brimming with youth. He no longer complains about his joints or his chronic rheumatism. He laughs out loud and in all directions. He's forgotten the peevishness that has accompanied him throughout his life.

Waves of empathy break over her as she recalls José dos Montes. A beautiful black man. Like me, we've both fallen into the same trap. Both of us suffering, victims of the same magic. She lets out the sigh of all betrayed women and acknowledges this: when it comes to pain, blacks and whites weep in the same way.

◆　◆　◆

Delfina penetrated into Soares's home with subtlety. She filled the white man's house with squabbling until she made him feel happiest when he was away from it. By her side. She made use of the favors of one of the domestic servants who joined the plot, and together they organized a real carnival of magic in the Soares household. They introduced a mystical atmosphere, placing totemic objects in various corners of the house: scorpions, toads, little snakes, black spiders. They would throw open and slam doors, simulating the mysterious presence of wandering spirits on moonlit nights. They terrorized the whole family, causing sleeplessness, bewilderment, sobbing, frights, neurotic illnesses, in a display of wizardry that was high-quality, brilliant, avant-garde, refined, successful, and ended up driving one of Soares's children insane.

"It wasn't the young boy's madness I wanted," Delfina exclaimed to Simba, "but my rival's head on a tray. Well, it paid off anyway. She took her children away and abandoned this land along with all its mysteries. Now Soares belongs to me!"

The black man's witchcraft had had its effect on the white.

Simba won his promised house. A large shed with a tin roof and a cement floor. Beautiful and spacious. But... it needed furniture and all the things to go inside it.

< 310 >

18

History repeats itself. The legends of old reproduce themselves and become real. Legends of the times when God was a woman and governed the world. Once upon a time...

A long long time ago, the goddess governed the world. She was so beautiful that men throughout the land sighed over her. They all dreamed of giving her a child. The goddess was so motherly and affectionate, that she swore she would satisfy the desires of all the men in the world. She sent a message through the voice of the wind, that there would be a dance one night by the light of the moon. She would come down to earth in her golden carriage so that human hands could at last admire the smoothness of her skin. The time came. She bathed, perfumed herself, and used the finest ointments. She ascended to the summit of the mountains of Namuli, took off her gown and danced. Naked. So that all the women could envy her charms. She summoned the menfolk one at a time and gave them the pleasure of her divine dance. She became pregnant by just one, because she obviously didn't have the power to give birth to the entire

< 3 1 1 >

universe. The discovery of her limitations proved fatal. Everyone was left knowing that the goddess after all was a mundane woman and her divinity resided in her diamond-studded gown. They discovered too that she was fragile and humble as a child. The men surrounded her. They stole her gown and pushed her over. They took up her place, condemning all women to hardship and servitude.

That is the origin of the conflict between man and woman. That is why all the women in the world go out into the street and produce a general racket so as to regain their lost gown.

< 312 >

19

They say it all began as if in a fairy tale. They say that on one particular night the mysteries of the world were being incubated and the
planet was spinning round at a new speed. In the dense darkness,
a partridge shaped like a woman was singing gurué, gurué! The
whole world was aghast because only owls sing at night. A partridge
singing on a moonless night was a bad omen. Many abandoned their
slumber, and with torches tried to light up the sky   to witness this
unexpected event. They glimpsed a vague shape near the clouds.
Could it really be a partridge?

It was a woman with the voice of a partridge, whooping triumphantly down at the world, dancing naked on the highest peak of the
mountain. The smell of eroticism, sex, the smell of kaffir bawdiness
wafting through the air. The eyes of the world asked the following
questions as of one:

"Who are you who scale the sides of the mountain with the speed
of light and whoop in triumph from the mountains of glory?"

"I am Delfina, the queen!"

"Who crowned you queen of the night?"

"I live on the highest peaks, I am queen, I am the white man's wife."

They say the whole world lit up with astonishment. Some blacks viewed it as the social rise of a young black woman. Some whites viewed it as the madness of an old colonist. Some blacks and whites agreed with each other and viewed it as the perverse behavior of their respective races. Delfina closed her ears to the gossip of the world and soared higher. She discovered that the paradise of Bacchus has the color of wine, the taste of olives and of baked salt cod à la Gomes de Sá.

They say that, on that night, Delfina's father, trying to save his daughter from the dizzy heights, bellowed hoarsely up at the sky. Delfina replied with an unhinged arrogance, imitating the song of the partridge.

"Delfina, my flower, is your life good up there?" Her worried father shouted.

"I'm the first black woman to live in the upper town, next to the whites. I'm awash with good fortune, I'm rich now, gurué, gurué!"

"My little butterfly, the top of the mountain is as sharp as a needle. The point of the pyramid can only hold one grain of sand. Up there,

< 314 >

your body has no way of sustaining itself. Delfina, come down! You can't live far from the soil. Up there in the sky, you can't grow cabbages."

"Ah, my dear father! My ignorant black, my poor old man, shut that mouth of yours, eat this grain of corn I'm giving you out of charity."

Dazzled by happiness, Delfina dances like an acrobat up there, oblivious to the magic powers of gravity. They say that at that very moment, the whole world was contorted with fear and suspense.

"I'm secure, anchored in the comfort of the ground, my dear Delfina. You should know that nature reaps its revenge on those who go against it. Even the waters of the River Licungo, whose source is high on the mountainside, abandon the heights and seek safety in the riverbed below."

"You curmudgeonly old black! You never wanted my happiness. You never agreed to become an assimilado so that I could get a diploma as a native teacher. Does your conscience feel sore now? I have become rich through my sweat and my sexuality!"

They say her old father wept. He foresaw the future curse hanging over later generations. Then he laughed. For, after all, his daughter was in the great hall on top of the great mountain, and on the edge of the great precipice. She was at the pinnacle of her ascent and her fall. Perched over the desert and the swamp.

"You will cross the desert, my dear Delfina, my partridge with a peacock's plumage!"

"Thank you, my dear old father, gurué, gurué!"

< 316 >

20

Delfina compared her two husbands. Soares talked about things of the sea, boats, parties and big cities, beautiful things that made her dream. José talked about lashes with the whip, labor camps and plantations. Sad things that made her cry. She didn't talk about anything. Neither life nor work. Of course, she knew about forbidden things, about sundown, about what goes on in the bedroom and sailors' orgies.

Amid smiles and embraces, Delfina and Soares woo each other and make their love pledges.

"Soares, do you love me?"

"I adore you, my little black girl."

My black girl, my little negress. An offensive expression — humiliating, demeaning. For she had surpassed the limitations of a negress. She already has a white man and mulatto children. She already speaks good Portuguese and her skin is lightened by creams, and she wears a wig. I'm black, yes, but only in my skin. I'm already more than a black woman, I married a white man!

"I'm not black, Soares, am I?"

"Well, aren't you?"

"I'm almost white, with the creams I use. I live with whites, I eat white people's food and I speak good Portuguese."

The signs of degradation send a chill through Soares's heart. It's as if someone left the light in order to follow the paths that led to the abyss, on a journey of no return. Can someone change their race? He tries to block off the abyss with words of affection.

"Ah, my little negress."

"You're going to take me to Lisbon."

"Take you? But of course. Someday, Lisbon will be the homeland of all races. Someday. Lisbon, ah, Lisbon! How I miss Lisbon!"

"Is that true, Soares?"

"Of course, my little saint!"

"A saint, me?"

Now that pleased Delfina. A saint in word but not in deed. For sin has the taste of honey and she loves sin. Being a saint is to abstain from the pleasures of this world.

"My jewel, my black pearl!"

A pearl, yes, but black? At that moment she became all tender and rummaged around for words in the drawers of her memory

< 318 >

to repay him with long words of love, elaborate melodies woven together like poems.

"I love you because you're white, you're civilized, you're good. Before you came along, everything was black, everything was poor. Today, we have radio and electricity. Here at home, everything is hygienic, there's no shortage of clothes, no shortage of food and we even eat salt cod.

"Delfina, my angel, you talk as if the poor weren't human."

"The blacks don't count for anything, Soares."

"My black beauty, I'm tired of hatred and am looking for love in you. Simplicity. The path to freedom."

"Freedom? What freedom?"

"A more just world where everyone has a place. A world without proprietors, or slaves, or masters."

"Where is that world?"

"We can try and build it."

"In this freedom you dream about, will there be salt cod and wine? Good clothes? What's this freedom you're telling me about, Soares, if I'm free, happy and well, and I have you to protect me?"

"Freedom, Delfina, freedom. A world where blacks and whites can live in harmony. A world where all are equal."

"Oh, Soares! You must be mistaken. A black is a black, a white is a white. It was God who made the world and set things up as they are. So if this freedom you talk so much of actually comes about, who's going to tend to the coconut grove? Who's going to harvest the coconuts? Who's going to wash and bleach my white skirts and leave them out in the sun to dry? Who's going to look after my vegetable gardens?"

There is fanaticism in Delfina's declaration. Tyranny and power, the stuff of earthly fascination. Confirming that even without the perverse effects of the cross and the sword, barbarian wars were bloody too. Long, long before the colonialists came, life was also harsh, bitter, impossible. There were other dogged motives that caused Soares to cross the oceans to reach Zambezia. And thus endure the despair of a life led far from his native land. This preserved in his heart a nostalgia for his homeland, which remains with him every moment of the day. To love and hate this land that has welcomed him.

"If you divide up this land with all these poor, what will be left for us? What is this freedom that takes away all our privileges? No, Soares, I don't want freedom of any kind."

"Think about your people's suffering, Delfina."

"This conversation about freedoms reminds me of my father and the enslaved dock workers. Talking all the time about freedom. A conversation among the poor and the blacks, Soares. Whoever hears you talk like this may even conclude he's listening to one of those terrorists against the regime. Oh, Soares! I just want to be with you, I don't want any sort of freedom!"

"I don't understand you, Delfina."

"I'm a woman like the rest. I would have been a good girl even, if life hadn't been so difficult, unequal and so brutal."

He understands: yes, Delfina, you would have been a good girl. A queen or a warrior woman if you'd been born in another world. You might have been the tenth wife of a man who was older than your father. But you would have had a dignity that was yours alone. But here, you've been transformed into something that's impossible to name. You don't want to be black. You dream of being white or mulatto. You dream of being a living object, without shadow or weight. The remnant of a race. An imagined white. Yes, Delfina, you would have been a good girl.

The truth lodges itself in the mind of Soares, increasing his vision of the world that has accepted him. The image of Delfina is reflected here. Sometimes childish. Other times an object. Other times thoughtful, penetrating.

Both of us are emigrants, Delfina. I came here to Zambezia from Europe. And you came from inside yourself to nowhere in particular. Neither of us have a secure perch. Victims of our time, we seek a breathing space in this world. Amid superiorities and inferiorities, we fell in love.

"Maria das Dores. Come and scrub my heels and cut my toenails."

"Yes, mother."

"Now bring me my slippers, my towel, my Vaseline, bring me my comb and my cream."

"Here they are, mother."

"Go and see if the table's been laid, go and see if Jacinta has eaten, if little Luís is asleep."

"Yes, Mother."

"Now bring me my clothes, I want to get dressed. Bring me my jewels."

She wants to enjoy once and for all everything that she never had, and does not know whether she will still have tomorrow. Underneath all that abundance, there are vestiges of hunger. That's why I eat everything, before it runs out. There are traces of uncertainty in all her acts. Before my day in the sun ends. Before life ends. Before the white man leaves. Before sadness returns. Adorn me with that silk whose texture attracts the sun's rays. Give me that cream so that I can sleep my beauty sleep. Give me that codfish, that wine, that potato, that shrimp, that turkey and that suckling pig. The white man will pay for it all today, but what about tomorrow?

"Delfina, my angel, why do you deny your own existence? I fell in love with you because you were black and not an imitation of a white woman. I've already had a white spouse. As white and as blond as could be, with a skin as white as a field of wheat. What I love about you is your earthen color, the color of fertility."

"Let me wear my bits of armor, my love, don't distract me. I need to draw all the sparkle of the firmament to my body. When it comes to the races, the road to the future has already been mapped out. Those who wear the color of the moon overcome life's pricks and thorns from birth."

"You should go back to school and fulfil your old dream. Get a diploma to be a primary school teacher, so as to learn the wonders of a new world and have a noble profession."

"I once had that dream, but then I lost it. To work is something a woman does without a man to sustain her. I'm with you, and I'm fine as I am."

"A husband isn't guaranteed security, Delfina. A man dies. Gets sick. Becomes poor."

"Listen, Soares, let me be, will you?"

Soares, old, exhausted by all his wars, tries to demonstrate through gesture what his words do not say. He shows the children too much affection. He showers them with gifts."

"I bought some clothes for Maria das Dores."

"They'll do for Jacinta."

"They're too big."

"She'll wear them when she's grown bigger."

"Delfina, why do you treat the children so differently?"

"Soares, these children are mine and not ours."

"Didn't you feel the same birth pains, didn't you bleed for each of these black children?"

"Everything's different, don't you see? The sky is different. The stars are different. The paradise is different. Mulattoes were born with the moon in their belly. The world is theirs. That's why everyone wants to be like them. The blacks by whitening themselves and the whites by getting a tan."

My black children represent the old world. The known. They are my past and my present. I'm me. I don't want to be me anymore. My mulatto children represent the allure of the new. They are the tools with which to open the door to the world. Zambezia is still virgin, it has no race. That's why we need to create human beings capable of meeting the needs of the moment.

"Delfina, I sought you out to show the world the futility of hatred. That love breaches the barriers of race. But you don't understand me."

"Do you believe in love between the races, Soares?"

Soares wept, without realizing he was weeping. He looked at himself and got a shock. I'm not myself, I'm somebody else. I'm the one who weeps for the flower that has poisoned itself. For the angels impaled on the pyramid of races. Equality is something to do with human rights that will be preached in days to come. Here, it no longer makes sense to talk of love. In Delfina's world, the term harmony doesn't even exist.

At mealtimes, the same discourse occurred. "Jacinta, have you washed your hands? You can't come to the table with your hands all dirty with soil, otherwise they'll be black like those of Maria das Dores. Don't eat those greens, it's we blacks who eat those. You can eat chicken, Zambezia style. You, Zezinho, eat manioc, you,

Luizinho, you mustn't eat it, otherwise you'll stink like a black boy."

"Why do you treat the children so badly, Delfina?"

"Do you want me to respect blacks, Soares? The father of these ones here, that fisherman, sepoy, planter of coconuts, what did he ever do for them? They should be grateful to me, for I gave them the good fortune of getting a white stepfather."

One day, the children were surrounding Delfina and Soares, firing off salvos of questions. With caustic words, just like the ones they had learned inside the home. Soares panicked. My God, these children are accusing me when all I wanted was to give them shelter, food. Where am I going to find the wise answers to explain the conflicts of the world to them?

"Mother, why did you make me black?" Zezinho asked. "I want light skin as well just like Jacinta or my white father."

"Ah, Zezinho! If I could have seen the future, I would never have married that wretched black man, your father!"

"Father, why did you make me with a black woman?" Jacinta asks. "I would like to have a white mother, just like your other wife."

"Be quiet, Jacinta," Delfina yelled. "If it hadn't been for me getting you a white father, you would have been born black like your brothers and sisters. If it wasn't for my care in your education, you would have grown up with a black girl's heart, like Maria das Dores."

Maria das Dores resented this and spoke up. She was twelve years old, and capable of thinking for herself.

"No, dear mother. Those weren't the words you wanted to use, oh no! You always wanted to feed us with the finest food this world could offer. Nor was that the tone of voice you used when our black father was here. I was my black father's princess, but everything's new in this house, everything has changed since our white father arrived."

A deadly arrow pierced Soares's chest. For heaven and hell live under the same roof. He took a close look at himself. We sailors, in order to exorcize our fears and superstitions, killed. We killed the other man's body without realizing that our soul was dying too. Delfina's behavior in part reflects our actions. Yes, of course, we should have come to these lands to shake hands and exchange knowledge, love, warmth. They welcomed us with love, dances and drumbeats. We could have listened to their harmonious songs as a comfort for our anguish. The lesson has been learned. Maybe our experience will serve history in times that only the future can reveal.

His sailor's eyes betrayed him. They caused him to see Delfina as both the boat and the river. The oars. He dreamed of sailing forth with her to distant places and to the depths of the sky. Discover the ocean and the length of the waves. His sailor's eyes made him see Delfina as the wings of the seagulls. He wanted to fly away with her in order to know the thickness of the clouds. To understand how mountains attract the first drop of water, when its rocks are hard and devoid of life.

❖ ❖ ❖

Soares walks along the seashore until his feet hurt. He sits down on the sand. In exactly the same spot as José dos Montes on the day he had said goodbye. His eyes take in the line of the horizon. He sees gulls, boats, masts. And he looks at the sea. A blue sea, a calm sea, a wild sea, a sea the size of infinity. He recalls stories of the sea from the times when he was young, as an army recruit, as a sailor. The countless voyages along the highways of the sea. The huge waves that swallowed up ships. He recalls the sea nymphs. Adamastor. Luís de Camões. Lisbon. The image of his wife emerges more clearly than ever.

< 328 >

Where can my wife be? What is she doing at this very moment, in Lisbon? I never heard from her again. Can it be that she remembers me? He counts up the years along the expanse of time: seven years away from her, living next to a black concubine. How did I end up here?

He feels he has just awoken from a dream and remembers: I smashed the glass displaying exotica, attracted by the honey that existed on the other side of life. I fell into Delfina's hands.

Ah! My sweet wife back in Lisbon! Why didn't you leave home waving your fists and yelling in a fight for your family's rights, and save me from the prison cell where I now find myself? Was it because you didn't want to wage war on black women? If it was the son you gave birth to who went crazy over the black girls on the dockside, would you have remained silent? Why did you fold your arms and just weep when it was me who was the victim? Did you ever feel any love for me? Weren't you jealous? Do you believe the story that men are the strong ones? Only another woman can save a man from a woman's talons. A woman's spell can only be understood by another woman. Did you prefer your status as a refined, pious, and well-mannered lady, on top of your pedestal, while leaving me to succumb to the power of a mad woman? You could have had Delfina arrested, sent into exile, to the plantations, but you didn't do that. You preferred connivance and silence. You left without saying goodbye. But you knew what you were doing wasn't going to lead anywhere, because sooner or later, I would miss you and our children.

Why are white women so passive in the face of their husbands' debauchery, leaving them to wallow in the bodies of black women without any complaint, their only reaction being tears that flow like resin from an old tree? Why do they limit themselves to praying and moaning, as passive and submissive as all the women in the world? I got lost because I didn't have a savior. Black women throw themselves into battle, hit each other in the street, create public disorder and end up at the police station. White women gravely witness their men's dissoluteness. Is there some kind of complicity?

He admires the black mermaids of the docks, excellent artistes. Tempting a man here, a man there, until they succeed. They do their research. They roll a few dice. They listen out to gauge the most intimate secrets in the homes where they work as servants. They study the most perverse bodily tastes of the husbands of their mistresses, so as to dominate them all the more effectively. He is impressed by the victory smile of some black women whose greatest triumph is to

< 330 >

destroy a white woman's marriage, in an act of pure revenge, turning the great ladies into great losers.

Ah, my wife over there in Lisbon. Thanks to your apathy, Delfina invaded our private life and destroyed us. I entered her family and destroyed it. In our mutual act of destruction, she and I built a new family full of endless questionings. Where were you to defend your home? Everything's your fault, it's all your fault, it's all your fault!

◆　◆　◆

He awakens from his dreams and questions himself. Who am I, and what am I doing here? He suddenly realizes the absurdity of his existence. Delfina? Did she really have any allure? Yes, she did. Her color is the black of night where souls sigh and bodies approach each other. She is repose and shade. The moonless night where the stars of the firmament shimmer and dance. The nimbus, pregnant with rain, the portent of abundance. The black clay of divine creation, with which the world is molded to perfection. She is the color of good earth, the earth of fertility. Her skin possesses the fragrance of coconut and in her blood, there is the taste of wild palm. She is the vast palm grove. She is all Zambezia!

21

Tired of his adventure, Soares woke up early and gave Delfina and the children a kiss. He spoke gently and concisely, words that Delfina would remember for the rest of her life.

"Take good care of our children. I don't want them to lack for anything, not even my black kids. Treat them all equally, for they all came from your womb."

"Oh, Soares! Since when have I ever forgotten to care for them?"

With her usual smile, Delfina accompanied her man to the front door. She waved goodbye, her hand in gentle undulation, unaware that would be the last time she waved to her man, her gold mine.

The white man Soares left for Lisbon on the same day, unaware that some ten or more years afterwards, many whites would follow him, leaving behind them, at the time of their flight, affection, yearning, and splendid booty that would be fought over with knives.

My white man has gone, what will become of me? I'm left helpless. Without a job, or husband, or lover.

* * *

Inspired, Delfina writes love poems in the air. Sitting in her rocking chair on the veranda. She says that great love is a dream. A drop of honey that is swallowed and then defecated. A morning song that comforts and then stops. Inspired by love, she places her misfortunes in the soft melody that gushes up through her throat, and she lets them fly on the sonorous pulses of her weeping.

She weeps for her two husbands. She analyzes the similarities and differences. José was the unadulterated soot in the chimney of her memory. But he was hers, hers completely. That was why she scorned him. Soares was hers too, but shared, a human trophy won in a great battle. He was hers but on loan.

In the distance, she sees a man walking toward her. A handsome sepoy. A manly figure. Who could it be? The image of her black husband rises up in all its splendor. Maybe he's bringing her news of José dos Montes. Of Soares, perhaps. The man draws near and smiles. His honeyed lips and his eyes full of desire.

"Good afternoon, good sir. What do you want?"

"I've come to tell you I love you, my pretty Delfina."

"What is your name, sir?"

"You don't know me. But I know you need a man. That's why I'm here."

"What?"

Delfina loves men and their pleading eyes. She pretends to be angry but inwardly she smiles. She is still beautiful after all. She is still the object of desire. A man leaves, but she fixes herself another. Only her mother is special. Only her father is special.

"Where have you come from, sir, because I've never seen you before?"

"From nowhere. I came here to love you and take the money the white man left."

"What money?"

"This is a hold up."

There's the glint of a dagger in the sunlight, in this mad sepoy's determined hand. Delfina trembles. She gets up. With the knife held next to her neck, she obeys this strange man's command.

"Come on, let's go! Fill my eyes with your tender smile. Come on, excite me. Sweep away the pain of my lust, and give me a kiss. Dance for me, ah! Delfina, I want you today, right now."

The man drags her into the house. There they are, beauty and the beast, on this early afternoon. Pushing Delfina off the peak of her mountain down into the dusty vale. She weeps. For José dos Montes, who loved her to perdition, until he led her to the altar and proclaimed her queen of all women. For Soares, who lost himself for her sake and destroyed his family. My tree, my shade, my goose that laid the golden eggs, have all died.

"I'm sorry for the unusual way I told you I love you," the stranger says, "naked, rich, poor, I'm besotted. The love I feel has driven me to this act of madness. I shall skewer your heart with this blade, my little barbecue, my piece of spit-roast meat, so you'll be mine alone. I'll kill you if you go with some other sonofabitch!"

Delfina stifles a fit of confusion, a flurry of tears, a scream. My God, my guardian angels, my dead ancestors, help me. Bring sun back to this house. Bring poison too for this wretched worm who is destroying me.

"You've no longer got an owner, Delfina, your white man has gone and isn't coming back. From now on, I'm your owner. We've got to share the white man's money. You want security? I'll protect you. You want a fight? I'll crush you. You want confrontation? I'll kill you."

"Leave me in peace, I haven't done you any harm, let me go, get out of my house!"

"Don't you believe me, princess? Assassins also love, my little saint. I'm one of them. The white man's gone and has left you many things, a palm grove, lands and cattle, I've come to help you take care of it, I'm married but that doesn't matter, you'll be my second wife."

I need to find some space for my hopes to breathe again, she thinks to herself, for the sake of this home's peace and quiet and for my children's health, I've got to find a way out. I've got to solve this problem. I don't know how, but God will guide me along the right paths.

"Leave me in peace, don't come back here again."

"That's where you're wrong, Delfina. I shall always come back just to make love to you."

And the man did come back. To empty out the larder and her stock of wine. Countless times, he headed straight for the kitchen to count the chunks of meat in the saucepan he'd eat, and the bottles of wine he'd drink. He'd sit down at the table, stick his tongue in the bowl of soup, and then holding it with both hands, tip it up and drink. He would eat with his hand, stuff his mouth full, and spit out the meat and fish bones left right and center. He'd bring chickens into the room to eat up the crumbs he spread under the table. He'd open bottles with his teeth and empty the wine straight down his throat,

< 336 >

in front of the startled looks of Delfina and the children. When he went away again, he left behind him chaos, disorder, and tears.

Maria das Dores and Jacinta hid under the bed and whispered to each other.

"Dores, my father's gone away," Jacinta whined tearfully.

"Mine too," Dores answered.

"We're both orphans," they said together.

"I didn't know it was hard not having a father."

"Oh, don't cry, Jacinta!" Maria das Dores consoled her. "That's life."

It was society's sadistic revenge bearing down on Delfina. For having crossed the red line and destroyed families. For having loved a white man and rejected a black.

My God, how many times am I going to have to fight in order to affirm myself? She asked herself. I thought the world was mine. Life is a burden, the world is a burden, the idea of being here is a burden. Here I am in the hands of a stranger, who sweeps me across the floor as if I were trash. For the first time, Delfina learned the suffering of a home without a protector, of children without a father. She swore she was going to resolve the problem, that she was going to get her own back, with the help of Simba's magic.

< 337 >

She sought out Simba and he placed rat poison in a bottle of wine that the intruder was bound to drink. It would kill him gradually, first with swellings, then diarrhea, then general weakness, madness and eventually death. The sepoy came. On that day, he was gentler than ever. He drank the wine straight from the bottle and liked it.

"Delfina, do you know who I am? Do you know why I'm here? I was paid to avenge the tragedy of Soares. To make you disappear from the face of the earth, after torture. Make you pay the price for your brazenness. You defied the blacks, and you defied the whites. You've got to die in order to ensure the morals of society are maintained. I'm good at killing, I'm good, I've already killed many people. But I haven't got the courage to kill you. Because I love you. I truly love you."

It was the snake hissing his love, after tasting a dose of poison. Delfina was overcome with a fit of pity. For the first time, she felt the strange sensation of comforting someone who would soon be dead. She embraced him.

< 338 >

22

I've got no port, I've got no anchorage, this is the only truth. I've got to get it. Find it. I'm alone again. A friend here, another there, I possess nothing that lasts.

Delfina looks for new pathways in old places. She goes back to Simba's house like someone in retreat.

"Here again, Delfina?"

"Bring Soares back, Simba. Come on, invoke him, and summon your spirits as well to bring him back to my arms."

"You want my spirits to do the work? When are you going to learn that happiness is cultivated and bread comes from toil? When are you going to understand that brilliance comes from the mind and our capacity to create? You have everything you need to be happy, Delfina. Everything. Instead of using your abilities, here you come asking for reinforcements. And then afterwards, you don't pay what you promised."

His words wound like the sword of justice. They condemn.

Censure. Delfina listens in silence. In Simba's voice there are sounds echoing from beyond. This conversation about my rise and fall was my father's favorite topic. The story of the calm sea, the sudden storm, boats and shipwrecks was my father's best loved tale. He used to love talking about the crossing of the desert. She then starts to understand the meaning of those conversations. She is startled. Can it be that the time has come to cross the desert?

"I pay what I promise, yes I do."

"You promised me a house, Delfina."

"And didn't I give you one?"

"But there was no furniture. Tables, beds, curtains."

"But...!"

"A house is only a house when it's full. You gave me walls..."

"Isn't that what we agreed?"

"If you want a service from me, you've got to settle old bills first."

Delfina humiliates herself by asking for clemency. Exposing her feelings in an actor's flourish.

"Ah, Simba! If you only knew the tragedy that's befallen me. The houses, lands, stores, the bakery and all its machinery, everything has been distributed among the children."

"And you, my little saint?"

"I didn't get anything. Even my black children inherited from the old man. Everyone except for me. For me, he left a paltry allowance that doesn't even last three months. That's why I'm here again."

"If your children are heirs to a great fortune, you are the executor as they are still minors. I don't see what your problem is."

"Soares even disinherited me from being the family's executor. He left it clear in his will that I shouldn't be allowed to administer so much as a cent of my children's inheritance. He treated me unfairly."

He was fully aware that no court would allow her to be the executor of an inheritance because of her bad reputation, vices and extravagance which were visible to absolutely everyone.

"I'm here for you to help me start all over again."

"That's impossible. You took your seat on the throne that I created for you. You didn't keep your promises. You set yourself up, you made yourself scarce, you ignored my appeals to you, and you forgot that I'm the one who holds the key to your whole life. I'm the one who sawed through your pedestal and you fell off it. Those who place their trust in the power of others should be aware of that lesson."

"What are you telling me, Simba? How? Why?"

"I had the key to your secret. When I got tired of waiting for my reward, I broke the spell. The white man woke up."

She is surprised, but not totally. The love of magic is made up of trickery, and it doesn't last.

"What shall I do with my life, Simba? Help me now. I promise, it won't happen again."

"I'll try, but before anything else, pay me. Give me an official document, a guarantee. Mortgage something of value."

"I'll give my blood, my life, everything."

"Your blood's no longer any good, it's sullied, I won't accept it. But tell me your plans."

"I want to build my business selling bread."

"Ah! Have you already started the business?"

"Yes, but it doesn't make any money."

"Bravo, Delfina! But... what will you give me in exchange?"

She thinks quickly. Of the things she still has. Of the furnishings he's claiming. The jewelry she can sell to pay for his services. She thinks of her countless dresses, capulanas, sandals. She thinks of Maria das Dores. For a woman, studying isn't important. Because love doesn't require one to read and write. You don't need schooling to give birth to a child. Grabbing a rich man is a question of cunning, not mathematics. Holding a man in bed is a question of magic and tactics. Living well is a question of finance. She, who could barely read and write, had managed to hunt a rich white man who swapped his entire family for her alone, leaving their children a large fortune. The most important thing for a woman isn't a diploma, but luck in life and the skill to catch a man who's any good. After a long silence, she returns to the surface with a macabre proposal.

"I'll give you my daughter's virginity."

"What? Are you capable of that?"

His reply hurts her, which is why she doesn't say anything. For it is not easy to give your own daughter up to a witchdoctor who is also your lover. She feels sick at herself. And she swears that if this act is going to be consummated, then it must be quick. Little time wasted and it's all over.

But she forgets that a split second is the most important facet of time. An explosion takes a second. An earthquake. A bullet fired. A lightning flash. The conception of a new being.

"Have you got the courage, Delfina?"

"Me?"

She says no more. She's not even sure of the decision she has made. But she believes in the curse that may fall on her if their pact isn't fulfilled. As she understands it, it's better to have one victim in the house than the whole family. She has no regrets. Where she comes from, a woman is a chattel who can be bought and sold. A seal on a contract. Money exchanged. A mortgage. A fine. Survival. She too had been used by her own mother in her distant childhood. Handed over to the white shopkeepers in exchange for food. For the rest, any contact wouldn't last long.

"Delfina, the faith that will save you, will also be your death."

"My luck has deserted me, Simba."

"That's what the good spirits are like, Delfina. They come and go. You didn't know how to hang on to the blessing they had given you. Don't blame anyone for your lack of success except yourself. You are the most fortunate woman in the world because God turned all the wonderful things that happened to you into material wealth."

Simba had worked everything out. Maria das Dores, that sweet little girl, isn't just a woman, but the inheritor of four rental properties in the upper part of the city, many lands and a whole parade of palm trees lined up as far as the eye can see. To have control of all this means a new life. It's worth accepting the offer. Filling her belly with children as soon as it becomes possible. Leading her up to the altar when she reaches the age of majority and managing all that inheritance himself.

"When is this promise going to be fulfilled, Delfina?"

"Today. Tomorrow. Whenever you want."

"Then let it be today at sunset. Today, do you hear, Delfina? Let it be today before the spirits change their mind."

Delfina leaves. Her heart tells her she loves that daughter more than ever, after having despised her and humiliated her for so long. She promises herself that she will protect her after the pact has been sealed.

23

Various incidents marked Jacinta's life. The most important of these occurred when she was strolling along the streets of the city with her schoolmates. She saw her father entering a huge building with lots of stairs. She got excited and went in. She looked for him in all the offices, corridors, crying out loud, daddy, daddy, as uninhibited as any child. When she saw him, she jumped up on his shoulders, full of delight. The man speaking to her father asked:

"Who's this little black girl? What's she doing here?"

Her father blushed and mumbled an answer.

"She's the daughter of a friend. An African."

"Who calls you daddy?"

"Yes."

"I knew it, I'd already been told and had pretended not to hear. You're a shame on our class, Soares, you're a kaffir. If things go on like this, the whites will all start wearing loincloths."

Her father was sent packing from that office with a great show of arrogance by the man who seemed to be his boss. Because he had

< 346 >

a daughter by a black woman. The worst part was discovering that her father didn't have the courage to say she was his daughter. He denied her. That day, she also discovered her father was weak and didn't love her as much as he said he did.

The second major incident: she was walking hand in hand with her grandfather through the suburbs. A white policeman looked at them in astonishment. A black man with a white child, out there in the suburbs? He called them over and confronted her grandfather.

"Old man, where did you steal that child?"

"She's my granddaughter."

"A white kid like that?"

"I swear, I give you my word she's the daughter of my daughter."

"Hey, you're a kidnapper. Sepoy, give the black guy a few lashes and make him tell the truth."

Her grandfather was whipped, broken, and spent months in bed, with lesions that eventually led to his death. Her child's heart was also broken. Her grandfather was the most marvelous person in the world. And he died as a result of being whipped for having a granddaughter of another race.

In the beginning, Jacinta was unaware she had any racial identity. Afterwards, she learned that the blacks were the servants. She

< 347 >

started to think that Maria das Dores was a slave, and Delfina her father's servant.

When she went out with her mother, blacks and whites would ask:

"Is she your mistress's daughter?"

"No, she's mine," Delfina would reply proudly.

"Oh! She's too white to be a mulatto girl."

One day, during school break, she went and looked for Maria das Dores to play. The teacher reprimanded her. Because she was playing with a black girl, and she should be playing with people of her own race. So she said: she's my sister. The teacher was shocked. She summoned her mother. She wanted to meet her and understand such a phenomenon.

"Madam, you're reducing the girl to being a black," the teacher censured her.

"But she's not a black and speaks good Portuguese, she's got a white father."

"Yes, she does, but she doesn't pronounce her double RRs properly. She must learn to say R correctly. Who does the girl live with?"

"With me and the father."

"But she spends most of her time with you."

"Yes."

< 348 >

"Well then. Isn't there anyone who isn't colored she can live with?"

"Her godmother. Her godparents."

"Well, send her to them. Do it quickly so she can learn her Rs. It would be a pity if such a perfect little mulatto girl couldn't pronounce her Rs as she should. It would be better to send her soon before she gets into bad habits. As the twig bends, so bends the tree, remember."

She was always excluded from the ring dance by the girls in her area. Because she was white, and a ring dance is for black girls. They didn't want to have to put up with Delfina's tantrums, in which she threatened them with prison or the whip and using the husband's influence, in the event of her getting hurt.

Maria das Dores playing with the black girls. Jacinta playing with the mulatto girls. At home, Maria das Dores scrubbed the floor while she got on with her school homework. Maria das Dores carried the firewood, cooked and cleaned, while she just played.

It was from that point on that she began to look around her. And she saw that the blacks were very black. And the whites were very white. When she was with blacks, they called her white. And they didn't want to play with her. They would keep her away, say bad things about her mother and use bad words. When she was with whites, they called her black. They chased her away too, said bad things about her mother and called her names.

Her little head was filled with a growing dilemma: where's my place? Why do I have to remain between two races? Can it be that I've got to create my own different, marginal world, only with individuals of my own race? She started to feel angry toward her father, who loved a black woman so as to transform her into a mulatto girl. She felt angry at her mother, who didn't make her black like Maria das Dores, which was why she couldn't join in the ring dances on the street corners of her district. She started to love Maria das Dores, who was oppressed within the home because of her race, and because she did her hair in an incredible way and told her stories until she fell asleep. They lived under the same roof, slept in the same room, but their mother kept their plates, glasses, and cutlery apart. She questioned herself without knowing that such moments would haunt her for the rest of her life.

It was strange living in a multi-racial household. She found it confusing having to absorb the behavior of blacks and whites at the same time. It was still more complicated to be divided at mealtime. The worst thing of all was not having anyone respond to her problems. She was already all too familiar with her mother's opinions. And if her father was present, he wouldn't answer her either.

< 350 >

Jacinta glares into the distance, as if challenging the mountains on the horizon. It's a gaze that dominates the world. She has her father's sense of security and has inherited Delfina's adventurous spirit. Maybe one day she will change. In order to acknowledge their destiny, people need to grow up and their paths need to be revealed to them. She learned from an early age to distinguish between races. To look at her dark-skinned brothers from her vantage point in the clouds. To hear the voice of hatred fall upon the human race. Her childhood lullaby was woven with notes of hatred.

* * *

Various events had a profound effect on Maria das Dores: the most important of these was the departure of her father, whom she dreams of all the time, asking the wind the reasons for his absence. When she woke up, she would sigh: but what's happened to my father, whom I'll never seen again? Where's he gone, and why didn't he take me with him? And then, there was another motive for heartache: when her mulatto sister was born, her mother's affection migrated to the other side of the river, and she never managed to regain it. She looked to the heavens to try and understand what was happening to her. She thought about running away, seeking refuge on the streets or anywhere else. But she was gripped by the idea that her father might return.

She silently put up with the fits of temper directed toward her by her mother. It was unfair, she knew, but she didn't want to complain. She had been born from that mother's womb and she didn't want to defy her, because to defy a mother is to defy one's destiny. She had heard the first song from that mouth, and received her first kiss. She couldn't go against her. For a mother's curse is a prophecy. That mother was her tree and her shade. She couldn't get rid of her. To get rid of a mother was to get rid of one's own foundation. She knew her mother loved her in a perverse kind of way, but she still loved her. As her daughter, she couldn't hate her. To hate one's mother is to hate one's own existence. From José, her black father, she had learned that suffering is a stage in one's own existence. That one should smile in the face of incredible pain. That one should accept this sacrifice in order that life should go on. From her white father, she had learned that joy is a right. That bonhomie generates harmony. She had learned that the beauty of the world is its diversity, all races, from all over the world, because we are all children of the sun.

< 352 >

Another moment that had a profound effect on her life was her black brother Zezinho's illness. On the fateful day, her brother had spent the afternoon playing soccer with his friends in the neighborhood. After his bath, and after he'd eaten dinner, he felt sick and vomited.

"My tummy aches, Dores, help me."

"What have you been eating?"

"Nothing."

"Well, have a rest."

Pearls of sweat appeared on Zezinho's brow. His skin was burning. His movements languid as he succumbed to fever, exhaustion, and dizziness. Maria das Dores tended him and packed him off to bed.

"Mother, mother?"

Zezinho was whining like an abandoned kitten, in that bedroom that was now too hot, now too cold, calling for his black father and for his white father. Maria das Dores responded in silence, recalling the words of a song of despair.

Mother's not here.
She's gone east of nowhere

And she wouldn't be back before dawn. She had sneaked off through the shadows of the tall coconut trees dancing in the moonlight, and headed to the bar to have a drink as the bats awoke in their gloom, and she would come home tired, disheveled, and drunk. My God, there's an owl hooting on the roof of the house, that's a bad sign, Zezinho is dying, maybe he'll die today!

Maria das Dores rushed off in alarm, defying the howling of the sea in the night, and in no time at all reached the quayside bar, where she tried to shake her mother, tugging at her desperately.

"Mother, Zezinho needs help."

"You don't need to raise your voice in the presence of my friends," Delfina shouted, lifting her glass to her lips.

That bar was a vision of chaos. There were no blacks, whites, or mulattoes to be seen there, for poverty reduces all races to the same. The atmosphere roused an inner lion in Maria das Dores that she never imagined she possessed. She let out a roar, shaking her mother with anger and resentment.

"Go away, Maria das Dores. I will not allow such disrespect in front of my friends."

She went back home to her brother. She waited, but her mother didn't appear. She set off again in search of her.

< 354 >

"Mother, Zezinho got worse. He passed out."

"How do you know?"

At that point she felt truly alone. Her father was away, far away. In this world perhaps, or in another. Her mother was near, very near. Her body was present but her mind was roaming through the world's mysteries. Her anxiety turned to despair.

"Mother!" It was a child's gushing cry of revolt.

"Stop shouting, can't you see I'm with my friends?"

"Mother?!"

A chorus of slurred voices shooed Maria das Dores away as if she were an intruder, go home, girl. Get out of here, a bar isn't a place for kids. The drunkards looked at her, raised their glasses, drank, stifling their fears and bitterness, surrendering to the decadence of their body and soul, without paying her any attention, because children don't exist, they never have existed, and they don't know anything. Maria das Dores was then assailed by a feeling of nausea and indignation. The place reeked of cigarette smoke, alcohol, cheap hootch, and the stink of sailors.

Maria das Dores's eyes popped out like glass marbles. Deep within her, she felt the sting of a scorpion.

She went home in a panic, like some lost creature in search of help.

She reached home. She looked at it. It was the most beautiful house in the neighborhood, its garden abundant with colors. She entered the room and blocked her ears so as not to hear her brother's groans, for there was no point in living for the sake of appearances, bitterness, and drunken bouts or racism.

Suddenly. She felt like blowing up all that luxury and turning the bedroom into one vast blaze that would turn the place to rubble and ruin by the morning, with her and her brother Zezinho's bodies turned to ashes, leaving Jacinta and Luisinho alive to occupy a place in their mother's heart. She decided to put an end to her brother's suffering, her own suffering as well, and give her mother more freedom to enjoy all types of drink from all manner of bottles, from all over the world. She squatted down and buried her head in her knees, animated by the laughter of the curtains as they were kissed by the flames. She no longer took any notice of Zezinho's despairing cries.

"Fire, Maria das Dores, fire!"

A loud thud smashed doors and windows, and from the other world, Maria das Dores felt the freshness: death had the taste of rain, clouds, she was soaring toward paradise. Suddenly she felt herself raised on high. It was the neighbors coming to rescue her, taking her and Zezinho to the hospital, each with light burns. Then

< 356 >

they took Jacinta and Luisinho in their arms and went and dragged Delfina out of the bar.

"Delfina, your house caught fire."

"I'll see to it in a minute, I'm here with my friends."

"Delfina, your children are dying!"

"What?!"

Delfina went home, reeling like a drunkard. She saw, through her glazed eyes, the vestiges of an averted tragedy, but she would only realize the extent of the disaster next morning. Or she wouldn't understand anything, blinded by her vanity. She went to bed fully clothed. Maria das Dores wasn't there to put the blankets over her. She complained to the walls. She huffed and puffed. And she hurled the same abuse as usual, but deep down, she wept.

Maria das Dores's eyes were timid, furtive, those of someone who sought shelter in her own absence. She inherited the mindset of someone who would allow everyone to trample on her. She was embittered and her despair was growing. Questions buzzed around inside her head like a swarm of bees. She started questioning everything in this world. Sometimes she would become aware of her tears flowing, but without knowing why she was crying. It was all very confusing.

She asked herself many questions and she was fast growing up. She looked for a place to hide within herself, ever timid and elusive. She envied her friends, who were badly dressed, barefoot, hungry even, but who always had a smile on their lips. She was smartly dressed, she had her packed snack of bread and cheese, but she didn't smile. She missed her black father terribly.

< 358 >

24

It is a beautiful scene to behold. Two sisters sitting on the veranda as evening falls, braiding each other's hair. One black, the other mulatto. Talking about things of the world's beginning, in the springtime of their lives. Their little heads in the air, discovering heavenly highways along the contours of the moon. Maria das Dores talks of a heavenly prince, the famous centaur, a man-horse in the form of a star, and tells the most fantastic adventures.

Delfina comes and looks in on them. She is moved. Her daughters are growing ever more beautiful. She feels a deep anguish emerging within her but even so, she puts on a smile.

"So, girls, haven't you finished fixing your hair yet?"

"It's hard to plait a mulatto girl's hair, mother, because it's slippery," Maria das Dores says.

"It's black girls' hair that's hard, because it's like straw, it's no good. Jacinta, you inherited good hair from your father, what do you want a black girl's hairstyle for?"

"It's so pretty, mother!" Jacinta exclaims.

Maria das Dores works on her hair in great detail, placing colored beads in each braid. In each braid, a dream. Delfina shivers, because it's getting late. Soon, darkness will fall.

"Maria das Dores, come on! Let's go!"

"Where?"

"I want to take you somewhere lovely. Hurry up, before it gets dark. You can go on with Jacinta's hair when you get back."

"It'll be done in a minute, mother."

"Let's go."

"Is Jacinta coming?"

"She's still a child. But her situation is different. The white world lives according to other laws, they don't need to go on this journey. For them, the school of books is more important than the school of life."

Mother and daughter set off along the path in the cool of the late afternoon. They walk quickly in order to arrive before it's too late. Before Delfina's conscience causes her to change her mind. Before the darkness of night and dreams provide her with new answers.

"Why such a hurry, mother?"

"Don't talk so much, just walk!"

They take quick, long strides, and cover the long distance in little

< 360 >

time. They reach their destination. There is a clearing. A straw hut. A black man sitting in Buddha-like meditation in the doorway. The man's eyes terrify the timid young girl. His smile reveals some secret satisfaction. He is disposed to acts of love and hatred on this afternoon that is about to end.

"Good afternoon, Simba," says Delfina.

"Welcome," the man replies, getting to his feet.

"Here we are."

"So much the better."

The man takes Maria das Dores by the hand. He pulls her firmly into the hut, with a look of triumph on his face. He is all prepared, his weapons polished and in position for combat. He goes straight into action without bothering with words. He directs all the energy of a man at the peak of his life at her, a parched bird in the cool of the lake. He dives in. He is the creator pounding the clay, molding a sculpture at the whim of his inspiration. That's what it's like to be a woman, it's easy. One knife thrust is enough, one moment of agony and one shriek:

"Father!" Maria das Dores cries.

Everything dies at that moment. Childhood. Innocence. All the stars go out as a sign of mourning. The act is violent, cold, with all the refinement of torture, Maria das Dores is being raped. Fleeced, Robbed. A young girl submitted to the sadistic obsession of those who should love her.

"Father, father!"

Vague memories flow through the mind of Maria das Dores. All the tiny moments come into her memory. Her black father's prickly chin when he kissed her in the morning. The color of his smile. The forest of hairs on his chest, which she could never finish counting. Her white father who gave her dolls, chocolates. Her black father who gave her bananas and coconuts.

"Father, dear father!" Her screams gain deathly tones.

Outside, Delfina trembles, soaked in fear and sweat. She hears everything. Her daughter's shriek. The man's groans. The grunt of sated bestiality. At first, she smiles, thinking about the debt that has been paid. Maria das Dores was a wild animal that had been hunted, she was food, bloodstained in her captivity. But she is also saddened. That daughter is now a woman. A woman who came from her. Inheritor of her genes, her destiny and her devilish love affairs. Awaiting the end of the torture in that act of sexual initiation, revenge sex, business sex.

After it is all over, the man goes to speak to Delfina, now satisfied.

The mission has been accomplished. In a mother's smile, there is a child's weeping.

"Thank you, Delfina. You've kept your word at last."

"So, can we go now?"

"She's going to stay here today."

"But!"

"She's in no condition to walk. She's fragile, exhausted. She's going to stay here."

Delfina is experienced enough to work things out and guess what's coming. The man is going to use her. Abuse her. No, that's not what was agreed.

"All right. So I'll come and fetch her tomorrow morning."

"She'll stay here. For good."

"What?"

Simba responds in an aggressive tone. In the argument that follows, there's one voice that rises in pitch and another that is lowered. One shouts and the other weeps.

"Give me back the girl. I've carried out my side of the bargain," Delfina complains.

"Don't deceive yourself. You gave me the girl's virginity without batting an eyelid, Delfina. Why?"

"Why didn't you tell me at the appropriate time? You've consummated the act. Why do you want to condemn me to more suffering now?"

Maria das Dores has concluded that her father, José, has left, never to return. It is useless for her to shout his name. And she has already understood that she no longer has a mother. And that she will forever remember this day when her life changed forever.

"You're my man, Simba. You can't have mother and daughter at the same time. What will become of me without her?"

"Go away and leave her. I shall treat her like a queen. Here, she'll have the love she never had. I shall take care of her like a husband and a father. I will give her the worthy home you stole from her and the father you denied her. You don't want her as a daughter. What you want is a slave. You won't get her back. You never wanted her. And she should never think of running away from me. Oh no! If that happens, I shall curse your whole family and make your life hell, Delfina."

There is conviction in the man's voice. Inspiration. Passion, Betrayal. But even so, in spite of her cunning, Delfina hasn't yet understood the man's true motivation. Maria das Dores hears everything. The offensive words, the conspiracy that has led her to the

< 364 >

longest night in her life, forcibly delivered by her mother into the middle of the flames of a war she barely understands.

"My good luck and misfortune are your work alone. Without your intervention, my life wouldn't have taken off in the way it has. Why are you deserting me now?"

"I'm a free man, Delfina, I slept with you but I was never yours. Casting spells is my profession. I'm skillful in this, you know that only too well. Don't provoke me."

"I shall complain to the police," Delfina cries in despair.

"What do those whites you're so sure of know about magic? Who will be the one condemned? You or me? Try, if you want. You know what I'm capable of."

"As soon as I've got the money, I'll pay all my debts."

"When?"

"When my bakery business takes off."

Delfina dreamed of returning in triumph, her hands full of gold coins, but she leaves vanquished, spattered with blood, regret, and shock. In her final battle, she has lost her daughter, her slave, and the white man's fortune which will remain in the witchdoctor's hands.

"Ah, Delfina! I caught you this time. She's a little piece of you. Oh! My God, she's so pretty! You are a whore and she is a saint. You are

< 365 >

coarse and she is refined, she has breeding. You sleep with everyone, but she is mine, mine alone. No, I can't lose her. If she tries to get away, I'll kill her, I guarantee, Delfina, and I'll kill you. I shall keep her under lock and key and protect her from any greed and lust."

"Let me see her one last time," Delfina implores, amid her tears.

Mothers are powerful. In letters of black or of gold, they fill the pages of their own destiny with their own handwriting. They transform their children into heroes or cowards, into saints or fallen women. They can give birth or abort. They hold their children's fate in their hands. That is why their children call them goddesses. Or witches.

"Get out of my house now! Walk away and don't look back, otherwise I shall unleash curses against you and all your family."

Delfina raises her eyes to the sky. Instead of seeing God, a bird poops in her right eye. She rues her fate and raves. My straw thatch burned. I shitted in my own boat and now I've no way of crossing the river. She abandons Simba's house like a dying toad. The moon is full and round, tempting, like a truckle of cheese.

*　　*　　*

< 366 >

There stands Simba, victorious. With a prophetic air. A poetic demeanor. His mouth full of subtle sayings and unintelligible wisdom. Madness disguised as luminous knowledge, which for years has fed Delfina's vainglory and made her think she had the power to pull the world's strings.

There is Maria das Dores, delivered up to the unknown. Words such as shame, pain, conscience, are lifeless stones in the mouth of her mother and in that of Simba, whom she barely knows. She recognizes the abyss into which she has been plunged and recalls the only happy moments sketched on the face of her childhood doll. In Jacinta's hair. In the arms of her black father and in the smile of her white father.

25

After the initial invasion, women became slaves. They fought for their liberation. They regained their realm once again and killed all the men. They decreed a law: any child born a male should be killed, in order to put an end to the curse of men. That is what happened. For a long time, women lived in a complete and absolute paradise. A modest paradise, without emotions, sex, childbirth, bonds. Then one day, a child was born who was as lovely as an angel. He was a boy. The midwives, hypnotized by the creature's beauty, hid the truth and declared the baby to be a girl. The child grew up dressed as a girl and learned how to do domestic chores. Time passed. Whiskers began to grow and the voice deepened. He started to make new incursions and impregnated all the women in the realm again, like a rooster in the henhouse. The queen ordered him to be killed, but the women were in love with the creature and got together, killing the queen and proclaiming the man their new king. And so this saw the emergence of the first harem. Women became slaves and everything

< 368 >

went back to how it had been before. For man is an indestructible, ambitious animal.

Rivalry between men and women intensified. To solve the problem, it would be better to stick the men on the earth and the women in the moon. That way, they would gaze at each other longingly in the celestial mirror, just as happens when the sun lights up the timeless images of the remote inhabitants of the moon.

26

Jacinta's life took off in unexpected ways. She saw the house being visited by other white men of the vicinity, who occupied the place previously held by her father. Delfina's drunken bouts became ever more protracted. But most painful was the absence of Maria das Dores. Out on the streets, people would come up to her and recount the tragedy of Maria das Dores in all its details. They talked about her mother and called her names. For a child, there is nothing more unpleasant than hearing wicked sagas about a mother being spouted by all and sundry.

Jacinta noticed the explosion of sighs emitted by her mother's clients in her presence. They were assessing her. Weighing her up, maybe preparing for a major assault. She felt like the virgin nymph her mother would sell to any sailor, just as she had done to Maria das Dores. Jacinta felt defenseless, with neither a father nor a mother to protect her from the lewd eyes of men.

She grew up fast. She wasn't a woman yet, but she was of a perfect age to be raped by any man. Fear impelled her to seek some form of protection, defense. She challenged her mother in her search for a solution.

"Delfina!"

Delfina quivered. She sensed in her daughter's voice, the portent of war. When a child confronts you, the day you must part draws near. She widened her eyes and sighed. She had discovered that her daughter was a woman and was beautiful. And had a steely courage. She would defeat her, annihilate her.

"Yes, my little flower."

"Where is Maria das Dores?"

Jacinta's look had a warrior's determination. Her voice was harsh, corrosive. Delfina felt butterflies in her stomach. Terror penetrated her, pummeled her until she bowed and knelt before her daughter.

"Jacinta, my flower, you must understand."

"Understand? What?"

Delfina searched in her mind for a word, a reply, a point of escape.

"She's with her husband."

"How did this love affair start, this marriage?"

"They love each other, and decided to be together."

"You're lying, you murderer. You sold Maria das Dores. Out on the street they hurl abuse. They all talk about you and call you names to my face."

Delfina came out in a sweat. Her silent daughter had spoken. That was a bad omen. She felt the same despair as a farmer, when he discovers that the most beautiful plants in his vegetable patch have been flattened in a cyclone. Or that after tilling the soil, it's not going to rain. Or it's going to rain without stopping. Or there'll be a great plague of locusts.

Jacinta's eyes showed that she had declared war.

"Did you ever think of me, mother? Did you ever ask me what I thought?"

"Oh, Jacinta! I've given you the best part of me. There are things you don't yet understand. You're still a child."

"I'm a child, yes. Is that why you used to carry me around in your arms to show me off to your friends like some trophy? You used my image in order to humiliate my darker-skinned siblings. Do you think I like that?"

Delfina had always been a fighter, she had won all her battles, had dominated the world and men, but had never prepared herself for a fight with her own daughter.

"Mother, bring Maria das Dores back."

"Yes, dear daughter. I'll try."

< 372 >

"If you don't bring her back, then I will. I shall fight for Maria das Dores to the end, I swear. And we're not staying in this house any longer. I shall take Zezinho and Luisinho with me."

"Yes, I'll go and get her. I shall carry out your wish."

Delfina was struck dumb by the commanding tone that José dos Montes had recognized on hearing her first cry. She looked behind her in order to measure the depth of the hole she had dug herself. Her daughter was demanding answers, weapon at the ready, making her sail to the very ends of her conscience, disposed to shake the malign tree until it fell.

"Daughter, I made a mistake, I know. In my mind, there was one formula: my black child had to die so that my white child could live. You'll never understand that, Jacinta, because you're from another world."

"If my father left it's because he couldn't put up with you any longer. You're a horrible woman, mother."

"Don't get at me so much, my girl. All I did was for your good. For you to have bread. For the business to run better. For you to maintain your position as a mulatto girl, your assimilated status, and not to sink socially."

"You make me sick, mother."

She discovered that bringing up a child is declaring a war. An annoying presence, a bell round one's neck, a rattle around one's ankle. Delfina decided to lay down her arms and submit herself to torture. One never comes out a winner in a fight when one's main enemy is one's daughter. In the struggle between parents and children, there are no winners. Everyone wins and everyone loses. The contest needed to quieten down.

"I'm ashamed of you, mother!"

"Maria das Dores's sacrifice was made for you, so that you wouldn't suffer."

Jacinta did all she could to bring back Maria das Dores. But she encountered a barrier, always the same answer: it's not worth it! Adults are predators of innocence. They grab a virgin, they stab her and bury her, with a frenzied waving of axes, like Indians dancing around the fire, celebrating the magical joy harvested from children's spasms, just as cowboys on the American prairies take delight in gunning down bison.

She sought counsel from the church and explained the problem. They folded their arms and declared: she is no longer chaste, there's no point, all this while the priest, in his sermons, screamed: slavery must end, exploitation and forced labor. The people must be freed and there must be greater harmony between the races. Deportations must stop, so that families may grow and live together. But what about the case of Maria das Dores? It's too late, there's no point.

Jacinta was in despair and conducted a silent monologue: Ah! Maria das Dores. No one's interested in you anymore, because you're no longer a virgin, you've been stained, dishonored. They're burying your body under rocks, you don't exist for them anymore. They'd rather go to the aid of a woman who's been held up by a robber of papayas, bananas, or manioc. As for you, they've deprived you of your existence, your life and your dream, no one helps you and they all say there's no point.

She despaired, unaware that a day would come when the whole world would prostrate itself before blacks to ask for their forgiveness over slavery. She couldn't even imagine when men from all over the world would get down on their knees to beg all the women for their forgiveness because of the oppression, exclusion and violence visited upon them ever since the world was born.

After all her frustrated efforts, Jacinta vented her fury on her mother.

"Mother, you killed Maria das Dores."

"Not at all. She's with her man. And she is well loved."

"Why didn't you make us all the same, mother? Why didn't you make us all either blacks or mulattoes? Why did you erect this division, this border?"

Ah, Jacinta! One day you'll acknowledge all the good I did for you."

"Mother, I'll never thank you for a crime. You buried your daughter alive. Why did you hate Maria das Dores so much?"

Delfina didn't hate Maria das Dores. Nor did she hate herself. She hated the world. The regime. She hated the differences that created masters and slaves. She couldn't hate her. Maria das Dores was an obedient girl, a tireless worker, a waitress in the bar, a cook, a seller of bread at the local market. She made sure the house and the children were clean, and did everything so that Jacinta was left free to study without any interference. The daughter who had put up with her mother's bad temper without ever complaining, because she was black and without a father. No, she couldn't hate her.

At that moment, Delfina missed Maria das Dores, as she sat on the veranda, her head in the air, watching the moon rise from the heart of the ocean. She missed the joy in Jacinta's eyes after she had had her hair done and listened to the stories about the stars and centaurs. She missed the time when she was often hauled away from the bar by Maria das Dores, and, drunk and exhausted, was dragged home, where her daughter would undress her, take off her shoes, and cover her with a clean, sweet-smelling sheet. And she would plant a kiss on her like someone sowing a flower. She never told her daughter how much she loved her, because love, like pain, has many ways of manifesting itself. Only love between a man and a woman requires songs and incantations. Love between a mother and her children is shown in outbursts of anger and ugly words, because it is sweet, supple, pliable, without artifice, and so natural that it doesn't require great speeches or praise.

"I hate you, Delfina. My presence here is a mistake, I wasn't born from you, nor are you worthy of a daughter like me."

"One day, you'll understand, even if you can't forgive me. You're a daughter of this black belly, like the green palms undulating throughout Zambezia. You're mine. Forever mine!"

Jacinta was seized by a sudden feeling of revolt. Of tears and hysteria. She screamed against a father who had left her alone in the hands of a mad woman. Who had brought her into the world via the womb of a black woman and not that of his white wife who was known for all her virtues. She screamed against the absence of Maria das Dores, so obvious in the squalor of the house, the disordered kitchen, and her grades that were dwindling by the day because she no longer had someone to check her handwriting, so evident from her untidy hair, in the stories about rabbits and monsters Maria das Dores told, in the lullabies she would sing until she fell asleep, while their mother tended to her own beauty and gazed at herself in the mirror.

Jacinta wept and addressed the wind.

"I'm all alone, Maria das Dores. Without a father or mother, with two little brothers who are as lost as I am. I don't know how to cook, I don't know how to wash, I don't know how to get food. Ever since you left, we eat badly, we eat trash. What's lacking is your artistic touch to everything we eat. We eat the greens from our grandmother's garden and the leftover fish given to us by the fishermen on the quay. Delfina eats salt cod on her own and drinks wine that tastes of sin. She is still as pretty as ever."

Some days later, Jacinta packed her bags along with those of her brothers, and they left. Their white godparents and the black and white nuns responded immediately and hastened to keep them away from that pit of perdition. They took all of them in except for Maria das Dores. She was already a lost cause, for she was pregnant and the prisoner of an evil witchdoctor, there was no point. To complete things, a social worker ordered Delfina to be issued with a certificate of moral ineptitude, and sent all the children off to college.

Delfina shivered when she saw her daughter carrying out all her threats, hitting her at all her most vital points until she could no longer breathe. She had suffered a defeat equivalent to death, and with all the cruel refinements. She was on her own. Late into the night, she called for Maria das Dores, before remembering she had left for good. She started to have a drink in the morning, in order to allay the pain of waking up. A drink in the afternoon to kill off the strength of her memory. And another at night, to kill off nightmares and fall asleep.

◆　◆　◆

Delfina sees herself as a heroine. She sees no evil in any of her acts. She taught everyone a lesson. She showed that the fierce white man was, after all, human, who could be domesticated through love. She showed that black women were people too, could love white men and set up a family. She inverted the rules of the game. If she had been a good little girl, she would have ended up just one among all the other women. Without a history. Anonymous. Who was born, gave birth, and died. But she is a landmark. A point of reference. Everyone talks about the times when Delfina was young. When she was married to a black man and when she was married to a white. She was the first black woman to live in a house that had electricity. The first to have a house built of concrete, with a tin roof in the black neighborhood. The first white man to live in the black neighborhood was hers. She was the first black woman to live in the white neighborhood. The older men sigh for her: Delfina, how beautiful she was! Delfina, the queen! Who defied whites, defied the system, waged war, won and lost, and was lost because of the life she led. That was why her life was turned into song, into stories, into poetry. She is a parable. A proverb. That is Delfina.

Delfina, oh so fina
She slept with white men
On account of tea and sugar

◆　　◆　　◆

Sunrise is as painful as bearing a child. Impregnating the womb of night. Breaking the membrane of the earth and the dawn.

Overcoming the force, remoteness, and baffling power of the dark clouds on the horizon. Sprouting out of the ground. Smiling. Releasing all its inner light to bring comfort to the earth, cause flowers to open and the world to be lit up.

From nature, Delfina learned how many flaming torches it takes to make a sun. She summons her remaining strength and carries out an old dream of hers: to open a brothel with young virgin girls on call. She embarks on a huge recruitment drive in villages, with the help of some sepoys. Some black mothers, moved by the myth of honor, lead their daughters by the hand to be broken in by Delfina's clients.

Her house hosts a parade of satisfied old colonists, drinking virginities and glasses of blood, trampling living bodies with their soldiers' boots, demolishing any moral qualms with the strength of their gold. And after all that, Delfina hands the girls one or two paltry coins, a basket of dried cod and olives and a bottle of quinquina wine. And her hands are once again awash with gold.

Many of those girls, trembling while displaying themselves, famished, hurt, barefoot, will bring into the world children of the new race, children of unknown fathers, who in future will have to rummage around among the roots of History in search of their identity.

27

In the beginning of all beginnings, the world belonged solely to women. They planted, hunted, built, and life flourished. Human beings, like the flora, were born from the soil. It was enough to plant a pumpkin seed, and pumpkins grew. After a few months, the pumpkins would open like hens' eggs, releasing the most beautiful women on the planet. One day, one of the women went hunting and caught a strange being. It looked like a person, but had no bosom. It had hair on its chin and, unlike other creatures, it sported a short tail in front and not behind. They seized this creature and took it to the queen. The queen looked and was astonished. She gave orders for the animal to be washed and brought back to her. The animal had a certain magic. A mere glance from it provoked concentric massages around the heart, the chest, and the mind. When she touched it, her blood raced and her heart thumped. The queen found herself doing the dance of the moon and the snake, while her lips spouted poems that had never before been recited. From the animal's tail, a serpent emerged, at first timid, then violent, which knocked the queen over while it sought a harbor for its head. It found a subterranean passage, and immediately burrowed into it and hid. The queen quivered and surrendered. She let out the first sigh of love and discovered that the animal was in fact a man. She started to get fatter and fatter until she couldn't hunt anymore. After some time, a child was born.

The animal went back to his own domains and spoke of his discovery. He was, in fact, also a king. He invited his people to embark on an expedition to the wonderland he had just visited. The men came, and colonized all the women and set themselves up as lords and masters. That's how the first episode of love and of hatred occurred. Received with love, they robbed the women of their power and that was why they were condemned to travel ever further to hunt and to work all the harder to sustain them.

That is why the men die in wars, in the mines and in the plantations, so that they can take their promised success back home with them. That was what happened with the sailors. Received with love, they ended up as masters. They tried to flatten everything and return home to their ladies in triumph. They failed. You cannot put the whole of Zambezia onto a ship. Or an airplane. Nor can you destroy all life with the force of your weapons.

< 383 >

* * *

In the world where the woman is boss, the children are José's, Abdul's, Ndialo's, Charles's, Lu Xing's, Stefan's. The family weighs the same as the wind, it is light and floats through the air like a cloud stitched with the blood of different colors, shapes and textures. Joy and freedom are the offspring of a matriarchy, where the laws of nature are obeyed because only the woman knows who the real fathers of her children are. Men are mere reproducers, minor actors. That's why they have to pay for everything. For leisure, and for the pleasure the women concede them. They have to pay for motherhood and for the dignity that women give them, because without them they wouldn't be able to build a family.

In the world where the man is boss, the children belong to one man alone. The family weighs as heavy as lead, stitched together by threads of the same blood. But it's a kingdom of tears and suffering. And violence, for the men ensure their women's fidelity by wielding a big stick. Violence is the product of patriarchy, because men robbed women of their power.

28

No, Maria das Dores's arrival didn't cause any drama. The two older wives felt what any woman would feel in the same situation: they were hurt, humiliated, and consigned to the scrap heap. They stifled their protests, but masked their pain with pursed lips. They accepted it doggedly. If it weren't with that woman, then it would be with another. If it hadn't happened like that, it would happen some other way.

Simba only had eyes for Maria das Dores. He gave her flowers, presents, chocolates, cookies, which she received like a lifeless goat. While he was doing this, he softened his other wives' jealousy with salt and beatings. That is why they lamented their own fate with sarcastic comments.

"Pretty woman, may you be blessed! With your arrival, there are three of us to occupy just one man's heart. Young woman, are you crying? Why, if marriage is such a painless state? Smile, for like us, you will be indulged by the magic spells of this house."

He taught her to drink. To smoke a bit of soruma to make her relax, while he gradually increased the dosage. Little by little, she began to forget the things of old. To find the poverty surrounding her normal. To live with that lack of cleanliness. To put up with the man on whom she was more and more dependent, because of the alcohol and drug she consumed. When, for some reason, she disobeyed him, he only applied one form of punishment: he withheld her drug, and filled her with anxiety. The other women openly expressed their delight.

"Beloved woman, do you think you're the only one? What do you have that we haven't got? Every day sees the birth of another beautiful woman. You are a sweetheart, for sure, but for only a short time. Soon, other women will come and you'll be forgotten. Women are flowers, they open in the morning, and wither away at night."

One day, she tried to pound maize with the eldest wife. She tried hard but failed. She was languid. Drunk. She reeked. The older woman remarked:

"You came here fresh and pretty, Maria das Dores. Now, you're old, and you smell of alcohol. You've become worn down in no time at all."

"Do you think so?"

Maria das Dores took a look at herself and agreed. I've grown old, yes. Eighteen years old. Three children. I'm no longer the same, I feel it. I was thirteen when I came here. How is it that time has gone by so quickly? Where was I that I never noticed the days flashing by? I have no father, no mother, and I'm here in this inferno where I was abandoned. This isn't my home. This man isn't my man, but my mother's. What would my man be like? Tall and handsome like a film star? Kind and caring like my father, José?

"You won't even need a coffin for your funeral, because you're already buried."

"I'm not dead," Maria das Dores replied defensively.

"Just look at yourself!"

"Love is beautiful, constructive, Maria das Dores. What love is this that kills you, sucks you dry, ties you down?"

She stopped and thought. Simba said he loved her deeply. But what kind of love was that if she was delivered here through hatred? Maybe it was the love of soruma they smoked together. The love of rum they got drunk on, while indulging in the biggest orgies in the world.

I think I really am dead, she said to herself. My first child was inserted into my womb, in a pregnancy I never really took in or felt, numb as my bodily organs were. Not even the birth hurt me, hypnotized as I was by the alcohol and the resentment. It was the same with the second child. The third time, I thought I was going to die. My muscles, anesthetized by the soruma, didn't react. They had to cut me open in the hospital for the baby to be born. It was a miracle I survived, according to the doctors.

"Can it be that I'm so worn down, so over the hill?" Dores asked, shocked.

"Can't you see?"

One day, the three women were talking about what happened in the bedroom, their favorite topic of conversation. Maria das Dores mentioned one or two intimate things and the others were horrified.

"That's devilish, sodomy, sinful, that's not something he should do to a wife. Men do that with prostitutes, you shouldn't put up with it. He's killing you bit by bit."

"Killing me?"

"Oh, dear girl, open your eyes and grow up. He is indulging in malign practices that will eventually kill you."

At that point, Maria das Dores got scared. Every time they talked, they repeated the same thing: he's going to kill you, he's slowly killing you. Can it be I'm going to die? My God, I'm nobody in this world, I don't exist. He's going to kill me because I have no father or mother to defend me. Because I'm Delfina's shadow. It's her Simba is angry at, not me. But I'm the one who suffers the torture. It's me he's killing, I'm not from this place, I don't exist. This life I lead here has nothing to do with me. The jealousy he shows toward me isn't directed at me, but at my mother.

Mother, why did you leave me here? The roof leaks, the floor is of beaten earth, I don't have a bed, I sleep on a mat, in the damp, shackled like the slaves of old. Simba goes off in the morning, leaving me shackled, and only frees me when he returns in the evening. And he brings me food himself. In this polygamous household, even the children insult me and smile when they would rather bite me. They lament my fate as a drunkard and then they feed my lethargy with other forms of poison. They pillory me and say I stole their place in their man's heart. How long will I go on living like this, mother? I'm involved in a war that I didn't even start. This is a home ruled over with military discipline, with whippings and punishments. Mother, these women have given me their heavy crosses to bear, I who did them no harm, I don't know why, mother, but why did you bring me here?

I am Simba's spouse, married according to religious law, in a ceremony that had no party and no wedding cake. I got married in a dress made from bed linen, bought in the market, and sewn by a street tailor, of the kind you see seated in front of shops. You didn't even come, mother. Nor were there any guests. The ceremony was short, hurried, it was just a question of entering the church, signing a few papers and leaving again. Simba was happy, he pocketed the certificate, took me home and then went out again. He then arranged to get a certificate of mental incapacity from the use of narcotics that he himself administered.

One of the women, furious, one day blurted out:

"What a marriage you got yourself into, Maria das Dores! Not even your mother was invited. With all that money you inherited, there wasn't even a wedding reception, nor any pomp, or special food, nothing! Why was Simba in such a hurry to lead you to the altar the moment you reached eighteen? He married your inheritance, that's what he did. Our lives got better thanks to your money. We're living well now, can't you see?"

It was then that she began to understand what before she had been blind to. The hurried marriage when she reached eighteen. The certificate of insanity. Then, she really became alarmed: the next step will be my death, I've got to get out of here. I've got to find a place

< 390 >

of my own, a shelter, where I can light a fire and tell my little ones beautiful stories, far away from this place.

She desperately set about thinking how to escape. But where to? The world is big but there are few hiding places. Maybe she should go and pick tea on the plantations. Or become a prostitute in the bars. She started to think more clearly. She wouldn't go to either of those places. She wanted to go somewhere open. Far from everything and everyone, where she could live unnoticed like a plant or a lizard. She wanted a house without any walls or a roof. Without a fence around the backyard. A place of freedom and silence. It was then that she recalled all the myths about sacred mountains that attract all souls in their hour of need. She started to dream about hearts of stone. Where stones go to die. And she felt the call of the mountains of Namuli coursing through her veins. Would she go alone? Would she leave her children in that wretched place? No. The death of the pumpkin vine portends the death of the pumpkins. She would relinquish her inheritance, it didn't matter. Life was worth more than any amount of gold.

◆   ◆   ◆

She waited for the right hour and slipped away quietly early in the morning. Her head was full of fears and dreams. She was carrying Rosinha on her back. Benedito and Fernando were walking beside her. They are going to have a bathe in the river while I wash the clothes — she explained, as she said goodbye. In the bowl used for clothes, she had hidden some food for the journey into the unknown, a journey to discover the world and all its luminosity.

Where am I going? I'm going in search of my father, in the sacred soil of the mountains. And if I die during this quest, it will merely be another death on top of all the ones I have already suffered.

She climbed aboard the early morning bus and savored the pleasure of traveling while seated and seeing the trees flash by. She covered great distances. One hour. Two. Six. The journey seemed endless. But she marveled at all she saw. During her years of captivity, she hadn't seen a single street or highway. And she didn't even remember what it was like to breathe in fresh air. Or the rattling of a bus. She smelt the pleasant aroma of the earth and the renewed green of the plants. She sat taking in the landscape of valleys and mountains, of rivers and bridges. She traveled with her face turned towards the window for fear of being recognized. Her escape had to be perfect. She decided to get off before the bus reached its terminus in order to slip away from any possible searches, just in case Simba had put the police on her trail. She wanted to reach her destination in the dead of night.

She reached the city of Gúruè in the early evening, and breathed a sigh of relief. She had arrived in the Promised Land. She looked. The mountains displayed their eternal profile. So high. A silver tear in the corner of the mountain's eye, the source of the river. The tea plantations, the pine wood, the eucalyptus forest. And she felt her mind go weak. With anxiety. Hunger. Fear of being found and returned to the place where she had lived as a prisoner. It became vital for her to reach a cavern high up on the mountainside that very night. So that she could live unnoticed for a while. She began to climb, loaded down with three young children who couldn't walk because they were so sleepy. Exhausted and hungry.

As she climbed. Remorse and fear began to disturb her conscience. She felt ashamed for not having had the strength to support a home, for not having been able to accept her destiny, eventually dragging her children off into a life where the future was uncertain. She admonished herself for her selfishness in taking her children away from their family ties. Suddenly, she felt hungry. She felt thirsty for liquor and wanted to smoke some grass to give her courage to face the future.

High up on the mountainside, she paused for breath. How hard it is to climb a mountain. How hard it is to find one's own space. How hard it is to find oneself. She summoned all the strength she had and began to climb again. Rosinha had long ago stopped crying. She started to panic and prayed silently: cry, Rosinha, cry and show me you can still get some air in those lungs of yours. She was scared of the night now falling. Of the people passing by in the distance. Of the owl now embarking on its gloomy serenade. Of the hiss of the snake she could hear among the bushes. She saw vultures flying around her, right in front of her eyes. Her knees trembled. Her body caved in, and she collapsed. She lost consciousness.

She woke up in a white room, with a white bed and white sheets. With white people dressed in white. Can it be I'm in heaven? She looked around her. For it to be paradise, there would have to be the sky, blue, trumpets and angels. The people around her had a gender, they couldn't be angels. They lacked the bodily swiftness caused by the absence of gravity. She felt her mouth dry. A pain in her arm. In heaven, pains don't exist, everything is joyful. She discovered she was in a hospital. How did she end up there? She looked everywhere for her children. She couldn't see them. She became delirious.

"Where am I? Why am I imprisoned here?"

"Sleep, girl, you need to rest," a nun said, with a smile like the sun.

< 394 >

"You were brought here on a stretcher by some soldiers who were training in the mountains. You're in the military hospital."

"Where's my little Rosinha? I want Benedito. Where is Fernando?"

"They're not far away and they're fine. Rosinha is out of danger."

"Danger? My God, my daughter's in danger!"

"Come on now, don't fret. The worst has passed. Calm down, and I'll go and fetch them. Look, I found these dolls for them. Relax, and I'll be back in a minute with Rosinha."

At that point, the lights in her mind were extinguished. In the sky, the stars suggested destinies. She advanced, a somnambulist, sailing in her moonlit vessel, roaming over the whole ocean and the earth until she had completed and surpassed all the phases of the moon. Seeking in every heavenly season: have you seen my children? My real children, not these who neither cry nor suckle. And the wind replied: yes, we have seen them. There. Over there. Over yonder. And when she reached that point, she got the same answer. Over there. Right there. And off she went again, until she had completed a full circuit of the earth.

Maria das Dores hurled her thoughts at the moon, while her body remained on the earth, in a journey that left all the inhabitants of the world dumbstruck. Her feet would come to know the entire surface of the planet, moved by the invisible wheels of hope. She would learn how to work out how many lines it takes to draw the frontiers of the world, how many people it takes to fill a country, and how many races it takes to build a nation.

In the hospital, there really were three babies, given birth to by a mountain, and carried by a nun in the beak of a stork.

"Your mother set off in the ship of the moon," the nun would tell them one day. "She lives up there at the top of the mountain, where only saints can go. You are the children of Namuli, and I reared you on goats' milk."

And she welcomed them and became their godmother. A protective mother. One day, your mother will return, she always said, and she will come down from the mountains on the wings of an angel.

❖   ❖   ❖

Two wives anxiously await the return of their husband who has vanished. They shriek. They weep. They lament. Their children too are anxious. Simba disappeared early one morning. After willing Delfina to be reduced to ash.

< 396 >

It was unusual for Simba to be gripped by a desire to destroy everything and leave without giving his anger time to abate. No one saw him leave. Where did this fevered, crazy reaction stem from? Where did his sudden love for Maria das Dores originate? He wandered, mad, ragged, unkempt. Was it out of love or injured pride? Many believe he went mad and threw himself into the sea after a frustrated attempt to commit suicide. Others believe he's just gone for a wander and will return. If he took all his belongings with him, it means he didn't die, but left. Everyone says it was Delfina who delivered the curse. Whatever she touches is reduced to dust.

29

Maria Jacinta is in front of the altar. She is getting married at the age of nineteen. Ah! How time has passed so quickly! It seems like only yesterday that she was born. It seems like only yesterday that she was playing with dolls and I was carrying her around, her hair tied with silk ribbons, mothers sigh, time has passed and we are getting old. One day, Maria Jacinta left college and met the love of her life. And now, there she is, to confirm all this in matrimony. A Jacinta who is now a woman. A Jacinta who is a flower. Young, lovely Jacinta.

Delfina is at the door of the church. She sees the bride, her dear Jacinta. And her eyes widen, hypnotized by the image. The whiteness of her dress makes her brown skin even lighter, so much so she even looks like a white woman. She is moved. There is love in the air, peace, the perfume of a romantic kiss. There is so much beauty bedecking the day, so many flowers, such a heady scent. A cry of triumph explodes deep within Delfina, she feels once again as if she is looking down on the world from on high, and singing like a partridge, gurué, gurué! I have won! Gurué, gurué, my dream has come true, Jacinta is now the beautiful wife of a white man! Everything has happened exactly as I asked for in my prayers.

How is my Jacinta feeling at this very moment? Delfina wonders, if I too felt emotional on my wedding day. My eyes all confused, my mind dizzy. A whole host of eyes on me. I was the queen.

Marriage offers a moment of peace. Delfina is there to beg her daughter's forgiveness, create a dialog with the past and effect some form of reconciliation. She didn't receive an invitation to the wedding, but she has come. She is determined to stay to the end, even if all the stones in the world are thrown at her. As Jacinta climbs the altar steps, Delfina weeps. That moment represents the crowning reward for all her sacrifices. She detects all the family likenesses in her face. She has the eyes of Soares, her father. Her grandmother Serafina's mouth. And she even sees her daughter Maria das Dores as well. They are both very alike. One black woman, the other a mulatto girl. Both of them her daughters. Zezinho is an adult, he's handsome, just like his father, José dos Montes. Luisinho, has a large head and slender fingers. Like Soares. Only Maria das Dores is missing from this scene.

At a moment of high emotion, one's lifetime is compressed. The beginning and the end touch each other. Recollections of a trajectory.

From the act of giving birth. Teething. The first steps taken. The sacrifices made. The little moments of joy.

A white woman stands next to the bride, in the role of her mother. Delfina seethes with jealousy. That's her place, for it is her daughter, the grandeur of that moment is hers too. But Delfina forfeited everything at the time of the angry exchanges. The family disintegrated, the children left, and that woman rescued the children from the wreckage of life. The white woman had become their godmother and had taken care of the little ones' education while Delfina enjoyed herself. Jacinta grew up in the convent school, where she led a harsh, sober life, which wiped away the recollections of a libertine mother that she had absorbed in her infancy. Now, she is reaping the rewards of her own efforts.

Delfina summons up all her courage to approach her. It isn't an easy step to take. A moment of expectation hangs over them and everyone awaits the outcome. What will happen? At first, Jacinta averts her gaze laden with surprise. As if she doesn't know her. Inside her, anger rages. What has this wanton woman come here to do? Images flash across her mind. Memories of her childhood. Racial animosities. The struggle to create a space that any mulatto is subjected to. To make

< 400 >

new friends, a new family made from the remnants of acceptance, of negation, by blacks and whites. To find her equals in a world without blacks or whites, where she can feel at peace, where she can be heard and accepted, without a finger being pointed at her, a weapon, some defect. A more humane world where people can be viewed with more seriousness, greater maturity. Blacks and whites accuse mulattoes of all the world's evils: criminality, prostitution, frivolity. Maria Jacinta takes a deep breath — I am the fruit of these conflicts, no, I shan't let you near me, mother.

Delfina senses she is going to lose that daughter for good. But what does it mean to lose a child? A child is never lost, it leaves. That is why it abandons its mother's womb. That is why it breaks the umbilical cord. That is why it wounds, draws blood, even kills at the moment of birth, because a child never belongs to the mother, but to the world.

All Delfina wanted was to hug her daughter in that instant. Touch her. She knows she can't. Her hands are full of stains, of crimes, that could sully the purity of that moment. But even without touching her, she celebrates. That daughter, after all, is hers. The honor, after all, belongs to her. She takes another step toward Jacinta and stops. She trembles. Her daughter's eyes are those of a warrior woman with her weapon at the ready, for a duel to the death. They look into each other's eyes. They are two souls fated to such an encounter. Foreshadowing a beginning or an end.

"You're beautiful, dear Jacinta!"

"Where's Maria das Dores?" Jacinta asks, hissing aggressively.

Jacinta's words are abrasive, cutting. Delfina responds with silence, emptily. She understands. The old war continues unflagging, and the return of Maria das Dores is the only measure that will bring about reconciliation. She releases two tears and snivels. With her eyes, she asks for forgiveness.

"She is still lost out there in the world."

"Delfina, I shall never look at you again until you bring back Maria das Dores to me."

"Forgive me, daughter."

"Don't touch me, don't sully me, you black whore. Keep away from me, forget you ever brought me into the world, you tramp."

Delfina resists. For a mother is a mother. All she wanted was to witness the marriage of the daughter who had been born from her womb, and then leave without trace. This is why she resists and mutters: "you are part of me and my blood flows through your veins. This white dress of yours is the product of my suffering."

< 402 >

Delfina feels comforted by the offence she believes she deserves. She retreats to the back of the church and sits down in the last row, unnoticed by all. History is repeating itself. It was that pew that welcomed her at the time when the nun accused her of distracting the priests with sinful desires. She huddled in her corner like an intruder, fearing being chased away at any moment. While the marriage ceremony is underway, she asks for a blessing and forgiveness. For herself. For everything. For everyone. In her silence, she dreams of the miracle of reconciliation and of Maria das Dores's return. And she feels pride in seeing that daughter at the altar, who has inherited all her virtues from her mother. To fight for her dreams. She knew she was a mulatto woman, and inferior. She followed the example of her mother, fished a white man and married him. A daughter who grew up cared for by the wind. Who learned how to remove the thorns on her road ahead and lay them with flowers. Pure. A virgin. With a diploma in her hand and a ring on her finger.

She goes to the reception, led by Zezinho, who was aware of the conflict and chose a quiet, unseen corner from where she could watch the wedding celebration continue. She sits there, huddled, contemplating the scene. Weddings are all alike. Food, music, and dancing. Gifts and flowers. Special speeches. Jacinta completely ignores her

< 403 >

mother. Even so, Delfina enjoys seeing her dream fulfilled. She feels she has reached the most beautiful star in the heavens and has opened up a route to the impossible. She feels as much joy in her heart as she would if that garland of flowers were on her own head. And it is. For it is her blood flowing through the bride.

Maria Jacinta gets to her feet to thank those present and Delfina is assailed by a feeling of panic. And shock. On their wedding day, brides are supposed to be beautiful and tearful. Give a speech? What has Maria Jacinta got to tell the world?

"I would like to thank all those present. Today is a very emotional day for me, for I finally have a family."

She then begins to understand what she hadn't seen before. That only a chameleon changes its color. That a black is always a black and should learn to take pride in being so. She begins to understand the messages of resistance conveyed in the strikes on the palm plantations. You can't be black and white at the same time. She remembers the rebel songs. The land was mine and they stole it from me. My body was mine, and they used it. This bride is my daughter and they have stolen her from me. Ah! If I were younger, I would take out a weapon and fight for my dignity and for everything they took from me.

"I was weaned on coconut milk and goat's milk. My mother died in childbirth. I never even saw her face. My father, I knew him well. He would carry me around in his arms and sing me the most beautiful lullabies."

Her speech is a brutal awakening to things of the past. Jacinta pays no heed to the grave consequences for her emotional wellbeing or that of her mother. She launches forth into a bombastic speech replete with caustic words. Delfina feels a shiver. She freezes. She discovers the color of her daughter's eyes. Sparkling blue like the eyes of a cat. Penetrating. Hypnotic. The strength of her voice. Undulating. Commanding. Vibrant. Gentle and rebellious. A committed fighter. A warrior woman. A heroine. She feels as if she's in a theater of war. Her daughter is disposed to shout until she has drained all the clouds in the sky and produced a great flood. She wants to free herself from the monolith of her nightmares, and sweep the thorns of time away from her heart.

"I had a sister who was taken away from me. She was kidnapped by a witch and got lost along the pathways of life. She was black like the color of the earth. She would braid my hair on moonlit nights and tell me dreamlike stories. Each night, she would collect a star for me and place it on my forehead, to chase away any bad dreams I might have."

Jacinta's voice dictates silence. Memories. It is a red sword edged with smoke. It is fire in the struggle for the beginning of life: the child tearing through the mother's belly amid screams and blood, in the centuries-long battle. A cry shakes Delfina and rises to the roof of her mouth. But her dome is of glass, and hermetically sealed, and stifles her shout. It is a fight between fire and time, in the decorative ambience of a wedding reception.

Where has that courage come from, that steely coldness of Jacinta? It came from Delfina, who had taught her the lesson of difference ever since she lay in the cradle. In her lullabies, she sang that humanity consisted of races. That races had stigmas, and were organized in strata, categories. That courage came from her hatred of her origins. From her need for self-affirmation and the pleasure derived from hurting. From the urgent need she felt to cut the umbilical cord that attached her to her origins and her past. From the need to wipe Delfina away from her life's path. From her need to predict the future. Eliminate any potential problem, for maybe her white husband is averse to the idea of having a black mother-in-law.

There is thunderous applause from the crowd. Among all those

< 406 >

present, there is a collective sense of jubilation and vengeance. This was a speech that earned the praise of the white women, who harbored their hurt in coffins of silence against Delfina, the queen of forbidden love. The desecrator of god-fearing households. At last the fiend had been unmasked. Delfina tries to get up and flee in order to save herself from the howls of a bitch who had emerged from her womb. But her feet are in the grip of sorrow, nerves, hatred. She curses under her breath.

"Ah, my dear Jacinta! You didn't come into this world borne by a stork! You came from me, you're the projection of my dreams as a woman. I went and fetched you. I brought you down from the mountains of darkness. I placed you on the pedestal of life and made you fit to be a white man's spouse. You personify my whole struggle and my triumph."

Doubts begin to hover in the minds of the guests. Who is the one being dragged down: is it the daughter or the mother? Can a daughter wash a family's dirty linen in public on a wedding day? To spit in a mother's face is the same as spitting at oneself. To insult a mother is to insult one's own destiny. Can it be that this girl has an education? Does she think?

"Jacinta, one day you'll call out for me. I'm more important to you

< 407 >

than all these whites who deceive you. My power is much greater than theirs. This light that shines upon you comes from my blood. I'm the one who holds the key to the box where your umbilical cord is kept. I am the pillar you lean against to rest. I know the direction your life will take. The stones on your road meet each other and come together. You will hoist white flags, in your search for me at the source of all shadows. And you will shed tears in the wind as you seek answers from my parched throat. And I will reply with words you cannot hear because I'll be on the other side of the world. I sold myself, I humiliated myself to provide you with bread and a roof over your head. I turned myself into a tramp in order to prepare your victory plinth. I never left you. You are the one who abandoned me, and who chose your own world.

There is dynamite in Delfina. There is an explosion. The high mountain collapses into boulders that roll down the precipice. Marriage is a celebration of love, not a manifestation of pain. She mumbles imperceptibly.

"Why are you denying me, Jacinta?"

She was looking for the origin but found the end. Her illusion diluted like salt and Delfina sipped salty water from her glass used to toast the bride.

< 408 >

"I don't regret anything. I went to live among a swarm of whites and became a queen bee to the astonishment of the world. I was stung so many times that I went dizzy, but I won. I entered the duel between the races and proved I was human. I fought with all the weapons at my disposal. I went from invader to victor. And today, it's the blood of a black person that's being celebrated. Today, love heralds new dawns. I found in life everything I was searching for. Your nineteen years are stages, steps, phases in my journey as a black woman. One day, you will understand what today you cannot see."

Delfina manages to open her mouth and speak out loud.

"Why are you doing this to me, Jacinta?"

The guests exchange looks of complicity and avert their eyes. For the speech is malign, as it turns a wedding feast into a funeral wake. People whisper to each other: poor bridegroom! He's taking home a viper in the shape of a queen. What kind of daughter is this who slits her mother's throat, and serves up her head on a golden platter at her enemy's banquet? If she despises her own mother, what will she do with her mother-in-law and all her other in-laws? A mother is always a mother, whatever her origins. It's a blessing to have her alive and by our side. You aren't given a mother in response to an official request or concession. A mother is what God gave us. Jacinta

< 409 >

will learn one day. That the cure also kills. And the hands that hold you on high to the heavens also bury you. The world that places a crown of gold on your head, can also give you a crown of thorns. In love, the mouth that kisses you can also humiliate you.

"Jacinta, my precious one! I came here to beg for your love so that I could break this chain of pain. I ask you for forgiveness! It is I who gave you this sun, this moon, this wonderful moment that dignifies you. You have beaten me. You have pulled down my throne, and spread my secrets among enemies. But I forgive you for everything, because I am your mother. After God and your father, I am the most important person in the world for you."

She shuts her eyes and shakes her head as if strange birds were pecking at her eardrums. A magic wand touches the middle of her head. She curls up tighter and tighter and feels herself getting smaller and smaller. She raises her head and tries to glimpse the world. All she can see is the monstrous creature she has created. From her tired chest, she lets out her last breath.

"Jacinta, my angel, you will know the desert!"

Delfina expresses all her agony with old words. Ancient terms. Ones that she heard so many times from her father, and which had come from her father's father. What Delfina does not know is that

< 410 >

these words contain magic. Words uttered in anger turn into prophecies, and come true. A word is a prayer.

A stifled scream is heard exploding within her. She feels a million needles pricking her stomach. She leans over the floor and keels over. She faints. Zezinho rushes forward to help his mother. And he picks the prostrate Delfina up from the floor. The ambulance is called and takes her away.

Life is made of contrasts. Weeping and singing. Screaming and dancing. The bride and bridegroom smile for the photographer and kiss each other on the lips. They cut the bridal cake, with its five layers and its silk ribbons. The guests clap their hands and the voice of Amália Rodrigues belts out one of her melodies.

São caracóis, são caracolitos
São espanhóis, espanholitos.

Delfina's heart dances in free fall. In shock. She sowed winds and reaped storms.

I turned my body into a cornfield where any sailor with a thirst for gold could drop anchor. The light that dazzles you, also dazzled me. Your words today, were spoken by me yesterday. The world you dream of, I dreamed of too, oh yes, my dear Jacinta!

< 411 >

Delfina sees a line in the sea. A highway in the air. She sees her daughter ever further away. The earth opening up into a great abyss and they are eternally separated by a fast-flowing river.

Jacinta has said what she had to say. What she said, she had learned from her mother. Despising the darker skinned, and preferring those of lighter hue. If her own mother despised her two children because they were black, what obligation did she have to accept a black mother, and in public?

"Where are you taking me, Zezinho?"

"To the hospital."

"Where am I? Stop, leave me here."

"No, you're not well, mother. You were delirious and passed out."

"I feel sick."

"Ah!"

"But that voice I heard? Was it hers?"

"Whose?"

"My Jacinta. What did she say?"

"I didn't hear. Did she say something?"

She jumped out of the car by the seashore. She vomited. A vomit of red wine, baked salt codfish and black olives. A black and red vomit, a vomit of blood. And she takes deep breaths of sea air. Of malediction. Of treachery. She opens her throat and speaks to the waves.

"Maria Jacinta! Be careful with the words you use! With your tongue you can tear up the flowers along your path, and you can also mold the clay of life. With your tongue, you can erect the bars of a cage and also sketch out the path to freedom. Jacinta, my precious one!"

The waves dance in their perpetual youth and she walks, her head bowed, vanquished by life. She kicks off her shoes and paddles in the waters on the shoreline. She feels a deep weariness and falls asleep in the embrace of the waves. She wakes with a start.

"What happened to me?"

She looks at herself. Her clothes are torn. All she has left is her mother's heart and her black skin. Footprints in broken circles left in the soil, revealing the geometry of her journey.

"I sought the pathways to happiness without knowing that happiness lies in the step you take each day. My struggle dressed in glory has lost its gown. I don't regret it. I entered the war and enjoyed the taste of victory. But my greatness was no more the chicken's feathers on my body. The paradise I looked for was the wind and the clouds in their aimless wandering. I betrayed the man of my life. I destroyed your father's home. Now it's you who despise me. Can it be that my wars were worth nothing at all?"

Was there really a wedding? It can't have been more than a bad dream. The voice she heard must have been the expression of her inner ghosts. She sees her satin hat floating. Yes, of course, there was a celebration of love.

"I know you love me, Jacinta, I know that deep down, you love me. But I am your shame and your disgrace. You don't want to see me like this, drunk. But if I don't drink, how am I going to face up to my night-time ghosts? You don't want to see me with many men, I know. But the war for survival made me what I am today."

True love lies in the full udders of a dairy cow. In the spring sun that causes the fields to come into flower. In the crickets that fill the ears of the world with peace. In the fire and ice that are the vectors of humanity, the incubator of life. In the night and in the light that produce the cycles of darkness and sunlight. In the black coal, the source of fire, which makes the winter more romantic and cozy. True love lies in the hands of the blacks and whites who together planted the palm groves of Zambezia, waged war, hated each other, succumbed to Cupid's bow and loved each other in the shadows, gave their hearts to each other, in the gestation of a new race and a new nation.

She lies down again on her back by the waves. The clouds in the distance are sheets of coolness. She feels a hunger and a thirst for tenderness and good feelings. But the sun is setting and night is falling. She will have to wait for day in order to taste justice in a bottle of rum.

< 415 >

30

Contemplating the world is all she has left. Nature is sustainable, perfect. When everyone leaves, there is a shadow awaiting you. When you have nowhere to stay, there is a cliff, dunes, a dead tree trunk along the way, waiting for you. A beautiful landscape on the horizon to fill the emptiness. Even if there's fire in your heart, there's rain. Wind, dew to mitigate your pain and calm your fever. When your heart penetrates the gloomy shadows, there is sun, moon, stars in the heavens to light the candle of hope. Nature is full of sounds and poems that fill your ears deprived of words of love.

Delfina is within herself, along with nature that encircles her, but with her mind up in the vicinity of the moon. She feels the pulse of the air, wind and water. And she has the impression of being alive in the memory of time that has passed and will never come back. From another dimension, she listens to voices from the past, which explode in her ears like bags of wind.

< 416 >

Delfina, my daughter,
You will cross the desert!

The desert makes all the sounds of your body clearly audible. And it reminds you that you exist. That you are flesh, ash, dust, and that you are ephemeral just like the wind. It teaches each one of us to be aware of our own presence and to appreciate the merest drop of water. Far from any vegetation, the desert mirrors your conscience. And it forces you to confront your own image until you reach a stage of dialog and reconciliation. The desert makes you understand that life is a sandstorm, a cloud that roams on high, that passes, releases rain and disappears. It shows you that there is no use in surrounding yourself with crowds because pain is solitary, intimate and unheeding.

Delfina who slept with white man Sousa
On account of tea and sugar

A thousand pathways intertwined like poisonous snakes. In her wounded heart, Delfina screams. You perfect folk, why don't you put an end to me, why don't you throw me into the inferno once

< 417 >

and for all? You, the powerless dead, the insane, take this sun away from me, this moon. Deaf and mute God, why don't you bring me news of my daughter? I'm a dried-up tree, shorn of branches, I am nothing. My name is the stuff of satire and of song. Acclaimed in joy and in scorn. A fugitive in the sweet memory of a glamorous time. I'm in the dance of the flesh roasting on the spit. I, sinner, confess... I'm in the desert of life dying of thirst!

She opens her eyes. Lively young schoolgirls pass by, in groups. In dark blue skirts and light-colored blouses. They swarm together like dark clouds near her. They sing. Clap their hands. Dance. Little bodies invoking moments of lust for times to come, when they are obliged to sleep with someone or other on account of tea and sugar. Because of their submissiveness. Poverty and human injustice.

Seagull, oh seagull.
Go and tell my mama...

In Delfina's ears, the buzzing grows fearsomely loud, awakening memories, moments, experiences. The song gains wings to fly backwards in time. It forces her to hold onto her pain like a treasure. To tear her heart out of her breast and place it in the palm of her hand in order to extract the thorn that is causing her so much bitterness. She feels the crackling of the flames in her body. Her blood boiling. Her body's temperature increasing. Her whole being is transformed into a dead forest, firewood, parched straw, gas, in the conflagration of centuries. The children's songs awaken other songs buried in the roots of her memory. And she sighs. That voice sounds like Maria das Dores. That scream sounds like Maria das Dores. That erotic dance of the young girls is the same Maria das Dores marveled at! That fun, that freedom, was the same Maria das Dores used to enjoy. Tell me, Maria das Dores, were you holding your unhappy fate in your clenched fist at the time you were born? Maria das Dores, how much you have suffered in this world. How you must be suffering now, if you are still alive. Where are you now, that you send us no news of yourself?

> ... *who sold her daughter's maiden head,*
> *To sell some loaves of bread.*

Ah, Maria das Dores! I trudged through valleys and across mountains. I swept entire landscapes with the antennae of my eyes. I spoke with the waves and lost hope. I tore stupid confessions from the

< 419 >

soothsayers' talking seashells. They told me you were alive and that I, in my emotional state, would meet you again. But all this was of no use. Neither hope nor despair, neither candles lit for the saints, nor the sacrifice of chicken's blood for the dead. Twenty years passed and nothing happened. I don't want to die before you return.

Delfina, oh so fina...

The world of the vultures feeds on my wounds. They won't let them scar, but keep them alive and bleeding with dead songs. She looks up at the sky, at the blue, and at the clouds. Then she starts a tearful dialog with her body. Womb of mine, see the misfortune you bore. See the pain you created. Womb of mine, unhearing womb, unseeing womb, why do you do everything in darkness and silence? Why don't you answer my questions, why don't you speak to me? Each time I was pregnant, I suffered anxieties, I had visions, fears shredded my heart in the face of your silence. I saw monsters, ghosts, highways, destinations, parading in my imagination like flocks of birds. I imagined abortions. Difficult births. Premature babies. Disabilities. Illnesses. Death. And my face was wet with tears. The superstitious fed my

< 420 >

fantasy with what they said. I dreamed I was giving birth to snakes, fish, black cats, toads, monsters with two heads on one body, and three legs. I learned when I was pregnant with Maria das Dores, that for a woman, eternity involves a nine month wait.

I bore you with a lot of love, Maria das Dores. But when you were born, life imposed adverse rules on me when it came to motherhood. The world dehumanized and disunited us. And it meant I forgot it was my womb that gave birth to you.

Delfina who gave birth to blacks
Who gave birth to whites

Your destiny is the same as mine. Full of pain, ashes, anger and cruel words. Attracting love and ending up tortured. You and I have known it all. Tears and laughter. Sun and gloom. We've had love in our hands, which everyone seeks, and we haven't managed to hold on to it. Simba loved you. His angry voice screamed protests at your departure. He went mad and uttered terrible curses against you. He accused me of hiding you and beat me brutally. Wielding a tree trunk he smashed up my whole house along with all its furniture and

< 421 >

glass. The envious people helped him and attacked me, setting fire to everything out of revenge. I was left with nothing. No one came to my rescue. The priest applauded them. The firemen laughed as they put out the fire. The police laughed and only turned up to free some captive girls who were terrified, cold, insecure, in the middle of those horrifying flames.

But Simba didn't win, oh no! I had enough money to have him killed, but I didn't want to sully my hands with the blood of a wizard, who was the father of your children. What did defeat me was the yearning I felt for you. Yearning for my children who abandoned me and left. Yearning for my husbands who fell in love with me and destroyed themselves. Simba disappeared. I only hope he threw himself into the sea and that his soul rests in peace in the stomach of piranha fish.

Your three children must be beautiful, I sense that they are still alive. I see them in my dreams, I miss you so much, I love you, Maria das Dores.

❖   ❖   ❖

Delfina always follows the same routine. She wakes up, sweeps the house and the backyard, so that everything is tidy for when

< 422 >

José dos Montes arrives. She tidies up the toys so that everything is neat and in order the day Maria das Dores gets back. And she tidies herself. She buys a liter of palm oil and dabs it all over her body. And she glimmers like a star. There she is. Magnificent. Queen Delfina tired of war. Delfina who abused blacks. Provoked whites. A lone fish outside the school, drifting aimlessly, with frilly skirts and lace torn by the wind.

And she lives with her gaze ever fixed on the ocean, searching for something hidden under the waves. Next to a bottle of rum, her faithful companion. Maybe resting from her former troubled life. Maybe recalling and reliving the time when the sailors were here.

< 423 >

31

National Woman's Day.

Delfina has decided to join the women marching to celebrate this day. The march makes her dream. The dream is about everything she wanted. She thinks of Maria das Dores.

Can you hear these voices, can you hear them, Maria das Dores? They sing of the word freedom. They remind me of the strikes when I was a young girl, up there in the tea and palm plantations. Today, it's the women who raise their voices and clamor against other forms of slavery. Hurling their timeworn bitterness against the wind. Burning their aprons, bashing their saucepans, smashing their brooms, abandoning their washing troughs and ironing boards, in order to sing their dreams. Their song expresses a world that doesn't exist. They want to have everlasting love. Everlasting land. Everlasting everything. But how can a woman be mistress of the world if she has short arms and small eyes? How can a woman be happy if love is fashioned from a flower and the flower is in fact herself?

This song awakens the ashes of time. All the souls of the girls killed

< 424 >

in my brothel rise from their graves. It is they who are singing the dreams I stole from them, the life I denied them. These songs speak of me and of you, Maria das Dores. Today, women sing in the street. On the radio. In my day, they sang to the wind. They sang to the waves on the river, washing clothes, washing their anguish. They sang at the mortar, as they pounded corn, as they pounded their dreams.

Ah! This realization has come late. I watch the changes in the world from the margins. Black people ascending. The sailors leaving. Poverty growing. I was born in a time when life had no direction, and I ended up the victim of my illusions. I steered my boat through rough seas. I ran aground. That is why I sold myself in order to satisfy the sailors in their erotic wanderings.

❖   ❖   ❖

The history of this march didn't begin on this particular date. The war between the sexes is ancient, timeless. It all began in a time beyond memory. Once upon a time…

At the beginning of everything there was a kingdom made up only of men. They were born from the banana trees and there were many, in just one bunch. Each banana was a baby. It must have been at this time that bibs were invented, for children were fed with coconut milk, as men can't nurse. Their task was to sow palms. Wait for the coconuts to ripen. Climb up, harvest, grate the coconuts, squeeze the flesh and prepare the milk for the babies. The worst source of unhappiness for the men at this time was having to wash the diapers, and clean them of baby shit.

They discovered the domains of the women on the other side of the world. They also discovered that they were more advanced, for on their chest they had two portable, automatic, electronic, digital dairies, and what's more each woman only bore one child a year, or in exceptional cases two. They devised a plan. If they conquered them, they wouldn't have to see to the diapers or rely on coconut milk. They invaded the women's domains. After fierce combats, came a peace treaty. The women would make the children and look after them and the men would look after security and provide food. At first, the men fulfilled their side of the agreement but sometime later, there were incidents of rape and the women were turned into slaves. That is why they are going out on the streets and reclaiming their lost freedom. In the demands made on National Women's Day, there is a threat: if the men don't stick to the pact, there will be a sex strike and everything will go back to being how it was before. Children

< 426 >

will once again be born from banana trees, men will depend on coconuts and will have a heap of diapers to wash. In order to prevent this ecological disaster, scientists have speeded up their research to develop human clone technology, test tube babies and hired wombs.

Women on their own are queens and are proud of existing as they did at the beginning of the world. Enslaved, they go out into the street, fight for freedom, but when they're in the bedroom, they beg once again to be enslaved and dominated by men. And the men, those triumphant heroes, are only kings when they're alone. In the arms of women, they howl like children.

< 427 >

32

As the day ends, they are exhausted. The two brothers sit down on the priest's veranda for a rest. Dusk, calm, and silence reign. Not even the crow of a rooster. Or the hoot of a nighthawk. Amid this silence, the moon appears. The moon and magic. Stubborn fatigue has taken flight, and no one wants to sleep. They talk about everything. And nothing. Never before have they talked so much about so little. Never before since they were born. Since they grew up and became men. The word is the only life force gravitating in the cosmos. They are together and exorcizing their fear of the bogeyman still hovering over their distant childhood. Words are the kindling wood in the fire lit to protect them from their fear. Within each, there is a heart dreaming of a mother's love.

The mad woman of the river appears in a flash. She seems to have been assailed by some strange terror. She sees a horizon shrouded in deep shadows and malign elevations that threaten to crush her. She sees ghosts the size of mountains and she flees from traps, ambushes and hurled rocks. She quivers like a navigator faced by the giant of the oceans churning up the waters in fierce waves. Without asking permission, she is seeking help and safety inside the priest's house.

"Each one suffers their own madness," the doctor remarks. And they let her penetrate the building and wander around freely. The two men get up at the same time. They follow her merely to observe her movements. Their curiosity draws them forward like some powerful magnet. They feel neither pity nor compassion, but something quite simply inexplicable. The magic of the night is largely responsible for this. Solitude reminds us there is a room inside us. To be inhabited by sounds. Feelings. Heat, cold. Movement. It reminds us that we are nothing without company to fill the emptiness of our soul. It reminds us that we are only someone when we have someone. The mad woman pauses in the priest's dining room. She looks at the wall. She sees a crucifix hanging there with a black Christ bleeding from his open wounds.

She stares fixedly at the figure of Christ hanging on the wall. Maybe she is transferring all the force of her rebellion onto that image. Maybe she is saying silent prayers. Or maybe she is quite simply appreciating a piece of clay sculpture. Or looking at the twisted body of a man on the wall. She discovers many unusual things in him. A black man's nose, nostrils the size of seashells. Lips

< 429 >

the size of conches. A bare torso and stretch marks on his belly like some famished individual. And eyes that are so sad, framed by long hair. Dreads. A Rastafari Christ. A Reggae Christ. Christareggae. Christafari. If he died so far away, why did they deliver him here? If he wasn't black, why paint him that color? She averts her gaze. She expected to see a white Christ, not a black one. A king and not a Bantu. None of this chimes with anything she has learned.

She sits down on the chair and travels out into the atmosphere through the open window. The mountains gleam in the light of the moon. And she sees a full moon, a white, round moon, illuminating the world with milky lamps. A virgin moon with beautiful people inside it.

They can hear the swish of a bird riding windy waves. A silent, hesitant breath emerges from the mad woman's throat. A sweet, sad, beautiful song coming from some nameless place. The two brothers listen, hypnotized. Without knowing that the magnetic power of that song would be forever etched on their minds.

Maria looks again at the clay Christ, who is now blinking, while his lips tremble and open like some ancient seashell displaying luminous teeth. He speaks.

"Hello, Maria!"

< 430 >

The wall can be heard cracking. The clay Christ liquefies the nails, also made of clay, that attach him to the cross. He climbs down and steps onto the ground. He stretches his arms a bit to get the circulation going again in his limbs, like someone who has just awoken from a two-thousand-year sleep. He brushes the dust off his shoulders and walks toward Maria. The priest and the doctor hold the mad woman who is screaming wildly. They don't have enough strength between them, and they summon the mute cook to help. They try and hold onto her until she calms down. As they do this, they have the strange sensation that they are holding the mother they never had. The mother who died or who may still be alive. Lost in the memory of times long gone. The mad woman is really mad, for she has confused the cook with the clay Christ. From the mouth of both, she hears the same voice lost in the depths of time.

"Tell me everything about yourself, Maria," says the man of clay.

"I'm me, Maria das Dores, the mad woman. She who left in search of love and lost all her treasure. She who wanted everything and has nothing. Daughter of José dos Montes and Delfina."

"Ah! Maria!"

"Why did you abandon me, father? Why didn't you take me with you to your kingdom of clay?"

"Ah, Maria! Tell me what's making you suffer, and I'll give you an answer today. Undo the knot in your heart, for I am here to support you. Come, Maria, tell me your wish, just one wish, and I'll give it to you."

Maria opens the floodgates of her soul and declares her wish in a fearsome cry:

"I want my Benedito, my Fernando, and my Rosinha, my real babies."

"Where are they?"

"I lost them in a cave on the mountainside. Long ago. They were taken by a nun."

"Tell me everything, Maria."

She tells her story. The mountains of Namuli. The climb. The cave. White soldiers on a military training exercise in the middle of the colonial war. The hospital, the doctors. The nun who took her children. Three men stand there quietly, listening to this unusual tale. They are present. They are absent. Hypnotized by the torrent of words flowing from the mad woman's mouth. The Bantu Christ lifts Maria up in the air and utters incantations. She closes her eyes and savors the moment.

The black Christ sheds a tear and smiles.

"Your wish will be granted, Maria, free yourself, fly, look for your belongings in space, then return to earth and I'll give you your answer."

A flash crosses the mind of Maria das Dores. It is her madness leaving for the moon. For she can now rely on the earth's protection. Maria roams through the heavens in a downward spiral. She bids farewell to all the constellations. The Bear. Centaur. Southern Cross. Cassiopeia. The Milky Way. She gathers up the fragments of her soul on the moon's surface and returns. She sheds the madness covering her and lays to rest the endless trajectory of her twenty-five years of barefoot wandering. She looks for the clay Christ with his lucid eyes, but he has returned to his place. She looks from side to side like someone waking up from a vast dream. She is shaken by a huge spasm. The priest and the doctor hold her with all their strength so that she doesn't run away and tell everything that she knows.

"Call old Simba to come and hypnotize her until she calms down, quickly! She's possessed," the doctor shouts.

Simba comes running and curses her trance. Maria calms down and awakens to the reality around her.

"What am I doing here?" Maria asks, embarrassed.

"Maria, where are you from?" asks the priest, stirred.

< 433 >

"I'm from nowhere. I come from a womb that was in mourning, covered in fire. A fire lit there by demons. I am a cactus flower in a distant desert. I am solitude and despair. My story will never be understood."

"We too had a mother and lost her. We don't know whether she's alive or dead."

"Ah!"

"We were found in a cavern on the slopes of Namuli," the priest explains. We are three siblings. Benedito, Fernando, and Rosinha."

"How did it all happen, Maria?" the priest asks.

"It's a long story."

Maria tells her story. Tales of blacks, whites, and mestizos under the same roof, residents of the same womb. Tales of business deals and witchcraft. Tales of violence, rape, sex, and torpor. A tale of unconscious childbirths, jealousy and polygamy. She recounts details of pathways taken, suffering and anxiety. Of virginity as a price to pay off business debts. She talks about the contour lines of every Calvary she experienced. About the water courses in the valleys and on the mountains. Of the highways, villages, cities, and towns that she knew.

"Tell me your real name, Maria," Simba, the medicine man asks.

"Maria das Dores, Mary of the Sorrows."

< 434 >

The two brothers look at Maria das Dores with deepening tenderness. They stare at the woman in her delirium, as she rummages through the darkness for her most distant memories. Yes, this was it. She was the motive for their eternal search. They encounter all the traces people look for in order to identify someone. They visualize the image of Rosinha in her facial contours. They compare the two. The silken arch that falls over her eyebrows like a crescent moon. Her full round lips, her blood and flesh. Her hair and abundant lashes like skeins of silk. Her skin of black gold and her catlike eyes. A cat that kills a mouse in the dead of night. Those abundant breasts. The voice of someone singing as she talks. The only difference is in the color of the skin. Rosinha's skin is lighter, a mixture of black and peach.

Maria das Dores seeks in the priest and the doctor all those childhood features that only a mother knows. Tiny stains, black dots, scars. Likenesses. Differences. Skin color. Looks. Skin tones.

"Can you be the mother we are looking for, Maria?"

"Can you be the children I am looking for? My Benedito has a birth mark on his shoulder blade. It's round and closed, like a lizard's egg."

The priest and the doctor were accustomed to the idea of not having a mother. Maria was accustomed to the idea of having lost her

< 435 >

children. Their shared truth is all they ever desired, but they wanted it to come out slowly, bit by bit. So that they should be psychologically prepared. They had lit many a candle for this to happen. But that it wouldn't happen this way. Which, after all, was the best way. Unexpected but desired, a yearned-for surprise.

Mother and children emerging from a scene of fire and storm. The end and the beginning touching each other. The miracle of the night has been fulfilled.

"Where have you been all this time, mother?"

Where? She had followed the paths westward. While she did this, ghosts and evil shadows had come to frolic in her children's tortured souls. She had set off for afar on the wings of night birds whose song is a deathly hoot. Where? On the roads to Ile, Namarrói, Gilé, Gúruè, Milange, Molócue, and unknown worlds. Searching for her three little children who cried and whom she nursed. Life gave her hard knocks, tugged her ears and pinched her hard. And the mountains filled her with fear, while they closed off any sight of the horizon. Sometimes they attracted her, turning into mirrors that spoke to her with the intimidation of phalluses.

They stand there hugging each other for minutes on end. They are still not fully conscious of their encounter. It might be a dream.

It might be real.

The mute cook opens his mouth. He speaks.

"My eldest daughter, my pain, my affirmation as a man!"

"Eh?"

"I'm your father."

"My father? José dos Montes?"

"Yes. Me. I'm the one who produced you out of love. From you, I first heard the word daddy, and I felt more of a man. I abandoned you with an aching heart, I sought refuge here and pretended I couldn't speak so as to stifle the need to recount my tragedy."

"Oh, my dear father!"

"I survived loneliness, distress. To see you like this, Maria das Dores? What happened? What did this evil world do to you? Who destroyed your heart, who? How many times did I think of assaulting you like some vagrant in order to fulfil the sense of manhood I still felt? At that precise moment, I stopped myself, as if some magic hand were holding me back. Because you were my firstborn. Ah! What a wretched life!"

The medicine man is crying like a child. From the emotion of it all. From something that no one understands.

"What's wrong, old-timer?" the doctor asks.

"Doctor, I am Simba, it's me. The man who loved Maria das Dores to perdition. It's me…"

"Who?"

"Her husband. Your father."

"Oh! You? We were all here. Why did you stand by while we suffered so many years of anguish?" Benedito cries, uncontrollably.

They stand there, more dumbstruck than ever. None of those present ever imagined that such an incredible miracle could occur right there in that very spot. None of them ever knew that there were no words nor seers in this world capable of describing the mystery of this instant. Nor priests. Or philosophers. Or clairvoyants. Or poets. Maybe that clay Christ hanging on the wall. Maybe God.

A thousand words rain down that night. Words capable of blowing asunder buttresses in space that were the moon's accomplices. They talk so much they can't stop. No, they can't. First come the heavy words, falling like hail. Then gentle ones like poems, and refreshing as the dew. A festival of tears is being held in that place. At first, dense and profound like stormy seas, then smooth like the waters of the River Licungo near its source.

The dawn chorus sings gurué, gurué. Maria das Dores feels a

dribble of honey running through her mouth, and falling straight from the source of a river. Once again she looks at the priest's room in the light of the sun. The clay Christ has returned to its place on the eternal prison of the wall. She suffered a hallucination, perhaps, but the reencounter was real.

They all go back in time, floating toward the past in a pirogue of tenderness. And they arrive at the same point. At the sky's navel. At the peak of a mountain. The point of arrival and departure. Then, they start their journey again toward the future, with a pause in the present.

Three generations dreaming of the same mountain. Endlessly searching for each other. Fragments of a piece of glass that are collected, stuck together to make a new pot, that reflects the light, that is fragile, that can no longer contain water but adorns the middle of a table. Seeking their identity that has been pecked at and stolen by a vulture.

The children's survival was an extraordinary story. Taken by soldiers on a training exercise, they were given to a nun, who lit candles for them to chase away their darkness. A white nun. Who had given them boundless love, as if they were her own. Who gave

< 439 >

them the name of the place where they had been found by way of a family name. Which in fact was their own mother's name. And which in fact was the name of a sacred mountain.

For those children, the age of daydreaming and unanswered questions is over. What would it be like to go to sleep in a mother's arms? Why does a lullaby put all the children in the world to sleep? Why do some children have mothers and others don't? What would life in a mother's womb be like? As comfortable as a cottage? Temperature controlled? Would it have chairs, tables, air conditioning? What might our mother's face have been like?

Maria das Dores doesn't want to sleep. Nor does she want to rest. Or blink. She wants to keep her eyes open, in order to regain all the images from twenty-five years of absence.

33

Early morning. Delfina is on the banks of her river. She wants to remain sitting there until the sun comes up so as to absorb, in each ray of sunshine, all the signs of hope. As if she is sure of an impending miracle about to arrive in the wake of the sun that is about to rise. In the murmuring of those gentle waves, she begins to invoke names, images, places, people.

Suddenly, she hears a man's voice calling her. She doesn't take any notice, it's just another illusion. She smiles. And speaks to herself out loud.

"That voice sounds like José dos Montes, who was lost and died more than thirty years ago."

"It was your fault he got lost, Delfina," the voice replied. "You left him for the love of other men."

She looks surreptitiously to one side. And she sees an old shadow that has emerged from the confines of the world. Fears and anxieties project live images that become reality to the eyes that want to see them. This has happened to her before.

"The shape, the smile, the deep voice remind me of my José. How I miss my dear José!"

"It was your fault, greedy Delfina. You threw him out of the house so you could sleep with white men in return for tea and sugar."

"Gentle shadow, wicked shadow, who are you and what do you know about me?"

"I know you are gentle, and wicked too, but that doesn't matter for the time being. Listen to the song of the partridges in the early hours and the rumble of the drums bringing good news. The dense forest is shaking to the nhambarro drumbeats, come and join the ring dance."

"Good shadow, shadow of yearning, where are you taking me?"

Within her, there is the question. Whose voice is that talking of pleasant things? Timidly, she raises her eyes. And what she sees is a figure that isn't human, it can't be. She has been divorced from the things of this world for a long time and she has nestled in the cocoon of absence. Everyone disdained her and no one even approached to utter a single word to her. It could only be some benign ghost originating in the furthest reaches of her longing. The voice has the gentle quality of a long-forgotten love. She opens her eyes and stares at the image. She identifies one or two features that have resisted the corrosion of time.

< 442 >

"Shadow of my José, tell me: where are you taking me?"

"To endless happiness, to the start of a new life. The crocodiles of the Zambezi have returned to life all the people they have eaten over the centuries. Over there in Morrumbala, Mount Juju has just opened its gigantic gateway and is feeding whoever is hungry."

José dos Montes awakens his Delfina. Slowly. And he prepares her for the great news gradually.

"What happened?"

"It's the celebration of the new century."

This time Delfina reacts, for José dos Montes is making her remember long-forgotten tastes. He speaks of bodily needs to someone who feeds herself on the leftovers from quayside restaurants. She is one of the old women who fill the streets on Fridays to collect alms.

"Shadow of José, you speak of the good foods I aspired to my whole life."

"Come, Delfina, come and celebrate the sun."

"No, I'm not going. I haven't proper clothes to wear, I can't go along just like that."

"Ah, you vain woman!"

"I am Delfina. The woman who will sleep in the earth with her head held high, a black queen on a throne of clay."

José dos Montes gives her a look of tenderness. And pity. He identifies her. She is a queen. She always was. Wars, misfortune, vanity, robbed her of her majesty for a while. But she gained new wings. She is a noble tree where birds perch and sing beautiful songs. A queen is always a queen even when her throne is one of sand, just like the Pia Mwenes of the great lineages in all Zambezia. Barefoot. Impoverished. More representative than any citizen elected in a democratic vote. They have no seat in Parliament, but they have a throne of gold in the people's hearts.

"I've brought you new clothes. A black skirt of pure silk. A yellow lace blouse. A yellow capulana, dotted with red flowers. A gold-colored headscarf for your queenly head."

He pulls her by the arm into the house. She allows herself to be pulled along like a shrimp at the will of the waves. Obeying the command of the souls from the other world, and which she has invoked in her belief that the dead are the true rulers of life. Fortune tellers have predicted the resurrection of dead souls at the beginning of the new century.

She bathes, gets dressed again, primps herself and is rejuvenated in time for the celebrations of the new century. This is when she realizes it isn't a dream, but all true. That the ghost is indeed her José, the man of her life. She absorbs a ray of light and smiles. Her smile chases away the gloom and revives in one single instant her heart that has been buried under the weight of unhappiness.

José dos Montes explores the labyrinth of the house he abandoned more than thirty years ago. In the sitting room, some gaudy furniture reveals vestiges of grandeur. The floor is clean, but there are cobwebs on the ceiling. How long is it since Delfina last looked up at the sun? Does she still remember that the sky is blue and contains stars? He touches the walls, the furniture, and all the objects. The windowpanes of this ruined building have all been smashed. With his touch, he brings the former nest back to life. He relives feelings and thoughts. He lives a moment of ecstasy, madness, discovery, rediscovery, in a rapid, violent process of rebirth. He talks, laughs. That bedroom is exactly as he left it. Forty years ago, he left his antelope bone pipe on the table. He left a shirt hanging on the back of a chair. Everything is there, exactly where it was. He feels his old underpants, his socks, his contract worker's clothes that smell of soap and camphor. His tin guitar is hanging on the wall. It is as if the gods have arranged everything, awaiting his return. It is good, when everything is taken into account, to have a past to regain and relive. He understands. This is a sanctuary and I was an object of veneration for her, one of her dead, maybe a god. In her solitude, she called for me, ah, my poor Delfina!

He takes a look under the bed. The dagger is there, where he left it. Bloodstains on its leather sheath. He quivers and is humbled by the power of memory.

He closes his eyes and savors the night for a moment. In the bloodstains, he seems to see the eyes and voice of Moyo, censuring him for all his crimes. This weapon fed my illusions and my cowardice. With it in my hand, I thought myself a real man because I had power over others. With it, I affirmed myself as a false black, a real white man and not merely an imitation of one. I showed all black-skinned people that I had changed race. I wasn't one of them. That bayonet there reminds him of all his deeds. Burning the grain in his own grain store. Killing a father or mother just to please his boss. Hunting people down in order to deport or sell them. Looking for dissidents in bars, on the streets, on the plantations, among the quayside prostitutes, in order to feed his bosses' wallets. That bayonet had got him the reputation of a killer of blacks.

"Why did you keep this weapon, Delfina? I killed my people with it. I killed my companions and friends, but I didn't kill the sailors who slept with you in the bushes, or in the bedroom and in this bed.

I silenced blacks with this blade in order to defend my position as a betrayed husband, because I was uncontrollably in love with you. Ah, Moyo! Why didn't I listen to your warnings, your wise voice? Why did I kill you?"

The past cannot be forgotten. It sleeps like a seed in the depths of your mind. It falls onto the soil and germinates thorns in the present.

"Why are you crying, José dos Montes?"

He conceals his tears and feigns a smile. He justifies himself.

"It's a characteristic of violent men. When they are softened by life's blows, they behave like women. Forgive me my tears and at least allow me to weep for a brief moment now."

They look at each other with love and hatred. Falling in love once more with the new image each of them has created. She thinks: here is the man I hurt. He thinks: here is the woman I lost myself for. Then, they look down at the ground, for they are far from the stars. Love? Has it ever existed? Does it exist? They remember the time of their dreams and their madness, their temptations, the illusions felt in the name of love. When old age arrives, hearts hold back and look at everything like mere onlookers at the craziness of the world.

"Do I look good in my dress?"

"You're beautiful. Very beautiful!"

< 447 >

"Well carry me away then. I'm no longer in charge of life," Delfina confesses. "Life is in charge of me. So carry me away to the vast tomb, to the end of the world, to oblivion."

"Mount Pinda killed the water dragon and cast it into the River Chire, so there's no longer any danger. Mount Tumbine swallowed the seven-headed dragon, which was destroying the mountain and devouring lives with its seven fiery mouths. The mountains of Namuli garlanded themselves with white roses and red anthuriums. Yes, I'll carry you away to the vantage point of the world. Let's go and join the grand celebration."

"All this festivity because of the new century?"

"It's because of the return of Maria das Dores."

"What? Eh? You're lying, José, you're lying, you mustn't do things like that! What are you saying? Maria das Dores? Where is she, where, where, where?"

Delfina spins round and round, yelling, weeping. Walking to the left, to the right, and in no direction at all. She circles around herself like a scorpion in its death throes.

"Don't die now, Delfina, get a grip on yourself, we've still got a long journey ahead. It's three hundred kilometers of dusty road from Quelimane to Gúruè."

"My God! Lend me your hiking sticks so that I can climb the mountain, say a prayer and pick a flower for my little girl."

"Crazy old lady! Climbing the mountain is easy. All you need to do is close your eyes and allow your soul to soar to the highest point, pick the most beautiful flower and place it on your breast. Let's go!"

Delfina walks as fast as she can, but all she can do is advance with the sluggish steps of a sleepwalker toward the vehicle that awaits them. The red sun is emerging from the earth. Tears are an oasis in the desert where plants sprout and flower. Suddenly she steps back. José gets worried.

"Do you think she'll forgive me? Will she welcome me, the one who killed her? I ruined her life and her dreams. Do you think she loves me?"

"She spent her whole life calling for you, Delfina. She called for me. She called for us both. Let's hurry, she's waiting for us."

"Just wait a moment."

"Hey! What for?"

"I just want to fetch something."

"What?"

"A magic pot. It's huge. It's big enough to cook an elephant in, along with its tusks. I kept it for her and I want to take it to her now."

< 449 >

"A huge pot? But how are you going to carry it?"

"You'll see."

"Let me help."

"No. You might die."

She disappears and comes back with a normal-sized pot, covered with a black cloth, full of jewels which she collected in order to pay Maria das Dores her debt. Jewels forcibly torn from the hands of sailors, given to Delfina to please her. She learned from Asian traders to keep her fortune under the bed, guarded by a tamed, venomous black snake, and trained to kill any intruder who might try and get hold of her possession. She takes a while. She had to kneel down, hold the snake. Kill it. Remove the pot from the floor. José dos Montes is astonished.

"Delfina? You were begging for alms every Friday while you possessed such wealth? Do you realize the true size of the fortune you've got in your hands?"

"Of course!"

"How did you come by all this?"

"Have you forgotten? I'm Delfina, the quayside mermaid!"

They begin their journey. The same one made by Maria das Dores

< 450 >

during her flight. Without any stops. Rushing headlong because of their anxiety. They reach their destination, where the whole family is reunited. They look at each other with intensity.

"You're disheveled, José dos Montes. Too slovenly for our daughter's party. Your shirt is badly buttoned. Haven't you got a mirror?"

José now realizes how solitude is an unhappy state. How his life has always been sad. He looks closely at Delfina and sighs. My woman, forever mine. How good it is to listen to her breath filling my chest, to inhale the perfume from every particle of her body. Oh, how good a woman's scent is! That's what it means to be happy: to hold in one's hand the soul of the person you love. To smile. To dream of the sun that is bound to appear. To long for the night that is sure to arrive. To feel one's body quivering with ecstasy. To listen to green and blue messages brought by the heavens, the ocean and the palms.

"I don't have anyone to keep an eye on me."

"Didn't you get married again?"

"Why, if you were still waiting for me?"

They embrace in silence. Their eyes journey towards the same target. Their hearts beat together to the same rhythm. They discover that the sun dwells inside them, and a heart can still produce honey

< 451 >

that provides life to all they do. They discover that they are once again ocean, ship, mariners sailing toward the immense unknown. All this story needs now is a kiss. But this won't come yet. For to love each other and feel happy, they must first be reborn.

At this point, José discovers something he has never noticed before. That a palm tree is a woman. With round, milky fruits like a mother's breast. With long green leaves like a mermaid's tresses. With a grooved, tattooed trunk like the body of a woman. That offers everything: food and wine. A house, a roof, furniture, medicine, fuel. Like the body of a woman.

It is then that Delfina takes a step toward her daughter. She stops. Something strange, painful, delicious, is sprouting from her inner self, filling the endless void. Her head is suddenly shaken by a violent buffeting. She is on a bottomless ocean fighting against her shame. The creature she sees there inspires pity. She is so small. Fragile. Defenseless. An adolescent frozen in time by her interrupted growth. A seed that has been kept in the grain store, awaiting the magic of a drop of dew as spring bursts out. How was she able to believe that her own daughter's virginity could save her life? Delfina is lost, overcome by fits of dizziness, remorse, yearning, and she lets out a cry of joy:

"My daughter, my angel, my one and only stroke of good fortune!"

Maria das Dores takes a step toward her mother. She too stops. In the archive of her mind, drawers open to reveal the words of an old song.

Your mother's not here
She's gone east of nowhere.
If you cry I'll give you a slap
Tug your ears and a rap-a-tap-tap.

Her mother's ballad is honey, that of her brothers is salt and lemon. With tugs of the ears and rap-a-tap-tap. She smiles. At last she can go home and see to Jacinta's hair, which she still hasn't finished. She can talk to the centaur again, that knight of diamonds, with the body of a horse and a man's head. She can go back and tidy her books left open on the table more than twenty-five years ago. Hug her doll in her childhood bed. She flies through space until she has turned into a smudge, a dot, a tiny germ ready to be incubated once more in that same mother's womb. She feels dizzy and light headed and furiously seeks something to support herself as she utters her cry of liberation:

"My mother, my mother, my mother!"

They rush forward to take each other in an inevitable embrace, and so protect themselves from vertigo. The whole world witnesses this perfect representation of rebirth. A mother giving birth to a new

< 453 >

daughter in her former body. A daughter giving shape and meaning to a mother's wandering existence.

"Mother!"

"Together at last, Maria das Dores!"

"Ah! My mother, my mother, my mother!"

They clutch at each other, nestle together, stand locked together. They laugh and cry.

"I was lost along the byways of the world, dear mother."

"You weren't lost, but you found yourself. I was the one who lost you, because I banished you from this world. I imposed burdens on you that you weren't able to bear. You left. For space and into your deepest self. You left your place among humans and gained the lightness of the breeze. Out of all of us, you are the most free, the one nearest to creation. Or the creator. You feared neither death nor the night. On hot days, you stripped off your clothes and walked naked, as innocent as a child. You tried to explain your dilemma, and you did so in the language of angels, and that was why the world didn't understand you. You smiled up at the heavens, in the song of the birds, because you flew. Your journey was between your innermost self and the moon."

"I was mad, dear mother."

< 454 >

"No, you were never mad, never!"

Delfina offers her daughter the most loving embrace in the world. She feels her rough skin. She is a piece of clay of divine creation, black clay with red blood. The victim of madness. The madness of hunger and of war. Victory and defeat. Of the hierarchy among races. Of social immorality. Union and rupture. The madness of destiny, the madness of good luck and bad luck, the madness of life and death. Madness in the city, in the countryside. The madness of the land in its struggle for existence.

"Separation? Never! Never again," Delfina cries.

"Are you speaking the truth, mother?"

"We shall be together forever! In joy and in sadness. In health and in sickness, until death separates us!"

A bird launches forth into a strain from on high. The flock responds and their voices join in a beautiful song. A thick cloud covers the sun and the mountains. And it is transformed into drops of rain that fall on their breasts dousing the fires of old. Washing away detritus. Crushing anguish and thorns that will germinate, when spring comes around again, as red anthuriums edged with clay.

"Accept this gift which I have kept with such care only for you all the time you were away."

< 455 >

"My eyes, long ago, grew unused to things that glitter in this world. Gold is a color, it is pure fantasy, children are one's fortune. For me to be happy, our very existence is sufficient. Life is worth much more than fortune. But in spite of this, I thank you, mother, for your kind thought."

Music and rain falling from the eyes of both mother and daughter. In the distance, the bucolic sound of flutes. Emotion hangs in the air. There are silences. Sighs. Murmurs. Tears. These lofty mountains were created to incubate the mysteries of fate.

Delfina and Maria sway together, animated by their giddiness. Maybe they both remember the day of her birth. The mother's smiles exploding in the heavens like fireworks, scattering the millions of stars surrounding the world like luminous tears. Dreams, visions, desires, prayers. A new reason to live. After the birth, the challenge. To turn a mother's dream into a mountain. To start the great ascent to the celestial peak in search of the newborn's happiness. To resist winds and storms to make the child blossom.

"I need you, Maria das Dores."

"I missed you so much, my mother."

34

They came with a centuries-old hunger. They were grains of sand, particles of clay that the divine hand had molded in order to inculcate it with the new breath of life. Figures, shapes, faces, souls begin to emerge. Life is beginning at this moment.

I am Simba, the poet, seer, prophet! I am the one who sees far, but can't see the color of my own eyes. Who cures the pains of others but who was never able to cure his own. I married your mother out of hatred, without realizing that it was love I really felt. I always sniffed around among other people's fates, but never explored my own grievances.

I am Maria das Dores, the wayfarer. My footprints have covered all Zambezia. The vibrations of the soil, the sea, the palms, banished me from my homeland and I wandered directionless until I found refuge in the world of the moon. I lived between lucidity and obscurity. On my journey, I encountered other suns and other galaxies. I am the sleeping beauty and I spent twenty-five years in hibernation. I envy the trees their luck, for they never leave their place or become separated from their children.

I am Maria Jacinta, the mulatto woman, a trophy of war, a white flag, a battle shield. I defended the family from slavery. Next to whites, I am white, next to blacks, I am black, on my own, I'm a mulatto woman. I move from one place to another in order to survive. I envy Maria das Dores and I envy my father. They never leave their place nor take pains to affirm themselves. It was my black mother who placed me above blacks. Faithful to the balance between races, I never experienced slavery or deportation. I belong to the caste of the ladies and mistresses, owners of land and slaves, power is my inheritance. When it comes to jobs, I am of course at the front of the line. The factories belonged to my father. The banks belonged to my father. The airline companies too. I belong to everyone and to no one. I am different and the same. Love me or hate me, depending on the degree of your feeling or your anger, but be careful: I'm yours, I belong to you! This is my land. This sky is mine and this ground belongs to my ancestors! I have come in my father's name. In order to get back all the inheritance that has been usurped and return it to Maria das Dores, its legitimate owner.

I am Zezinho. Delfina's son. I don't know what my magic power is, but I am beautiful and make all the white women fall madly in love with me. I married a white woman for love. In our home, we have abolished any racial hierarchy, blacks and whites eat with the same spoon and drink water from the same pitcher.

I am José dos Montes, the assimilado! A brave warrior! I crushed all the strikers and silenced all those opposed to slavery. It was the blood of the people that elevated me and made me important. I changed my identity and kept my mouth shut for forty years, I went around on my own, I hid, in order to protect myself from possible acts of revenge. When night falls, the voices of the past are raised against me and torture me. I'm a sleepwalker.

I am Delfina. A woman who is loved and hated. I flew, just like the wind that has no wings but still flies. I sailed the ocean of life using only one limb. Like a fish. A fish woman. A mermaid. I am everything: pure and profane. Serene. Mad. A whore and a saint. A seer, a witch. Truth and myth. A goddess and a demon. A cannibal. I turned my home into a battlefront, with victims, victories, allies, enemies, dead, wounded, traumatized. In the manner of a jet bomber, I destroyed my nest while in full flight, but I was freer than all the

< 459 >

other women in the world. The mountains on the horizon were mine, along with the swallows high in the sky.

We are Benedito, Fernando and Rosinha. We are the children of a white nun and the black clay of the mountains. We traveled in the carriage of yearning among the stars because we were the offspring of the heavens, and we were brought from a distant constellation in the beak of a stork. Maybe from Cassiopeia. Or from the Southern Cross. We are the children of a celestial bear, Ursa Major or Minor, and we were like Romulus and Remus, except that we were reared by a bear.

I am the nun, the earthly bear they speak of. One day, a stork delivered a bundle with three marvelous chicks who, barely had they opened their eyes, chirped: Mommy! My heart was moved with tenderness as that new dawn was born. I fell desperately in love that very instant! I raised my hands to heaven and prayed with fervor. Instead of milk, God placed in my right hand a lit candle. I was alarmed: what am I to do with this candle? Good Lord, I need three bibs and a lot of milk, why have you given me this? You cannot imagine what a panic I was in. The divine answer had been given and my fate sketched out. And so I became a mother and a godmother. With the light of that candle we defeated the monsters on our journey, we sailed against the darkness inhabiting us, and we kept the light of hope going, which sustained us over those twenty-five anxious years. Every day, we prayed for this reunion. I was terrified by the idea that I might die before this encounter, because God would ask me: what did you do with the lit candle I gave you? I did what I could until the chicks fledged. These three creatures proved to me that wealth is achieved by giving life to another life. Wherever there's a human being, there's a family. They made me forget that I'm a woman and that I'm white. What do race and sex matter when the work to be done is of this world?

The eyes of the three siblings identify Simba, the man who was the object of dreams, fantasies, nightmares, hallucinations. They see similarities in that lean man. That man who had always been there, healing their bodily and spiritual wounds. Giving them hope that one day they would meet the father they yearned for so fervently, without realizing that he was their father. They look at their mother like a broken eggshell at the moment of birth. They look at each other. They discover they now have wings but they can't yet fly, and they need a great deal of comfort from their mother.

They walk from person to person. They recognize the genetic traits in each one. Benedito has inherited the philosophical demeanor of his father. Fernando the feline walk of his mother. Rosinha has

< 461 >

inherited everything from everyone. From Maria das Dores. From Simba. From Delfina.

Moments of liberation are experienced in the festival of the anthuriums. In this celebration, a kiss becomes bread and sustenance. The human body, fragile like the breeze, needs sounds and living words in order to gain strength. Delfina and José dos Montes assume the leadership of the party, masters of the word. They raise the veils and open up the battlements of their minds. It is they who are the guardians of life's wisdom and of stories about the birth of the world.

In order to smooth over the truth and penetrate the depths, José dos Montes tells time-honored tales. The best stories always start the same way. Once upon a time…

"The call of your blood summoned you all to this magnificent encounter," José dos Montes explains. "Through our veins flows the sacred blood of the stones. The blue sky was incubated on the mountains of Namuli, inside the egg of a partridge. It was born with the wings of a bird, flew off and colonized all the land. Then, the first star was born from the egg of that same partridge, and it shot up into the sky, exploded and spread like a firework to form the Milky Way. This was the beginning of the world. The end of the world. All the races were born at this point. They spread around the world and then returned, because the mountains of Namuli bring together all those who wish each other well, so that they may eat from the same shell and drink the water from the same spring."

The sugarcanes wave their leaves in the wind, rustling loudly and widely. Bringing back memories of their origins and the reason for human enslavement around the cultivation of coconuts, tea and sisal.

The River Zambezi, the sea, the palm grove and the mountains of Namuli are united in a multi-faceted diamond. God created this land in a moment of happiness and endowed it with great beauty, causing each wayfarer to feel an even greater passion and that is why, once upon a time...

Stories of navigators who set sail searching for chili peppers in a distant land. Stories of the eleven mermaids, all of them sisters, the most beautiful of them being Zambezia. Stories of sailors and the whips of settlers granted land. Stories of ladies and mistresses. Of the Zambezia Company, the Boror Company, and of the palm groves. Stories of warrior women who penetrated the invader's fortress, stole the men's seeds and constructed a barrier of life, thus showing the world that, faced with the women of Zambezia, the invader was not all-powerful. Proving that racial superiority was just so much nonsense. Stories of mountain gods who blessed Zambezia with the divine blood of blacks, whites, and yellows, in a racial soup that had more substance to it than a traditional hearty broth from Portugal.

"We are makers of rain and guardians of water," José dos Montes explains. "Commanders of thunder. We were born to the song of the partridge, gurué, gurué! We built in caves. We cultivated cereals with antelope horns. Out of the long bones of gazelles, we made pipes for our warriors to smoke their tobacco. Then, the whites came and we were caught like mice. They enslaved us."

They all raise their eyes once more to contemplate the image of mother earth in this nascent world. Allowing emotion to flower in the heart of Eden. Contemplating the mountains in the distance, and confirming all they already knew. You are a child only when you are in your mother's womb. Once you are born, you are alone and you will live your life alone. You are a mother only when your child inhabits your womb. After you give birth, each of you gains their own identity and follows their own destiny.

"We are quiet of step, and tread the ground in secret. We do not accept a house as a prison. We set off to discover the world. We built our home on the sides of mountains and we were washed away by raging torrents, we were children of pumpkin vines planted along the sides of the road, and gathered by any wayfarer. We trudged

< 464 >

across the surface of the soil to the ends of the Earth. We completed the circuit silently and here we are again at the place of departure. Here, everything begins and everything ends. The world is round."

They now hear their children asking questions. If the ancestors were heroes yesterday, they do not understand why their descendants only get a taste of the bitterest part of their journey.

"Why did you bring us into the world in order to make us suffer?" the children of Maria das Dores ask. "Our father was here, and we didn't know. The mad woman of the river was our mother and suffered wherever she went. How did it all happen?"

Simba has come to the meeting disposed to settle old accounts and fulfil a stale old promise. To tear the witch's eyes out with darts of fire. The witch was Delfina, it could only be her, it had to be her. He averts his gaze and justifies himself in a voice that is worn like a piece of moth-eaten cloth.

"I was a withered branch ruled by the night. I withstood the desert sun because I loved you. I came looking for you in heaven and hell. I followed you far beyond the horizon. Those were twenty-five anxious years. In my search, I drank the water of the swamps and ate the fruits of the wild. I walked across rocks so as not to leave prints for fear of enemies. I lived through years of bitterness. It was all Delfina's fault."

Delfina penetrates the gloom of time. And she feels she's in an arena fighting a past that is coming back to life. Every woman is a witch, that's true. Because she governs the mysteries of creation, she ends up causing all the world's disasters. Every mother should be tortured for bearing a child without asking its permission.

"Why was it all my fault, dear God?"

"You came into the world to destroy men's hearts. You didn't know how to educate your daughter for love, but only for pain. Maria das Dores abandoned me in order to run away from you, not from me."

In Simba's world, heart and dream hibernated in each other's arms, waiting for spring to blossom. Amid the thunder of words and the abundance of tears, it was evident that the man was a spoilt child who was just throwing his toys out of the pram. He is fully aware of his guilt but he invented his witch as a way of giving himself a life raft. It could have been his own mother or any other woman. And because he had become isolated from the world, his eyes had lost their clarity of vision, which meant that he couldn't see his beloved in the figure of the mad woman of the river, proving that one's eyes only see what the heart reaches first.

"I kept a poisoned arrow to kill you, Delfina, but the weapon was corroded by the wind and the poison consumed by time."

Delfina feels a pang in her heart and looks down as a sign of sadness. Lives, passing moments, feelings, bob around like islands in the ocean of her mind. She lays down her arms, now willing to allow herself to be hacked about like a woman on the point of giving birth.

"You lazy woman!" Simba shouts. "Because of your laziness, you became a woman for white men. You divided your family up into blacks and mulattoes. You deserve to die!"

The death sentence? The laws of today don't judge the actions of yesterday. The past has gone and it took with it its suns and its dreams. Of the crimes of old, all that is left are recollections revived on the chessboard of memory.

"Ah, Delfina, you old shrew! I caught you. You'll pay me for all my suffering. I never saw my children grow up because of you, wretched Delfina!"

Maria das Dores is delighted. She never expected to see a man cry over her, completely lost because of his love. She discovers that Simba isn't at all like her father, and nor is he her mother's man. He was hers and he was handsome. Sensitive. Romantic. She learns to appreciate that elusive figure, with his refined, poetic words, his gray beard and his hair turned white by life. She mourns the time wasted fearing a man who, after all, was hers.

< 467 >

In spite of his ranting, Simba appreciates his Maria das Dores and promises that his woman's dull, rough skin will gleam once more. The skinniness of her body will be a distant memory. Her backside will fill out and occupy the wide space of an armchair and flatten the strong springs of a bed. He will take care of her physical and mental fragility, renew her and make her smile once more.

"You were the reason for all the wars, Delfina."

She understands the insinuation behind these words. But she has learned from life that nothing is gained by fighting wars with one's children. Behind that anger, there are the adolescent palpitations associated with passion. Her anger will abate. Her voice soften. Her heart will rest.

"I was the cause of disaster, yes. I attracted warfare into the same home. Those black and mulatto children inherited a conflict, and they will have to go on fighting until they come to an understanding."

Different generations composed endless melodramas on the strings of the same guitar. The ingratitude of children is an ever-present theme in a mother's songbook. The lack of parental understanding is the litany of offspring. The elegy for time lost is the sad sigh of each father. José dos Montes struggles against conflict and tries everything in order to banish discord.

< 468 >

"It wasn't your fault at all, Delfina. We were a man and a woman building our world. You and I were assimilados. Voluntary servants of the regime. Lackeys. We killed and we died. While I made use of the strength of my arms, you surrendered up your belly so that we shouldn't lack food on the table. We betrayed, we suffered, and we paid the price for our way of life. All we want now is to celebrate the reunification of our family.

As far as José dos Montes is concerned, happiness is nearer and pain further away. The time is right for discord to be overcome and a new world to be born. The time has come to bury suffering.

"What we have to do now is to nurture new life," José dos Montes pleads. "Forget the struggles of old and face up to the new ones. Let us now sign a pact that we will live together. We have built the new world, now we must tend to its defenses."

"No, José, we didn't build anything," Delfina laments. "We killed so many people!"

"It's necessary to destroy in order to build, Delfina. The history of the world is full of barbarity and bloodshed. You women played a key role in that history."

Delfina is willing to tear out the thorns and exorcize all the ghosts and nightmares of the past in order to be reborn. She places her lips

< 469 >

next to José dos Montes's ear and whispers.

"Why are you lying to me, José dos Montes?"

"You and I were living through a dark night. The rivers burst their banks and all the paths ahead were closed. The sky fled afar. The clouds on the horizon hid the mirror of our origins. We lost our land for a while, but we gained the palm grove. We lost our women but a new people emerged in all parts of this Zambezia of ours. Our earthen ramparts were broken down by the invaders' gunfire, but we gained edifices of stone. The palaces the sailors planned and our arms constructed are now ours.

Delfina smiles, the sun brings hope of a new world. She sighs. I survived. I was victorious. Then, she immediately starts to feel sad. The palms suffer from a yellow fungus disease. There's no cure for it yet, the scientists will have to find one, and quickly. Self-affirmation for the native of Zambezia depends on the height of its palm trees, so the palm grove mustn't die. The manor houses of Macuse, Quelimane, Chinde, Pebane, the warehouses and the old ships have all become ghostly monsters, for they miss the sweat and blood of the black forced laborers and the sailors' whips to breathe life into them, they miss the wailing of the mothers as their children were snatched from their arms. They miss the cries of revolt of the men during the strikes and the massacres. Death and mourning have abandoned the land, and in the air the joyful song of the partridge prevails, gurué, gurué! Slavery is over and won't come back! We are independent. We defeated colonialism. The palm grove will also live. It will live!

"Don't deny the past, José dos Montes," Delfina insists. "We were murderers, that's what we were."

"You are right. But tyrants like us were necessary in order to give the nation new images."

"You surprise me, José dos Montes. You haven't changed, you haven't evolved. There wasn't any need for tyrants, there never was."

"You were the greatest visionary in this process, so what are you accusing yourself of? Your old alliances built a new empire. The blacks who resisted, Delfina, died in prisons and in massacres, they were eaten up by the earth, and were only offered dead statues in the middle of the square. Their descendants are orphans suffering the worst poverty in this world."

"That's true. Life is made up of injustices. But there was no heroism in our life, José."

< 471 >

A flash crosses through José's mind, and he looks toward the west. He is confused. He closes his eyes. In that silence, his troubled journey with sudden eddies of wind dislodging stones, thorns, dust, trash, lumps of deadened heartaches. Sweat bathes his body, which the breeze refreshes. His heart gains wings and flies up to meet the sun, which re-emerges with fair-weather colors, over yonder in the dawn of the world.

"Delfina, my goddess. You are absolutely right."

"Just see how ironic this life is, José. The language previously rejected is the one that's now sought after and treated with fondness. We assimilados consigned the people to suffering. We facilitated oppression, exile, deportation. The people struggled, resisted, and the land is free. When everything was ready, we stormed into command again. It's our children who have taken over the leadership with their knowledge of the sailors' language."

Delfina is right. Colonialism was incubated and grew vigorously. It invaded the most intimate recesses and corroded all the foundations. It no longer needs a whip or a sword, and today dresses itself in silence and with a cross. It has branded itself in the skin and hair of the women, assiduous seekers of light skin, in imitation of another race. The mouths of black mothers spit their rage against their fate

< 472 >

and waste their best energies in the futile reproduction of a perfect god. Thirty years of independence and things are going backward. The children of assimilados have re-emerged as violent as ever to show the world their pride in their caste. Colonialism is no longer foreign, it has become black, it has changed its sex and become a woman. It lives in the uterus of women, in their fallopian tubes, and their sexual organs have turned into a trap for the white man.

"In this respect, Delfina, you were a pioneer. All of Zambezia should erect monuments to women like you, who gave their lives and their blood so that this new nation could be born."

José dos Montes's memory travels along sound waves of guerrilla songs. When feet stamp the ground to the rhythm of the drum, dust is raised and makes you smell the scent of the soil. José feels the need to kick off his shoes, tread the ground and feel the earth's vibrations strengthen his bones. To hug the ground, roll around like a child, until his entire skin is covered in sand and dust. To be born in Zambezia is a blessing. To live in Zambezia is a stroke of good luck. To die in Zambezia is the greatest gift the world can provide. José feels he should have fought for his land and not against it. Fortunately, there were courageous men, visionaries, who loved it so much that they gave their blood for it and brought it back. To be free you first need to dream of it. And when it is attained, it must be preserved from all possible storms.

"My dear Delfina, the paths ahead are still covered in fire and thorns. We assimilados helped the powerful to blame God because we thought he had made a mistake in the formula for his creation. We wanted a world with only one voice and only one race. That's why we decided who should die and who should live, as if our hands could somehow help God to rectify this possible error. We obliged some to fight for their survival and beg for mercy. We placed the blacks and whites in a racial battle, but they beat each other so fiercely, that they fell in love with each other's bravery. They ended up married, wrapped up in one binding passion, and forming one family. They killed each other, burned each other, until they became the same dust that the rain moistens and artists use to sculpt monuments to eternity. When this war is finally over, we shall be one people. These half black, half white, half Asian children will be the fossils from which our history will be understood. In the coming generations the races will fall in love, without hatred or anger, inspired by our example. Humanity will conquer other heavenly bodies with folk who are green and blue. Then, the time will have come to invent new races and recreate new humanities. The blacks, whites, and their mulatto offspring should free themselves from all remaining hatred, anger and resentment.

"What will the future be like, José dos Montes? What magic words should be said to this new people?"

"Let us be the ones who give thanks for our meal after we have digested it well," José dos Montes counsels, "so that we are not betrayed again by the food."

"How?"

"Because we two assimilados, inebriated by the food of the sailors, went crazy and destroyed, with our own hands, all that we had received from our ancestors, from our friends, and everything we had built."

Peace assumes its role as leader, on its throne of stone, and Delfina hugs all her children and grandchildren. An obliterating silence prevails. It is the past and the present exchanging kisses on the invisible frontiers of the future. Delfina clamps her lips together and sways. In her breast, the gentlest of all lullabies can be heard.

35

The voices of mothers are magical, they constitute the music of the angels. A note. A stanza. Two. Yet one more stanza to complete the poem. Finally, the refrain. A lullaby, an invocation to honey. Reuniting all the beneficial forces in the world, and weaving a blanket of petals to lend color to the destiny of a new soul.

Mother and child. A weeping voice and a melodic one. Exchanging affection. Looks. Secrets. Kisses and dreams. Unique moments that will cease to exist in the near future, once the umbilical cord is severed. A mother swaying, a child swaying. An unbreakable code, a language of signs. The baby listens to the song up close. And the song gradually fades away as the eyelids droop and sleep comes. Paradise resides in a mother's arms.

The baby falls asleep but the mother's mind wanders, carried by the waves. Traveling so far and so near. To the beginning and the end. For she knows the origin of all things. She knows the number of cells it takes to shape a child. The sperm and egg it takes to produce a soul. The extent of anxiety over the nine months of waiting. Will

< 476 >

it be a boy or a girl? Will it be born chubby or skinny? Will it grow? Who will it be? A whore or a saint? A murderer or a doctor? Will it get married? Will it have children? Will it be normal? Will it be poor or rich? What will its destiny be?

Rocking her baby, the mother's soul rocks, riding on the rear end of life's ruddy river. And she recalls the pain of giving birth. The sleepless nights and the heartache at her little creature's illnesses. The drunken bouts and violence of her partner. The nights she wept at the happiness she didn't have. The candles she lit for a different future she still awaits. And so she clutches the child with all her strength and protects herself. From the separation that will inevitably come. From the weaning that is bound to occur. And she smiles. To hold a baby is to hold the world. To rock a baby is to rock the future in a woman's arms.

No woman ever suspects the fate of the child she rocks in her arms. She does not know if it will be a star that will make her smile or a thorn that will make her heart bleed. A mother defies all the perils and the sinister shadows and fills her soul with gentle songs. While she rocks her child, she rocks herself as well.

My sadness is having nowhere
To lay my fatigue to rest
If I were a bird
I would lack for nothing

Hey little bird, hey little bird
Sing, sing
Rock me in the sweetness of your song!

GLOSSARY

ASSIMILADO — in the Portuguese colonial era, an African who adopted the language and culture of the colonizer

CAPULANA — a colored gown or wrap akin to a sarong

CHICOA — a fresh water fish of the tilapia family

MADJINI, *mandiqui, matoa* — spirits in the Lomwe and Changana languages

MAPIKO — a ritual dance in the Tete and Cabo Delgado regions

M'SIRO — a facial mask used by Makua women

MUKHUTO — a prayer to the dead in the Lomwe language

NHAMBARRO — a dance from Zambezia

NHAU — a ritual dance in Tete and Cabo Delgado

NIPA — a variety of alcoholic spirit distilled from cashew and other fruits

PENDE — variety of tilapia found in the Zambezi

PIA MWENES — queens in the Lomwe and Makua languages

SURUMA — marijuana

TUFO — a dance from Zambezia